ZERO

TITLES BY JACOB WHALER

JACOB WHALER READERS CLUB

Looking for a rich source of reading enjoyment?

Join the **Jacob Whaler Readers Club** with just an email and be the first to find out about new novels. You'll also get free short stories, sneak previews and more.

You won't be spammed, your email won't be shared with anyone and you can opt out at any time. Just go to **jacobwhaler.com** and click on the button to join the **Jacob Whaler Readers Club**.

Thank you!

Jacob Whaler
jacobwhaler.com

ZERO

Jacob Whaler

ISBN-10: 0-9984162-3-1
ISBN-13: 978-0-9984162-3-6

And, for an instant, she stared directly into those soft blue eyes and knew, with an instinctive mammalian certainty, that the exceedingly rich were no longer even remotely human.

— William Gibson

Table of Contents

Red lights flared in the control room.

Link's eyes fluttered open, jarred out of half-sleep. A loud siren cycled up and down. Uniformed soldiers rushed to their stations behind him.

"Got her!" Wilson yelled.

"What'd you find?" Link muttered, his mind still in a fog.

"The ghost girl, boss! Surveillance drones just nailed her!" Wilson raised his arms in victory and let out a whoop. "After all these months, we finally got her."

"Are you kidding?" Link leapt out of his chair, pulse pounding with sudden clarity. "Throw it onscreen!"

"Working on it, boss."

Link couldn't believe his luck. As the commander on deck, he'd get credit for catching the girl and stopping the rebellion. There'd be a big bonus. Whipping out his jax, he couldn't resist a quick glance at his account balance. It was about to jump, maybe enough to bump him up a notch in the rankings.

"Don't let the Fringe scum get away!" Link roared, liking the way his voice filled the control room. He couldn't wait to be the first to see her dirty Fringe face. "Get a close-up. I want to see her eyes when she gets destroyed."

Wilson nodded, legs spread for stability, hands working the holoscreen at his station. "Adjusting the drone visuals now. Should have it up in a second, boss."

"I hate it when you call me *boss*." Link smirked, fully awake and exhilarated, blood pumping, psyched for the chase, enjoying the give-and-take with Wilson.

"Sorry, but that's what you are," Wilson said. "It says right there on your badge. *Patrol Commander Lincoln Wells.* That makes you the boss."

"Drop the formalities, Wilson. That's an order. We're friends."

"Only after work. Right now, you're the boss on deck." Wilson glanced up at the giant holoscreen at the front of the room. "Take a look, boss. You've been dying to see her. There she is."

The Fringe, an endless slum encircling the city, materialized on the holoscreen in all its filthy, savage glory. From the drone's-eye view, it was a chaotic spiderweb of broken-down shacks, toxic ponds and bombed-out buildings, reaching to the horizon. In every respect, it was the exact opposite of the Sanctuary—no color, no slender structures of glass and steel reaching to the sky, no sign of technology. Just relentless, soul-crushing, dirty grey.

And then, he saw her.

A lone, chopper style motorcycle shot down a dusty road driven by a skinny girl with long, black hair. Civilization was rare in the Fringe. Vehicles were rarer. Choppers were unheard of. Until now.

"You're a genius, Wilson. You found the ghost." Every muscle straining, Link stared into the huge holoscreen that took up the whole wall at the front of the room, as he angled for a better look, sizing up his enemy. Who was she? What did she want? It was the first clear visual they'd gotten of her, and they'd been tracking her for months. All they knew from their spies was that the girl was a *healer*. She cared for the sick, and the Fringe was full of them. Lately, she'd been making the rounds, whispering about change, raising the people's hopes. Talking about revolution.

Which was dangerous. The Fringe functioned best as a world without hope or change. Hope would destroy the delicate balance between the Sanctuary and the Fringe so carefully constructed over the last century and a half.

At least that's what President Quinn always said.

"How'd you find her, Wilson?"

"Easy. Air sniffers picked up strange chemical signatures in the northwest quadrant, something that's not common in the Fringe, even with their rotten air quality. Made me curious. So I launched a squad of scout drones and started scanning. Didn't take long to pick up that crazy trike she rides. It's old tech from the last century. Uses home-brewed hydrocarbs and leaves a vapor trail that screams at our sensors. Drones got a hit on the first pass, while you were snoozing in your chair." Wilson yawned and stretched.

"Look, I had a late night. Don't rub it in."

"Sorry, boss."

"For the last time, stop calling me *boss*."

"Yes, sir." Wilson executed a perky salute with a contagious half-grin.

Link stroked the stubble on his chin. "Any intel on why the girl's on the road? I mean, it's broad daylight. She usually moves at night. Like a ghost."

Wilson nodded. "If you ask my opinion, she *wants* us to find her."

"No one asked your opinion, Wilson. I need cold, hard facts."

"But sir, with all due respect, this is too perfect. She—"

"Look, Wilson, just don't lose her. That's all you need to worry about. We have a lot riding on this. There's a promotion in it for both of us. And our account balances will get juiced by President Quinn. Could be the big break we've been looking for. So get a lock on her, Wilson. Quinn's orders are clear. Kill her on sight."

"Working on it." Wilson pored over a mass of images and gridlines on his desk holo—sorting, magnifying, refining. "Initiating a tracking algorithm to plot her course. She won't get away."

The view of the girl on the screen zoomed in. The first thing Link noticed was her scarlet leather bodysuit. He'd never seen anything like it in the Fringe. As she gunned the motorcycle, her front tire lifted, and she rode a wheelie down a narrow alley, balancing on two rear slicks, hands high on the handlebars. On either side, the flimsy huts seemed to lean in as if pulled by the force of her attraction.

"She's cocky. Get the drones in position. Zoom in more." Link leaned forward onto his toes, feeling his adrenaline kick in. "I want to see her eyes."

"There's some kind of digital interference." Wilson thrust both hands into his holo, grasped her image and tried to expand and focus it. "Wait, I think I have it."

At last, she filled the screen.

Like all Fringe scum, she was skin and bones, pencil-thin arms hanging off the handlebars, with the outline of ribs visible under the bodysuit. The ragged black hair and vaguely green complexion contrasted wildly with the bright red leather.

"Why do they all look like that, Wilson? Skinny and green. Less than human. A perfect zero."

"I hear it's the cornboo. It's all they eat. Turns them into sick, little demons."

For an instant, she looked up as if listening to their conversation and gazed directly into the drone camera, not a shred of fear in her face. Only smiles and taunting.

Link couldn't breathe, like he'd been punched in the solar plexus. She was staring directly at him. Or through him. The room fell away into silence. He stood alone in the dark, spine tingling as if on fire. Afterward, all he could remember was her eyes. One was blue, the other brown. The intensity of her stare struck him with the force of a hammer.

"Weapons locked on," Wilson said. "Ready to fire on your command, boss. Let's wipe that pompous smile off her dirty little face."

"Wait." Link leaned forward, grasped the rail and pulled himself up with a white-knuckle grip.

With his hand poised over the trigger on his desk, Wilson paused. "Ready for the kill, boss."

Link stared, unable to take his gaze off her. Unable to breathe.

"Boss?"

The soldier part of Link wanted to give the command to shoot, but all he could see or think about was her eyes. Blue and brown.

"I'm going to shoot, boss. Three, two—"

"Wait!" Link roared.

On the big holoscreen, a cloud of pixelated haze rose like smoke from behind the chopper.

"What's that?" Link's eyes narrowed.

Wilson checked his desk holo. "I don't believe it."

"You still have the lock, right?"

"Sorry, boss." Wilson shook his head. "It's some kind of EM disturbance. Triggered a partial system failure. Our cameras can still follow her, but our drones can't acquire a target lock. I'll have to go full manual."

"Do it." Link said. "But first, have you confirmed her identity? Are you sure it's even her, the ghost girl?"

Wilson nodded at the holoscreen and pointed, his light carbon armor stretching like glass over his skin. "It's her, boss. I'm 90% positive."

"What if that isn't even her, Wilson? What if it's a trap? A diversion? We need 100% confirmation before we pull the trigger. You know President Quinn. He doesn't like messy mistakes. The Fringe is a delicate place right now. Tempers are high. He wouldn't want us to make things worse than they already are." Link folded his arms, surprised at his search for excuses not to shoot the girl.

Her face still floated on the holoscreen.

"Come on, boss. You know we'll never get 100% confirmation." He pointed at the holoscreen. "Even if she's not the leader of the rebellion, she's still just Fringe scum. I say we kill her."

"Who's the commander on deck, Wilson?"

"You are, boss."

"Then follow my orders. Run her bios through our intel. I want to be sure who she is and that we aren't walking into a trap."

"Already did, boss."

"Do it one more time."

"Right away, boss." Wilson cleared his desk holo with a sweep of one hand and pulled in the facial shot of the girl. "She's something, isn't she? Not typical Fringe scum. Especially the eyes. They remind me of something. No, someone. Can't put my finger on it. A shame to have to kill her."

The girl on the screen stared back, blinking slowly. She looked to be in her early twenties, but you could never tell with Fringe types. They lived a rough life and aged fast. Link studied her rough-cut, jet-black hair, small nose, full lips and the random scars on her face. Not exactly a world-class beauty. But those eyes. It was impossible to look away.

"Facial recognition algorithm confirms 99% match with the intel we got. It's the best we can do." Wilson looked up. "It's got to be her, boss."

"Do we have her name?"

"Not yet. She may not be in our database. I've got people working on it."

The visual of her on the chopper still floated in the holoscreen. She slowed near a group of children playing in the road. They all rushed her together, half-emaciated but still giggling and smiling. She kissed one on the head and waved as she rode off. Then she executed a quick right turn, leaning in as the chopper went into a power slide and nicked the corner of an old building. Dust trickled to the ground.

Link thought about the incredible scene he'd just witnessed. Children never played outside in the Sanctuary. They hardly ever played together anywhere. But there were kids all over in the Fringe, always in groups, always having fun. How could they be so happy in a dirty slum? He'd heard rumors that a virus was running rampant. It was almost like they didn't care.

"Keep your drones on her, Wilson. Where's she going?"

"The tracking algorithms aren't detecting a pattern. There's no grid system in the Fringe. It's just a crooked maze of streets and back alleys, and she's taking random turns. It's a jungle down there. They live like animals. New shacks go up overnight and disappear the next day. Especially near the junk piles. Like an anthill. Our latest maps are already—"

"Outdated. I know, Wilson. I don't need a lecture on Fringe architectural tendencies." Link sunk back into his chair and gazed into the holoscreen with its sea of drab houses buried in layers of dust and rot, like a spreading fungus. Here and there, the skeletal remains of old steel structures rose out of the chaos.

No matter how many times he saw it, the Fringe was always a foreign world to Link. It began just outside the Wall, only meters from the city. But they couldn't be more different. The city had a neat pattern of wide avenues, pristine skyscrapers, plentiful parks and, most of all, normal, healthy, educated people. People in the city worked hard to keep their account balances growing. They cared about their ranking. They valued peace and security and progress.

That's why the city was called the *Sanctuary*.

After staring at the Fringe for so long, a wave of nausea rose in Link's belly. The chaos of winding streets and off-kilter houses was unsettling. He grabbed a dispenser from his pocket, raised it to his mouth and popped a tiny blue pill. It instantly dissolved on his tongue. Calm and clarity flooded his brain.

"Did I ever tell you how much I hate the Fringe?" Link tried to forget about the girl's eyes and, instead, channel his revulsion for the slums. Maybe it would help him focus on killing her.

"Ten times a day." Wilson turned back to his desk holo with a wry smile, his fingers a blur as they weaved and sorted through a collage of images. "Can we start shooting yet?"

Link cocked his head to the side. "With no lock on the girl?"

"No worries, boss. I can shoot on full manual."

"Don't get trigger-happy, Wilson. Just keep the drones in position, and be ready for the order. I'll tell you when to shoot."

"You sure?" Wilson grabbed a drink from a tall, thin cup. "I could let off a Reaper round right now. Kill the girl and clear out a couple of blocks. A few hundred might die, but we'd get her for sure. And who would care? It's only Fringe scum."

Link frowned. "Too risky, Wilson. Might show up in the evening feeds. You've seen the reports. Sympathy for the Fringe is on the rise. Kids are dying there at a faster rate. Some kind of new virus. Anyway, we need to keep this operation clean and quiet. I can't authorize more than a surgical strike. Can you do that on full manual?"

"No problem, boss." Wilson cleared his throat. "Drones are in standard attack formation. Ready when you are."

The girl's eyes were still burnt into Link's mind. He'd never felt such an intense reaction. But that was behind him now. With the help of the blue pill, his mind was pleasantly numb.

The girl slowed the chopper. With one hand on the handlebars, she lifted the other to the sky, pointing directly at the drone camera, wagging her finger and shaking her head.

It was more than Link could stomach.

"Wilson, I'm getting tired of this. Time to put her out of her misery. Have you plotted an ambush point?"

"Yeah, boss."

"Alright. Listen up. I want a neat, clean shot, OK? No mess. Something nice for the evening feeds. Is that clear?"

"Got it, boss." Wilson steadied himself in front of his desk holo. "Just give me the signal."

Link turned back to the main holoscreen at the front of the room. The girl had both hands on the handlebars now, as if bracing for the attack. With a long tail of dust behind her, she was moving faster through the streets.

"Show me the line you've plotted to the ambush point." Link sank back into his chair.

A superimposed green line appeared on the main holoscreen just ahead of the girl, as if she were following it. It zigzagged right and left until it terminated in a dot.

The girl approached a point where the green line abruptly turned right.

"Watch this." Wilson grabbed the joystick rising from his desk and tapped a red button on its side. "Bombs away."

A thin line of smoke shot down toward her. An instant later, an orange explosion bloomed just off to her left. She abruptly turned to the right, remaining on the green line.

"Nice shot," Link said. "You've got her right where you want her."

"I know." Wilson laughed and shot off more pinpoint strikes, each one forcing the girl to keep to the green line.

"Almost there." Wilson rubbed his hands together. "This is too easy." He stopped and stared at his desk holo. "Wait a minute. One of the drones has an error message. Some kind of glitch. Says it lost system access and requests a reboot. This will just take a second." He moved his hand across his desk holo and wiped it clean.

"Wait, Wilson, are you sure—"

At the front of the room, the main holo flickered out.

"Wilson?" Link jumped out of his chair. "What's going on?"

"Just rebooting the camera drone, sir. Give me 10 seconds."

Link held his breath, eyes on the holoscreen, silently counting.

Nine, eight—

When he hit *two*, the holoscreen lit up.

"All systems are back on." Wilson pointed at the big holo. "There she is. In the trap. Right where I want her."

"Shoot!" Link yelled.

Wilson grabbed his joystick. "Fire in the hole!"

The girl had stopped, and she stood next to her chopper in the middle of an open square. Lifting both arms into a spread eagle, she raised her face to the camera, opening herself to the attack, embracing death.

And then—no explosions. Nothing.

"Wilson?" Link shouted, his voice rising to a crescendo. "What's going on?"

"I pulled the trigger, boss. She should be dead, nothing left of her, but I can't confirm weapon launch." Wilson poured over numbers and symbols flooding through his desk holo. And then he slumped back into his chair, slowly shaking his head. "It's in our system."

"What's in our sys—"

As if on cue, every jax, slate and screen lit up in the control room. Link pulled his own jax out of his pocket.

A holo image of the girl floated above it. She smirked, one hand on her hip, leaning on her chopper, head tilted to the side like a puppy. Link couldn't believe it. She was posing for the camera.

Everyone in the room stared at her image floating above their jaxes, as if transfixed by her eyes. Like Link had been before he took the blue pill.

"Wilson!"

"Oh no." Wilson dropped his head into his hands. "This is bad."

Link took a deep breath. "OK, Wilson, start from the beginning. What's going on?"

"There's a worm in our system, boss. She's taken over every screen in the Sanctuary."

"Every screen?"

"Yep."

"This *is* bad. President Quinn is going to—"

The girl's lips bent into a slow grin. "Have I got your attention, Sanctuary? Good. Now listen up. The revolution starts now. Come along for the ride." Carefully and deliberately, she grabbed the handlebars, swung her leg over the saddle, kick-started the engine and gunned the throttle.

For a few seconds, Link stared in silence, mesmerized by the girl's eyes. And then he realized what was happening. The whole Sanctuary was being pulled in, just like him.

"Kill the image!" he shouted. "Pull the plug! Destroy the feed! Do something!"

Wilson shook his head in disbelief. "I'm trying, boss. The reboot inserted a worm into the root system. We've been kicked off. It's propagating throughout the Mesh. There's nothing I can do."

"Where's the source of the attack?"

"You won't believe it, boss, but it's coming from the Fringe."

"How can that be? They don't have Mesh access." Link glanced up at the holoscreen. The girl was weaving back and forth on a wide street, drawing long arcs, mocking them.

"Hold on." Wilson peered into his desk holo, scanning lines of code. "I still have the laser cannons on full manual, under my control. It'd be messy, but maybe I can shoot her, boss."

"Do it." Link sank back into his chair, jaw tight, fists clenched.

"In front of the whole Sanctuary?"

"Kill the scum."

2

Alix Yamaguchi knew the Patrol was watching, helpless to stop her, seething with rage.

She stood on the pegs, shifting her weight from side to side, carving long, lazy turns in the dirt with the chopper just to make them mad. With adrenaline pumping, her fear had vanished. She was in total control. Lifting her face to the sky, she drank in the sun and smiled big for the drones. Just being in the light filled her with intoxicating joy. It had been months since she'd been above ground in the daytime. The drones were everywhere, and she'd been forced into hiding. But now, for the first time in her life, she was glad to see the insect-like forms with their rotors, cameras and guns.

It was all part of the plan.

Three months before, when Alix had quietly spread the word about a revolution, Sanctuary spies had heard the rumors. Overnight, she shot to the top of their most wanted list. The reward for turning her in was life-time admittance to the Sanctuary, a dream come true for Fringe dwellers. At least that's what the public holoscreens were saying. The only problem was, it didn't work and never would. Fringe folks might be poor, but they weren't stupid. They protected their own.

The crazy thing was, Alix had never wanted to start a revolution. Like everyone else, she just wanted to survive. She'd tried to work in the brain labs, but her mind had rejected the trodes and the neural interface. Then, she had tried the chemplants and gotten scarred with acid and toxic waste. The only path left was to be a healer, going from house to house to comfort the sick, hoping for an extra portion of cornboo. And somehow, she was a natural at it. The people loved her quiet voice and gentle touch, and she loved them in return.

The truth was, there wasn't much extra cornboo to go around. The Sanctuary made sure the workers in the brain labs and chemplants barely got enough for their families. But in the Fringe, sharing was a way of life, a natural part of the culture, the only way to survive. No one had money or rank, not like they did in the Sanctuary. And yet, with all the sharing, they managed to get by.

It had been a hard but quiet life for Alix until the children started dying for no reason.

One day, Merf, a Mesh-hacker who had been severely disabled by the brain labs, had visited her house. He said it was time to start talking about change. He had proof it was a Sanctuary-engineered virus that was killing the children, and there wasn't much time. They needed a revolution and a leader to bring all the people together. And he wasn't just talking about the Fringe. The Sanctuary would be part of it too, and the leader would have to unite everyone on both sides of the Wall.

"How is that possible?" she'd asked.

Merf had said he'd been thinking about it for a long time and had a plan. The ideal leader would be someone who grew up in the Fringe and understood it completely. But they'd also have to be wildly popular with the Sanctuary.

In other words, Merf was talking about finding a Mesh-celebrity, the kind who appeared on the big public holoscreens and had a cult-like following.

But that was impossible. There weren't any Mesh-celebs from the Fringe and there never would be.

"Where would you find him?" she'd asked.

"That's the thing," Merf had answered. He'd already found that person, the perfect leader, and it wasn't a *him* at all.

It was Alix.

Sudden nausea had filled her stomach. She'd wanted to run away where no one could find her. After a couple minutes of silence, she'd figured out that Merf was serious. "Look, you know me, Merf," she'd pleaded. "I'm no Mesh-celeb. Not even close."

"Yeah, I know," Merf had said, smiling. "But that's OK. *I'll make you into one.*"

She had protested, over and over. But it didn't seem to matter. Merf said he knew what he was doing. He had a plan, and he said it would work. It was just a matter doing it right.

And so, with his encouragement, Alix changed. She started talking about revolution and how everything could be different. It was hard, even painful. She'd never liked the spotlight. She's always been the quiet one in the background. But when she talked about revolution, something strange happened. Her pulse beat faster, and she became a different person, a person with confidence and courage. And people listened. The more she talked about it, the more she believed what she was saying, and the more people looked at her in a different way. They started calling her a leader. The one who could free them.

But Alix never felt like the one, at least not in the quiet moments when she had time to think.

Merf had finally broken the Patrol's encryption and hacked into their Mesh files. He'd found out about a certain young commander. His name was Lincoln Wells, or just Link, and Merf said he was hungry for Alix's blood and the money and rank it would bring him. Merf made sure Alix rode her chopper on the day Link was the commander on deck. Merf said that was important.

Right now, against all her instincts, she was doing her best to attract attention. *Link's* attention.

Merf's plan was crazy. She wondered *Would it work?*

It had to. Masses of children were dying from the new virus. Alix had been doing her best to comfort the sick and bereaved, but there was only so much she could do. More and more, she saw parents carrying the bodies of their children to the toxic dumps, the only safe place to dispose of the dead. It was heart-wrenching. The Sanctuary had the cure. They were just waiting for the virus to burn itself out.

Culling the herd, they called it, according to Merf.

The more Alix thought about it, the more it filled her with a new and uncomfortable emotion. Rage.

A familiar voice pushed through her earphones, pulling her back into the moment as she raced past a line of shacks on the chopper.

"Alix, it's me. I muted your audio. No one can hear us. We can talk."

"Hey, Merf." Alix took a deep inhale. "I was waiting for you. You sure the Sanctuary heard my opening line?"

"Are you kidding?" Merf chuckled. "I'm positive. It was great, Alix. *The revolution starts now.* Don't worry, they heard you. Loud and clear. And now they're frantic to shut you down. Especially Commander Lincoln Wells. I'm watching him right now. I wish you could see it. See him."

"So, the whole Sanctuary is watching little old me?" Alix still couldn't believe any of it. There she was, an unranked nobody, with their full attention.

"Yep," Merf said. "More than just the Sanctuary is watching. I mainlined the video feed to every jax, slate and holoscreen in a hundred mile radius. It's on every building and street in the Sanctuary and all public screens in the Fringe. Even the Wall. It's *everywhere*, Alix. The event of the century."

Alix tried to wrap her mind around the scale of what Merf was doing and found it hard to breathe. It made her want to run away. Part of her wanted to call the whole plan off and just disappear. The other part was having a blast.

"Are you sure this is a good idea, Merf?"

"What, are you scared?"

"Yeah, you could say that." She zoomed past a group of kids and waved. "I'm not used to being a Mesh-celeb."

"Get used to it, Alix."

"What about the drones?" Alix could hear the buzz 30 meters up. "They're shooting at me."

"Don't worry, no one's going to lay a finger on you."

"I trust you Merf." Alix relaxed into her position on the chopper, calm settling over her. "Just keep an eye on those drones."

Merf was good, easily the best Mesh-hacker on either side of the Wall, but that didn't begin to describe him. The Mesh was his natural habitat. He'd logged more time with trodes and a neural interface than anyone else alive. Merf called it *swimming*, and it gave him the freedom he'd never had in the real world. He could go almost anywhere without leaving his wheelchair. As he'd told Alix many times, only a few ultra-high-security nodes inside the Sanctuary could keep him out.

"There's something you need to understand, Alix. After this, you'll be famous. A real Mesh-phenom. The first ever from the Fringe."

"Look, Merf, all I want is a way to talk to the Sanctuary so they'll listen." Alix sat down on the chopper and gunned the engine. The wind lifted her hair. "I don't want fame, Merf, just a megaphone."

"Sorry, Alix. You can't have one without the other. I know the Mesh, how it works, how the Sanctuary folks think. They've got a word for what we're doing. *Marketing*. It's the language of money, the only one the people of the Sanctuary understand." Merf chuckled again. "Trust me. When you go, you have to go big. And you can't get bigger than 100% screen saturation. Until now, only President Quinn could do that."

President Quinn: leader of the USA, the United Sanctuaries of America. Just hearing the name triggered nausea in the pit of Alix's stomach.

"I don't know, Merf. That's not my style."

"It is now. Look, I've surfed all the latest feeds. No one will listen to you unless you get on their screens. That's the world they live in. It's what they eat, drink and sleep. It's what they crave."

"You've shown me their world, Merf, their Mesh-celebs and superstars. They're all idiots. Meaningless. Empty. I'm not going to be one of them."

"You will be after this, Alix. There's no going back."

"For the record, I don't like it."

"And, for the record, you don't have to like it, Alix. You just have to use it. For the revolution. For the Fringe." Merf abruptly stopped, taking slow breaths, as if he were thinking. "OK, look, Alix. We've had this conversation before. I'm not going to force you to do anything. There's already enough force in the world. I could disconnect and give their screens back to them. And you could go back to being a nobody and watching kids die."

Alix exhaled long and slow, thinking about the children playing in the streets, laughing in spite of being half-starved and liable to die of the virus at any time. If no one did anything, they'd have no future.

"No, Merf, that's not what I want."

"There's no turning back if we do this, Alix. You're OK with that, right?"

"What choice do I have, Merf?"

"I want the same thing you do, Alix. Just trust me, OK?"

"Merf, you *know* I trust you."

A 20-story high-rise flew by in a blur, the broken-off skeletal remnants of a structure from centuries past that used to be 10 times as high. Alix had the throttle wide open now. Hopefully, the old engine wouldn't blow apart.

"So, what exactly are you doing, Merf?"

"It's just like I said." Merf's voice was low and smooth, pure confidence. "I'm inside the Patrol Mesh node. Their military tech is sloppy. They think the whole Fringe still lives in the Dark Ages."

"Most of us do, Merf."

"Yeah, but not me. I found the chink in their armor: a back door into one of their drones. Didn't take long to break the encryption and upload a fake error message. It got them to open the door. Then I worked my way up the chain to the main facility and forced a system reboot. It opened a crack in the firewall long enough to slip in one of my specially designed AIs. It took over the video feed, and it's working on their weapons systems right now. You just got a free pass."

"How much time do I have?"

"15 minutes max before they shut us down." Merf chuckled. "15 minutes to start the revolution. That's all I can give you."

"What about audio? You sure they'll hear me?"

"Absolutely." Merf could hardly hide the glee in his voice. "As soon as I take it off mute, you'll be live, Alix. Just talk into the microphone on your collar. Nothing like this has happened in decades. Be natural. Don't think about millions of people watching and listening. Hanging on every word."

"Thanks, Merf." Alix throttled down for a moment, collecting her thoughts.

"Anything for the leader of the revolution."

"That's you, Merf. Not me."

There was no answer, and Alix didn't expect one. With a twist of her wrist, she shot past a stretch of low-level dwellings made of organics and other materials scavenged from the massive garbage dumps that dotted the Fringe. A patchwork of uneven roof lines and off-kilter walls floated by. On a regular day, the street would be buzzing with a free market, where people gave away items they'd made, but right now, nobody was there. Word had gone out early in the morning about the operation, and people had cleared out to minimize the collateral damage.

Merf's voice crackled back into Alix's ears.

"Bad news. I can't disable the laser guns on the drones."

"What?" Alix felt her chest tighten. "But you said—"

"They put them on manual before I got control, and they locked me out. But don't worry, Alix. This may be even better. My AI found a way to scramble their targeting algorithm. The lasers are going to be jumping all over. Should look good on video. You'll be like a superhero dodging bullets. The Sanctuary will eat it up." Merf laughed, long and deep. "They'll be able to shoot, but I doubt they'll hit you."

"You *doubt*?"

Merf cleared his throat. "Unless they get lucky."

"You mean unless they use one of their Reaper bombs. Like last winter. Wipes out everything within 50 meters."

"They've gotten bigger since the last one. Now it's more like a hundred."

"Thanks, Merf."

"Here comes the first wave of laser cannon shots. Be careful, Alix."

She slowed to make a turn. Two meters to her left, a line of holes ripped through the soft wall of a house, opening up a massive perforation.

It collapsed like a tired elephant. Debris exploded across the road into her windshield.

"OK, everything's set." Merf paused. "You ready to go live with the audio again?"

"Can't wait."

"Three, two, one." Merf's voice took on a distant tone, as if a pane of glass had slid between them. "Video and audio feeds are synced. Ten million people are watching here and elsewhere, including President Quinn. You're the star, Alix."

She took a deep breath as she imagined countless eyes staring into holoscreens on the sides of buildings, on sidewalks or on the jaxes in their hands. Should she be humble or cocky? Condescending or earnest? Maybe it was best not to worry and just deliver the message. Be herself, whatever that was in the moment.

Gunning the engine again, her adrenaline surged. Her fear instantly vanished, replaced by calm invincibility. "Ladies and gentlemen, it's another perfect day in the Sanctuary. I'm the one on the chopper. Alix Yamaguchi. Nice to meet you."

Bullets ripped the road in front of her like an angry dotted line.

"I know most of you don't get outside the Wall much, so I thought I'd give you all a quick tour of the Fringe. Oh, and don't mind the shooting. Your friends are trying to kill me."

Light flashed ahead. A hole the size of a house opened in the dirt road, spewing dust and pebbles.

Alix leaned hard and made a power slide into a deserted alley on her left. Killing the engine and coasting, she distinctly heard the swarm of drones buzzing overhead. Like always. But these were closer. She reengaged the engine and gunned the throttle.

Her chopper split a puddle of water neatly in two, throwing spray high onto the sagging walls on either side. A massive impact shook the ground behind her, like a giant foot slamming into the ground. She was an ant about to be squashed. Bits and pieces of black debris rained down. Her chest tightened, squeezing out her breath. It took effort to relax back into the adrenaline.

Concentrate on the words, Alix thought. *Just deliver the message. Tell them the truth.*

"I'll let you in on a little secret: folks in the Fringe are just like you. We have hopes and dreams, fears and doubts. We try to improve our lives. We do our best with what we have. We need food to eat, air to breathe, water to drink and a roof over our heads. We need family and friends."

A flash of fire erupted from a building just ahead on the left. Alix hated the property damage, but people in the Fringe were used to it. The structures were simple enough that it didn't take a lot to fix them. Surplus organics were easy to obtain. The Sanctuary discarded tons of them every day in the ubiquitous trash heaps. Veering to the right side of the street, she guided the tires up a low flight of wooden stairs to an open porch. With a burst of power from the engine, she pulled up the front wheel and shot through the air over the flames and black smoke.

Alix gazed down at her crimson-red bodysuit. It made her look like a superhero. No one in the Fringe wore anything like it. Merf had secret friends in the Sanctuary who had created it especially for her and smuggled it out only a few days before.

"If you're going to be a celebrity," Merf had said, "you've got to dress like one."

"Ever wonder why folks in the Fringe are slightly green?" Alix looked at the skin on the back of her hands. "It's the cornboo, the miracle food made in gigantic vats and engineered from corn and bamboo, a gift from the Sanctuary to keep us alive. I suppose we should be grateful. It's nutritious but turns us green when it oxidizes. They say it was designed that way to make us look different, to mark us as Fringe scum."

On both sides of the alley, walls and doors burst into black debris in a rain of laser darts. Holes danced across the ground. To the right and left, rising fireballs left craters in the raw ground.

The Patrol was throwing everything they had at her, desperate to stop the truth from emerging. But Merf was right. Their targeting systems were going crazy. They couldn't hit her.

It made her smile again.

"I'm going to tell you another secret, my friends. You won't like it, but you need to know. It's the reason I'm talking to you today. Your perfect life in the Sanctuary is only possible because of the suffering you inflict on the Fringe. It's true that the Fringe lives off the refuse of the Sanctuary, but it goes both ways. The Sanctuary lives off the pain of the Fringe. It's the dirty little secret Quinn doesn't want you to know about."

The narrow alley widened into an open field that was home to a busy free market on a typical day. It was empty now, the perfect place to make her last stand.

Merf's voice cracked in Alix's ear. "Less than five minutes to go, Alix. I'm doing my best to keep the lasers off you. I just looked at some random visual captures inside the Sanctuary. The whole population is mesmerized right now. They've never seen anything like this. A Mesh-celeb from the Fringe. They already love you, Alix. I told you they would. Now hit them with the final punch."

With another rush of adrenaline, Alix gunned her chopper and rode a wheelie through the middle of the field. Dust and smoke hung like shrouds in the air as a barrage of laser shots slammed into the ground.

"So, my Sanctuary friends, let's start with the Mesh. Ever thought about what powers it?" Alix slowed the chopper so she could concentrate on the words Merf had given her. "Decades ago, the Sanctuary's bioengineers made a discovery: the most powerful computing device isn't a silicon-based chip, but a live, carbon-based human brain. They didn't stop there. They built the actual technology to suck computing power from human brain slaves to run the Mesh."

She paused to let that thought sink in for a minute, doing figure eights in the open field with eyes to the sky, staring at the drones overhead.

"Guess where they found the brains to power your Mesh games? Right here in the Fringe. No, they don't kill anyone, at least not at first. But every day, hundreds of thousands of workers trudge to the brain labs for 12-hour shifts. They work in warehouses that look like giant, shiny cubes, a kilometer long. They're filled with endless stacks of cheap cots. The workers lie down like slaves in the hold of a ship and connect to the Mesh with trodes.

I've tried it, and it's torture. Feels like drowning and sets off a full-blown panic attack. Imagine doing that every day, all day, for most of your life. The brain is like a wild animal and fights to get away. Over time, side effects take their toll. The connection between brain and body erodes, little by little. After a few years, the brain lab workers are paralyzed and used up. *Mind-blown*, as they say. Most turn into paraplegics. Many die young. Why do they do it? For the cornboo. People will do anything to keep their families from starving."

Just thinking about their living conditions made it hard to control her rage. The brain labs had destroyed Merf's body. But he'd been one of the rare ones who'd found a way to fight back by adapting to life inside the Mesh. Millions less lucky ones languished all over the Fringe, with broken bodies and shattered minds. Alix wanted to scream, but she gunned her engine instead. Merf had told her only a few of the Sanctuary elite knew about the brain labs. Well, now everybody did.

"It takes a hundred brain slaves to power one of your jaxes. Life is cheap here in the Fringe."

The drones were floating down in long, steady spirals. There hadn't been any shots in the last 30 seconds. Maybe they'd run out of ammo. Maybe they were about to drop the Reaper.

"Ever wonder why the Sanctuary is so pristine and clean? All your toxic waste is processed right here in chemplants so it can be made into more stuff for you to buy and discard. Most of the time, the air isn't safe to breathe. Throwaway workers from the brain labs do the labor. The first things to go are their teeth and fingernails. Some say it's better than starving, but I'm not so sure. And the fumes and acid take their toll. I tried it, and that's why I look like a scar-face."

Alix made slow turns around the field, trying to suppress thoughts about her childhood. The long hours in the chemplants and the acid burns. But the drones caught her attention. They were coiling together into a tight double helix. Her instincts told her there wasn't much time left.

"Just one last thing. Let's talk about the Wall. At a thousand meters high, it does a good job of keeping us out of sight. Maybe you've forgotten it's even there. On your side, inside the Sanctuary, the Wall projects gorgeous images of sunsets and mountains and lush jungles. I hear the view changes every day. Must be great."

Alix fought back the tears.

"Ever wonder what the Wall looks like on our side? I'll tell you. It's transparent. Folks in the Fringe gather there at night for a glimpse of the paradise you live in. To gaze at what they'll never have. Clean air. Enough food."

The drones hung above Alix, emitting a subtle buzz.

"Maybe you've heard about the virus that's killing our kids by the thousands. Rumors are that the Sanctuary knows what's going on, that maybe it was engineered by your scientists to reduce our population. You've got the cure, they say. If it's true, we need it."

The drones went silent.

"You may think we have nothing to offer you, but that's a lie. Over the decades, we've evolved a new way of life. We've learned to give and not take. We share all we have. There aren't any rich and poor here. We're all the same. We have free markets where people give away what they've made for the sheer joy of it."

She'd seen it before. The drones were separating into attack formation.

"So, that's your history lesson for today. The Sanctuary is an island of beauty in a sea of misery. It's time you understand your way of life can't exist without ours. We pay all the costs, and you get all the benefits. It's a system out of balance, created to sustain a wealthy elite by preying on millions of the poor. It can't last. It won't last. That leaves all of us with one final, inescapable truth."

Her rage welled up. This time, Alix didn't try to push it back.

Glancing to the sky, she saw the drones diving for her. She punched the engine, and the chopper lunged away as she barely held on. A dozen drones slammed into the ground where she'd been two seconds before. But there was no explosion, just a crater and a rising cloud of dust.

Merf's voice floated in Alix's mind, like a creature barely alive at the bottom of a pool. "They're trying to detonate the Reaper. I'm fighting back now but can only give you 30 seconds. Make it count."

She rode over to the smoking debris and found a live camera lens, still glowing red. Bending close to it, she imagined her face filling every holo-screen in the Sanctuary.

"Let's do this together." Alix smiled, unafraid to show off her uneven teeth and flawed skin. "The Fringe and the Sanctuary have been separated for long enough. We need you, and you need us. Change is coming. Let go of your fear and embrace it."

3

The Words

The control room fell silent.

Alix Yamaguchi's blue and brown eyes filled the holoscreen at the front of the room and shredded Link's soul to the core as he stared, helpless. With his last remaining strength, he was desperate to push back, searching his mind for a weapon to break the spell.

Digging deep, he found the *words*. He'd heard them in school. He'd read them in the mandatory propaganda on every Mesh node. They'd been drilled into him over and over at President Quinn's compulsory rallies. They were pumped through his brain at night when he slipped on the trodes and found his way to the public dreamscape.

The words:

Why a Wall? People in the Fringe are different from you and me. They're foreign. They hate us and our civilization. They're socialists, forced to share everything and live together in herds, like animals. They hate capitalism. They hate private property. They hate peace and prosperity. Our culture rewards independence and success. It rewards winning. In the Fringe, they have no ambition, no drive, no winning. And that's why they have no money or rank. They're zeros. Losers and criminals. A cancer that must be quarantined. They want to pull us back into the dark past. Make no mistake, here in the Sanctuary, we are protecting the future for ourselves and our children. That's why there has to be a Wall.

Link had heard the words so often, they'd been engraved so deeply on his psyche, that they had mostly lost their meaning. But now, as the words flowed through his mind like water through a deep channel, he held onto them, repeating them aloud and tasting their feel and texture. Slowly, the words gave him the rage he needed to push back against those eyes from the Fringe.

"Blow it up! Detonate the Reaper!" Link shot to his feet, screaming. "Kill her! Now!"

Wilson's hands moved furiously on his desk holo. "Trying, boss. Trying to take control from the worm that infected our system."

On the big holoscreen, Alix Yamaguchi was oblivious to the words. She smiled, turned and walked back to her chopper in her red leather, her jagged black hair swinging with every step.

"Do it!" Link listened to his voice as if someone else were screaming. "Before she gets away!"

"Almost there," Wilson said, hands a blur. "Just have to delete the root code inserted by the worm."

Alix Yamaguchi swung her leg over the saddle of her chopper. It flexed under her weight. She brought her hands onto the throttle and gunned the engine.

"Now, Wilson!"

The chopper shot across the field, kicking up a cloud of dust and smoke.

Link shook his head and tried to erase the afterimage of the blue and brown eyes, but they still haunted him from behind his closed eyelids. The image of her chopper racing away floated in the holo above his jax. Millions of people were watching her every move, including President Quinn. They would all wonder why Link had failed to kill her. Twisting, he launched his jax against the wall. Sparks exploded into glowing crystals that fell to the floor like snow. With his lips firmly pressed together, he held back the urge to scream.

Breathe, he thought, *just breathe and forget her.*

"I killed the worm," Wilson whispered. "We now have full control of the drone. Shall I engage the self-destruct protocol?"

"Do it!" Link sunk back into his chair, stunned.

There was a burst of fire, and the holoscreen faded to black.

"With your permission, boss, I'll try to trace the exact location of the

AI that wormed into our system. Initial indications show that it came from the Fringe."

"But that's impossible." Link stared out of the corner of his eye at the black holoscreen. "Look harder. That kind of tech doesn't exist outside the Wall."

"I would have agreed until now." Wilson shook his head. "It'll take time, but I promise you I'll get to the bottom of this."

"Thanks Wilson, but it's too late." Link's voice was lower and weaker now, and he gazed at the floor. Somewhere deep in his cranium, a headache gathered strength. "How did all of this happen, Wilson? How did it all go so wrong?"

"As near as I can tell, sir, we walked into an extremely well-designed trap." Wilson's fingers skipped over a grid of green and blue lines on his desk holo. "The sudden appearance of Alix Yamaguchi—"

"Just don't say her name." Link raised a finger in Wilson's direction. "I don't want to ever hear it again."

"Understood." Wilson cleared his throat as if to purge his system. "The sudden appearance of the woman on the chopper triggered our automatic surveillance drones. Once the squadron was tracking her, a high-frequency transmission from the Fringe penetrated our security shield. It uploaded an error message that, unfortunately, exploited a vulnerability we didn't know about. It took over video and targeting. The Fringe sector was evacuated beforehand to minimize casualties. The open field was waiting for her. It was all an elaborate plan. She was the bait—"

"And we took it." Link's head was a raging storm. "Tell me, Wilson. How would someone from the Fringe have the resources to pull this off?"

"Hard to say, sir. But whoever did this has deep knowledge of our systems, capabilities and security vulnerabilities."

Link stood, making it clear that the conversation was about to end. "I want a full investigation, Wilson. A thorough report."

"I'm on it, boss. We'll plug all the holes. Next time she tries, we'll be ready."

"No, Wilson, that's not good enough." Link pulled out the dispenser and downed another blue pill. In a few seconds, his headache was gone and forgotten. He leaned on Wilson's shoulder on his way out of the control room. "There won't be a next time."

"That's a great idea, boss, but how—"

"Easy." Link walked to the exit. "I'm going into the Fringe to hunt her down myself."

4

Lifting the scanner to his eyes, Link peered out from under the roof and scoured the landscape for survivors from his assault unit.

There weren't any.

Drone fighters hovered overhead, targeting all movement with pulse cannons. The skeletal remains of burnt-out heli-ships and incinerated dwellings made the ground a graveyard. Smoke coiled skyward from smoldering organics. Off to the right, a hostile in grey rags burst through a window and raised his rifle. Link snapped the hostile's spine with a roundhouse kick to his head. A fighter in red pajamas jumped off the roof, rolled and lunged at Link with a dagger in his left hand.

"Hey, it's me," a voice whispered in his earbud. "Did you forget about my birthday? I turned 20 today. Finally an adult. Daddy's got this huge celebration for me. You ready?"

In the split second that Link hesitated, the fighter drove the dagger into his heart. Agony exploded in his chest, dropping him to his knees. Two more hostiles appeared out of the darkness, tackling him to the ground. A fourth fighter pointed an old pulse rifle at Link's chest and touched off the trigger.

The pain was excruciating and delicious, purging the stress of the day.

"Daddy told me he wants to make the announcement about us," the voice in his ear purred, "when the time is right."

Link took in a deep breath. "Delete Fringe invasion simulation V2.1 and create V2.2 for execution tonight with the following settings: hostile skill level 10, chaos level 7, pain level 5." He stood and rubbed his chest where he had taken the shot, feeling refreshed. Next time it would hurt more. The buildings, drones and soldiers faded into sparks that slowly died away, leaving him in complete darkness. "I'll be out in a second, Chelsea."

A rectangle of light opened in the side of the holo-cube. Link walked into a bright room with high ceilings and felt the cool air on his chest. Other than the cube, the only furniture was a bed, a desk and small holo, a walk-in closet and scattered workout equipment. That was the way Link liked it: neat and empty. Minimalist. A single window ran from floor to ceiling, wrapping the whole penthouse in a ribbon of glass.

In the Sanctuary, the height of anyone's view was tied to their rank. Link had worked hard to earn a 500-meter-high view above the street. It might not last. Another dismal performance like the one today in the control room, and he'd find himself kicked back down to ground level with an account balance drained to nothing. President Quinn gave generously to those who performed well, but he also punished failure severely.

Chelsea stood near the glass, staring at the middle reaches of the Sanctuary. "Are you sure you can take a pain setting of 5? Sounds too hardcore to me."

"I need to increase the cost of failure in my training scenarios in the cube. It's the only way to improve. I know what I'm doing." Link pulled the bud out of his ear and tossed it on the desk where it landed and stuck. "By the way, happy birthday, Chels. Glad you came. It's been a hard day."

"Yeah, I heard." She walked close, flashed a too-perfect smile and slid her arms around his neck.

"Sorry about the sweat." He looked down at his moist biceps. "Give me five minutes to clean up and throw on a shirt. Had quite a battle on my hands a minute ago."

"Did you win?"

"Almost."

"Daddy says there's no *almost* when it comes to winning. What were you doing in the cube, slaying demons?" Chelsea looked up through long eyelashes. "Working off steam?"

"Yeah, that and *practice*."

"For what?"

"An operation. In the Fringe. I'll explain later."

"Let me guess. You're going after *her*."

"Yep. You always know everything."

Chelsea pulled him closer. "That's my job."

Link relaxed into her embrace. The last of the tightness in his muscles drained away as he enjoyed a long kiss.

She pressed her forehead into his sternum. "I'm here for you, okay? Everything will be fine. Daddy—"

"*Daddy* is going to kill me." As soon as he'd said it, he realized his mistake. Irreverent talk about President Quinn was never appropriate, especially in the presence of his daughter.

Chelsea trembled. She moved, as if to speak, and then hesitated. "Look, I can talk to him. Maybe he'll listen. You're not just anyone. You're my boyfriend. We're going to get married. Someday."

"Chelsea, I don't want to be a liability to you. Maybe you should just forget about—"

Her finger on his lips stopped the words. "We don't talk like that."

"You've done enough for me already, Chelsea."

"Stop it, Link."

"But your rank is 8Z, Chelsea. That's eight zeros. Five more than me. Totally out of my league. You could date—"

"Any man I like. It's true. But you're the first one I've met who actually cares about me more than about my bank account. That's rare. I'm not going to let anything happen to you, okay?" Chelsea took a step back. "After all, you're trying to protect our life here in the Sanctuary. Leave Daddy to me. I'll make him understand."

"Come here." Link slid his hand down Chelsea's arm until he found her fingers and squeezed. With his eyes closed and lips moving over her neck, he took in the sweet fragrance of her hair and tried again to open his heart to love. But there was always something missing. He wasn't even sure what love was. A feeling that just came on its own? Or one you had to work for? Maybe it didn't matter. He liked being with Chelsea. She was beautiful, charming, smart and ultra-rich. No reason to overthink the situation.

Out of nowhere, the image of the blue and brown eyes came back to haunt him. He shook his head, trying to forget *her*. Trying to forget the eyes.

"Something wrong?" Chelsea said.

"No, just thinking about you," he lied.

Pulling her to the window, they stared out together across the scenic view of gorgeous structures inside the Sanctuary. In the exact center stood Quinn Tower. At 1,500 meters tall, it had a massive square footprint the size of a city block, a skin of glossy titanium and no windows except for a thin band of black glass at the top. It was half again as high as any other building and the only place where you could see over the Wall. Chelsea lived with her father on the top two floors.

No matter where you were in the Sanctuary, your eyes were drawn up to Quinn Tower, a constant reminder of the power and ranking of the Quinn family.

"What's it like to live there, Chelsea?" Link had often tried to imagine the effortless perfection of her life.

"I know it sounds trite, Link, but it's lonely to be at the top. It'd be so much better if I had someone to share it with."

"What about your father?"

"Don't be stupid." Chelsea shook her head. "You've heard him talk. He doesn't believe in sharing."

From Link's window, they could look down a long boulevard for a full view of the Wall. It surrounded the Sanctuary, protecting it from the Fringe like a giant membrane. A thousand meters high and one meter thick, it was taller than any structure except for Quinn Tower. Right now the Wall's glossy surface projected an idyllic image of a snow-capped mountain range on the far side of a crystal blue lake. Yesterday, it had displayed a majestic waterfall in the heart of a tropical rainforest. The image changed every few hours, like having an exquisite work of art always in the background.

With the Wall wrapping around it, the Sanctuary was like a glass box stuffed with precious jewels. Pure beauty, but fragile.

"Daddy says it's a great achievement, all of this. The fulfillment of the hopes and dreams of thousands of years of civilization in the pursuit of paradise." Chelsea leaned in, palms pressed against the window. "A perfect world, Link. And someday, it will be *our* perfect world. Free and beautiful."

"We have a saying in the Patrol: *freedom isn't free.*" Link narrowed his eyes. "The enemy is just beyond the Wall. Constant vigilance is required."

"So, any idea why *she* wants to destroy all of this?" Chelsea stood closer to Link, stirring the air with the intoxicating scent of her hair.

"She?"

"Don't play dumb, Link. She was on every jax and screen. Even the Wall. The whole Sanctuary was mesmerized by her, including Daddy. Everyone's talking about her."

"Alix Yamaguchi?" Link's back stiffened as he spoke the name, pulse quickening just a bit. "Why does she want to destroy the Sanctuary? It's not complicated. She's typical Fringe scum. They all hate us. They want what we have. And if they can't have it, well, destroying it is the next best thing."

"And you want to go after her, into the Fringe?"

"We have to stop her. There's no other way."

"Did you see her eyes?" Chelsea asked.

Link flexed his jax, shaking his head vigorously. "Stuff like that doesn't matter."

"You don't think so? I don't know. People on the street are strange. They can be swayed by little things like that. Take it as a sign."

"Come on, Chelsea. Don't worry so much. By this time next week, no one will remember Alix Yamaguchi."

Chelsea stared outside, never taking her eyes off the Wall. "I can see the Fringe from my bedroom window. I've been fascinated by it ever since I was a little girl. It's massive and dangerous, Link. Like something wild. I don't like the idea of you going there. Can't you just try the drones again? Do some kind of surgical strike to take her out?"

"That's exactly what we tried today." Link took in a big breath and let it slowly bleed out. "It's not that easy. There are thousands of places to hide. People help her. Our tech is good but not good enough."

"Then send someone else. Maybe Wilson?"

"It wouldn't be right." Link shook his head. "I'm the one who lost her today. It's my responsibility."

"I've heard stories about the Fringe. Sounds like the closest thing to hell on earth. What's it really like there?" Chelsea pressed against Link, hands still on the glass. "I wonder if it's true?"

"What?"

"That the Sanctuary dumps toxic waste there. That it's processed in the Fringe by children. That they're dying from a virus, and the Sanctuary has the cure."

"She's lying." Link shook his head. "Nobody's dumping waste there. And I'm sure she's making it up about the children. But the place is a living hell; that much is true. We all got a good look at it today. Endless shacks of recycled scrap and surplus organics, cesspools everywhere. They've made a real mess of it."

"Who? Us or them?"

"The Fringe freaks and zeros that live there."

"What about my jax?" Chelsea slipped her hand inside her dress and came out with a slender, curved cylinder of finely chiseled ivory, laced with gold. Tiny lights, like miniature jewels, flashed along its surface. She tapped one with her pinkie. A holoscreen with the latest celeb feed jumped above it. "She said they use brain slaves in the Fringe to power my jax. Doesn't sound like something Daddy would do, but—"

"Don't believe her." Link shook his head. "The Sanctuary isn't built on slavery. Freedom and liberty are at the foundation of our society. Everyone's equal. There's the Constitution. The rule of law."

"Sounds like one of Daddy's public speeches."

"I'm telling you, Chelsea. Having a revolution is ludicrous. There's nothing to revolt against."

"What about the virus?" Chelsea folded her arms. "Do you really think the Sanctuary would do nothing if children were dying in the Fringe?"

"There isn't any virus. If there were, don't you think we'd know about it? We'd share the cure with them if we had it. Even though they don't deserve it. It's the civilized thing to do."

"Exactly what I was thinking."

"Don't believe anything she says, Chelsea. The revolution is fake news. She's just stirring up trouble."

"And it's working." Chelsea peered out the window to the streets below. "That live holo feed today had the most detailed footage people have ever seen of the Fringe. You know Daddy doesn't allow that sort of thing on the Mesh. When it pops up, it's immediately scrubbed by censor bots. So, of course, everyone's talking about it now."

"Your father's angry, isn't he?"

Chelsea shrugged. "*Angry* may not be the right word. He's always angry, but when I left, he was *livid*. In a rage like I've never seen before. Smashed a whole collection of vintage Ming Dynasty vases. I was afraid he'd take a dagger to the Mona Lisa hanging in his bathroom. He was popping blue pills like crazy. But don't worry. He's not mad at you, exactly."

"Hard to believe." Link felt a heavy weight the size of a boulder in his stomach but tried to ignore it. "I was the commander on deck when it happened."

"That was just unlucky." Chelsea turned to face Link with her back to the glass. "Anyway, I think Daddy is wrong."

"About what?"

"About the Fringe. About not letting anyone see it." She shuddered. "It reminded me how good we have it here. If I become President—"

"You mean, *when* you become President?"

"Yes, well, you never know. We have a democracy here. There is an election, after all."

Link nodded. "You know the saying. *A Quinn always wins.*"

"When I'm President, I'll pass a law that makes it mandatory to view life in the Fringe."

"If there's still a Fringe when you're President."

"Daddy says there'll *always* be a Fringe. There'll always be Fringe people. People that can't adapt. People that don't want to adapt. They're just different from us. They made the Fringe. It's where they belong. It's where they feel at home. It's what they like, I guess." Chelsea reached up and ran cool fingers down Link's bare spine. "You better get dressed. Daddy is waiting."

"Right." Link walked away from the window to a closet. Its doors slid open without a sound, and he entered an enclosure larger than most family apartments. He stepped into a shower where a mist of water and air blasters cleaned away the sweat in a few seconds, leaving him clean and dry. "How should I dress for the party? Military or corporate style? Or a little of both? Or, maybe something whimsical, like those feather epaulets that have taken the Mesh by storm?"

Chelsea leaned on the side of the closet entrance, arms folded. "Don't do the epaulets, Link. That was *last* week. I know you don't have time to keep up with the latest fashion, with all your Patrol duties, but I can't have you dressing so hopelessly out-of-date. And considering what happened today, I'd skip the military. You don't want to remind them."

"I have a feeling they'll remember no matter what I wear."

Chelsea turned and lifted a black box off the desk. "Here. Wear this. I picked it out myself. It goes with my outfit." She handed it to him.

Inside was a carbon silk tunic and matching black leather leggings.

"Thanks, Chels. Always thinking of me."

Link slipped the tunic over his head. As soon as it rested on his shoulders, it became semi-rigid, with enhanced pecs and shoulders.

"What do you think?" Chelsea said. "It's got the latest tech from Fiji."

Link walked to a mirror. "I like it."

"And so will Daddy."

"I'll need all the help I can get."

Chelsea put a hand on her hip. "So, what do you think of *her*?"

"Her?"

"Come on. Everyone will be talking about her." Chelsea folded her arms. "Alix Yamaguchi? People are going to ask your opinion. You better have the right one."

Link's eyes narrowed. Blue and brown eyes flashed into his mind. "The girl from the Fringe? I don't think anything of her, other than that she's a traitor and deserves to die." He tried to wipe her image out of his mind, but it wouldn't leave. His stomach tightened.

"You're lying."

Link pulled on the black leather leggings and took another glance at the two of them in the mirror. "Perfect match. Shall we go?"

Chelsea hugged him from behind as he walked by. "Stop trying to change the subject. You can't get her out of your mind. You're distracted. I can tell."

"I really don't want to talk about it." Link shook his head. "Or her. She's a nobody. Like I said, pure Fringe scum."

"That may be. But she's a Mesh-phenom now. The whole Sanctuary will be talking about her."

"It's just a fad. Cheap propaganda. They'll forget about her in a few days."

"Right after you capture her?"

Link flexed his jaw. "You mean *kill* her?"

"I still don't know if I approve of your idea to go into the Fringe after her. That's why we have drones. Daddy's always talking about the Wall and how important it is. He doesn't like it when people cross over to the Fringe."

"Don't worry. I'm sure your father will make an exception for the man who's going to marry his daughter."

"What?" Chelsea curled her arms around Link's neck, pulling him close for another kiss. "You think you're special?"

"That's what you always tell me." Link grinned. "I hope it's true."

5

Alix left the chopper leaning against a wall inside the lobby of the old library, her favorite place. Well-worn books lined the shelves. She'd read many of them, some more than once. The library was usually crowded, but it was empty now. People had gotten the word to evacuate the area.

Merf had told Alix how stealing was common in the Sanctuary. Motorcycles were usually stored inside apartments for that reason. Anything left outside was chained up. Doors were locked. It seemed like a lot of bother. Life was simpler in the Fringe. There weren't any locks on anything, doors or otherwise.

She glanced back at the chopper, which actually belonged to Merf. If someone needed it, they could use it and bring it back. Why hoard stuff? Just use what you need and let other folks use what they need. It all worked out.

Walking away, the adrenaline rush of the last hour faded, leaving her legs and arms heavy. What followed was a sudden craving for sleep and a longing to go home, where she could rest and hide. And the fear began to seep back in. Like a wall of cold water, a thought hit her.

I'll be dead tomorrow.

She'd openly defied President Quinn, the latest tyrant in a long line of Quinns stretching back six generations. The Sanctuary liked to talk about democracy, but they all knew Quinn was a dictator. And yet, millions of folks on both sides of the Wall had watched her challenge him. She'd shown them all that it was possible, that he wasn't a god-like emperor, that with enough guts and tech, you could take him down.

She'd crossed a red line. No matter what, she could never walk away from what she'd done. Only two possible outcomes remained. Either the people of the Sanctuary would open their eyes and demand change, or they'd close their eyes and demand her blood. Either way, Quinn would send soldiers like Lincoln Wells to come after her in the Fringe, to find her and kill her.

It wasn't a question of *if*, but only a matter of *when*.

She'd talked about the possibility with Merf. It was a risk she'd been willing to accept in the excitement of the moment. Merf said the Fringe was ready. He'd promised to use all his powers to keep her safe. Folks would step up and protect her. It sounded plausible at the time, but what could Fringe folks really do if an invasion came? There were only so many places to hide. With enough soldiers and tech, they'd find her and kill thousands of innocent people on the way.

Why hadn't she seen it before?

Her chest seized up. Unable to breathe, she stopped and leaned her forehead against a cracked door frame, smelling the reek of mold and rotten organics. Eyes closed, she forced herself to take long, slow breaths and wait for the terror to pass.

Think logically, she told herself. *You already know the risks. You're not alone. It's all part of Merf's plan. Nothing has changed. Shake it off.*

People had launched rebellions before. All of them were dead. She hadn't thought much about it in the past weeks and months. All the talking and brainstorming with Merf had been a game, an exciting way to dream about taking down the power structure. They'd convinced themselves that things would be different this time. Merf was a better Mesh-hacker than anyone inside the Sanctuary. They had resources. This time, they were smarter, and they'd win.

She broke into a sprint.

The heaviness in her legs drained away, taking the fear with it. Dashing through an empty house, she jumped out an open window on the other side and darted across a wide street, taking care not to show her face to the sky. A ramp of crumbled concrete steps led down into a hole. She plunged into the darkness.

The old subway.

It was a relic from a time before the Wall, like the skeletal remains of buildings scattered through the Fringe, some of them as large as the ones in the Sanctuary. It was evidence of a distant past none of them remembered, a time before the Quinn family had taken over, before the nightmare, proof that the world had once been different and could be different again.

The deeper Alix pushed into the subway, the darker it got, until she no longer needed eyes. Like all Fringe natives, she had a detailed map of the underground network in her head. It was how you got around when the skies were full of drones. Walking in utter blackness was easy and relaxing. She'd done it so much that she instinctively sensed where the tracks, walls and turns were. And except for the roving packs of cat-sized rats and the wild dogs that hunted them, the old tunnels in the subway were safe.

In the darkness, with nothing to see, the image of Lincoln Wells blazed in her mind. He was coming after her, maybe already making plans. He'd drop down with his battle armor, pulse weapons and overwhelming force from the Patrol. And this time, they'd do it the old-fashioned way. Boots on the ground and no drones. Merf wouldn't find it so easy to disrupt their targeting algorithms. Her chest tightened. Unable to breathe, she staggered to the left over two lines of railroad tracks and past a set of columns until her hands hit the wall. Pressing both palms into it, she brought her face close and took a big inhale of the earthy odors of concrete, dirt and rat dung.

After 10 deep breaths, her pulse settled down. But that didn't last long.

She had a sudden urge to stay there, enveloped in the dark, away from the omnipresent eyes of the Sanctuary. Lots of people lived below ground. The air and water were cleaner there. When the Patrol started looking for her, she'd move around inside the subway, stay hidden.

But they'd still come. They'd fill the tunnels with soldiers and searchlights and wouldn't stop until she surrendered. There'd be battles and endless fighting. It might destroy the Fringe.

Inevitably, Quinn would win.

Eyes still closed, she turned and dug her shoulder blades into the wall until they hurt, waiting for what she knew was coming. When the wave of panic hit, she didn't try to push it back. She embraced it, facing it full on until it swelled in her veins and filled the empty spaces in her mind.

Once the terror had her completely in its grasp, she knew what to do.

Bursting off the wall, she raced into the heart of the blackness, pushing herself to run faster. With each stride, she penetrated deeper into the void and let the fear bleed out like a slow leak. If there were demons in the dark, let them come out.

Rounding a long curve, Alix opened her eyes to a light in the distance. She slowed her feet and her breath. The adrenaline and hunger for oxygen had beaten back the panic. It was a trick she'd learned as a child.

As she focused on the light, her fear dropped away.

The underground market came into focus. You could get old electronics and assorted military paraphernalia, some of it from the prior century, stuff not available on the surface. The crowd here was different, too. They had sharper opinions about Quinn and were Alix's most enthusiastic converts when she began talking about revolution. She'd known most of them since she was a kid doing scrounging missions for Merf.

The din of voices reached her while she was still half a klick away. When she finally stepped into the light, her terror had mostly evaporated. She was back to pretending to be confident and met the crowd with a smile.

"Hey look, everyone, here she is," a woman yelled. "Come on over, Alix."

At the mention of her name, the rabble fell silent.

It was the same old crowd with the same old faces, but they'd changed. Alix had seen that look before. It had happened a year earlier when a new Mesh-celeb named Licious had come to life on the public holoscreens in the Fringe to brag about her perfect glass condo on the summit of Kilimanjaro and the exquisite taste of sushi from the last bluefin tuna ever caught in the wild. Alix had looked into their faces and seen open-mouthed awe.

And now they were staring at Alix in the same way. Merf had been right. With his help, she'd become a Mesh-star.

The rollercoaster of fear instantly resurfaced. Her first impulse was to turn and run back into the darkness, away from the eyes and the staring. Away from the weight of impossible expectations.

She shuffled through the market, hoping to avoid conversation and eye contact. She was the same Alix she'd been the day before. All she had to do was act as if nothing had changed. Maybe no one would speak to her if she just kept moving.

And then the voices started.

"You did good, Alix."

"You really told them, Alix."

"We got your back, Alix."

Hands reached out to touch her. Voices got louder. She nodded and kept walking, smiling but not speaking, not wanting to stop and answer, not sure she even had an answer to any question.

A teenage kid stood under a bare lightbulb, hands thrust into his pockets, pencil-thin legs swimming in baggy pants cut from scavenged cloth. Like everyone in the Fringe, he had a pale green pallor from the cornboo. His eyes traced her movements. As she walked by, he stepped into her path, blocking the way.

"You know he's going to punish us. He has to. Quinn's like that. You spit in his face. Now he's got to do something to show the people he's still in control. What are you going to do when the soldiers come and tear the Fringe apart?"

I have no idea, Alix thought.

She slowly brought her gaze up from the ground to meet the kid's eyes. "What am I going to do? Depends. We'll figure it out when they come." She cringed.

The kid tilted his head. "What do you mean by *we*? *We* didn't do anything. You came here and talked about revolution and change, but this is off the charts. You haven't started a revolution; you've started a *war*. Whatever happens, it's on you."

"If you want to be a stinking coward, go hide with the rats." A young woman with an old pulse rifle and a buzz cut pushed past the kid. "I think she did good. Exactly what Quinn needed to hear. If there's going to be a war, I say bring it on." She pumped her pulse rifle and let off a couple of shots, the echoes reverberating in the darkness.

An old man in a broken wheelchair pushed through a sea of legs. "You got a plan, Alix, right?"

The kid in the baggy pants cocked his head to the side. "Well?"

The woman with the rifle also looked at Alix quizzically.

Alix stifled the urge to escape.

Yeah, there was a plan. Sort of. She and Merf had talked about it for months. Eventually, they figured out that the real revolution had to happen in the Sanctuary, not the Fringe. But how do you *plan* to open people's eyes so they see the truth? How do you *plan* to give them courage to demand justice, not just for themselves but for everyone in a weaker position? What kind of *plan* could change the way people see the world?

The beginnings of a plan had been stirring inside her from the time she was old enough to go to the Wall on hot summer nights and peer through the transparent glass at the perfect lives of seemingly endless joy, all of it just out of reach. At some point, she realized that people in the Sanctuary couldn't see her, and they had more than just cornboo to eat. They had more than one dirty shirt and homemade pants to wear. They lived in paradise.

Then there was the annual lottery. Every year, one person was chosen at random from the Fringe for a life in the Sanctuary. One person out of millions. When she was small, Alix had dreamed it would happen to her. She was sure of it.

But every year her dream died a little.

It wasn't until she was a teenager that she realized all the other kids in the Fringe had the same fantasy. That was when she threw away her dreams.

The truth was, she'd never be part of the Sanctuary, and she knew it. No matter how hard she worked, no matter how much she longed for it, the effortless happiness of the Sanctuary was forever beyond her reach. When the full realization dawned on her, the utter unfairness of it was seared into her mind to the point where she could think of little else.

The only thing that saved her was working on a way to change the world. Working on a *plan*.

"Yeah, we got a plan." Alix stared back at the kid, his pale green skin pocked with sores and scars from the chemplant.

"What you going to do, raise an army?" The kid folded his arms, casting a side-glance at the woman with the pulse rifle. "Scale the Wall and invade the Sanctuary?"

"Do I look that stupid?" Alix smirked, her confidence coming back as her pulse rose.

"Then what?"

"Tell us." The old man in the wheelchair pushed closer to her, peering up from beneath a mostly disintegrated baseball cap with a faint NY emblem. "What's the plan?"

"We're going to change their minds," Alix said. "That's the plan."

The kid threw up his hands. "How you gonna to change their minds? The Sanctuary-born love life at the top. The last thing they want is change. And then you've got the Quinns, a family of thugs. They have all the power. You think they want change? What could you possibly do to change their minds? We got nothing that can do that."

"You're wrong." Moving close to the kid, Alix stared into his eyes. "We've got the ultimate weapon."

"What?"

"The truth."

6

Ocular

The instant they stepped onto the express sidewalk in the sky tube, Link looked down through the glass to the streets 500 meters below and noticed it.

People in scarlet everywhere.

"What's going on?" Link blinked his eyes.

With on-demand clothing fabricators in every home, fashion moved fast in the Sanctuary, but he'd never seen anything like this. Within the past hour, crimson attire had become the style of choice, a new social phenomenon.

"I wonder how she knew." Chelsea stared down at the streets.

"Knew what?"

"Daddy hates red. It infuriates him." Chelsea pointed down. "I have to hand it to her. It's working even better than anyone could have predicted."

"Who are you talking about?"

"Her," Chelsea whispered. "She's smart. Look what she's done."

"Her? She?"

"Come on, Link." Chelsea exhaled. "Don't you get what's going on?"

It hit him like a wall of water. "Alix Yamaguchi?"

"Who else?" Chelsea moved her finger along her jax, parsing through multiple video feeds as she talked. "Have you seen any celebs wearing red on the Mesh?"

"No, but—"

"And you never wondered why?"

"Not really."

"It's simple. Daddy has an understanding with them. They know he hates it. Reminds him of China." Chelsea stared out the glass window of the tube. "But now look."

It was incredible. A crimson tide of humanity flooded the boulevards and sidewalks. Link couldn't remember the last time he'd seen so many people outside at the same time.

Link and Chelsea made the rest of the journey in silence. He did his best to ignore the red, and it looked like Chelsea was doing the same. Brushing shoulders, they each got absorbed in their own Mesh feeds. Chelsea had her jax on mute, listening to the audio with her implants. It was a live show from Licious, a Mesh-celeb with a swarm of mini-drones broadcasting her every move 24/7. She lived in a personal skyscraper in the Sanctuary. He remembered how she had once paid a huge sum for the last wild tuna on the planet and had carved it into sushi with her own hands. Now she was hunting whale calves off the coast of Antarctica. He quickly looked away from Chelsea's jax, unable to stomach the pop-celeb garbage that everyone loved. Instead, he grabbed a video feed from a ninjutsu studio in a gritty part of the Akihabara section of Tokyo.

After 10 minutes of travel through multiple buildings in the tube, they arrived at Quinn Station, a sky hub across the street from Quinn Tower. From there, they'd take an elevator down.

Quinn Tower had the tightest security of any installation on the planet. Most Sanctuary-born had never even stepped inside the lobby. Signal dampeners made civilian jaxes inoperable within 100 meters of its titanium walls. And it was the only building in the Sanctuary with no sky tube connections. Naturally, people tended to avoid the neighborhood. It only had two entrances: one at street level and the other 1,500 meters up on the roof. Not only was Quinn Tower physically disconnected from the rest of the Sanctuary, Link's security clearance as a Patrol commander wouldn't even get him past the guards outside the front door without Chelsea. Everyone knew the Tower's Mesh-node was hacker-proof and had never been penetrated.

Link wished they'd had that kind of tech at Patrol HQ. It might have stopped Alix Yamaguchi.

Stepping off the express sidewalk in the tube, they passed a crowd of ecstatic teenagers, children of the elite, gathered near a window. It was rare in the Sanctuary to see groups talking or walking together, young or old. People liked to be alone, their full attention absorbed by a jax, audial implant or other tech.

But these kids were deep in conversation.

"Can you believe it?" A girl in crimson leather gushed while pointing through the window in the direction of the Wall. "She was so *real*. So *earthy*."

The boy next to her nodded vigorously, licking a red narco stick and weaving a jax through his fingers. "Wonder where she lives. Love to get a holo of her for my room."

"Don't be crazy." Another girl with red hair rolled her eyes. "She's Fringe scum. You can't go there."

"Why not?" the boy asked.

"You'll die. They're animals."

"I like animals. Besides, sounds like maybe we made them that way. Maybe it's our fault. Maybe we should help them. Extend some sisterly love."

The girl shook her head. "Talk like that will get you in trouble."

"Yeah, well maybe there needs to be more *real* talk around here—"

They looked up as Link and Chelsea walked by.

"Shut up!" The girl whispered. "Don't you know who that is? Quinn's daughter."

Link waited until they were alone in the elevator. "Stupid kids," he said.

"Stupid or not, you realize what's going on, right?"

Link nodded. "Yeah, I get it. They've found a new hero. Alix Yamaguchi." Rage flared, and he had to consciously uncurl his fingers from a fist. "She's crossed a line. Those kids are the proof. They've been brainwashed. They think she's *cool*."

"Think about it, Link." Chelsea flicked off her jax. "That's what all Mesh-celebs do. It's just marketing. A genius plan."

Decelerating, the elevator hovered and stopped. The doors opened. Link followed Chelsea through the lobby and open doors to the curb outside.

"I don't care about her plan. All I care about is stopping her." Link gazed up as they crossed the street to the titanium monolith of Quinn Tower. A great glass arch marked the doorway. Armed guards stood on each side brandishing shoulder cannons. Link recognized them as former Patrol soldiers. They nodded to Chelsea. As she and Link passed under it, the arch glowed green.

The guard on the right nodded. "Enjoy your evening, ma'am. And happy birthday."

They walked through an open lobby with gold leaf walls, a massive crystal chandelier and wall-to-wall guards. Link could almost feel the presence of data sniffers, security cameras and hidden laser knives. At the far end of the lobby, he and Chelsea took another elevator up to the second floor and stepped out into a hallway. Voices emanated from a ballroom.

Link's chest tightened. "Here goes."

"Don't worry. I'll be here. Can you feel it?"

"Feel what?"

Chelsea gripped his arm. "My love. What else would I be talking about?" She pulled his head down and pressed her lips into his. "You'll do fine."

"Thanks, Chels."

Link was lucky to be with her. Any guy in the Sanctuary would trade places with him in a heartbeat. To have a shot at marrying into the Quinn family was the ultimate dream of dreams.

He'd caught her eye at a party six months prior and they were still going strong. She'd made the first move, and it wasn't long before she'd looked into his eyes and confessed her love. She liked to talk about her hunger for love and the ecstasy of finally finding it.

Love was a common theme in the Sanctuary. Thousands of Mesh

nodes were devoted to the topic of real love and how to find it. Like everyone else, Link felt the same hunger for love as Chelsea and wanted to give her what she craved. He'd dug deep trying to feel it, but there was always a certain emptiness, a nagging feeling that his romance with Chelsea Quinn was too convenient, too perfect to be real.

"Remember, this party is just another kind of battle," she said. "Like in the holo-cube of yours. You can do this."

"Maybe, with your help."

"That's why I'm here." She brought her hand up and gently pulled his face close. "Turn your *ocular* on."

"Do I have to? It's so annoying. I hate the constant pestering. Too much information."

"Trust me. You'll need it to get through this party, and I'll need it to talk you through the meeting with Daddy. He's not in a good mood."

"OK." Link pressed his tongue to that spot on the roof of his mouth to engage the ocular. Faint grid lines appeared in his vision along with floating bits of data about everyone in his view, including their all-important rank. "It's on now."

"Are we connected?" Chelsea's icon floated in the lower right corner of his field of vision.

"Yep, I can see you."

"Look, I know how to work Daddy." She squeezed his arm. "Pay attention, and it'll be alright."

"Thanks, Chels."

Link hated the ocular interface. At Patrol headquarters, he never used it. They had to be a tight-knit group, and the ocular was prohibited because it emphasized rank and tended to push people apart. But Chelsea was right. Tonight was different. Every VIP would be at the party, and they would all be using their oculars. Information was a weapon, and he would need all he could get to navigate through the events of the evening. It would help to have the voiceless connection to Chelsea. When he glanced at her, her data appeared in green below her face.

Chelsea Quinn

0.000000027

"Eight lovely zeros. Looks like your rank's clicked up a notch since last week." Link lifted his eyebrows.

"Crazy, I know. Money flows into my account 24/7. It's constant and effortless. I don't know how Daddy does it."

It amazed him every time he saw Chelsea's low number and had to remind himself she was one of a few dozen ultra-rich people in the world. The more zeros, the higher your ranking. Everyone knew that President Quinn's rank was 0.000000001, the lowest possible number and the highest possible rank. It's what you got when you divided 1 by the 1,000,000,000 ranked people in the world. He had nine zeros in all, so his rank was 9Z.

Link hated it, but everyone in the Sanctuary had a wealth ranking based on the total market value of their accounts and investments. With an ocular, you could see the rankings at a glance. It was public information, clear evidence of one's worth to society. Coming in with a rank of 0.000000027, Chelsea was the 27th richest person of the billion ranked people on the planet. The eight leading zeros in her rank made her an 8Z, one of only a hundred in the world.

Link looked down at his palm and saw his own rank floating in the ocular.

0.007385612

Only three zeros. An ordinary 3Z. It put him solidly in the top 1% of the ranked population, but he yearned to make it into the top one hundred, like Chelsea. That would instantly happen on the day they got married.

It was just like the old saying: *access equals success.*

It could be worse. Thanks to his Patrol job, he was ticking higher every day, taking a bigger cut of the government revenues controlled by the Quinn organization.

Alix Yamaguchi, the Fringe freak, was so far down in social status that she didn't even have a rank. If rank was a measure of one's worth to society, then she and all the other Fringe scum were literally worthless. With that in mind, he walked to the open door with Chelsea, passing more armed guards.

Words appeared in his field of vision by Chelsea's icon as she subvocalized the words.

Here we go. Stay close to me. I'll protect you.

The instant they stepped into the room, the hubbub of voices lowered, then stopped. Faces turned. Link took a deep breath against a tight chest.

"Happy birthday, Chelsea, my little girl!" A familiar voice boomed from the other side of the room. The guests parted. Link saw the man standing alone on a raised platform. Link's ocular provided the pertinent information.

Franklin Alexander Quinn.

President of the United Sanctuaries of America.

0.000000001

Nine zeros followed by a single number one. It was beautiful, utter perfection. Quinn was the highest ranking 9Z on the planet, literally the most valuable man in the world. Number one.

"Daddy." Chelsea smiled widely and walked through the crowd, pulling Link behind her. Her palms were sweaty.

Link scanned the faces of the Sanctuary elite. With his ocular engaged, names and ranks cascaded across his field of vision. President Quinn's entire cabinet was there, every one of them a 7Z or higher.

Together, he and Chelsea made their way up the broad stairs of the platform, taking care to stop a step below Quinn. Chelsea's words glowed in Link's field of vision.

Stay behind when he invites me up. Only a Quinn can mount the top step. Daddy's rules.

Quinn smiled down on his daughter. The room was silent.

"Chelsea, my dear, I hope you like this. It's all for you." Quinn stretched his hand down to her. "Please join me." He cast an ambiguous glance at Link.

"I'd love to." She took her father's extended hand. He gently pulled her up to his level and turned her around to face the crowd, large hands on her bare shoulders.

The room exploded in applause and then abruptly stopped as Quinn raised a hand.

"I couldn't be more proud of my daughter. Chelsea's a true winner." Quinn's face relaxed into that terrible smile known coast to coast in the United Sanctuaries. No doubt the scene was being broadcast on all the public holoscreens here and elsewhere. "She's so young and already an 8Z. A fabulous achievement."

"Thank you, Daddy." Chelsea had that plastic grin on her face that meant she was in robot mode. "I owe it all to you. You've shown me the way."

As everyone knew, Quinn loved and demanded public adulation. His smile filled his whole face, neon-white teeth gleaming.

"All I want is to keep the Sanctuary safe and prosperous." Quinn's gaze swept past Link on the lower step. "It's clear we must be even more vigilant to protect our way of life."

As the room reacted with applause, Chelsea reached up and pulled her father close, whispering in his ear. At first, his face was rigid and stern. He shook his head and whispered back to her. Her eyes went wide. It was a negotiation. They were working out the terms of a deal. Link could see Chelsea's fear. She spoke quickly, and Quinn's features relaxed back into a smile. With an expert flick of her finger, she wiped a single tear from her eyes and turned back to the crowd, beaming.

What sort of concessions had she been forced to make to him? As if in answer, Chelsea's words appeared next to her icon in Link's field of vision.

You have to personally kill Alix Yamaguchi. If you fail, you'll be forbidden to see me. He's giving you two days. It's the best deal I could get.

"My friends," Quinn stretched his arms out wide, as if embracing the crowd. "I wish to say a few words about the terrible events of today. The perfect society we have created is under attack. Ever since the first Wall was built by my distinguished ancestor, the great John Quinn, we've had no choice but to separate ourselves from the outside world."

As Quinn talked, Link found it hard to concentrate. Like everyone else in the room, he'd heard this particular speech a hundred times before. No doubt every word of it was true, but all Link could think about was two eyes, one blue and the other brown. Without thinking, his eyelids dropped, and in the darkness, Chelsea startled him awake with the ocular.

Pay attention, Link. Act fascinated. Daddy is always watching.

"We are a free people. We believe in freedom. We love freedom. That's why we keep the Wall. Here in the Sanctuary, we have the freedom to live life to the fullest. And we allow the people of the Fringe to live their lives as they choose. No one forced them to build slums. But they have made their choice, and now they must live with the consequences."

Link scanned the room. It was filled with greens and blues, but not a single person wore red. Link wondered if Quinn knew what was happening outside.

"And now, a word of advice for us all. Ignore the lies you heard today from the Fringe. It's a cesspool of incompetence and failure. We already help them. We provide food that's practically free. But their idleness and ingratitude knows no bounds, and they clamor for more. Remember, my friends, we have achieved perfection in the Sanctuary. To accept change is to accept defeat. No change is needed. None will be tolerated."

With a wave of his hand, Quinn signaled for all that discussion of the incident was to end.

"This is a party for my daughter. We hear from her so rarely. How about a few words from the birthday girl?" Amidst the applause, Quinn motioned to Chelsea, the signal for her to speak.

She responded with a nod of easy confidence and a practiced smile, the same plastic smile Chelsea used to navigate the world of the ultra-rich, a world within the Sanctuary as foreign to Link as the Fringe.

Now to give the speech Daddy prepared for me.

"My friends, thank you for your support. I wouldn't want to be anywhere else on my birthday. From the time I was a small child, I've looked to my father for guidance and support. He's a man of integrity, experience and wisdom. He's always been here for me. I know he can be trusted to do what is best for the Sanctuary and all the other great cities in our great nation." She pulled her father closer.

No doubt Chelsea was streaming on all channels.

"We live in a blessed time, a time when we are reaping the fruits of the work started six generations ago by my forefathers. Never forget, the

Sanctuary represents the pinnacle of civilization. Here, we have made a society where each of us can achieve our ultimate potential. Nothing holds us back, especially not foreigners or outsiders. The Wall guarantees our freedom by keeping them out. We must be vigilant against forces that try to destroy our paradise."

When Chelsea stopped talking, Link realized he had stopped listening and couldn't remember a thing she'd said.

Everyone in the room applauded. Quinn whispered in Chelsea's ear and then released her to mingle with the crowd. As she turned away from him, her smile disappeared.

Daddy just added one more condition. You won't like it.

Link looked up in time to catch Quinn's gaze. Both of them locked eyes for an instant. Link dug deep for a confident grin. Quinn's eyes narrowed slightly.

Chelsea descended from the platform, slid her fingers into Link's hand and pulled him with her into the safety of the crowd.

"You've got five minutes to get ready," she said.

"Ready for what?"

"Daddy changed the deal on me at the last minute." Chelsea peered at the floor. "You're going to have a personal meeting with him. In his special room."

7

Secret

Alix walked up the ramp, out of the subway and onto the street just as the sun dropped below the horizon. Only two things mattered: food and sleep. She'd think about the rest later. Moving across an open square to a row house on the other side, she saw a man in tattered overalls step out of a door with a bundle in his arms. As she approached, Alix could only see the small toes that stuck out of the blanket.

"Hi George. How is little Lilly do—"

In an instant she was close enough to see that the child's eyes were closed, her small face lifeless and pale.

The man shook his head. "It happened so quickly. She was out playing kickball just this afternoon. And then—" He choked and moved past her, walking across the square.

Alix reached out a hand of comfort, but it was too late. He was gone. She watched until he disappeared around a corner into the dusk, headed for the nearest toxic dump. Lips pursed, she wanted to scream with rage.

Turning in at her row house, she dropped down four steps to where a door hung open. A dim light burned inside. The aroma of boiled cabbage, not cornboo, pulled her through.

"I'm home," Alix said, lingering on the deep meaning of the words and wondering how much longer she'd be able to say them.

"Glad you made it." The voice came from the kitchen in the far corner, where a shadow moved behind a paper partition. "Just in time for dinner."

There was something about the voice of Muse, the woman who'd adopted and raised Alix, that always had an instantly calming effect. Alix's rage bled off, mellowing into sadness.

"I passed George outside," she said. "He was carrying—"

"I know. Little Lilly is gone. I just came from their house. The virus is out of control. All I could do was cry."

"I feel so helpless, Muse. How is this all going to end?"

"How will it end? By you doing exactly what you did today, Alix." Muse popped her head out from behind the partition, eyes red and puffy. "Keep telling them the truth. Push for change. It will come. Now sit down. What you did today took courage. We're going to celebrate."

The aroma of the cabbage overpowered Alix's senses.

"Where'd you get the greens, Muse? Can't remember the last time I ate a real veggie." Alix closed her eyes and allowed herself to feel joy with a deep inhale of the cooking aroma. She took four steps across the room past the lopsided old piece of plywood that served as a table and dropped into a large bag of rough nylon filled with carefully chosen small pebbles. It was the softest chair in the house, one of her prized possessions. "That takes real money, which we don't have. Where'd you get them?"

"The money or the vegetables?"

"Both."

"Can't you guess?"

"Merf?"

"The one and only." Muse stepped out of the kitchen into the room, strings of gray in her hair, like moonlight on the water. "He said he hacked a Sanctuary account and borrowed the cash. Had a friend deliver the cabbage with a small drone over the Wall. According to him, you deserve special treatment for that little ride on your chopper."

"It was all him. I just played along."

Muse paused as her eyes scanned Alix from head to feet. "I like red."

"Apparently, President Quinn hates it."

"I didn't tell you that, did I?" Muse stopped, as if trying to remember. "No, it was Merf."

"I wonder how he found out. He must have hacked more than a few accounts in the Sanctuary."

"Merf is good at finding out things like that."

"By the way." Muse wiped her hands on her apron. "You were magnificent."

"You saw it?" Alix arched her back in the chair and let her head relax so she could stare at the ceiling.

"I couldn't miss it, my dear. You were everywhere, including all the public holoscreens here in the Fringe. Merf made sure of that." Muse softly giggled and shuffled back into the kitchen. Alix stood, mesmerized by the rhythmic sounds of cooking. "You're exhausted. Take a nap. I'll wake you when dinner's on the table."

Muse was like that. No matter what you said or who you were, she saw the truth and knew what you needed. And if she could give it to you, she would, usually in the form of gentle words. The thing was, she made you want to be better. Alix tried to learn from Muse, to be like her. It was hard, especially when Alix got excited or angry. And then she became like the version of herself that had ridden the chopper. Fearless and cocky. Merf said it was a good trait. "To rise to the occasion," he called it. Alix didn't like that version of herself. She would rather have been like Muse all the time, calm and steady. Before Alix could think about it more, a wave of fatigue crashed down on her.

I should be helping Muse with dinner, she thought as she drifted to sleep.

It was always the same dream.

A collage of colors mixed with the sound of surf on sand. Sunlight descended from above through a filter of branches and leaves. Shadows resolved into cedar trees with enormous trunks and mossy sides. The ground was soft, and it flexed with every footstep. Birdsong played in the canopy. Golden daffodils bloomed at her feet.

She stood on a trail that passed under a rocky ledge and around a corner.

Discovering an apple in her fingers, she inhaled its aroma and bit deep into its cool flesh. Sweet nectar exploded through her mouth as she consumed it down to the core.

Alix felt the presence of another gazing upon her. She searched for the source and found nothing.

Behind her, the fine mist of a waterfall drifted in from a distance. Moving off the trail, she followed the mist through the trees until she came to a pool. Water cascaded from high cliffs above, breaking into sheets of lace.

Bending close to the water, Alix dipped both hands in and brought them up to her lips for a long drink. And then another. Sweet and cool. Still, Alix couldn't shake the feeling that she was being watched. Her thirst satisfied, she rolled onto her back on the bank and stared up through the canopy. A lone hawk glided in tight circles just above the trees.

But then she looked again, more carefully this time.

It wasn't a bird.

There was a burst of light. The first drone shot grazed her shoulder. The sky went dark like a lid had slammed down. Behind her, the underbelly of a huge mechanical beast crashed down through the trees into the pool, throwing up a fine white mist that engulfed the forest.

She was up and running. A voice called her by name and commanded her to stop. As she weaved through the trees, bits of wood and bark exploded on all sides. They were firing pulse projectiles. Crossing the trail, she kept running for the beach and the surf. If she could make it to the ocean, maybe she'd get away.

A sharp pain in her right thigh dropped her to the forest floor. Ignoring the agony, she stood and hobbled forward. The voice was getting closer, and the shooting had stopped. Whoever it was, they probably knew she was wounded and wanted to take her alive.

"Sanctuary Patrol! Stop!"

The beach was in sight through the trees. Alix struggled to her feet and kept running.

When she broke out of the forest onto the sand, a dozen drones floated overhead. A sharp pain bit into her neck, and she pulled out a red dart. In seconds, her arms and legs froze, the muscles simply refusing to move. Like a statue, she tipped and fell to the sand, landing face up and staring at a beautiful sky.

Booted feet emerged from the forest to form a ring around her. Black helmets and goggles gathered to gawk.

"Stand back."

The helmets moved away until only one soldier remained. "Are you Alix Yamaguchi?" he asked.

"Who wants to know?" She tried to move, but her body was stone from the neck down. Paralyzed. She couldn't even grab a handful of sand.

"We're from the Patrol."

"Why are you chasing me?"

"Cyber terrorism." The soldier brought the tip of his pulse rifle down to rest squarely on Alix's forehead. "You're trying to destroy the Sanctuary."

"Wrong." Alix shook her head, feeling the gun barrel scrape against her skull. "I just want them to know the truth."

"About what?"

"Everything. How the Sanctuary isn't the perfect paradise they think it is. It's a parasite that feeds off the Fringe."

"That's a lie." The soldier ripped off his helmet to reveal brown eyes, dark hair and a snarl on his lips. "The Sanctuary is built on freedom and justice. We prosper because we work harder, make better choices. We choose civilization, while the Fringe chooses chaos. We deserve what we have."

"I've seen the public broadcasts. We get them in the Fringe, too. You're parroting President Quinn. Have you ever had a look at the Fringe for yourself?" Alix smiled.

"I don't need to."

"Thought so."

"You're going to die." The soldier pressed the rifle harder into Alix's head. Warm blood ran down her cheek.

"Don't I get a trial?"

"You're trying to bring down the Sanctuary."

Alix closed her eyes. "No, just trying to tell them the truth."

"We already have the truth!"

"I thought you said the Sanctuary is built on justice. Does that mean I get some?"

"Yes, Fringe scum, here's your justice. Exactly what you deserve."

As Alix looked up into the soldier's eyes, he pulled the trigger.

Alix jolted awake.

"Are you okay, my dear?" Muse looked down. "Bad dream?"

"The same one I've had for the last couple of months, ever since they started looking for me."

"Did you die?"

"I always wake up before that happens. But he always pulls the trigger."

"Who?"

"The soldier from the Sanctuary. The one who's coming after me."

Muse shook her head. "It's just a dream."

"Maybe. But I know he's coming."

"I think you're just hungry." She pointed at the table, smiling. "Come. Eat. You're going to like it."

"Can't wait!" Alix sprung to her feet, pulled by the aroma of the incredible feast on the table, straight out of a fairytale book like the many she'd read. She stood a moment to take inventory. "Boiled cabbage with flecks of bacon, bread with butter. Milk! Is this real?"

"As real as the morning sun on the Wall," Muse said, eyebrows rising.

"Wait a minute." Alix searched the table, bending close and squinting. "No cornboo mush? How's that possible? I must still be dreaming."

Muse sat down on the opposite side. "We owe it all to Merf. And his connections in the Sanctuary."

"I don't know where to start." Alix reached for the small glass of milk.

"Take it slow."

She meant to sip, but the taste of whole milk was too much. She couldn't hold back and downed the glass in three gulps. It lingered on her tongue like sweet nectar. "Is Merf coming over?"

"Maybe later, after dinner." Muse pointed at the steaming cabbage. "Chew your food carefully."

"Can't." Alix stuffed a forkful in her mouth. "Might still be a dream. Got to eat it all before I wake up."

Muse sat back to watch, palms on her knees.

Cheeks bulging, Alix looked up. "Aren't you going to have any?"

"That would spoil it. I'm having too much fun watching you. Besides, I'm really not hungry." Muse folded her arms. "Do you have any idea how proud I am of you, Alix? You did good. Real good."

"Maybe too good." Alix spread a square of butter on the bread with a fork and then licked the fork clean. The taste was overpowering, beyond heaven. "Merf said it had to be big. Make an impact. I guess it did."

Muse nodded slowly. "Oh yeah, you made an impact. There hasn't been anything like it in the Fringe since I found you crying by the Wall 22 years ago. What you did took a lot of guts, Alix. I couldn't be happier. Or more scared."

"I know," Alix said with her mouth full, trying to wrap her mind around the overpowering taste of bacon with its subtle saltiness. "They'll be coming after me soon, maybe tomorrow. And I'm sorry. You'll need to hide, at least for a while."

"Don't worry about me, child." Muse took a deep breath and carefully let it out. "You're the one we need to worry about. Like it or not, you're the face of the revolution."

"For the record, I *don't* like it. And I don't see why it has to be me. Should be Merf."

"Don't be silly. You've seen his face. I mean, can you imagine him riding the chopper?" Muse let her head fall back to laugh at the ceiling. Her skin glowed in the evening light against the backdrop of long, dark hair, streaked with gray. She leaned in to grab a tiny piece of bread. "Merf is smart, but he'd be the first to admit he's not the type."

"Neither am I."

"That's not what I saw today." Muse chewed on the bread. "I know you better than you know yourself. You've been tough your whole life, but today, you looked—" She stopped.

"Like what?"

"The leader we've never had in the Fringe. The one we need now." Muse nodded. "All these years, I've been right about you. Like it or not, you are the one."

"Don't say that, Muse. It scares me." Alix slid the last of the succulent cabbage into her mouth. The bread was already gone. Stabbing the small spot of butter remaining on the plate, she gazed at it longingly and put it back, leaving it for Muse to enjoy later. Alix rose and pushed her chair away from the table.

"Of course it scares you." Muse put her elbows on the table and focused all her attention on Alix. "I know you. You're shy by nature. You like quiet places out of the limelight. You're happy to let all the attention focus on other people. That's what makes you such a good healer. But you're going to have to let that part of yourself go. And that's scary, isn't it?"

"I saw it on the way home. People had that look in their eyes. A hunger. They weren't seeing me. They were seeing someone else." Alix thought of the market in the subway, the old man in the wheelchair. The kid demanding to know if she had a plan. "I'm afraid I won't be able to give them what they want."

"Listen, Alix. It's not about what *they* want. It's about what *you* want." Muse stood from the table, stacked the empty dishes and walked into the kitchen.

"It's not that simple."

"It is, my dear. And you don't have to *be* the revolution. You don't even have to be a leader, not like President Quinn. All you have to do is plant the idea in their minds. On both sides of the Wall. Once the idea takes hold, nothing will stop it. The revolution will happen on its own."

"I wish I could believe that." Alix let out a long exhale and then noticed the look of concern on Muse's face. "I'm sorry. You've given me so much. At least let me do the dishes. Please."

Muse laughed. "OK, I'll let you." She put the dishes on the counter. Then she picked up a cup of cheap tea made from toasted cornboo, walked out into the main room and dropped into the chair by the table, holding the mug close.

From a container in the corner of the kitchen, Alix took a handful of sand and sprinkled it over the dishes. She began to rub the surface of each one clean.

"You were born to do this," Muse said over her shoulder.

"Wash dishes? You're probably right."

"You know what I mean. Spark a revolution."

Alix kept working on the dishes with her back to Muse. "I don't understand. I was abandoned at the Wall by a mother I never knew. Like thousands of other babies. You found me and raised me. How does that qualify me?"

"Because you're different."

"I'm just Fringe scum, like everyone else."

"No. You're not."

"My whole life, you told me that I'm special. Different." Alix could feel the confidence and courage slipping away. "I almost half-believed it today while I was riding the chopper. But I know the truth."

"No. You don't." Muse sighed again. "Look, Alix, there's something I need to tell you. A secret I've kept for too long."

Alix stopped. "Huh?"

"You're not Fringe-born, Alix. You're from the Sanctuary."

8

Alix stared at Muse, mouth open, not talking, not knowing what to say. "My mother was from the Sanctuary?"

Muse nodded. "Yes, your mother and father were both from the Sanctuary. That's where you were born."

"Then why—"

"Maybe your mother wanted to protect you, to keep you safe." Muse stood and walked into the kitchen to rest her hand on Alix's shoulder. "She loved you. I'm sure she had a good reason to do what she did."

"Did you know her—my mother?" Alix felt the room closing in on her, her vision blurring. It was hard to breathe.

"Please don't ask me that."

"Did you?"

Muse turned Alix around and squeezed her hands. "For your own good, I can't tell you right now. But someday, I will. I promise."

"So you did know them. My mother and my father."

"I can't tell you any more."

"Why not?"

"You have to trust me."

"But you knew the rules when you found me, right?"

"I knew. Anyone born in the Sanctuary has a right to live there. I could have sent you back. You could have grown up in an orphanage there, had a completely different life. An easier life. I don't blame you if you hate me for that."

It hit Alix. "I could go there right now, couldn't I? I could pass through the Wall into the Sanctuary."

"Yes, you could." Muse walked back to her chair, put both hands on her cup of tea and brought it close to her lips. "You have the implant that all Sanctuary-born children get at birth. It'll activate any portal and let you through. Whenever you want. You can just walk away and leave the Fringe behind."

Somewhere in the far distance within her mind, Alix felt a shift like a deep earthquake. A wave of emotion was taking shape, gathering strength. She did her best to push it back. Instinctively, her hand went to the back of her neck where her spine connected to her skull, as if feeling for the implant that was the birthright of all the Sanctuary-born.

"But, why, Muse?"

"Why did I keep you? Why didn't I send you back?" Muse put down the mug and covered her eyes with her hands. Tears leaked through her long fingers. "I don't know. I was young, desperate and alone. You were alone, too. I thought we needed each other, that we could make it together."

"Does anyone else know?"

"Just one."

"Who?" The wave of emotion was moving, coming closer. "Wait, it's obvious."

There was a knock on the door, which was still ajar. Alix and Muse both turned to see who it was.

Merf.

He stood in green pajamas, erect as a wooden board, his shriveled body held up and controlled by an impossibly articulated exoskeleton. A wide band cradled his bald head. A network of trodes ran up the back of his neck to his crown, flush against his skin. A river of black titanium flowed down his spine where it exploded across his chest, shoulders, back, arms and legs like a giant squid. It all ended in metal rods that extended along each finger and toe. All across the exoskeleton, telltale lights of red and green flickered on and off. A multitude of servos hummed and hissed at every mechanical joint. The human part of Merf, paralyzed from the neck down, seemed slight and inconsequential compared to the machine that wrapped him. It was already dark outside, but he wore mirrored glacier glasses to shade his eyes. Or maybe it was a fashion statement. But that was Merf.

"Bad time?" he said.

Alix glared at him. "Have you been standing there the whole time, Merf?"

"Yup."

"So, you heard my conversation with Muse? Everything she said."

"Uh, yeah."

Alix glared at Muse, then back at Merf. "So, you've always known?"

"About you being Sanctuary-born? Yeah." Merf looked away and lifted his hand to scratch his nose as a tiny chorus of servos sang in his exoskeleton.

They knew. Both of them. For all these years they knew, and they never told me!

Alix couldn't hold it back any longer. The wave of emotion that had been building inside her crashed down. Legs going wobbly, she looked one more time from Muse to Merf, stumbled backward and dropped into the pebble-bag chair, folding into a fetal position with her face buried in her hands. It was embarrassing, but she couldn't hold back the tears. With every breath, her body shook from the inside.

Alix tried to hate Muse and Merf for betraying her. And she almost succeeded. In the end, though, it wasn't possible. They'd done too much for her over the years. If they'd really wanted to hurt her, they'd have done it long ago.

A warm hand came down on Alix's shoulder. Muse kissed Alix on her forehead. The softness of Muse's dark hair brushed her face with the familiar smell of sand.

"I'm so sorry, Alix. If I could have figured out a better way to do this, I would have done it. Long before now." Muse stroked Alix's hair as if she were still five, running the fingers over her scalp and down her neck and back. "I wanted you to have a normal life here in the Fringe, to feel like you belonged. I tried to tell you the truth more than once, but it was too hard. I couldn't do it."

"Me too." Merf took two steps into the house, his exoskeleton whirring softly. "And honestly, I didn't want you to run away to the Sanctuary. We need you here. For the revolution. I know, that's selfish, right?"

Alix still convulsed in the chair, the supposed leader of the revolution acting like a baby. She tried to stop crying, but it was like sliding down a steep slope with nowhere to get a handhold.

Muse stood and walked toward Merf. Moving off to a far corner of the house, they had a hushed conversation, Merf nodding his head with the soft motion of servos.

And then, as quickly as it had come, the tide of emotion turned and receded. Finally, Alix stopped crying. There was still the residual anger, but it wouldn't help to focus on it, so she exhaled and let it go.

"I'm OK." She lifted her head.

Muse and Merf looked up.

"Look," Merf said. "We get it. This is a lot to take in, especially now. We should have told you sooner. You'll need time to process it." He shot a glance at Muse. "But try to think about it objectively. This makes you the perfect bridge."

Wiping her eyes, Alix sat upright in the pebble-bag chair. "Bridge?"

"Yeah, bridge. You know, born in the Sanctuary, raised in the Fringe." Merf walked to the table and sat in a chair with his typical jerky movements. "A foot in both worlds. In more ways than you know." He shot a glance at Muse. "That's why you're the one. You can bring them together."

Muse slowly moved to a chair on the opposite side of the table, keeping a delicate gaze on Alix. "It's what you were born to do."

"You've told me my whole life that I was born for a purpose. Not sure I agree, but now I know why you said it." Alix felt control of her life slipping away, as if it had all been a lie. "You've been grooming me to do this. To be the face of the revolution. All along, I thought that my ideas mattered, but that's not really true, is it? I'm just a tool."

"No one's manipulating you, Alix." Muse gently smiled, her lips coming together, one side slightly lower than the other. "You have such great potential. More than anyone else in the Fringe. People look up to you. You're perfect—"

"But I'm not who I thought I was!" Alix slammed her hand on the table. "I'm not—"

"What? Fringe scum?" Merf shook his head, face devoid of sympathy. "Yeah, I guess not. It's true. You're not from the Fringe, if you think that sort of thing matters. You could walk away whenever you want. Just find a portal and go right through the Wall. But don't you see? That's the beauty of it. You could leave, but you choose to stay. For most of us, it's not an option. But you're different. You stay here because you want to be here. You refuse to turn your back on the people."

"So what? That makes me a hero?" Alix chuckled. "Wow. Sounds like the perfect propaganda. A great story."

Muse moved closer. "But it's not just a story, Alix. It's who you are. I know you. I raised you." She took Alix's hand in hers. "You won't turn your back on the people here. It's not in your character to do that. Whether you like it or not, it's inspiring. For all of us. Don't run from it, Alix. Embrace it."

As she heard the words, Alix wanted to hate Muse but knew she was right. In the end, why did it matter that she was born in the Sanctuary? Her heart was with the people of the Fringe, the people who were dying, the people who were losing their children to the virus, the people whose lives were being sucked away in the brain labs and chemplants. She could never leave them. Her anger slowly drained away.

"I'm sorry." Alix leaned back into the pebble-bag chair. "It's obvious. You're right. It doesn't really matter, being born in the Sanctuary. Just came as a surprise, that's all."

Muse nodded with moist eyes. "I love you. More than you know."

Merf tapped his fingertips on the table and stared at the ceiling. "Look, I don't want to rush you two. I'm more than half human, and I'd be the first to give human emotion its due. But as soon as you get over the shock, Alix, we need to talk. I've got a lot to tell you. A lot."

"Like, for starters, the big plan?" Alix found a wooden chair and pulled it to the table. "I know you've got one. Probably have the whole thing already figured out. Beginning to end. But you're keeping me in the dark about it. Why?"

"It's the logical thing to do," Merf said, not a hint of apology on his face. "Didn't want you to know enough to spill the beans if you got caught. Besides, I don't know if it's really a plan. It's more like an audacious idea. A way to fight fire with fire. You ready to hear it?"

"It better be good, Merf. You've made me wait long enough." Alix folded her arms.

"Agreed," Muse said, turning her eyes on Merf. "We've both been patient and played by your rules. Now it's time. Tell us the *plan*."

"OK, here goes." Merf stood, or rather, his exoskeleton stood and took Merf with it. Plunging his hand deep into a pocket, he produced a green cube the size of a die, held between his index finger and his thumb. "Behold, the key to a bold, new future."

Alix narrowed her eyes. "A memory cube?"

There was a loud knock on the door. It burst open. Old Jim stumbled in, a man in the neighborhood with a missing arm who had looked out for Alix ever since she could remember. "They're coming. For Alix."

They all heard the distant sound of human voices, hundreds of them.

"A Patrol invasion?" Muse jumped to her feet. "Alix! You have to—"

"No, not Patrol." Old Jim pointed outside. "Just local folks, all stirred up. They're talking about marching to the Wall. Storming the Sanctuary. They're on their way here to get Alix to lead them."

"I was afraid of this. Alix's performance today is rousing the masses even more than I thought it would. But we need more time." Merf moved to the door, stuffing the green cube in his pocket. "Come on, Alix, we have to get to a secure location. Over to my place." He turned to Muse. "Can you handle them?"

"Handle them?" Muse laughed as she waved Alix and Merf away. "Leave it to me. I'll speak to them and let them know Alix is doing fine. She's just hiding for her own safety."

"That should work." Merf nodded, or rather, the exoskeleton executed a nod of Merf's head.

"What if they ask about the plan?" Muse raised an eyebrow.

Merf gave a robotic shrug of his shoulders. "Don't say anything about the cube. Make something up."

"OK, how about this? *Please be patient my friends. The revolution is in good hands.*"

"Good luck with that." Merf pulled Alix out the door.

9

On the elevator ride up, Chelsea warned Link. Daddy liked to test people. It was one of his endearing quirks. He had a special room—he called it a chamber—where he received guests and, invariably, played mind games to get what he wanted. It was all harmless, of course. As the leader of a powerful nation, Quinn had to understand people, and he did it through games. He might try this tactic on Link. In fact, it was almost a certainty. "Just be careful," she said, "Daddy's smart. He likes to have fun. Sometimes he acts crazy. But don't think for a minute that he is, and don't let it get to you. Just hold on until it's over. You won't die. That doesn't happen all that often. Oh, and don't touch anything, don't smile too much, and don't look at the walls. Just stare straight ahead."

"You'll tell me what to say, right?" Link felt a wave of nausea rising in his stomach. "With the ocular."

"Sorry, Link." Chelsea shook her head. "Other people's electronics don't work in Daddy's special room. Only his do."

"What?"

"You'll be on your own."

Link took in a deep breath to keep from throwing up. "I need you Chelsea. I won't know what to say."

The elevator slowed.

"You'll be fine," she said. "Just be careful."

"What do you mean?"

"Don't be too honest. The truth doesn't always play well with Daddy. Tell him what he needs to hear."

"What if I don't know what he needs to hear?"

"Make him smile," she said. "And one last thing. Daddy doesn't talk. He *negotiates.*"

"What does that mean?" Link had asked.

"You'll see."

As the elevator glided to a stop, Link felt his pulse spiking and backed up, shoulder blades pressed against the wall. The doors opened. Chelsea pulled him through and across a small lobby.

"We're here, Daddy." Chelsea stepped into a long, narrow room.

"I've been waiting."

Franklin Alexander Quinn sat in a jewel-encrusted chair with his back to them as he faced an enormous window. Only the top of his head was visible, and his luxurious hair gave off a subtle rainbow effect. At his side, a stool waited, empty. Cigar smoke snaked above him in a thin ribbon.

"The party is excellent, sir," Link said, desperate to make a good impression and stifle the tremble in his voice. He stood behind Chelsea, using her as a shield.

"Glad to hear it." Quinn's head turned slightly, revealing a hawk's nose with a high curving bridge. "Welcome to my receiving chamber."

More like a torture chamber, Link thought.

Chelsea pulled him deeper into the room. Despite her warnings, Link couldn't help sneaking a peek at the exquisite dark wood paneling that made the walls appear unstable, a sort of floating effect. And then he was staring, unable to look away. In seconds, his stomach went queasy and he collapsed. Before he knew what had happened, he was lying face down on the floor.

"Choose your path wisely, young man." Quinn didn't bother to look up. "The walk across the room can be treacherous."

Carefully, with Chelsea's help, Link gathered himself back onto his feet. He didn't want to look, but there was a line of portraits on the right-hand wall, generations of dead President Quinns, going back to the first one. The stern faces brooded over Link and Chelsea as they shuffled by. A narrow table cut the room in half. Warm and smooth, its surface invited Link's touch. Without thinking, he ran his hand along the polished top.

"No, Link," Chelsea whispered.

A sharp pain stabbed his finger, and he yanked it back to see spots of blood beading on his skin. And then he saw the cause: tiny, transparent spikes poking through the wood.

"Be careful of the table." Quinn blew a column of smoke above his head. "It can be deceptive."

Licking his wounds, Link turned back to the open door behind him, ready to run. Chelsea gently grabbed his shoulder, smiling and shaking her head as she steered him toward her father.

"How are you enjoying the view, Daddy?"

"Brilliant, as always, Chelsea. I never tire of it." Quinn cleared his throat. "As I mentioned, I'll need some time alone with—what was his name?"

"*Lincoln*, Daddy. Lincoln Wells. One of your best Patrol commanders."

"Yes, well, our negotiations will be completed in short order. Assuming the results are satisfactory, we won't be long. Go back to the party. Enjoy yourself. If all goes well, he'll rejoin you shortly."

"Of course, Daddy." Chelsea turned to leave.

This wasn't the way it was supposed to be. Link couldn't imagine being alone with Quinn. In desperation, Link caught Chelsea's hand and stretched out her arm, his eyes begging her not to leave. She smiled, shook her head and blew him a kiss as she slipped out of his grip and walked away. He stared at Chelsea until the doors clicked shut behind her.

He was alone with the President. No way out.

"It's just you and me, Lincoln Wells," Quinn said, as if reading Link's mind. "Now come sit beside me. It's important that we reach an *understanding*." Quinn's hand motioned to the small stool at his side.

Legs trembling, Link moved deeper into the room, keeping his distance from the long table, avoiding the walls, each step taking him closer to the window, where Quinn gazed out on the Sanctuary.

As quietly as possible, Link slipped onto the stool, feeling like a child at the feet of his father. It was impossible to miss the intricate carvings of ivory and gold and the jewels and diamonds adorning Quinn's chair. Link would have burst out laughing at such an ostentatious display of decadence if he hadn't been so consumed with terror. With a deep breath, he tried to find a way to disappear.

An elegant Hawaiian sunset floated on the Wall. But that wasn't what caught Link's eye. At 1,500 meters high, Quinn Tower was the only structure in the Sanctuary taller than the 1,000-meter Wall. He stared, open-mouthed, over the Wall into the Fringe, spreading like an endless, grey spiderweb of shacks and ruins off to the horizon.

A cool summer breeze stirred Link's hair. He realized, to his horror, that this wasn't a typical window. No glass separated them from the outside air.

The silence lasted for minutes.

Doing his best to calm his pulse, Link waited for Quinn to speak, anticipating questions about the Alix Yamaguchi disaster. It shouldn't be hard. Chelsea had helped him rehearse a detailed explanation for the fiasco and a precisely calibrated acceptance of blame, mingled with a promise to do better.

Finally, after an eternity of waiting, Link executed a quick sidelong glance at Quinn, who sat puffing on his cigar, relaxed and seemingly oblivious to Link's presence.

Exhaling a long horizontal column of blue smoke, Quinn finally spoke. "Breathtaking, wouldn't you say, Lincoln Wells?"

"Yes—"

"I come here for inspiration. Whenever trouble strikes, the view helps me comprehend what's at stake. The contrast is so clear and conspicuous. The Sanctuary. The Wall. The Fringe. Perfection side-by-side with chaos, separated by nothing more than a thin line. A constant reminder of the realities we face. Have you ever wondered why Quinn Tower is the only structure that rises above the Wall?"

"No," Link said, but then he saw Quinn narrow his eyes. *Wrong answer.* "I mean yes, of course."

"The Fringe is my cross to bear. I'm the leader of the Sanctuary and the only one who needs to see it, the only one who should have to deal with it." Quinn flicked a finger down at the Sanctuary. "The less they know, the better. For them and me."

Link's gaze drifted down to the canopy of building tops far below. It was his first trip to the top of Quinn Tower, and from here, the Sanctuary was like a magnificent crystal forest, a multicolored monument to the glory of the Quinn family. At street level, it all blended together, but from the top of Quinn Tower, with the miserable grey Fringe as a backdrop, the contrast was impossible to miss.

The Sanctuary was more than exquisite. It was the embodiment of perfection. Whatever Quinn might say about the burden of living at the top, Link had the feeling that there was another reason for Quinn Tower: to save the superb view entirely for himself. And Chelsea.

Standing there, Link was sure of one thing. The Quinn family, the creators and nurturers of the Sanctuary across almost two centuries, deserved all the vast wealth they had achieved.

"It truly is breathtaking, sir," Link said.

Quinn blew smoke out the opening. "Thanks to your actions today, all of it is in mortal danger." Quinn spoke as if stating a simple fact, with a voice devoid of emotion.

"I'm sorry, Mr. President. If you'll permit me, I can explain—"

"No." Quinn raised his hand. "You have lost the right to make an explanation. Save the promises, the excuses and the memorized apologies. They are of no use to me. Maybe you did your best. That doesn't change the result. The Fringe girl was smarter than you. Better prepared and hungrier. For her, it was life or death. She wanted it more than you and risked everything to get it. What did you risk? Nothing. I hate the girl, but I know talent when I see it. Hers was a brilliant performance. You lost, my young friend. Badly. Now the whole Sanctuary is wearing red, a color I despise. In the space of five minutes, the girl managed to morph from unknown Fringe scum to Mesh-celeb. Astonishing. And what of me? I'm a laughingstock. Thanks to you. End of story."

Link winced at every word.

"Yes, sir. I accept full responsibility." Link looked at the floor. "But I can assure you it won't happen again. Next time—"

"What makes you think there will be a next time?"

"Please, sir. My whole staff is working on a plan—"

"You don't need a plan."

"Sir?"

"Plans are nothing more than excuses for not taking action. What you need is to throw away your fear. And act."

"With all due respect, sir, I'm not afraid."

"Is that so?" Quinn nodded. "Good to know." He twisted his head to the side and spit between Link's feet. "We'll see."

"I'll get her, sir. I promise."

"Duly noted. Let's move on to a lighter topic."

"Sounds good," Link said, at first relieved but then embarrassed at sounding so cliché.

"In any negotiation, what is the most important question to ask yourself?"

Link wasn't sure how to answer.

"I'll tell you," Quinn said. "It's rather simple. Four words. *What do I want?* You need to have a crystal clear grasp of what you want. Do you understand me?"

"Yes, I think so, sir."

"I know what I want, and I've never wavered from it. But I'm not sure about you. What, exactly, do you want?" Quinn puckered his lips and blew smoke, watching the wind take it away. "What do you hunger for more than anything else? Be honest."

"I'm not sure—"

"It's not a trick question." Quinn took another long pull on his cigar. "But it's vital to be clear. What do you really *crave*?"

"In the world?"

"What else is there?"

Link took a deep breath to calm his pulse and think clearly. Quinn had a reputation for being demanding and cryptic. Was this a test? What was Quinn fishing for? It was confusing and terrifying, but Link had to try to tell Quinn what Quinn wanted to hear. Just like Chelsea had said.

"I want what's best for the Sanctuary."

"Good answer, if you're being broadcast to the public or surveilled. But this is a secure room on the most secure floor of the most secure building in the Sanctuary, maybe the world. No scanners or data-sniffers or Mesh interfaces of any kind." Quinn motioned to the portraits of the five staring Quinns. "We're completely alone, except for them, and they're dead. No one else will ever know what you tell me. What is your deepest wish, Lincoln Wells? Be brutally honest."

Link was confused. "I was honest, sir."

"Then you'll have to dig deeper, past the shallowness and half-truths we all tell ourselves to calm our consciences." Quinn stood and walked to the open window, his feet only centimeters from the edge. "What do you *really* want?"

"What's best for Chelsea. To make her happy." Link hoped that would work.

"If you're referring to my daughter, she has nothing to do with this conversation." Quinn cocked his head to the side with just the hint of a sneer, still looking intently out the window. "What happens to her is entirely within my control. You needn't trouble yourself. She'll get every-thing she deserves."

It was time for Link to be bold. "But it's true. I have strong feelings for her. If she's happy, I'll be happy. It's what I want."

"I'm flattered." Quinn let the smoke pour out between his lips with each word. "You really believe that?"

"I do." Link moved out of the chair and stood shoulder-to-shoulder with Quinn, staring down 250 floors at the grid of streets below.

"I see." Quinn took another puff on his cigar. "You have high principles. You strive for the happiness of others. Their well-being motivates you. You're an altruist. A rare gift."

"Yes, sir."

"I have some advice for you. Become a monk or a foot soldier. Sacrifice your life for the good of the Sanctuary and its noble people. Better yet, start your own religion." Quinn's mouth twisted to the side. "But stay away from my daughter."

"Sir?"

"You're a do-gooder. People like you are fine in the upper-middle ranks or even the lower-top. But not above 7Z. You'd be a danger to the system. More likely than not, you'd bring it all crashing down."

"I don't understand," Link said, and for the first time in the conversation, he was completely honest.

The side of a colossal pyramid half a klick away lit up with a full-color ad for the newest model jax, an exquisitely carved cylinder of braided ivory and platinum, with embedded diamonds, boasting 10 times the speed of its competitor. A woman twirled the jax through her fingers until it slipped into place at the center of her palm. As she tapped its side like a flute, a holoscreen jumped above it displaying her 5Z rank and bar graphs of a stock portfolio. She touched a bar, effortlessly moving money from one investment to another. She smiled into the screen as her rank climbed to 6Z. Words appeared next to her face.

Want it. Live it. Be it.

"I asked you what you want, what you hunger for." Quinn shuffled forward a few centimeters until the tips of his shoes were flush with the edge of the building. "If you intend to marry my daughter, there's only one acceptable answer. Would you like to know what it is?"

"Very much, sir."

"Everything."

"Sir?"

"The correct answer is *I want everything.* I won't accept anything less."

What was Quinn talking about? Link thought back to each broadcast, talk or textbook entry he'd listened to or read about Quinn. They were all about freedom and duty and opportunity. Putting the good of the Sanctuary above the good of the self. Nothing about greed.

"With all due respect, sir, I don't follow."

"That is precisely why the girl got away from you today." Smoke curled out between Quinn's frowning lips.

Link was ready. "I can assure you that it's all under—"

"Control?"

"Yes."

"Is that why everyone's dressed in red? She played you to perfection. It's a declaration of war."

"I can explain—"

Quinn raised his hand. "*Explanation* is a polite word for *failure*. I need solutions. I need to win. And you need to understand how the Sanctuary really works, what's at stake." He glanced at Link, reading the data on his own ocular. "I see you're a 3Z. Do you know what that means?"

"It puts me in the top 1%."

"It's all a matter of perspective. The way I see it, millions of people have *more* money than you. That makes you a minor mediocrity. It should keep you up at night."

Link's gaze dropped. "I'm working on it, sir. I'll get more."

"Everybody wants more. But *more* is not enough." Quinn shuffled forward until the tips of his shoes were hanging over the edge. "I know your problem. You think you understand how the Sanctuary system works. But you don't. Not even close. You need to wake up, open your eyes. You need a dose of reality. Here it comes."

Link looked over the ledge at the street below. "President Quinn, please be careful. You're—"

"What? Don't you trust me?"

"Yes, of course, but—"

"Jump."

"Off the edge? I don't understand."

"Do it."

Link rose on one foot. The whole of the Sanctuary floated below, every surface glowing with images and light, pulling him closer. "There's a safety system, right?" Chest tightening, Link couldn't breathe.

"Maybe. Maybe not." Pulling his cigar from his lips, Quinn flicked it far out into the night air and watched as the glowing tip dropped out of sight. "Let me put it to you as simply as I can. You have a choice to make, Lincoln Wells: jump now, or lose Chelsea and your job and your pathetic 3Z rank."

"But sir—"

The next three seconds were a blur. Quinn placed his fleshy hand squarely between Link's shoulder blades and shoved hard. Link lunged into empty air, arms flailing. All sound got sucked away. Colors faded into black.

Chelsea was wrong. Quinn had decided to kill him.

10

Silent Hinges

"Hey, wait for me." Alix sprinted to keep up with Merf. "Did you get a new exoskeleton or what?"

Merf was moving faster than she remembered. Slightly jerky movements carried his withered body effortlessly over the ground.

"No, just an upgrade. New code module. A few tweaks here and there." Merf stopped to let Alix catch her breath, taking the form of a relaxed man with folded arms and legs crossed at the ankles. "Plus some new titanium inserts from the Sanctuary. My usual source."

"You've got a mole on the inside?"

"More than one." Merf pointed with his chin in the direction of the Wall. "Let's just say I'm cultivating a new admirer."

"Let me guess. It's a she, and she's in love with you."

"How'd you know?"

Alix let her eyes do a slow roll. "No doubt she thinks you're a handsome, rich idealist from the Sanctuary living in the Fringe trying to make a difference."

"Which is mostly true, from a certain point of view."

"Where'd you meet her? Virtual reality chat room?"

"Yup."

The far-off voices of a crowd drifted closer.

"Let's go." Alix took off jogging, with Merf gently catching up and passing her. A whiff of acrid air forced her to stop with a coughing fit. "They must be working overtime at the chemplant tonight."

A mechanical breathing mask folded itself out of the exoskeleton and slipped over Merf's mouth. "Been happening a lot lately. Too many kids are dying from the virus. It's cutting down on the number of workers."

Alix shuddered with memories of working at the chemplant when she was eight. It'd been hard to keep the acid splashes off her skin. After a few days, Muse couldn't take it anymore and pulled her out. Over the years, nothing had changed. You could still spot the chemplant workers, children and adults, from the white scars on their arms and legs.

They crossed a wide street with disintegrating pavement and arrived at the base of an ancient 20-story structure built decades before the Wall.

"So, this is the new intellectual center of the Fringe?" Alix glanced up at bent steel girders, shattered windows and exposed interior offices. It looked as if the building had been sliced open on a diagonal by an enormous laser sword. "When you going to fix it up, Merf?"

"There are limits to what I can get smuggled out of the Sanctuary. Tech and electronics are hard enough. Industrial building materials are considerably more difficult." He led the way to the entrance. They passed steel doors blown off their hinges long ago by rioters with homemade bombs in the civil war that had torn the old city apart. The odor of dust hung in the air as they stepped into the open lobby.

The cracked marble floor was etched with a complex design, the remains of a massive map of the world. Alix had been here before, and she always bent down to study it. A spiderweb network connected dots on all the continents and islands with long, arcing lines. Muse had told her that, back before they built the Wall, just about anyone could travel. You didn't have to be rich. Now it was only the most wealthy in the Sanctuary who ever saw foreign countries on the other side of the ocean. Alix craned her neck to read the dust-covered words inscribed around the map's outer edge in massive letters:

Industrial Bank of China, New York City Branch.

"I know how much you hate money, Merf. So why'd you move into a bank? I like the old library where you used to live, with all its books." Alix stood in the middle of the Pacific Ocean on the map, just a hop away from Japan.

Merf snorted. "The library was good, but this is better. The old Mesh network is still intact here. The security's good, too. Have a look." He pointed across the room. "Tell me what you see."

"A big pile of broken concrete and steel beams. Looks sketchy, like it might collapse any second and cover the lobby. You sure we should be standing here?"

"Exactly. That's the idea." With the help of his exoskeleton fingers, Merf pulled a sleek-looking jax from his pocket and pointed it at the pile. "Watch." He tapped the end.

The pile of rubble faded like a mirage, replaced by a clean-looking wood counter separated into four equal sections. Alix had seen similar setups in the ruins of other banks around the Fringe. She'd heard stories about how people used to stand behind the counters and actually count money.

"You got a holo projector, Merf?"

"Yup. Brand new with a 30-year battery."

"From your new contact in the Sanctuary?"

"Yup. She's amazing."

"What did you tell her?"

"That I'm coming soon to see her."

"Is that true?"

"I hope so. All depends on how the revolution progresses." Merf walked across the floor with a robot-jerk motion, like he was standing still and the floor was moving under him. With one hand on the counter, he launched himself over it with a smart hop. Alix scrambled to keep up, following him behind a wall into a back room. At the far end, she saw an enormous metal disk four meters across.

"What's that?"

"My front door." He walked up to it and passed his palm over its surface, like he was petting a cat. "Beautiful, isn't she? Pure titanium on the outside. The vault's programmed to only allow one person through at a time. Retinal scan. I uploaded yours already."

"Why all the new tech? You've never been worried about security."

"Didn't need to be. The Fringe has always been safe enough. There's not much here to fight over and, besides, we share all we have. But the world is changing, Alix. We have to change with it. I want to be ready when it happens."

"When what happens?"

"When they come after us, Alix. When the war starts."

"You think it'll be that bad?"

"After what you did to them today? Absolutely."

Alix didn't try to suppress a smirk. "You're always so optimistic, Merf."

"Just a realist. I'll go first." He moved closer to the metal vault and leaned in to let a small camera scan his eye. "Stand back."

The glossy-black, meter-thick disc swung open on silent hinges, surprisingly quickly.

"Now that's a door," Alix said.

"The whole inside compartment is enveloped in a seamless sheath of carbonite. Strongest material known on Earth. Laser cannons can't touch this stuff." Merf moved through the opening in the interior. "It's a little dark inside. You OK with that?"

"Who said I was afraid of the dark?"

"Everyone's heard the stories." Merf shrugged. "About what happened to you in the brain lab. So I thought—"

"I'll be fine."

"Good. Give me a few seconds to slip out of my suit." The door swung shut behind him like an pressurized air lock, decompressing to a satisfying click.

Alix counted to 10.

Bending close to the camera, she felt a subtle buzz on her eyeball. The door popped open again, air blowing in her face. She stepped through as the door swung shut and bumped her on the backside.

It was pitch black, and this wasn't the wide, open subway.

"OK, Merf. Mind turning on the lights?"

The whirring sound of Merf's exoskeleton, like the whole thing was moving at once, was followed by the sound of a huge hand slipping out of an even bigger glove.

A tiny light barely illuminated the room. Merf lay on a cot in the corner without his sunglasses. His exposed eyes were almost colorless, with small black dots for pupils. His body looked even more weak and fragile, as he lay there in green pajamas. The exoskeleton stood beside the cot, bent at the waist, knees flexing, arms extended down, as if it had just gently placed him on the bed.

Which it had.

"Sorry about the light. It's part of the security setup here. And the fact is, I work better like this. It's how the machines raised me from the time I was a baby."

It was the same dim, red light she remembered from her first horrific experience in the brain lab. Nausea swelled in her belly.

The exoskeleton stood up, turned and walked with an effortless robotic gait to the opposite corner where it sat on its haunches, waiting like a loyal dog, status lights glowing red. Alix couldn't shake the thought that Merf belonged to it, instead of the other way around. It seemed that the exoskeleton was the part of his body that was most alive.

"Creeps me out every time I see it do that." Alix found a chair and sat next to the cot.

Without his exoskeleton, Merf was a shriveled bag of translucent skin pulled over thin bones. From the neck down, he was mostly dead. And from the neck up, he wasn't much better.

"Mind if I dive in?" He pointed at the holoscreen on the wall with his nose. "The exoskeleton tires me out. I need to get back home to the Mesh. Where I belong."

Alix waved her hand. "Be my guest."

Merf relaxed and sank deeper into the cot. A skull-sized cup rose up behind his bald head and slid down over it. The sound of suction and a vacuum seal signaled that the trodes had connected. Merf's eyes slid shut, and his face fell into a weak smile.

"Much better."

The voice didn't come from Merf. It came from the holoscreen behind her, which was lit up with the disembodied face of an impossibly healthy-looking man with a full head of hair, bright green eyes and no wrinkles. A full-blown Mesh-star.

"Is that you, Merf?"

"Yup, the real me."

"You upgraded your avatar, too?"

"Why not? There's no law against a little style, is there?"

"There's no law, period. But, yeah, you do look stylish. Makes me jealous. No wonder you've got multiple girlfriends in the Sanctuary."

Merf chuckled, his eyes making contact with Alix from the middle of the holoscreen. "You need to do a deep dive into the Mesh with me. Tonight. I think you'll like it."

Of course, Merf would think that. He'd grown up in the brain labs, back in the old days when the previous President Quinn had started the experimental program to harness human brains as a new source of computing power for the Sanctuary. The story Alix heard was that it had been announced as a life-changing jobs program to eradicate poverty in the Fringe.

The rumor was that Merf had been born in the brain labs and made his first Mesh-dive five minutes later. He was a natural. Over the years, his brain adapted in an organic way to fit the Mesh. It was his first, last and only home. He could Mesh-dive without a buffer, something no one thought possible. It had scared the authorities so much, they never tried it on another baby. But, like everyone else in the brain labs, the connection between his mind and body grew weaker and weaker until his arms and legs had all but ceased to function. At 30, he got thrown out of the brain labs and left to die. But that didn't stop him. He'd already set up equipment to run his own secret operation. He could go anywhere in the Mesh, breaking through encryption, like water through a sieve. As far as the Sanctuary knew, Merf was long dead. And in a way, it was true. But he'd created a new identity as a minor Mesh-celeb in the process.

"I'll be honest, Merf. Deep dives scare me. Too many bad memories. But I'll give it a try someday, after the dust settles."

"The dust is never going to settle, Alix. Someday is tonight. Let's do it."

"No way, Merf." Alix felt a thin film of sweat already clinging to her back. "You're the expert. I leave all the tech stuff up to you. I'd just get in the way."

"Look, Alix, I know about your issues, OK? You don't like Mesh diving. You had a bad experience once."

"Bad experience? Once?" Alix shook her head. "I almost died."

Ten years ago, she'd shown up for her first day of work in the brain labs, lured by the promise of unlimited food. She still remembered how delicious the grape-laced punch tasted. And then, lying on a cot in a dim, red room shoulder-to-shoulder with thousands of other kids. The trodes comfortably slipped over her head, but the next instant, it was as if a black lid had slammed down over her face. Colors exploded in cascades of ear-splitting sound. Snakes crawled under her skin. The air was gone. When her lungs filled with cold, viscous water, the hunger for oxygen only got worse.

She still remembered the instructions: *don't try to breathe.*

Of course, it was all in her head. Her lungs didn't fill with water; it just felt like they had. That was the point. In the brain labs, your mind got hijacked so that a rich Sanctuary queen could use it to run an app on her jax. All you had to do was kiss your freedom goodbye, relax, enjoy the ride and let it all go. Like dying. Night after night after night.

Alix couldn't do it.

The more she resisted, the worse it got. She'd gone into cardiac arrest. The system automatically unplugged her and mainlined adrenaline into her veins to wake her. Guards escorted her to the back door and kicked her out.

And that was the end of her brain lab dreams.

"It'll be OK this time," Merf said. "I've set up a new system that's much easier on the mind."

"Is this why you brought me here, Merf? To take me for a dive?" She thought about the airtight carbonite walls enveloping her. The red lights made it feel like the walls were closing in.

"It's the best way to show you what we're up against." Inside the holo, Merf turned to look at a single, blue dot as it turned into a line that branched into more lines until the holoscreen was full of a schematic of fine nerves. The lines morphed into a cube. "I could explain it to you, but you won't understand until I show you."

"Show me what?"

"A look inside the Sanctuary. What we're trying to change."

"Do I have to do this, Merf?"

"You need to see this. Trust me, OK?"

"No offense, Merf, but having a direct brain interface with the Mesh does things to a person. Strange things. I mean, take a look at what it did to you."

"Fair enough." Merf smiled from inside the holo, while his physical body rested like a dead lump of clay on the bed only a meter away. "You got me there. Look at me. I actually feel more at home in the Mesh than outside it. It's where I feel free. It's where I do my best work. Now lie down, and put on the trodes."

"There's no other way?"

"I offer you the rarest of experiences. To see into the heart of the Sanctuary. You'll enjoy it. I promise."

Alix pulled in a deep breath. "OK, Merf. You win. This better not kill me."

11

Amazingly, it didn't kill him.

Link remembered Quinn shoving him off the edge of the window, but instead of falling to his death, Link crashed onto an invisible, glass platform extending out from the building less than half a meter below the window. With his cheek smashed against the glass and arms spread-eagle, the fingers of his right hand reached out and felt the edge of the platform only centimeters away. Pulse pounding, he carefully pressed himself up to his hands and knees as he stared down.

Quinn stepped onto the clear platform beside him. "I find this exhilarating. Do I have your full attention now?"

Body trembling out of control, Link swallowed and nodded. "Yes, sir."

"Good. That's all I wanted. Come with me into the receiving chamber. You are far too close to the brink." Quinn turned and stepped back into the room. "Please sit and calm down."

"Thank you, sir." Link stepped back into the room and dropped into a chair at the table, resting his hands on the wood. A tiny spike pricked his little finger, and he pulled his hands away, letting them fall to his sides.

Quinn raised an eyebrow. Like a university professor about to deliver a lecture, he positioned his hands behind his back. "May I presume that, like all good citizens of the Sanctuary, you've been taught its history, starting with *them*?" He pointed to the portraits on the wall.

"Yes."

"Tell me what you know about the first President Quinn."

Blood beaded up on Link's finger. Resisting the impulse to lick it, he cleared his throat, took a deep breath against his pounding heart and tried to think. "The first President Quinn built the Wall."

"Correct, but why?"

"There were deep social problems at the time. A lot of people were lazy and poor, with no food, no job and no place to live. They were demanding help from the government. They started a civil war. Society was on the brink of collapse. He had to act to protect civilization."

Quinn motioned outside, as if pointing at the Fringe. "If the poor had really wanted to work, they could have gone to the coal mines and the chemical processing plants, but they refused."

"They thought the government should just provide for them." Link remembered words from elementary school history lessons he'd had to memorize. "They wanted free money, food and a place to live. They were lazy. A few people worked hard and got rich. They deserved it because they started companies, took risks, built businesses, manufactured cars and computers and jaxes. But the lazy poor hated the rich and fought back. They marched in the streets, started riots, blew things up. They wanted a revolution. The army had to protect the good citizens from the mob. It turned into a civil war. There were battles, people died, but there were still too many poor people who wanted to pull everyone down to their level. It got out of control."

"So the first President Quinn had a brilliant idea." Quinn grinned, turning again to the hanging portrait. "A way to restore peace and save civilization."

"Yeah, he decided to create a place where good people could be safe and free to succeed. He called it a Sanctuary of hope and built the first Wall to keep the criminals out. That's how all of this started." Link pointed outside the window.

Quinn nodded, hands clasped in front of him. "Yes, the Fringe, the Wall, the Sanctuary. The perfect system."

"Exactly." Link glanced at Quinn, confident he'd done well. "We owe a great debt of gratitude to the first President Quinn for his foresight and wisdom."

Quinn squared his chin and nodded. "You've done well. Exactly what I expected. I'm glad to know our education system is performing to perfection." He walked to the opposite side of the table and stopped, eyes focused on the portraits. "They would have been proud to see what became of their ideals."

Link couldn't think of anything to say, but he needed to keep the conversation moving, so he parroted a line drilled into his head by his junior high school math teacher.

"The Sanctuary progresses; the Fringe regresses. It's all part of—"

Quinn raised a hand. "That's enough. Just stop."

"Sir?"

"Look, it's fine for the other 99.999999% to believe the propaganda. In fact, it's absolutely necessary. The Sanctuary functions only so long as the majority believes what we tell them. But you're different. If you're going to be a 9Z like me, you've got to rise above slogans and silly stories."

"Silly stories?"

"There's another version of history. Alternative facts, some might say, but this version is true."

The tropical sun projected on the Wall dipped below the horizon, leaving behind an impossibly orange sky.

"Another version?"

"Brace yourself. What I'm going to tell you will be surprising, maybe even painful. It's best that I tell you quickly, like ripping off a scab. Just relax into it. In time, you'll understand and appreciate this history lesson. Are you ready?"

"Yes, sir." Link was confused at the sudden change in the flow of conversation. He studied Quinn's face for any clue about what was coming next.

"The Sanctuary started as an investment, a way for the first President Quinn to make money. A lot of money. As hard as it may be to believe, the Quinns weren't always the richest family in the world. Long ago, before rankings were introduced, the family had only enough money to be in the top 1% of the top 1%. A lowly 4Z. Polite society told the first President

Quinn to be satisfied with the position he had achieved. To borrow a Southern phrase, it was gracious plenty. Instead, he made a bold decision. He took the lid off his ego and allowed himself to want *everything*."

A strange lightness entered Link's body, as if he'd become a hologram and the world wasn't real.

Quinn paced along the opposite side of the table. "You already know about the riots that the first President Quinn had to quell. They were a gift. In fact, he incited them himself by playing on the secret fears of the populace. It was classic demagoguery. Blame all the problems on a particular segment of society—the uneducated, the poor, the foreigners, it doesn't really matter—and watch that society tear itself apart. Much of the city was destroyed. Fires were set. Bombs were detonated. People fled. The same story played out in cities across North America. At the height of the chaos, the conditions were ripe for President Quinn to execute his final plan. That's when he showed his true genius."

"What did he do?" Link said, dutifully asking the obvious question.

"He declared martial law and ordered the government to seize all land and buildings in the cities. Then, he unleashed the army, ordering them to go block-to-block and door-to-door to drive out the poor, the sick and the weak. He secretly directed the government to transfer the property to a special trust for safekeeping. It was a time of great conflict and chaos. No one dared oppose him, which he knew would be the case. In due course, President Quinn took the final step and had himself personally appointed as the trustee in control of all the seized property. It was a brilliant move. Essentially, he got it all for free. In the end, he owned the cities, this one and all the others, the buildings, the land, everything. And then he leased it all back to its former owners for a fortune. It was a beautiful deal. Pure genius. They had no choice but to accept it."

Link tried to wrap his head around the words. "Was that legal?"

"With enough money and power, anything can be made to appear legal. Whether it actually was or not was of little concern, especially after the lawyers were silenced. Of course, President Quinn spread the money around. Everyone got a share. That's how the ranking system started. The higher your rank, the bigger your cut of the revenue. With the help of technology, it became the perfect system. No one stood in his way. Peace was restored. Rich folks felt safe again. They had what they always wanted—the best places all to themselves. But Quinn wasn't done. He understood it was vital to protect his investment from the outside. So he took the logical next step."

"He built the Wall?"

"The people clamored for it, so they got it. When the poor were thrown out, they took over everything outside the Wall and turned it into the Fringe. It was the same story in every city across the old United States. And President Quinn owned most of them. In the space of a few months, peace had been restored, and a new society had been born. It was genius in every sense of the word." Quinn turned and walked to the table, sliding into a chair opposite Link.

"And that's how the United States of America became the United *Sanctuaries* of America?"

"How else?" Quinn grinned big, showing his larger-than-life teeth. "It's still the USA, but with only the best parts. It worked so well that other countries copied the concept, and it spread around the world."

"So, you *own* the Sanctuary?"

"Yes, for all practical purposes. There are others who share in the pie, enough to guarantee their cooperation. By definition, Quinns have always ranked number one. It's baked into the system that we get the biggest cut. And with each generation, my pile of money grows, effortlessly, without limit. It's like winning the lottery every day. Wealth attracts wealth, like a black hole. It's not rocket science, just basic economics and human nature. I have access to the best investments and financial instruments. I control the banks, and the banks control everyone else. The rich below me do all the work. My money grows by itself. And it always will. That's the secret."

"I don't understand," Link said.

"The Sanctuary, this one and the other cities, all exists for one reason: to keep me rich and in control. You can say all you want about freedom and civilization. None of that matters. What matters is that it all works for me. That is the truth you must embrace. Otherwise you won't be able to do what I ask of you."

In the silence that followed, Link stared at Quinn but didn't see him.

"Does Chelsea know?" Link asked.

Quinn grinned. "She could if she wanted to. The signs are all there. She has full access to the financials. But she's an idealist, like you. She prefers to live in a dream. I'm asking you to wake up from the dream and face reality."

Link realized he was still staring at Quinn and dropped his gaze to the floor. "Why are you telling me all this?"

"That's easy." Quinn motioned to the window. "The system only works if the person at the top has their eyes fully open. Unfortunately, I may not be around forever. Don't worry, I'm paying billions to a team of scientists to remedy that situation, but let's assume the worst. After a few more decades, I'll die. Of course, I'll hold onto the reins of power until the bitter end, like all my predecessors. But there will need to be a successor. I think you might be that person."

"But I'm not a Quinn." Link felt his pulse surging. "What about Chelsea?"

"Oh, it may be hers in name, but there will need to be a guiding hand behind it. Someone who fully understands what's at stake."

So that was it. Quinn wasn't mad; he was offering Link the top slot in the Sanctuary. It was completely beyond belief. "What do you want me to do?" Link said.

"It's simple, really." Quinn leaned forward with an elbow on the table. "You have to want money and power as much as I do, which means you have to hunger for it more than anything. More than freedom. More than love. More than life itself."

"So that's why you asked me what I really want?"

"Yes." Quinn leaned back and rested his feet on the table. "It's easy to be selfless, kind, compassionate, charitable, loving. It relieves you of real responsibility. You just sit back and help everyone, make them happy, be nice. But then, one day, you find you've been replaced by that ruthless one-in-a-billion individual who wants it more than you. Too bad. I won't let that happen to the Quinn family. That's why I'm talking to you."

"Honestly, I don't know what to say." Link slowed his breathing so he could talk. "I still can't help thinking that you should be talking to Chelsea about this."

"She's smart. But she's got too much of her mother in her. Too nice. Too much of an idealist. She lacks the killer instinct. I need someone with more greed to be in control."

"And you want me?"

Quinn stood and walked to the window. "That's the real question, isn't it? There are thousands of others who dream of marrying my daughter. She could have anyone, but she says she loves you. She wants you. It's an efficient solution."

"I love her very—"

"Of course you love her." Quinn waved his hand. "She's an 8Z. Five orders of magnitude richer than you. When that much money is involved, love is easy. It'd be impossible for you not to love her. But I have a harder task in mind. And I think you already know what it is."

"Kill Alix Yamaguchi?"

"Yes, but that's the easy part. I don't want you just to kill her, I want you to kill the very idea of her. And then I want everything she started to die with her. She's a threat to the Sanctuary. A threat to all the Quinn family has achieved over six generations. All of it absolutely depends on maintaining the status quo. People must not be allowed to question the system, to even entertain the possibility of change. And there's only one way to do that." Quinn stopped.

"How?" Link asked.

"We numb their minds with a million trivialities. Do I have the latest jax style of the week? Did I watch the hippest Mesh-celeb eat a French pastry last night? Do my eyelashes match my fingernails? Do I own the best underwear? These are the only kinds of 'deep' questions the people can be allowed to ask. This Alix Yamaguchi wants to open their eyes to the possibility of change. If she succeeds, the whole system will collapse. I could lose my rank, and that means I lose everything worth living for. So do you. We can't allow that to happen."

"No worries there, sir. I'm going after her."

"She's smart. And she's got help. The question is whether you're smarter, whether you're up to the task." Quinn gazed over the Wall, as if trying to find *her*.

"I am, sir." Link walked to Quinn's side and stood shoulder-to-shoulder with him. "The Patrol is far superior to anything in the Fringe. She won't get away next time."

"Military force is useful in a battle of raw strength, but this woman has started a different kind of war, one more difficult to fight. A battle of ideas. Dangerous ideas."

"Ideas?"

"The Fringe is different from the Sanctuary. I'm sure you've heard that over and over. But do you know why?"

Link thought back to what he'd learned in school. "They're lazy and—"

"Don't parrot back to me what you've heard your whole life, or you'll miss the point." Quinn looked up. "I'll give you a hint. What is Alix Yamaguchi's ranking? Did you look her up?"

"She's not ranked. She's a zero."

"And what does it mean to be *not ranked*? What is the essential item she's lacking?"

"Money?"

"Exactly." Quinn pointed over the Wall. "The Fringe is a lot of things. Filthy, low-tech, and yes, lazy. But it's something else, something dangerous: a society that has found a way to function without money. Some might call it the ultimate technology. I rather think of it as a weapon. One that's pointing at us."

"It's hard to imagine how that even works."

"I've heard they call it a gift economy. People do things for free, just for the joy of doing it, apparently. And here's the scary thing—it works."

Link laughed. "I've seen drone shots of the Fringe. It's nothing but a dirty slum. So much for their gift economy."

"You're missing the point again. Not seeing what's there. Just like before." Quinn's gaze went over to the invisible glass platform extending out from the building. "Think about it. A society that functions without money. What if an idea like that caught on in the Sanctuary?"

Link shrugged his shoulders. "Honestly, I don't think people here want to give up money."

"It's crazy, but like all rare viruses, there's a chance it may spread with catastrophic consequences. It's a chance I'm not willing to take. The Sanctuary system only functions with money at its core. It's how I control it, the foundation of all I do. Alix Yamaguchi has dared to call it all into question. That's why you have to kill the very idea of her. Do you understand?"

"Yes, sir. Find Alix Yamaguchi, kill her and wipe away her memory."

"You'll have unlimited funds for this operation. I want you to personally see that it's done."

Link smiled. "With pleasure." It was all going to be so easy.

"I take it we have an agreement."

"Yes, sir." Link extended his hand, but Quinn ignored it.

"After I've confirmed the kill, the full power of the Quinn propaganda machine will be engaged to transform you into a hero worthy of worship by the masses. You'll cooperate with all efforts to vilify the memory of the girl and erase her from the public consciousness."

"Yes, of course."

"When I'm convinced that the damage has been undone, and not before, I'll permit you and Chelsea to announce your engagement. And then we'll see about making you a part of the family."

"Thank you, President Quinn." Link could barely breathe with the sudden adrenaline shooting through his system. He was on his way to joining the Quinn dynasty!

"That is all." Quinn motioned toward the door. "Please join my daughter at her birthday party. Give her my love, such as it is, but not a word of our conversation to her or anyone else. I mean that sincerely. Not a word to anyone. This conversation never happened. Your life depends on it." Quinn paused to stare into Link's eyes. "Do we have a deal?"

"Absolutely, sir." Link kept a reverent gaze on Quinn, waiting for the proper time to look away.

"Good. I am exceedingly tired." Quinn slipped a tube out of his pocket and brought it to his mouth for a deep inhale. Then he rubbed his bloodshot, blue eyes. As he pulled his hands away, a contact lens fell out of his left eye. "Leave me now."

"Understood." Link found himself still staring at Quinn's eye. The left one was no longer blue. It was deep brown.

For an instant, Link was frozen by the contrast in color.

"Something wrong?"

"No, sir." Link nodded and turned to leave, moving past the portraits on the wall with the sense that they were watching him. Just before he passed through the door, Quinn took in an audible breath.

"Do not fail me, Link."

12

Mesh Diver

Alix tried but couldn't suppress the trembling in her fingers. Ten years ago, when she was just a child, she'd been thrown out of the brain labs. Like 10% of the population, her brain rejected the technology, making her unfit for Mesh diving.

Now she was doing it again.

"OK, listen carefully." Merf's face floated in the holoscreen. "The key to a successful dive is simple. *Let it happen. Don't fight back.*"

"Easy for you to say."

"Look, this tech is different. I've modified it. We're not going to hijack your brain. Just take it for a ride."

"No drowning? No claustrophobia?"

"Not like before. Trust me."

Alix eyed the massive, closed door of the vault behind her and contemplated making a run for it. But then she thought about all the work Merf had done to get them this far. He had a plan. He was always thinking two or three steps ahead. "OK, Merf. Let's get it over with before I decide to bail."

"Excellent." Merf pointed to the other side of room. "Grab that black cot and set it up here, next to me. And then lie down. I'll do the rest."

She settled into the cot, stared up at the ceiling and wiped her moist palms on her pants. "Now what?"

"Shut your eyes."

The exoskeleton woke up in the corner and crossed the room to stand over her. She peeked and found it looking down at her with its head cage.

"Merf, this is creepy."

"Don't worry, I'm in control. It's just going to put the trodes on you."

Ten icy metal fingers rested gently on her forehead and worked their way backwards over her scalp. "Merf, why's that thing got its hands on me?"

"Alix, please. Just relax. The exo is measuring your head for optimum fit. Nothing works unless the trodes make a perfect connection. OK? Now close your eyes. I know you like the ocean. Imagine a peaceful scene on a beach. You'll be there soon."

Without thinking too much about the meaning of his words, she let her eyelids close. Once, when she was five or six years old, she'd been rummaging through dusty, old books in the library where Merf used to live, when she found a small picture book. She could still remember the photos of a gently arcing shoreline with palm trees and lines of waves. And white sand.

White sand, she repeated to herself with each breath. *White sand.*

The cool tentacles of the trodes caressed her scalp in a hundred places as a soft cloth dome slid over her head like a skullcap.

Pulse racing, she repeated the mantra: *white sand, white sand.* But other thoughts got in the way. *Was the titanium door still closed? Was it too late to jump out of the cot and make a run for it?* Maybe Merf was crazy, maybe he was going to trap her in the Mesh forever. Maybe . . .

That thought and all others flickered out, like the slender flame of a candle in a breeze, leaving her with no fear, no longing. Nothing. For a few seconds, her mind was a complete blank. Peaceful nothingness. Merf's voice, a far-off whisper, floated down to her, like the voice of God.

"The algorithm is running a scan, searching for the optimal neural connection point. Brace yourself."

Alix was enjoying the nothingness too much to care. If she could have opened her mouth, she would have told Merf to leave her alone, at least for a while, maybe forever.

Out of the void, lightning shot down her spine. The floor disappeared, and she felt a sudden weightlessness. When she opened her eyes, windows moved by in a blur.

She was in free fall only meters away from the side of a Sanctuary skyscraper.

"Merf!"

"The neural interface has initiated the connection protocol. You need to be looking down on impact."

Every muscle straining, she arched her back and executed a half-twist so that she was facing down over what looked like a mirror extending from horizon to horizon. And then she realized it was a huge, still ocean. Just before she hit, she turned to see Merf walking on the water toward her. Smiling.

Blackness engulfed her.

"You OK?" Merf was still there, but now they were on a white sand beach beneath a palm tree.

Alix stood next to him. "What was that?"

"The neural interface protocol. It has to trick your mind into thinking you're going to die. It's the only way to get the mind to open up enough to get a good connection across all channels."

"It's rough, Merf."

"True, but much better than the old method used in the brain labs to mimic drowning. I changed it to a free-fall scenario." Merf sported a deep tan, perfect abs and a full head of dark hair. He stooped down and scooped up a handful of sand with his muscular arms. "What do you think?"

"I think you're way too hot, Merf. Where are we?"

"It's a dreamscape, a virtual world inside the Mesh. Sanctuary folks above a certain level have unlimited access. One of the perks of money. They plug in when they go to sleep to dream away the stress of the day."

"Are you kidding me?"

"It takes massive computing resources to run the dreamscape. Any idea where all that power comes from?"

Alix felt the nausea start in her stomach. "Please, tell me it's not true."

"Afraid so."

"The brain labs." She paused as she considered the reality. "People in the Fringe are selling their minds and ruining their bodies so a few ultra-rich insomniacs in the Sanctuary can—" She didn't want to say it. "—Have sweet dreams?"

"I wanted you to see it with your own eyes. That's the kind of system we're up against."

Alix dropped to her knees in the sand. "How could anyone justify doing that?"

"It's not that hard. After a while, any organization becomes its own justification if it isn't constantly challenged to grow and change. The status quo hardens. The system built by the Quinn family is simple and clean, from a certain point of view." Merf picked up another handful of sand and studied the particles as they slipped through his fingers. "You can boil it down to one rule: the value of a person is exactly equal to the amount of money they control."

"And since no one in the Fringe has any money—"

Merf nodded. "We are literally worthless to the system, nothing more than an inexhaustible supply of computing power to be exploited."

"That's how they justify hijacking the brains of a hundred innocent workers to power a single jax."

"Or a thousand for every dreamer here in the dreamscape." Merf paused for emphasis. "Now that you understand the theory, you need to see the reality. That's why we're here."

"To do what, Merf?"

"To enter the Sanctuary. An idealized version of it. To see it from the inside."

"Where is it?"

"Just over there." Merf took off on a brisk walk up the sandy hill and into a thick grove of trees. "Follow me. You've got to see this."

As Alix jogged into the grove, she ticked off each of her senses. She could *see* bright yellow flowers, *feel* the lush, green grass between her toes, *hear* the birds in the trees. Bending, she brought a flower to her nose and inhaled deeply.

Nothing.

Then, she licked a finger. Again, nothing.

"Hey, Merf," she said.

"I know. The simulation isn't perfect. They still haven't worked out smell and taste. That requires even more computing power. More brain labs."

A thought hit Alix. *How many people in the brain labs were generating the computing power for just one flower?* It made her shiver.

Emerging from the trees, she looked up to see a city of gleaming, glass buildings floating a 100 meters off the ground. "Is that it? The Sanctuary?"

"Beautiful, isn't it?" Merf walked in its direction.

"No Wall?"

"You don't need a Wall if there's no Fringe."

"Good point." Alix stopped. "So, there are real people from the Sanctuary dreaming in there?"

"You'll see their avatars walking around when we get inside. They're in their beds asleep, but their minds are here, dreaming."

"Do they remember what they dream?"

"Hard to say. I think it's like any other dream. Some of it's remembered. Some isn't."

"Merf, are you sure it's safe to go in there?" Alix glanced at the trees and the ocean behind her. "They'll see us. Isn't that a bad idea?"

"All they'll see is our avatars. Anyway, I've hacked the system to make us invisible. The super rich do it all the time. I'm guessing Quinn is here right now. But don't worry. Haven't you always wanted to see the Sanctuary from the inside?"

"What if I said no, Merf?"

"Then you'd be lying. I know you want to see it. Everybody in the Fringe wants to see the Sanctuary. That's why people sit and watch it for hours through the Wall."

"OK, so maybe I'm a bit curious."

"Thought so. Let's go."

They walked the last klick in silence up a green hill. The Sanctuary floated in the air above them, a city in the sky.

Alix craned her neck to look up. "How do we get there?"

Merf pointed with his chin.

A glass compartment descended until it rested in front of Alix. Its side opened, as if inviting her to step in.

Alix looked at Merf to ask permission.

"Go ahead," he said. "I'll catch the next one."

She stepped through the opening and saw it close behind her. Light as a feather, she ascended. As the ground pulled away, the ocean came into view on the other side of the trees. Then, the elevator passed through an opening and emerged onto ground level in the Sanctuary.

When the glass opened, she stepped onto a street that looked like a river of gold.

She'd never seen anything so gorgeous in her life. Brilliant, lush, sensual. A place worthy of dreams.

On the other side of the street, a tall woman stood with supreme confidence, arms relaxed at her sides as she looked up. With scarlet leather leggings, a matching crop top, neon-yellow thigh boots, tiger-eye implants and a jewel-encrusted fashion dagger, she was the opposite of anyone Alix had ever encountered in the Fringe. Mobile tattoos swam across her delicate, dark skin.

Merf came into Alix's peripheral view. "Meet Licious, mega Mesh-star, ranked 7Z and rising fast. She's asleep on her private island off the coast of Fiji right now and just plugged into the dreamscape. And like everyone else, she saw your video. Notice the red leggings. She's definitely a fan."

Still staring, Alix took a step closer. "She can't see me, right?"

"Nope. You should move in for a closer look."

Alix walked across the street, staring into Licious' eyes and examining her from every angle.

"So, what do you think?" Merf said.

"I've never seen anyone like her."

"Why don't you strike up a conversation?"

Alix flinched. "Are you kidding?" Talking face-to-face with a Mesh-celeb from the Sanctuary was the last thing on her mind right now.

"No, I'm not. You're here to learn. Next to Quinn, she's probably the most famous person in the Sanctuary. She could help you understand how they think."

"If she's even willing to talk to me."

"True," Merf said. "But you never know. I doubt she's ever talked to anyone from the Fringe. You might be able to get her attention. Besides, you have something in common."

"What?"

"You're both famous."

Alix still couldn't wrap her head around it. She wasn't sure she wanted to. "But she can't see me."

"It's easy to make you visible."

"Can she talk if she's asleep? In dream mode?"

"Absolutely. And you'll find out even more. People are the most honest when they're asleep."

Alix looked at her own body and saw she was wearing faux fur pants and a purple hoodie, standard Sanctuary attire that shouldn't attract attention. "It's not going to trigger any alarms if she sees me, is it?"

"Maybe. I don't know. The dreamscape is monitored. I got us in with stolen identities."

"Can you get us out quick if anything happens?"

"No problem."

She thought about it. "OK, I'm game. Make me visible." Her words surprised her, bringing a sudden spike of fear and the rush of adrenaline.

"Done." Merf nodded.

Licious' gaze stopped on Alix and they locked eyes for an instant. She surveyed Alix from head to foot. Without a word, she turned and walked away, leaving Alix standing alone.

The meaning of her look was clear. *Nothing here worth my time.*

Alix rushed to catch up. "Hey, Licious," she said, pushing the fear aside again. "I want to talk to you. Tell me about your life."

"My life?" Licious stopped and turned to face Alix with blank, colorless eyes. "What's there to tell?"

"You're rich and famous. I'm neither. I'd like to know what it's like to be you."

Licious' face was devoid of expression. "Everyone's interested in me. That's my job, and I'm good at it. But I only talk to people I'm interested in, which is rare. So the question is, how interesting are you?"

It was a challenge Alix couldn't resist. Like always, her adrenaline kicked in.

"You've never met anyone like me. I'm different."

"From what?"

"Everyone in the Sanctuary."

"Oh yeah? What's your rank?"

"Rank doesn't matter."

"Of course it matters." Licious couldn't stop laughing. "It's only the single most important fact about a person. A neat summation of your life. I'm a 7Z and moving up fast. President Quinn is only two magnitudes above me. Only a few hundred people on the planet are richer than me. It's clear you aren't one of them. Now leave me alone." She walked away.

"Wait!" Alix stood her ground. "I have no rank. That's why I'm different."

"No rank?" Licious stopped and turned back for a closer look at Alix. "You're lying. I could see it if oculars worked here."

"I'm not even in the database. I've never had any money or rank. Don't need any. Don't want any."

"Everyone has a rank. It's how the system works."

"Not me. I'm Fringe scum, here in your dreamscape paradise to learn about your perfect world."

"Impossible."

"Maybe. But it's true."

"How did you get in? You have to be a 3Z or higher to afford access."

"I hacked my way in." Alix jumped to the heart of the matter. "But back to your life. Are you happy?"

"What do you think? I'm a 7Z."

"That's not what I asked."

"Everyone in my rank is happy. By definition. It's not even a valid question."

"What about President Quinn. Is he happy?"

"Are you stupid? He's a 9Z, two magnitudes happier than me."

The more Alix thought about it, the more simple and clean and logical it sounded. "So, rank equals happiness?"

"Is water wet? Rank equals money equals power equals success equals happiness. Simple math. Different words for the same idea." Licious tilted her head. "You ask strange questions."

"And I've got another one. If you're happy, you must have a nice family or a ton of friends, right?"

"Family? Friends?" Licious gazed skyward. "No family. They'd just hold me back. But I have millions of friends. Everywhere I go. All over the planet. That's why I'm rich."

"You must have a lot of fun with them. What do you do?"

"It's not what I do; it's what *they* do."

"Which is?"

"Worship me."

"Sounds pretty one-sided." Alix shook her head. "Those are fans, not friends."

Licious forced a grin. "There's no difference."

"What do you do for fun?"

"I'm doing it. Sleep."

"What do you believe in?"

"Myself. Money. The Sanctuary. What else is there?"

"Do you love anyone, Licious?"

"I could only love a 7Z or higher. Anyone else would just be a parasite or a distraction."

"So, love is a function of rank?"

"What else could it be?" Licious paused to stare at Alix. "I've never met anyone from the Fringe. What's it like there? Does everyone wear red? I hear it's worse than hell."

"There's no money, but we do what it takes to survive."

"How?"

"We have our own kind of system. Mostly, we try to help people around us, family and friends. We sacrifice a lot and share all we have. We work together and, somehow, it works."

"But you have no money, no rank. A literal zero."

"That's true. The Sanctuary won't let us have money. So we got used to it. Found another way to live. Evolved. Maybe we could teach you a thing or two."

Licious took a step back as she appraised Alix. "You remind me of someone I saw today. She was strange, like you. Entertaining and scary at the same time. What's your name?"

"Alix Yamaguchi."

13

Link found his way back to the party, still reeling from the meeting with Quinn and his revelations about the origin of the Sanctuary and the Quinn family's role in it. He couldn't stop thinking about President Quinn's offer to make Link part of the family. Stopping by the door to the ballroom, he listened to a band playing wordless improvisations. His mind wandered with the music. What was it with the color of Quinn's eyes? A genetic defect? No wonder he hid it with a contact lens. The Sanctuary was no place for imperfection. It reminded him of—*her*. No, couldn't be. Link shook his head and instantly discarded the thought.

He felt a soft nudge on his shoulder.

"How was Daddy?"

Link turned to see Chelsea. Her arms slipped around his neck.

"It was . . . How can I put this? . . . A moving experience," he said.

"Daddy knows how to move people." Chelsea gazed between Link's eyes. "Did he consent?"

"Yes, sort of. But only if I can deliver on Alix Yamaguchi."

"Alive or dead?"

"Dead."

Chelsea pursed her lips. "I'm not surprised. I haven't seen Daddy this upset in months. The whole Alix Yamaguchi thing has caught on much too fast. You'll have to go after her into the Fringe yourself, won't you?"

"Promised I would kill her and then work to eradicate her memory. And there can't be any mistakes this time. But don't worry, Chelsea. I'll be fine. And when I come back, we'll announce our engagement to the world, with your father's blessing. Everything will be different."

Chelsea surveyed the party and looked back at Link. "Our work here is done. Let's get away."

"Couldn't agree more. Your place or mine?"

"I'd rather just go for a walk."

Link followed her out the big doors into the elevator where they both stood in silence on the long ride down. At the bottom, they walked out past the guards to the street.

"Where to?" Link asked.

"Anywhere away from here."

The sun had set. A soothing, blue glow lingered on the Wall and reflected off the glass skins of a hundred buildings. Feeling the cool breeze, Link felt more relaxed than he had in a long time.

"So, what did you and Daddy talk about?" Chelsea said.

Link gazed up past the tops of the buildings. "The Sanctuary, how it came to be, where it's going from here."

"Daddy gave you a history lesson?"

"I guess he just wanted to make sure it was all in good hands with you. And maybe me, too."

"I think it is," Chelsea said. "You and me, working together. We can take the Sanctuary to new heights. Do things that Daddy never dreamed of. Make him proud. Maybe even surprise him."

Chelsea was right. What President Quinn told Link about the Sanctuary and Quinn's motivation for protecting it didn't really matter. What mattered was where the Sanctuary went in the years ahead, after Quinn was dead and gone. He'd just need to be patient. When he and Chelsea were finally in charge, things would be different, better. Link didn't have to be motivated solely by greed, like Quinn. He and Chelsea could work together on creating a more fair system, a system that worked for everyone, no matter their rank, maybe even people in the Fringe. They'd make reforms. Take the society in a new direction. A *revolution*.

Wait.

Why had word had popped into his mind? Isn't that what Alix Yamaguchi was calling for? Her multicolored eyes floated in the darkness of his mind. He tried to wipe the image away, but it wouldn't leave. Sweat beaded up on his chest and ran down his spine.

The important thing was to be with Chelsea to inherit it all from *Daddy*. Link would have to find a way to please both of them, each in their own way. He'd have to strike the word *revolution* from his vocabulary. It wasn't safe to speak of it, at least not until Quinn was gone. Chelsea was the key. He had to keep her happy.

After fumbling for her hand, he squeezed it. "You and me together, Chelsea. I'd like that very much."

"I feel like celebrating." Chelsea reached for her jax and spun it around in her palm. "Can I see yours?" she asked.

"Sure, why?"

"Just give it to me." She had a devious look in her eye.

"OK, here you go."

Dropping both jaxes to the street, she smiled up at him as their jaxes landed, bounced, wobbled and came to rest. Then, putting a finger to her lips, she lifted her boots and stomped on each one, carefully grinding them to fine, white powder.

"Oops." Chelsea giggled.

"What are you—"

"Daddy likes to listen in on me. And you. Don't worry, I'll get you a new one." She took Link's arm. Her face looked serious. "Now that we're alone, I have a question."

"Sure."

Chelsea took in a big breath. "I know it's silly, but I'll ask it anyway. Are you happy?"

They passed a woman sporting a flowing, red dress and matching bandana. She was staring at a holoscreen replaying Alix Yamaguchi's famous chopper ride from earlier in the day. A man with a buzz cut rode by on an ancient motorcycle, dressed in scarlet.

"Am I happy? Of course I'm happy. I mean, it's not even a question, is it? I live in the Sanctuary. Everyone here is happy, right? How could we not be happy living here? We have all that we could possibly want." He thought about Quinn's words about wanting *everything*. "Well, almost." He saw a group of middle-aged women crowding together on a park bench, an unusual sight. People in the Sanctuary rarely gathered in groups. As he walked by, they were all watching the Alix Yamaguchi video in silence, eyes big, staring in wonder. "I wonder how many views that thing is getting?"

Chelsea shrugged her shoulders. "Who cares?" She stopped and held on to Link's arm, forcing him to look at her, something close to desperation in her voice. "Happiness is the whole point of the Sanctuary. It's fundamental to our existence. We have more of everything. More education, more technology, more sunsets and sunrises. More cappuccino and lazy mornings and fresh flowers and Mesh-celebs. They don't have anything in the Fringe. Zero money. So we're *more* happy, right?"

"My point exactly." Link nodded, vigorously. "How could it be any other way?"

They walked in silence for a block. And then, Chelsea let go of his arm and stopped. When he turned to look at her, she was crouched on the sidewalk, crying.

Bending down, he lifted her chin with his finger. "What's wrong, Chels? Is it something I said?"

"No, you said what I needed to hear." She wiped her eyes. "I have it all, more than I want, so I guess that means I'm happy."

"Yes, Chelsea, you're happy. I'm happy. We're all happy. Just accept that."

"Got it." She stood. From her purse, she found a golden dispenser and tapped it on the side with her finger. A small blue pill rose to the top, and she slipped it into her mouth, under her tongue. "That should calm me down, help clear my head. All I need is sleep now. It's been a long day. Will you walk me home?"

"Wouldn't miss it."

The instant Link stepped back inside his apartment, the dim lights came on. He gazed out at the immensity and splendor of the Sanctuary. It was a sight he'd seen most of his life, but tonight, as he thought about the possibility that it all might be his someday, its jewel-like beauty was intoxicating.

But first, Link had to kill Alix Yamaguchi, the one person that stood between him and all the rest of it. With his staff at Patrol HQ, he'd formulate a bulletproof plan of attack tomorrow.

Now, it was time for a restful sleep to put all the Alix Yamaguchi craziness behind him. As he moved toward the bed, the lights faded. He fell back onto the soft surface, his body sinking in. He needed a guaranteed good sleep.

He grabbed the trodes and slipped them over his head. "Engage dreamscape. Take me to the Arena."

He wondered if he'd see Chelsea there.

14

"What did you say your name was?" Licious turned around as if searching the air. "Hey, where did you go?"

"I'm right here." Alix waved her hands, but Licious looked through her like she wasn't there.

Merf's hand came down on Alix's shoulder. "I have to say, that was shaping up to be a great conversation." He pulled her to the other side of the street. "I was looking forward to the rest of it."

"Why can't she hear me, Merf?"

"I had to put you back on invisible/inaudible mode. Licious can't see or hear you. She just saw you disappear into thin air. Which may not be an altogether bad thing. She'll think about it when she wakes up. Maybe even talk about it. She has an audience of millions. Your legend will grow. I can see it now. *The Fringe girl appears here and there, in the real and the virtual world, vanishing like a ghost.*"

"Why did you have to kill our conversation?"

"It was over the minute you said your name. The dreamscape has AI algorithms monitoring all conversations and interactions. The dreamers don't know it, but this whole setup is actually a sophisticated surveillance tool, a way for Quinn to monitor the population. It's marketed as entertainment, but it's all part of the system. The moment you told Licious your name, it triggered an alert. System bots are already looking for you."

"Sorry, Merf. Guess I blew it."

"Don't worry, I'll make sure they can't track us."

"So we can stay a little bit longer? Have more of a look around?"

"Sure."

They strolled down the golden boulevard, past the tallest buildings Alix had ever imagined. With outer skins of glass, gold, silver or diamonds, there was more grandeur than she could comprehend.

A place you could get used to without a lot of effort.

The laws of physics didn't apply inside the dreamscape. Sure, there were people walking around on the streets and in the parks. But they were also in the air. Floating, flying.

She stopped and stared up.

"Want to give it a try?" Merf pointed at the sky.

"How?"

"It's all tied to the neural interface. If you can imagine it, you can do it."

Alix closed her eyes and thought about floating upward. Nothing seemed to happen until she opened her eyes and saw she was two meters above Merf. "Whoa!" Panic exploded behind her eyes, and she dropped to the street and rolled.

"You expected to fall just now, right?" Merf had a knack for pointing out the obvious.

"Yeah, so?"

"It's easier if you're dreaming. People don't expect the laws of physics to apply. Flying is just, well, normal."

Alix rubbed the back of her head. "I'll stick to walking for now."

An octagonal building far down the street caught her eye. Faint sounds of cheering came from inside. Crowds of people walked toward it.

"Let's take a look." Merf said. "See what's so exciting."

The closer they got, the louder the cheers became. When Alix and Merf finally walked through the outside gate, Alix understood why.

It was an arena, like the Colosseum she'd read about in ancient Rome. The stands were filled with wild people, thousands of them, relaxing in luxurious, jewel-encrusted chairs, yelling, fists raised to the sky. Far below, two people were engaged in combat. A closeup of the fight was projected on an enormous sphere floating in the center of the arena. One of the fighters lunged forward. With a slo-mo kung fu kick, her heel slammed into the other fighter's face, throwing him back. Twisting in the opposite direction, she swung a dagger that bit into his neck.

When she yanked out the blade, he fell limp to the ground.

Cheers rocked the arena.

"Are you kidding me?" Alix looked over at Merf and smiled. "They have fights here?"

"I guess everyone needs to let off a little steam now and then, so Quinn gives them bread and circuses."

They moved to open seats and relaxed into the decadent surroundings. Alix took it all in with a single glance, and she liked what she saw.

More cheers erupted from the crowds as two new fighters strode into the arena from opposite sides.

Alix studied them closely.

They were dressed in form-fitting bodysuits from head to toe. An overlay of ornately designed armor protected a few vital areas. One fighter was blue; the other, yellow. And because this was a digital dreamscape inside the Mesh, it was a physics-free environment. The fighters hovered around each other, lunged high in the air and executed slow-motion backflips with exotic kicks to disable their opponents, like an old Hong Kong martial arts video Merf had shown Alix. As far as she could tell, the only weapon they used was a single hand-held blade.

The yellow fighter bounded high in the air, arms outstretched, opening himself to a thrust from the blue fighter.

"Who gets to do it?" Alix felt the rush of adrenaline kicking in.

Merf pointed to controls on his chair. "Look at this. It says *Volunteer*. You press the button and you get to fight."

"Are we still invisible, Merf?"

"Yep."

"Make me visible, Merf." Alix pointed to the arena floor, where the two combatants were circling each other. "I want to do it."

Merf's eyes went big. "Are you kidding? The system already knows you're here. It won't take long for them to find you."

"You can pull me out any time, unplug and take us back to your little nest in the Fringe, right?"

"Yeah, but—"

"Look, Merf, I'm a good fighter. You've seen me working out. Lots of people are dreaming this right now. The elite of the Sanctuary. You're all about getting in front of an audience, aren't you?"

"I can't argue with your logic," Merf said. "But you need the right opponent. Not just anyone will do. I'm searching through the dreamscape data files right now, and it looks like he's here, dreaming, watching."

"Who?"

"The guy who tried to kill you today. The same guy who's going to try to kill you again tomorrow or the next day. Lincoln Wells. You game?"

Alix stood, her body feeling loose and strong, her mind suddenly clear, all fear gone. More than anything, she wanted to fight him.

"Bring him to me, Merf."

15

The dreams were always good.

Link didn't dive into the dreamscape most nights. He preferred falling asleep the natural way. The artificiality of any digital environment bothered him, but the dreamscape was stranger than most. The intense colors, vivid detail and sensual overload were unsettling. The residual effect always carried through to the next day, leaving him strangely unconnected to the real world around him. But it was intensely relaxing, better than the best meditation pills, and there was pharma to take care of the aftereffects.

He felt it, an urgent need for ultra-calm to wipe away the stress of the disaster Alix Yamaguchi had caused for the Patrol and of the meeting with Quinn at the party. For once, the dreamscape would be the perfect way to unwind.

For the next few hours, he'd take in the fights at the Colosseum. It was rumored that Quinn was there every night, invisible and observing. Chelsea would be somewhere in the crowd, but it was understood that she and Link would never look for each other. The dreamscape was a world apart—not a place to meet friends, but a place to forget and indulge in a deeply personal space.

On occasion, Link had fought and won at the Colosseum, drawing on his daily fighting practice in the holo-cube. He was good, maybe even one of the best. When he was in the mood, it was exhilarating. But not tonight. Tonight he needed rest, not excitement.

And so, as he entered the Colosseum, he surrendered to the soft embrace of his favorite seat, three rows up, on the east side, a little to the left of center. Settling deeper into the dream, reality slipped away as his mind let go of worries and inhibitions and opened up like a flower blooming in the moonlight.

Half a dozen fights went by in a blur.

And then, he saw the button light up on the arm of his chair.

Volunteer.

Must be a glitch; he didn't recall touching it.

But in a flash of white, there he was, on the floor of the Colosseum, in a bodysuit and armor, a fighter in the next round. He'd never seen this happen before, but there was always an element of randomness built into the dreamscape. Maybe it was a new protocol introduced by the Sanctuary leadership. Maybe it was Quinn.

It didn't matter; he could handle it. If he couldn't relax away the stress, he'd blow it off with a quick battle to the death and then get back to gentle dreaming.

Stepping onto the arena floor, he felt pumped up. He knew his body was lying on the bed back home asleep, but the dreaming part of his brain was very much awake. He executed a couple of side stretches and felt the perfection of his avatar fighting body. He wore the usual blue bodysuit with flexible black armor, something he'd designed himself and uploaded to his profile in the dreamscape. Daggers rested in slits on each thigh. A couple of Japanese throwing stars rested in a pouch at the small of his back. Fingering one of them, he walked toward the center of the arena floor.

The usual cheers rose from the crowd. Maybe they recognized him from past fights. Chelsea would be watching inside her own dream. She'd be surprised to see him in the Colosseum after all the excitement of the day, but she'd be proud. He hoped Quinn was watching. This was probably a test. A small chance to redeem himself.

On the far side of the arena, the opponent moved closer, walking with confidence, maybe even some battle swagger. It was a girl, and she had fighting experience. He could tell from her loose gait and the way she held her head and arms.

But the strangest thing was her colors.

She was dressed all in red, including a mask that hid her face. All the more reason to kill her quickly.

Link stepped inside the fighting ring and, as was customary, announced his name to the adulation of the crowds. As a commander in the Patrol and a suitor of Chelsea Quinn, he was well-known, the typical crowd favorite.

The girl on the other side of the fighting ring stepped in. Looking up at the crowd, she turned in a circle. And then, raising a hand, as if to quiet the spectators, she announced her name as she cast her mask aside.

"Alix Yamaguchi."

Her words echoed through the Colosseum. They were met by silence, as Link and the spectators struggled and then achieved comprehension. All he could see were her eyes. Blue and brown. A wall of emotion hit him like a tidal wave, teetering on the knife edge between love and hate. He stared, unable to look away, unable to move.

In unison, the crowd surged to their feet. With fists to the sky, they raised a deafening roar that buzzed the inside of Link's dreaming skull. A wave of red moved through the Colosseum as the crowd signaled a change in their allegiance.

If Quinn were not watching before, he had surely been alerted and would be taking a keen interest in the outcome, if he even allowed the fight to proceed. Link wanted to fight Alix and instantly realized the fight was for more than personal victory. The stakes were clear.

It was the Sanctuary against the Fringe.

With effort, Link shook off the effect of her eyes and dug deep to focus his hatred. The image of Quinn from earlier in the evening materialized in his mind. It was a face filled with rage at Link's failure to kill the girl. A face that would determine Link's entire future.

So Link turned Quinn's rage into his own.

He didn't try to hold back the snarl on his lips. "I don't know how you hacked into the dreamscape, but you shouldn't be here. You're nothing but a worthless zero." His voice reverberated through the Colosseum for everyone to hear.

"Oh, I see, Lincoln Wells. Or should I call you Link? You want me to leave now without a fight. Afraid you'll lose? Just like the chase today?"

Roars from the crowd made it difficult for Link to think.

"I'm going to destroy you. Now and later."

"Destroy away, then." Alix stood with her arms folded, waiting for Link to make the first move. Exactly what he wanted.

Slipping two fingers into the pouch at the small of his back, Link pulled out a throwing star, cradled it in his hand and twisted to the right, opening his palm to the sky and releasing the star.

As the dreamscape algorithms kicked in, all motion slowed. Link watched the star exit his palm, dip to the left and spin toward Alix Yamaguchi.

Standing across from Link in the fighting ring, Alix's feelings surprised her. She knew she could never hate him. It wasn't just his eyes or the vulnerability beneath the bravado, although that was part of it. There was something about the way he stood, part of him leaning forward to kill her, yet part of him holding back. She could see the conflict. He wasn't all bad, maybe not even mostly bad.

It was only his dreamscape avatar, not the real Link, but it told her everything she needed to know.

"I can help you beat him," Merf said, his voice playing inside Alix's head. "I've hacked into their algorithms and found a way to give you an advantage. Just like with the drones today during the chase. The dreamscape algorithm defaults into slow motion when a fighter attacks. It's supposed to make the action more dramatic. But you won't be constrained by the slow motion effect. Link will move slowly, but you'll move fast. It'll be no contest."

"You want me to cheat?"

"Don't think of it as cheating," Merf said. "Everyone's watching. It's critical that you impress the crowd."

"I don't like it." Alix subvocalized the words. "It's not fair."

"To whom?"

"To him. Lincoln Wells." Alix stared across the circle at Link. He was flexing his jaw, trying to show her how much he hated her. But it all looked forced. Like it wasn't the real Link. Like he was suppressing something.

She folded her arms as Link launched a throwing star. The instant it left his hand, he and the star phase-shifted into slow motion. It was going to be easy to dodge it. "I don't like to fight like this, Merf. It's still a rigged system, even if it's rigged in my favor. It's the way the Sanctuary operates, not the Fringe."

"Don't forget, he tried to kill you a few hours ago. For real."

"I know, but he was just following orders."

"Do you have feelings for him? It's dangerous if you do."

"Who, me? Yeah, I have feelings for him, and they're not good." Alix knew it was a half-lie as soon as the words left her mouth. So she dug deep, summoned her hatred of Quinn and magnified that hatred to focus on Link. But no matter how hard she tried, it didn't work.

Merf's voice lowered, the way it always did when he was making a point. "For six generations, the Quinns have rigged the system in their favor. It's the source of all their wealth and power. Don't you think it's fair to turn the tables and give them a tiny taste of their own medicine?"

"It's not his fault. Link isn't a Quinn."

"But he wants to be one. It's only a matter of time before he marries Quinn's daughter Chelsea. Think of the millions of hours of brain lab power he's exploited just to get a good night's sleep in the dreamscape or to play some inane Mesh game on his jax. How many Fringe lives has he destroyed?" Merf swore under his breath, revealing a vast ocean of rage just below the surface. "Now stop arguing and fight the dirty scumbag. If you can't find a way to hate the Sanctuary and the Quinns, do it for the love of the Fringe. Do it for me. Do it for Muse."

"OK, Merf, if you put it that way—"

"How else can I put it? Now fight!"

The throwing star made a slow arc to the right and navigated in a perfect line to sever Alix's carotid artery. She had to admit, it took skill to throw like that. With ease, she ducked, reached up and grabbed the spinning star, feeling the full force of its momentum as her fingers closed on it and held.

Slow motion stopped.

She stared at the star in her hand and flipped it in the air with her thumb, like a old coin. "Is that the best you can do, Lincoln Wells?"

The arena exploded with laughter and yelling.

Link's eyes went wide. "How did you—"

"I'm faster than you. Sorry."

Alix jumped and felt herself carried high in the air. Link followed after her. They hung two meters apart and circled each other.

"Worthless Fringe scum." Link bared his teeth. "Go back to the cesspool you came from."

"All of us in the Fringe are human, Link, human beings just like you. None of us are worthless, none of us are scum, and the Fringe isn't a cesspool. Think about it. Those are just words you've been taught to say. But you can unlearn them. You can learn the truth."

"I already know the truth!"

Alix scanned the arena. "I have to admit, it's fun here. I can see why you like it."

"You don't belong."

"I don't plan to stay. Too many of my friends in the brain labs are suffering right now to power this game, to power the whole way of life of the Sanctuary. They give their lives so you can be rich."

"Stop the lies."

"There's an easy solution, Lincoln Wells. Destroy the brain labs and the chemplants. Tear down the Wall. Bring the people back together."

"That's crazy!" Link whipped a dagger off his thigh. "The whole Sanctuary would be flooded with Fringe scum!"

"Come visit me in the Fringe, Lincoln Wells. I'll show you the truth. We'll build a new society together. One that works for everyone."

"We already have the perfect society right here!"

"The Sanctuary only works by sucking away the life of the Fringe. Like a parasite. It could never survive on its own."

"No!" Link gritted his teeth and swung with his dagger. The slo-mo algorithm kicked in. Alix tilted her head as the blade floated a centimeter from her eye. When the blade receded, she went into a speed twist and dug her heel into Link's jaw. The force of the blow threw him backward in somersaults to the floor. It wasn't fair, but it must have looked impressive.

Cheers rocked the arena.

"Doesn't really sound like they're rooting for you, does it Link? I think they agree with me. Why don't you listen to them?"

Alix floated down to the arena floor as Link picked himself up.

"You hacked the system. That's why you move so fast. I don't know how you did it, but you hacked the system. There's no way I can win."

Boos rained down from the stands.

"Now maybe you understand. That's what it's like to grow up in the Fringe. The Quinns hacked the system to keep us at the bottom. But it doesn't have to be that way. We can change it all."

Chanting started.

Al—ix! Al—ix!

With a smirk on her lips and a hand on her hip, Alix let one eyebrow rise. Link had a full measure of rage in his eyes. Each of his hands found a dagger, and he staggered to his feet and charged.

Then, the slo-mo algorithms kicked in.

"How much longer, Merf," Alix muttered under her breath. "This is getting old."

"You're working the crowd like a pro. Keep it up until they come."

"They?"

"The Sanctuary system has detected your presence and is mounting an attack. Drones are on their way inside the dreamscape. It's going to be epic, Alix. Everything we've been working for."

Link lunged with both daggers, arms outstretched, taking his time to reach Alix. She studied his face and could see the menacing lips, the clenched jaw. At the last second, with little effort, Alix arched her back to let him pass.

She moved in closer to study his eyes. There was rage on the surface, but below that, she thought she saw more. Uneasiness. Fear. Maybe even panic. As she looked more deeply, one of his blade tips opened a crimson streak across her cheek.

There was a flash of pain. Alix grabbed Link's wrists and rolled with him to the arena floor, still in slow motion, coming to rest on top, her legs pinning his arms. He struggled, unable to shake her off.

"Life in the Sanctuary is good, isn't it Link? Maybe too good. You should work harder to practice your moves." Alix slipped out her daggers and flicked them across Link's cheeks, giving him matching diagonal cuts.

Link was beyond rage and fury. "She's hacked the algorithms!" he yelled. "Just like when we chased her in the Fringe! No one can move that fast!" He struggled to escape her grasp, but Alix had him securely pinned to the ground.

Looking up at the arena audience, she twirled her daggers in her hands, as if to ask what she should do next.

The reply came, a muffled, scattered sound at first. Then, louder and clearer.

Kill him! Kill him!

"Looks like the Sanctuary has deserted you, Lincoln Wells."

"It's not a fair fight!" Link kept struggling to get free. But then he stopped as he looked to the sky. A smile formed on his lips.

Alix looked up and saw a swarm of black drones circling above the arena. Raising her hand, she silenced the crowd. "You're right. Life isn't fair. But we can change that. All we have to do is be willing to see the truth." She brought both daggers down and pointed the tips at Link's chest.

Kill him! Kill him!

The black drones broke from the circle into a dive, coming straight for Alix.

"There's nowhere in the Fringe you can hide!" Link yelled. "I'm coming for you."

Alix leaned closer and looked into Link's eyes, trying to see what lay behind them. "I'll be waiting." As she glanced up, the drones were only a couple of meters away. "When you come, we can—"

The air flashed white, and the arena disappeared.

Link awoke in a hot sweat and ripped the trodes off his head. No matter how he tried, he couldn't get her eyes out of his mind.

When you come, we can—

How did she know he was coming for her? What was she going to say? We can do what?

His jax glowed purple. Chelsea wanted to talk. No doubt she'd been in the dreamscape and had seen everything. It was another disaster, and the whole thing had played out in public. Just like the chase. Word had certainly reached her father by now, if he hadn't seen it himself. Things were worse than ever.

Link didn't have the energy to talk but couldn't ignore Chelsea, so he grabbed the jax, slid his finger along its length and dropped it on the bed next to his head. Her face came up on the holoscreen that opened above the jax.

With nothing to say, Link stared at the ceiling and waited for her to talk. He dreaded the conversation. She would have questions. Lots of questions.

"I'm here for you, Link."

He flexed and unflexed his jaw and let out a long sigh. "Sorry Chels, I'm so tired right now. Can't really think straight. OK if I call you in the morning?" Link closed his eyes, erecting a wall of silence between him and Chelsea that lasted half a minute.

"Link, we need to talk."

"Not now, Chels." Link reached for the jax to turn it off. "I'm not feeling—"

"Please don't cut me out of your life, Link. None of this is your fault. We can work through it together."

Link pulled his hand back and stared at the ceiling. His nose started to run, and he sniffled.

Then it happened, catching him by surprise. He tried to push it back, tried to hold it off, tried to ignore it, but nothing worked. From nowhere, a wave of emotion broke over him.

All he could manage was a whisper that turned into a whimper. "Did you see it, Chels?"

"Yeah."

"It's not fair. I wanted more than anything to beat her. I tried, but the slow motion algorithm got me. It's not supposed to work like that. I couldn't react. Couldn't stop her. It wasn't a fair fight."

"I know, Link. She breached the security protocols on the dreamscape and hacked the fighting algorithm. It was another setup. There's nothing you could have done."

Link buried his face in his hands, trying to hold back the tears, but they came anyway, forcing their way through his fingers. "It's over, Chelsea. Everyone was there. Everyone saw what she did to me, how she played me. Your father—"

"I'll talk to him, Link."

"It's no good Chelsea!"

"He'll listen to me."

"I know what he wants, Chelsea. I know how he thinks. What he's really after. It's not what you think, Chelsea. He doesn't really care about the people in the Sanctuary. All he wants is—"

"Money and power, right? That's what he told you?"

"Yeah, basically."

"That's only one side of him, Link. He's not really like that."

"I don't know, Chelsea." Link put his hand up to his forehead to suppress a rising headache. "He's not going to forgive me this time. Probably won't let us get married, either. It's all—"

"It's not over, Link. I'll talk to Daddy. He loves me. He'll listen."

"But Chelsea, the whole Sanctuary is against me. You heard the shouting. *Kill him! Kill him!*" He buried his face in his hands again.

"It was the dreamscape, Link. People aren't themselves there. They say things they don't mean."

Link shook his head. "You know that's not true. It's easier to talk in the dreamscape. People say what they're really thinking. They can't help it. They're all against me. The whole Sanctuary hates me."

"Not me, Link."

He wiped his eyes. "I don't know what's going to happen, Chelsea. It's all so crazy. Things are moving too fast."

"The dreamscape has been closed down."

"What?"

"I'm sure it's just temporary, but it's dangerous until the security breach is fixed. They've got to figure out how she's hacking in. So they shut it down."

"That's just great, Chelsea. Now everyone's going to blame me for killing their dreams. You know how popular the dreamscape is. They'll hate me even more." Link's mind raced. "Who told you they shut down the dreamscape, Chelsea?"

"Daddy."

"You've already talked to your father?"

"He called me just before I called you."

Link was almost afraid to ask, but it came out anyway. "He was livid, right?"

"He wasn't happy. He said—" She hesitated.

"What, Chelsea! What did he say?"

"He's running out of patience."

"I'm dead." Link's face went into his hands again. It was hard to breathe.

"Stop it, Link."

"That girl, Alix—" He stopped mid-sentence, not wanting to say her full name. "What's she trying to do?"

"It simple, Link. She's using you as a tool to bring down the Sanctuary. Listen to me. You have to be careful. She has a plan to destroy this perfect world we've created."

"She never said that, Chelsea. She only talked about fairness, about how the system is rigged. You heard her. She just wants to talk to me. Show me the truth."

"She wants to tear down the Wall, Link. You know we can't do that. It'll shatter everything my family has built over six generations."

"I know, but—"

"Do you really want to marry me, Link?" Chelsea lowered her voice. "Do you want to join my family and share what we have?"

"Of course I do, Chelsea. You know I do."

"Then there's one thing you've got to do. You talked to Daddy. You know what it is, right?"

For an instant, Alix's eyes stared back at him, and her words echoed in his mind.

I'll be waiting. When you come, we can—

What was she about to say? It drove him crazy. He'd never seen a girl who could ride a chopper like her, who could fight like her, who could talk like her, who had guts like her. Whether his eyes were opened or closed, he saw her face and brooded over her. It was impossible to think of anything or anyone else, impossible to shake her from his psyche.

"Are you listening, Link?"

"Sorry, I was just thinking about—"

"Her?"

"Yes, but—"

"What do you have to do, Link? What did Daddy tell you?"

The mention of President Quinn was like a splash of cold water in Link's face. It jerked him back to reality, and he sat up on the bed. "I'm going into the Fringe, and I'm going to kill her."

"Without mercy, Link. Do you understand?"

"Yes." Link looked at Chelsea and repeated her words. "Without mercy."

"For the good of the Sanctuary."

"Yes, for the good of the Sanctuary."

Link wondered if he'd be able to kill her when the time came. He'd have to do it quickly, without thinking, before she started talking to him. Catch her by surprise. It would be too hard to kill her if she was talking, her eyes on him. Maybe he could just hover over her in a heli-ship and shoot her with a laser cannon.

"Good. Bring back evidence that she's dead. Then, everything will go back to normal. We'll finally be able to forget about the Fringe." Chelsea's face fell into a forced smile. "Now try to get some rest. I'll swing by tomorrow. I love you." She waved her hand as the holoscreen collapsed back into the jax.

Everything will go back to normal . . .

Chelsea talked about it like it was already done. But even if he killed her, would he be able to forget about her?

Exhausted but wide awake, Link walked to the window. It was still dark outside as he looked past the lights and perfection of the Sanctuary, trying to see Alix Yamaguchi on the other side of the Wall.

17

Alix opened her eyes in Merf's dimly lit room inside the bank vault, her body soaked in sweat.

"Well, now you've seen it, the dreamscape, the cutting edge of Sanctuary technology. Any reaction?" Merf's face hung in the holo.

"It's amazing and terrible, all at the same time. To think that they're using Fringe brains to help them dream—" Alix shuddered at the thought of how many of her neighbors' lives had been destroyed for the sake of Sanctuary recreation and relaxation. "Does the average Sanctuary resident even know?"

"Everyone knows about the dreamscape, but only a small, inner circle knows about the brain labs. The general population has no idea what's going on." Merf seemed to be lagging, his voice and lips falling out of sync in the holo.

"You OK, Merf?"

"At the moment, I'm fighting off an army of trackers sent by Quinn to pinpoint my location in the Mesh." Merf's avatar face floated in the holo, but his human body flinched on the cot, as if jolted by an electric current.

Alix tried to imagine how Merf was able to fight an online battle while talking calmly with her. "Be careful, Merf."

"Don't worry. I'm the best."

"Tell me more about the dreamscape. I saw a whole city."

"You're right. The arena we saw is only a small part of the package.

The dreamscape has endless entertainment of every kind. Shopping, games, role-playing, to name a few. You can be anyone and do anything."

"What does Quinn get out of it?"

"It's simple. Quinn uses the dreamscape to control and pacify his subjects. And he's making a fortune off access fees. But we're going to turn all that technology against him."

"Sounds great, Merf. How?"

"I've got ideas cooking that will help. The Mesh is a two-edged sword, and we can turn it against Quinn. More about that later. For now, your performance in the arena was a great start. The dreamscape will never be the same."

"It was strange, Merf. I felt a connection. With Link for sure, but maybe more."

"It was definitely more than Link. A hundred thousand Sanctuary elites are going to wake up in the morning and remember how they cheered for you in their dreams." Merf nodded, as if talking to himself. "You've got the stuff, Alix. The secret sauce. People believe in you."

"I don't know, Merf."

"The thing I like about you is you're unpredictable. Most of the time you're quiet and shy, but throw some danger at you, and you go crazy. In a good way."

"Adrenaline helps me think."

"All I have to do is put you in the right situation, and you do the rest. You'd be a celebrity like Licious if you'd grown up in the Sanctuary."

"Don't say that, Merf." Alix wiped her face with her sleeve. "I'm just an average Fringe freak trying to change the world."

"Well, in that case, I'd say it's been a productive day. The whole Sanctuary loves you."

"Maybe not the whole Sanctuary. I'm pretty sure Lincoln Wells hates my guts."

"That was the idea."

"Maybe I pushed him too hard." Alix closed her eyes and recalled the image of Link's face in the dreamscape. It was just his Mesh avatar and not really him, but she couldn't help thinking there was more there, behind the anger and the name calling. Like he was trying to suppress something deep down. "What do you think of him?"

"Link? I've had a look at his file. He's not evil. Seems to have a conscience. Generally plays by the rules. Doesn't take advantage of his position like others do. It's been noted that he never steals from his subordinates' accounts like most commanders in the Patrol. But, at the end of the day, he thinks he's earned every shred of privilege and success that's graced his life. He may never be able to comprehend the simple fact that millions suffer because people like him go along with the system."

"I don't know, Merf. I think there's more to him than that." Alix thought back to the face she saw in the dreamscape. "Link just needs to wake up. The question is, will he be willing to listen?"

"We won't know until he gets here. He's got a lot of Sanctuary learning to undo." Merf looked more and more tired in the holoscreen with all his multitasking, part of him here in the holo, part of him swimming the depths of the Mesh. "Some people can see the truth and change their minds. Others can't see it even when it's staring them in the face."

"Do you think he'll come alone?"

"That'd be my guess. From his perspective, he's made a mess of things and needs to clean it up himself."

"I don't know, Merf. Maybe they'll send an army to destroy the Fringe."

"It's possible, but they have so much to lose." Merf flashed a mischievous smile. "If there's going to be an invasion, I'll broadcast it, just like your chopper ride. Once they figure out everyone is watching, I don't think the Patrol will risk a full-scale search and destroy mission."

"I hope you're right, Merf."

"No plan is perfect. This one is risky, but it's the only shot we have."

"So, what's next?"

"You've done your part. All we can do now is wait for Link and/or his army to come."

The sky was already turning pink in the east when Alix left Merf at the bank and began the walk home. Like Merf said, she'd done her part. All she could do now was wait.

But waiting didn't suit her. Maybe it was the time spent in the dreamscape, but she was wide awake. Link probably wouldn't come for a couple of days. He'd need time to create a foolproof plan of attack. That meant she had a few hours before going into hiding.

She decided to take the long way home, through an industrial neighborhood and past the Wall. After months of moving from place to place in the dark through the old subway, it would be refreshing to walk in the open air.

Before she'd gone half a klick, she saw a man with his arm around a woman. As they came closer, Alix saw a small body wrapped in a blanket in the woman's arms.

As the couple approached, Alix fought the urge to turn her face and walk away. The woman stumbled and stopped as the man steadied her. Looking up, the woman turned around and looked in the direction of the Wall.

Alix followed her healer instincts and drew closer to comfort them. The man tried to smile but had only tears. Extending her hand, Alix touched the woman's thin shoulders. "I'm so sorry." She walked to face the woman. "Let me help. Anything."

The woman brought the child close and kissed the tiny, perfect forehead. Then, without a word, she handed the child to Alix. "Please. I can't."

Nodding, Alix took the lifeless bundle, still warm, in her arms. The father bent low to kiss the child and then looked up with bloodshot eyes. "Thank you."

Without a word, Alix walked away from the two grieving parents on her way to the toxic dump, saving them the horror of having to dispose of their child's body themselves. As she walked, her eyes were drawn to the child's face peeking out from the folds in the blanket. The outline of a smile was still there. One blue eye was half open.

The telltale purple dots of the virus snaked a crooked trail up the child's neck.

How many other children were going to die before the Sanctuary recognized what was going on?

As Alix walked down a wide dirt road to one of the many toxic dumps, the buildings lay farther and farther apart. The road bottomed out and turned uphill. From this point on, there were no more structures of any kind. Blue pools of metallic liquid dotted the ground. The caustic stench of a chemical stew stung her nostrils.

That's when she noticed the others walking behind her. Three people, two women and a young man, each bearing a similar burden. Just before she crested the top of the hill, an old man passed her on the way down, his eyes almost closed, deep lines of grief etching his face. In one of his hands, he gripped a tiny shoe.

At the summit, an enormous hole opened below her, filled with turquoise liquid. On the far side of the hole, she saw the top of a building—the chemplant where precious metals were extracted from the toxic stew to be shipped back to robot-run factories in the Sanctuary. Robot drones poured toxic waste from the sky into open pits like these all over the Fringe. At the edge of the pit, people stood, some of them still holding the bodies of children in their arms. The bleached remains of small human bones were strewn among the rocks around the rim. As she watched, an elderly couple flung a bundle into the air to land in the pool five meters from shore. The body floated until, little by little, the caustic chemicals covered it like millions of tiny fingers pulling it under and out of sight.

Alix knew what she had to do.

Opening the blanket wrapping the child she held, Alix bent and picked up half a dozen of the largest rocks she could find, most of them no bigger than her fist, and stuffed them into the blanket. And then, pulling the cloth tight around the tiny body, she tossed the bundle with all her strength. It landed in the middle without a splash. Alix stayed long enough to see it sink.

On the walk back down the hill, she passed more people carrying bodies, mostly small children. A generation was being wiped out. The toxic dumps were turning into graveyards. She kept walking through the dead landscape past cesspools and the twisted remains of ancient trees, as she tried to *un-see* the image of the child in her arms.

Finding a crooked street, she walked past a row of low buildings cobbled together from the cast-off hulks of used transport vehicles. With walls at unnatural angles and protruding pipes and cables, it looked like a New Age metallic insect. Blue steam rose from multiple locations along the roof, a telltale sign that the inhabitants were already up and cooking cornboo for the day. A Sanctuary junkyard the size of a mountain lay just a klick away, and the living quarters reflected a creative use of steel siding and rusty shipping containers pulled from the scrap heap. When Alix was a little girl, she used to come here to watch the beautiful drone ships drop twisted metal and depleted plastic from the sky.

She learned when she grew up that sorting Sanctuary trash for usable materials was another way to make a living in the Fringe.

As she walked toward the morning sun, Alix found herself wanting to avoid the enormous, silver cube off to the right. A thousand meters on each side, it towered over the neighborhood and reminded her of a giant, metallic box that seemed to have dropped from the sky to lodge firmly in the black Fringe soil. From the meticulously shiny exterior, it looked like a building you might find in the Sanctuary itself.

There was a reason for that.

This was a brain lab.

With an air-conditioned interior and plentiful cornboo for the workers, it was a magnet for half-starved Fringe folk looking for a way to support themselves and their families. The work was easy. All you had to do was find a spot on the long plastic tables, take a hit of Sleeper, put on the trodes and lie down shoulder-to-shoulder with the other workers. From there, you could relax into oblivion for a 12-hour shift. At the end of the shift, if you could still walk, you'd stumble home with a bagful of cornboo before you came back 12 hours later.

The brain labs were at the heart of the Fringe economy and the major source of food. Whole families participated until, one by one, they lost control of their bodies. Most didn't last more than 20 years in the brain labs. Many died young.

The unlucky few whose brains rejected the trodes did the best they could. Some tried their luck at the chemplants or the garbage dumps. Alix was a healer, making the rounds in the Fringe, helping the young and comforting the old, doing what she could with the resources she had. Like a monk, she received offerings of cornboo from the families she helped.

But with every bite, she remembered it was bought with the lives of her people.

She passed the giant cube near the river of humankind flowing through the entrance into the dark interior. The exit was on the opposite side of the cube, where workers emerged in a drunken daze to find their way home.

Identical cubes lay scattered through the Fringe like shiny ships floating in a sea of refuse.

Alix hadn't been close to a brain lab for months, and she had to suppress the nausea that rose in her stomach as images returned of long rooms running for hundreds of meters with low ceilings and dim lights. Skull-shaped trodes hung over communal sleeping platforms. Put on the trodes, close your eyes and you got the sensation of your lungs filling with cold water. She shivered as she moved past the polished skin of the building, and she broke into a jog until the brain lab was far behind.

She passed all three pillars of the Fringe economy during her morning walk. Chemplants, garbage dumps and brain labs. Each of them represented a different way the Sanctuary stole from the Fringe, bleeding it dry, building a pristine paradise on a foundation of broken minds and bodies.

The sun was about to peek above the horizon, filling the sky with deep orange. Turning down a empty road, Alix headed for the Wall, visible from almost any location in the Fringe. Its transparent beauty resembled a fresh-cut rose in the morning light. As she approached it, the buildings within the Sanctuary came into view, their glass exteriors shining like diamonds in a jewel box.

No one else was there this early in the morning. They would come later to the Wall, some on their way home from the brain labs, some on their way to work in the chemplants, some to the garbage dumps to scavenge for materials to trade for cornboo. All of them would stop and stare, as Alix was doing, and wonder at the terrible beauty of the Sanctuary.

Something drew Alix closer to the Wall. She remembered what Muse and Merf had told her, that she'd been born on the other side, that she had the implant given to all the Sanctuary-born that gave her access, that she could become one of them whenever she wanted.

Without thinking, she found a spot by a pile of rocks marking the location of a portal. She remembered watching the portal open once when a platoon of Patrol soldiers stormed the Fringe, hunting criminals. Her hand rose, as if on its own, palm against the Wall. It felt warm, inviting.

A pleasant melody played like a tiny symphony. A round section of the Wall where she stood glowed green.

And then, as if by magic, it opened.

She stepped through.

18

Unthinkable

Link stood at the window in his office at Patrol HQ. He'd been the first to arrive in the morning, and in the quiet, he watched as the pre-dawn sun filled the sky with deep orange. Only one item occupied the agenda for the day: finalize the plan to kill Alix Yamaguchi.

There was no room for mistakes this time.

Link understood the challenge. Alix and her people in the Fringe were tech-savvy enough to hack into the Patrol's drones and the dreamscape. In spite of all the talk about worthless Fringe scum, they were smart. They'd be expecting retaliation. They'd be ready. It was likely they were preparing for an invasion by the Patrol. Provoking an invasion might even be part of their plan. No doubt they would broadcast it to the Sanctuary to get more sympathy.

But Link had other plans. He'd throw them off, do the unexpected. And, in the end, he'd make an example of Alix Yamaguchi by beating her at her own game. All he had to do was wait for Wilson.

It didn't take long. Just as a stylized projection of the sun was floating into the horizon on the Wall, Wilson arrived at the building. He came straight to Link's office and stood for a moment at the door.

"Figured you'd be here early, boss." Wilson leaned his back against the door jamb. "Rough night last night."

"You saw it." Link said, without turning around. "The whole fiasco?"

Wilson looked at the ceiling. "Yeah, I saw it, boss."

"At ease, soldier. We're alone. You can drop the *boss* stuff. We grew up together, best friends since grade school."

"Right, boss."

"Wilson, don't make me tell you again." Link motioned to a chair on the other side of the desk between them. "Come in. Have a seat. We need to talk."

"Ready when you are." Wilson sat and let his legs fall open.

Link dropped into a chair, leaning back. "We need a plan, Wilson. A good one. Nothing short of perfection."

"OK, what's the specific goal, if I may ask?"

"It's simple, Wilson. Make Alix Yamaguchi disappear with the least amount of fuss. Make everyone forget about her."

"A quick, pinpoint strike would be best. Send an advance recon unit to confirm her location. Three dozen battle drones on auto-target mode to take out anything that moves. Half that many heli-ships with heavy armor and laser cannons. Four snipers floating above it all to pick off the stragglers. On a moonless night, surround her hiding place. Concentrated firepower should be enough, but I'd suggest you lob in a couple of bunker busters, just in case they're deep. Turn the whole neighborhood into a smoking crater. Confirm casualties with remote DNA sniffers. No one ever needs to touch the ground. Nice and clean. Capture it all on video with a squadron of drone cams. Upload it to President Quinn's Mesh-site." Wilson smiled. "I'll work out the logistics and have a detailed battle plan on your desk by the end of the day.

"Hold on, Wilson. We're talking about taking out one person in the Fringe, not World War V."

"OK, so you'd like a lighter touch?"

"Yeah, more subtle. Quick and smart."

"We'll go light on the heavy weapons. Only use half the battle drones. Leave out the bunker busters. Rely more on laser targeting. Use infrared. Maybe hit them in the early morning." Wilson pulled out a slate and started working on it. "I like where you're going with this."

"If we go in with guns blazing we'll have too many casualties and draw too much attention. The last thing we want to do is turn Alix Yamaguchi into a martyr, a unifying figure worshipped by the Fringe masses. That may be exactly what she's hoping for. A way to jumpstart the revolution."

"Smart. We can go even lighter. I'd say a half dozen drones should do the trick."

"No, Wilson." Link shook his head. "No drones. They're tech and all tech is *hackable*. You saw what happened last time we used them. You saw the dreamscape last night. We need to go old school on this."

"Old school?"

"Yeah, you know, keep it all on the ground, out of the air."

"No air support?" Wilson asked, a skeptical look on his face. "Are you kidding? That's a fundamental component of any attack."

"The more I think about it, the clearer it becomes." A new plan was already taking shape in Link's mind, and Wilson wasn't going to like it.

"With all due respect, boss, the last full-on ground assault in the Fringe was a generation ago to quell some kind of a general strike, before you and I were born. I've seen the files. It didn't go so well. Fringe scum aren't afraid of guns. Thousands died. Turned into a bloodbath and a PR nightmare." Wilson shook his head. "We went back to drones after that."

Link pulled his feet off the desk and stood. "Here's what I want. Light and quick. No tech. Catch them by surprise."

Wilson took a deep breath. "The question is, who do we send in? We've got that squad of young ninja guys you train with. Maybe they're ready."

"No, Wilson. I'll go in myself. Alone."

"Boss?"

"You heard me."

"But I don't see why or how—"

"I have to do this."

Wilson's mouth hung open. "Let me get this straight. You want to go into the Fringe after the girl alone?"

"They'll be expecting an invasion force. Lots of Patrol personnel." The more Link talked, the more it made sense. "If I go in alone, I'll be able to blend in, slip through undetected until I find her. Simple. Clean. Perfect."

"Link, I strongly advise against this. Your life will be in serious danger if you go alone. At the very least, let me go with you. We'll do it together, like when we were kids."

"Sorry, but I need you here to be my eyes and ears."

Wilson stood and leaned into the desk between them. "Look, Link, what you're talking about, it's suicide. Why do this?"

Link leaned into the desk until they were nose to nose. "It's simple, Wilson. I had a one-on-one meeting with President Quinn last night. He ordered me to personally handle the Alix Yamaguchi problem. It's what I have to do. For the Sanctuary and for Chelsea. You understand?"

Wilson lingered for a few seconds, his gaze still fixed on Link. And then he nodded. "For Chelsea. I see. The king wants you to slay the dragon before you can marry his daughter. Classic."

"Yeah, something like that." Link sat back down in his chair. "Are you with me?"

Other Patrol personnel were beginning to arrive and take their positions in the control room in front of the main holoscreen.

Wilson dropped back into his chair. "No need to ask. You're my commanding officer. You give the orders. I execute them."

From the steely look on Wilson's face, he didn't agree with the approach, but he'd make it work. Wilson was like that, always a professional.

"Get me all the intel we have on the girl," Link said.

"Done." Wilson scratched the stubble on his chin, eyes wandering up to the ceiling, a sure sign his mind was already miles ahead. "The R&D department's come up with new prototype armor. Maybe you've seen it. Light, flexible, puncture-proof. Never been field-tested, but I think you should take it. That and a couple of pulse rifles and hand units. Survival gear. I'll come up with a list of basic—"

"No, Wilson."

"Sir?"

"I'm going in without armor or heavy guns."

Wilson stared at Link, eyes wide. "Look, there's no way—"

Link raised his hand. "Wilson, listen to me. I've been thinking about this since last night. Our whole approach has been a mistake."

"But boss—"

"Hear me out, Wilson." Link reached for his translucent gold water bottle and took a sip. "If we really want to get this Alix Yamaguchi, the last thing we should do is treat it like a military mission. That's why we've been failing. Marching into the Fringe with armor and weapons is a dead giveaway. I'll never find her. The mission will fail. I can't let that happen."

"But, boss."

"Can't you see? She's been playing us the whole time. She wants us to mount a major invasion and come after her. She's practically begging for it." It was becoming clearer to Link by the minute. "So, we'll do the last thing she expects. I'll go in alone."

"And then what?"

"I'll find her."

"And just walk up to her and kill her?"

"Yes. It's the only way to stop the movement." Link stood and returned to the window. On the Wall, the too-perfect sun was climbing higher over the fake horizon. The beginning of a new day. "Just get me all the intel you can on Alix Yamaguchi. I'll do the rest." He turned to leave the office door.

"Where you going?"

"For a walk. Just need some fresh air to clear my head."

As he left the room, Link slipped his hand into his pocket, took out his jax, the new one that Chelsea had given him, and tossed it on his chair.

Stepping onto the street, Link pulled in a lungful of sweet air, pointed himself in a random direction and walked. In the Sanctuary, if you walked long enough, no matter the direction, you always ran into the Wall. Like 99.99% of the populace, Link had never actually been beyond the Wall. You had to be a 7Z or higher to afford the right to travel abroad. But he'd seen plenty of live drone footage of the Fringe, and he was sure he wasn't missing anything.

The last 24 hours had been crazy. He needed time to think. There was

President Quinn's little speech in the boardroom, about the origins of the Sanctuary and how Quinn owned it and its only purpose was to keep him rich. On the outside, the Sanctuary held itself up as the bastion of freedom and liberty, the protector of civilization. Even Chelsea viewed it that way. But she was an idealist. The truth was, it was the perfect system for perpetuating a single family's wealth, power and mastery over the whole population.

He stared at the flawless buildings, the perfect streets, people whose lives were filled with pleasure and entertainment and endless novelties and information. Plentiful food from all over the planet. Health and prosperity.

Was it so bad to know that Quinn controlled it all? Was that such a heavy price to pay for a system that gave people safety from the outside, from places like the Fringe, where everyone was on their own?

And since it all belonged to Quinn, he had the incentive to confront any danger that threatened it. The actions of Alix Yamaguchi were raising questions in the mind of the populace. It hadn't yet turned into a full-blown movement, but Quinn apparently sensed that a revolution could happen. He was smart, like his fathers, and his instincts told him the Sanctuary and his control of it were in danger.

For the good of the system that Link would someday inherit, Alix Yamaguchi had to be stopped.

Now that his head was clear, it made sense.

How would it be to marry Chelsea? The gap between him and her, between a 3Z and an 8Z, was huge. She was always careful about what she said, but she'd let a few things slip now and then about her life.

There were the usual family compounds built by the 8Z and above. The Quinns had estates on multiple islands, including, but not necessarily limited to, New Zealand, Hawaii and Iceland. Each had a private security force for protection and centuries of supplies. Chelsea flew all over the globe to attend *gatherings* on the family properties, which she described as boring affairs. He'd heard rumors that they even had a compound on the moon and another at the bottom of the Pacific Ocean. He'd never asked her if it was true.

Then there was the fleet of air transports. The older Chelsea got, the more freedom she had to use them. She'd disappear for a few hours and then show up in the evening. Afternoon trips to Tokyo for sushi were common. Like other members of the exclusive 7Z and above club, she could afford to go anywhere on the planet she wanted, whenever she wanted. It was whispered that Quinn had an off-planet cruiser in orbit, with another under construction in China. Someday, Link imagined, he and Chelsea might take their kids to Mars for a family getaway.

There were other whisperings. People not sufficiently deferential toward the Quinns might go missing. The courts never handed down convictions for friends and allies of the family. The Quinns were untouchable by the system because they were the system. How else could it be?

The Sanctuary provided such amazing benefits for its inhabitants that the thought of opposing the Quinns was, well, unthinkable.

And yet, Alix Yamaguchi was doing exactly that. She was making it thinkable.

"Out for a walk?"

Chelsea stood on a corner, two steps away, arms folded as if waiting for him.

"You tracked me down." Link reached for Chelsea's hand. "Without my jax."

"I left my jax at home, too. Daddy was trying to get me interested in handling the interior design for one of our new family compounds near the summit of Everest. It's all so boring. When I called, Wilson told me you'd gone for a walk. I thought I'd get away and join you. Where are you going on such a beautiful morning?"

Link pointed ahead. "It's been a while since I went to the Wall. Thought I'd have a look."

"Sounds intriguing."

They walked in silence down a broad sidewalk, past scattered crowds of other people, each walking alone.

Link was the first to speak. "What do you think about the Sanctuary, Chelsea?"

"What kind of question is that?"

"It's a wonderful system, don't you think? The Quinns were geniuses."

"Thanks for the compliment." Chelsea gave him a sideways glance with a little eye roll. "You feeling OK?"

"No, I mean it. No sarcasm implied. I've been thinking about it all morning. After the craziness of the last 24 hours, I'm trying to understand the Sanctuary, why it's worth saving."

"From her?" Chelsea raised her hand and pointed up and over the Wall.

"From anyone or anything that wants to change it. It's already perfect. We don't need a revolution to open our eyes."

Rounding a corner, they both saw it at the same instant at the far end of the street.

The Wall.

It rose a hundred meters higher than the nearby structures, a surface of glassy smoothness and nearly infinite resolution. Today it displayed an exquisite morning sun in a mountain meadow setting. Butterflies flitted in the breeze against a background of violet and yellow wildflowers. A pristine lake of pure turquoise shimmered in the light.

The closer they got, the richer the colors became.

"I'll be doing it soon, Chelsea." Link pointed ahead. "Going over the Wall. Into the outside world. You do it all the time. What's it like?"

"I remember the first time I went over the Wall. I think I was eight years old." Chelsea stopped. "We boarded an air transport on the top of Quinn Tower. Daddy said he wanted us to see the real world. When we got airborne, I held my breath until we crossed over the Wall."

"What was it like?"

"I was expecting the outside world to be wonderful, full of deep meaning." She paused, as she gazed down to the street. "But you'll be disappointed, just like I was."

"How?"

Link glanced across the street at a tubular structure of windowless gold that reached skyward for almost 1,000 meters. Everyone knew it was the home of Licious, the mega-Mesh-star.

"It's just grey and gloomy and dead. As far as you can see in every direction. That's when I knew."

"Knew what?"

"That the Sanctuary was—" Chelsea looked up and froze. Link followed her eyes. A figure walked slowly down the sidewalk on the other side of the street, her gaze drawn upward.

"Is it possible?" Link turned to Chelsea, but she was already walking across the street.

erf and Muse were going to be furious when they found out Alix had stepped inside the Sanctuary on her own without telling them.

Merf was smart, but Alix was tired of letting him call all the shots. Maybe it was time for her to take action on her own, to do the unexpected, inject a little chaos into the Sanctuary system. And what would cause more chaos than for her to do the opposite of what Link expected? He said he was coming to the Fringe for her. Well, she was coming to him. At least for a few minutes. It wasn't really dangerous. She promised herself she would stay within an arms' length of the Wall and would slip back through the portal at the first sign of danger.

After passing through the Wall, she paused with her back against the smooth glass and waited for her pulse to slow. When she opened her eyes, she saw the flowers. On both sides of the wide street, bright red roses were in full bloom. She'd read about them in books and seen them through the Wall.

She checked up and down the street. It was empty. Local residents were probably still asleep. The roses looked delicious enough to eat. From her reading, she was sure they had a lovely fragrance. Maybe she could walk across the street for a smell.

Taking a tentative step away from the Wall, she made a mental note to go no further than the opposite side of the street. She'd come this far. Merf couldn't deny her the fun of picking a succulent rose. She was close enough to make a run back through the Wall if things turned sketchy. She planned to be back in the Fringe in five minutes no matter what.

So she crossed the street. The roses were magnificent. After picking one and bringing it to her nose, she took a deep inhale. The sweet aroma caught her off guard and triggered hunger pains. She noticed it didn't have any thorns. Before she knew it, the rose was in her mouth and she was chewing the petals. And then she was picking more, feasting on the soft red flesh. A dozen green stems littered the sidewalk before she could stop herself.

A man across the street stared.

Alix stared back and smiled, rose petals falling out of her mouth. The man's eyes darted back and forth between her and his jax, as if he were doing some kind of comparison. Did he recognize her? She wasn't sure, but she made no attempt to hide her face.

Pulled by the roses that lined the street, she walked deeper into the Sanctuary. More people came outside, whispering and pointing. No one tried to stop her. They just stared like they were seeing a ghost. She did a quick check and didn't see any Patrol forces on the street. As long as she didn't wander too far from the Wall and didn't stay too long, she'd be fine.

As she walked, Alix couldn't stop herself from glancing up the sides of the buildings to the sky. She had thought the dreamscape version of the Sanctuary was incredible, but now that she was actually in the real thing, the reality was almost more than she could comprehend.

An elegant golden tube 10 meters across rose from the ground and soared skyward. Its outer skin was nothing short of perfection. No windows or wrinkles or flaws. For a long time, she stared at its infinite smoothness.

When she looked down, a man and woman on the far side of the street were glaring at her, mouths half open. Alix's gaze couldn't help being drawn to the woman. The perfection of her skin and eyes was beyond anything Alix had ever seen. The woman crossed the street to Alix and stopped a few meters away.

"Alix Yamaguchi?" The woman spoke in a low, calm voice. "Why are you here?"

Why hide the truth?

"I was curious. Wanted to see it for myself." Alix point skyward. "Have to say, it's exquisitely beautiful."

"How did you—"

"Get in?" Alix nodded. "Easy."

"But the Wall." The woman pointed, apparently dumbfounded.

Alix turned and glanced back. "I know. Too high to climb, too deep to tunnel. So there was only one option left. I just walked through."

"But you're not—"

"Sanctuary-born? Yes, afraid I am. Surprised? So was I when I found out."

The man came up behind the woman, slowly raising a hand. "Stay where you are."

"Or what?" Alix glanced at the Wall, just down the street. Her muscles tensed, and she was ready to run. But something about his voice made her look again. This time, she recognized his eyes from the dreamscape. There was the same anger on his face as before, like he was conflicted and using the rage to suppress deeper feelings. Alix wanted to say something kind, but she couldn't think of anything. So she opened her mouth and just let the words come out. "Lincoln Wells? Is that you?"

"Yes," the woman said. "How do you know his name?"

"Hey, he's a commander in the Patrol. Word gets around." Alix took a small step back, closer to the Wall. "Looks like you recovered nicely from the beating I gave you in the dreamscape."

"You hacked into the Patrol files, didn't you?" the woman said.

"What, you're surprised that Fringe scum can do that?"

"Yes, to put it mildly."

"What's your name?" Alix said.

"Chelsea."

Alix thought about it. "Chelsea," she whispered. She liked the smooth way it rolled off her tongue. "That's a great name. You must be rich."

"Yes," Chelsea said. "I am."

"I've always wondered. What's it like?"

Before Chelsea could answer, Link exploded past her. "Look, I don't know what you're doing here." He grabbed Alix by the shoulder. "But you're coming with me."

"Stop, Link." Chelsea took a step forward. "I want to talk to her."

He cocked his head to the side. "But—"

The grip of Link's hand triggered a fight response Alix couldn't control. Before Link could react, she doubled him over with a hard elbow to the ribs and twisted to slam her booted heel into the side of his head, laying him out on the sidewalk. Landing on his chest, she pinned him to the ground, whipped the short blade off her thigh and brought the tip to his neck.

"Just like old times," Alix said, grinning down at Link and surprised at what his touch had unleashed inside her.

"Please, Ms. Yamaguchi. There's no need for violence. I'm sure we can talk over our differences." Chelsea stepped back, raising her palms in an offer of peace.

"What kind of a girl do you think I am?" Alix balanced herself carefully on Link. "I'm not here to hurt anyone, just wanted to have a look around."

Link twisted, trying to get Alix off his chest.

"He's my fiancé," Chelsea said. "Please let him go. I promise he won't hurt you."

Link struggled in vain.

"Tell him to settle down."

"Link, stop," Chelsea said. "We need to talk to her."

"I don't talk to Fringe scum."

"Link!" Chelsea's voice had steel in it this time. It was a nonnegotiable command.

Finally, his body went limp. "OK. Have it your way."

Slowly, Alix pulled away her knife and stood, stepping to the side.

"Good," Chelsea said. "Now get behind me, Link."

He stood and, without looking at Alix, obeyed the command.

"At least he can take orders," Alix offered, wanting to say more, especially to Link, but not sure where to start. She recalled Merf telling her that Link had a fiancé. Alix shouldn't have cared, but somehow it made her angry, and she hated herself for it.

Link's body stiffened, as if he were about to pounce, but Chelsea put out her hand to stop him.

"So, you're not Fringe-born?" Chelsea asked, her gaze jumping back and forth between Alix's eyes.

"Nope." Alix studied Chelsea's perfect skin and hair and her air of effortless authority. "My Sanctuary parents abandoned me in the Fringe. So I guess that makes me one of you. Only I have green skin, and you don't."

Chelsea consciously sucked in a breath, like she was trying to stay calm. "Why do you want to destroy us?"

"Funny, I was about to ask you the same thing. And, besides, I never said anything about destroying you or the Sanctuary. All I'm looking for is a little justice." Alix glanced up at the jewel-like structures glistening in the morning light. "The Sanctuary's a glorious achievement but one only made possible by a system that feeds on the Fringe like a parasite."

"That's a lie!" Chelsea went stiff. "Daddy would never allow it."

"Daddy?" Alix smiled. "Are you serious? So you're the only daughter of His Royal Highness, President-for-Life Quinn? I guess he hasn't told you how things really work."

Link shot forward like a mad dog. "Insult her father one more time, and it'll be your last breath."

"We have time for that later, Link. For now, let her talk." Chelsea gently pulled him back. The only thing missing was a leash around Link's neck. "So tell us, Alix Yamaguchi, tell us how the Sanctuary preys on the Fringe."

Alix could see the fury behind that perfect face and those flawless eyes. But she had to admit, Chelsea Quinn was good at hiding it. No doubt she'd grown up in a household where it was wise to keep one's feelings to oneself.

"It's simple, really." Alix took a step back, out of range of Link's long arms.

"We're all ears," Chelsea said.

"It all boils down to food."

"You're complaining about the cornboo?" Link said. "Provided by the Sanctuary so Fringe scum won't starve. What do you want, sushi and dumplings? Why don't you show a little gratitude?"

Alix looked down at the faintly green skin on her arms. "Call me ungrateful, but we don't get the cornboo for free. We have to work for it. And there are only two ways to get it from the Sanctuary: the brain labs or the chemplants."

"More lies," Link said. "You get the cornboo for free because you and your people have forgotten how to work. It's a humanitarian gesture by the Sanctuary to avert mass starvation."

It started in Alix's belly, a deep rage that suddenly woke up, searching for a way to the surface.

"Let her talk," Chelsea said. "Tell us about the brain labs and the chemplants."

"First, the brain labs." Alix closed her eyes for an instant and saw the giant, silver cube she had passed only an hour earlier. "Massive cube-shaped structures where Fringe folk go to sell their minds."

"Come on, you know that's not—"

Chelsea glared at Link and then turned back to Alix. "Please, go on."

"All of your tech, the Mesh, the dreamscape, jaxes and slates, everything that runs the Sanctuary, it all derives its computing power from human brains in the Fringe, people forced to trade their sanity for food."

Chelsea let a cute smile hang on her face. "Before you came along, I'd never heard any of this, and I assure you, I'm in a position to know."

"Then there's a lot your father hasn't told you about the Fringe. Maybe you should ask him." Alix cast a glance at the Wall and calculated she could sprint there in under 15 seconds.

Link stiffened. "Look, we know what you're up to. Making up lies. Fake facts. Trying to start a revolution. The only problem is, we're smarter than you expected. It's not going to work."

"Are you afraid, Link?" Alix asked.

"Afraid of what?"

"The truth."

"I have no idea what you're talking about."

"Come to the Fringe. I'll show you the brain labs and the chemplants. See for yourself. It'll open your eyes." As Alix whispered the words, her rage died down, and she took a step closer to Link.

"Even if it were true, sounds like a fair exchange to me. People work, and they get paid. The same thing happens here in the Sanctuary." Link snapped his fingers. "Oh yeah, I forgot. Fringe scum don't like to work. They're a bunch of lazy bums who want food for free. Too bad. The world wasn't made that way, at least not on this side of the Wall. We earn our keep. If your people don't like these brain labs, they can just walk away."

The words came like a slap in the face for Alix. After a couple of deep breaths, she uncurled her fists.

"It's not that simple. For a century and a half, the Fringe has been the Sanctuary's toxic dump. The ground is so contaminated, we can't grow our own food. We either eat the cornboo, or we starve. There's no walking away." Alix glanced at the Wall again. Sanctuary cameras had probably already identified her. Patrol soldiers might show up any minute. There wasn't much time and so much left to say. "The brain labs and the chemplants kill our people, use up their minds and bodies and leave behind a damaged husk. People understand this, but they still have to eat. They sacrifice for their families. That kind of work isn't a free choice. It's desperation."

Link's eyes ran up Alix's body. "You don't look like you're suffering."

"That's because I can't work. I tried, but my brain rejects the interface." Alix pulled up one sleeve, showing deep scars. "I went to work at the chemplant instead, processing the Sanctuary's toxic waste, until I had an accident and got these scars. Guess I should consider myself lucky to still be alive."

"The Fringe has created its own special kind of hell. Bad choices tend to do that." Link sneered. "And now you come crying to us to solve all your problems."

Chelsea allowed a slight smile to play on her lips.

"Our children are dying from a virus. A whole generation is being wiped out. The Sanctuary could help us. All I want to do is open your eyes so you can see the facts. There's no *us* and *them*. We're one people. The Sanctuary can't function without the Fringe. We need each other."

At the far end of the street, a battalion of Patrol soldiers ran toward Alix in unison, weapons raised. She scanned in a quick circle, checking the other streets. Soldiers were closing in on all sides. Last of all she checked the Wall. A line of soldiers had gathered in front of it, cutting off any escape.

She'd waited too long. Now she understood why Chelsea had wanted to talk.

"By the way, thanks for saving us the trouble of going into the Fringe to find you." Link stepped past Chelsea. "As long as you don't resist, you'll be accorded all the rights of Sanctuary due process before your sentencing."

"You mean *execution*, right?" Alix said.

Link nodded. "That is the usual punishment. Cuts down on the need for prisons."

"What laws have I broken?" Now it was Alix's turn to stall for time to find a way out. Merf and Muse were going to be livid if she didn't make it back. Then she noticed the little, silver pulse pistol hanging on Link's side.

"Oh, for starters, destruction of Sanctuary property." Link raised a finger, as if about to rattle off a list. "I'm referring to the half-dozen drones you hacked and destroyed the other day in the Fringe." He raised another finger. "Then, of course, all the hacking itself. Electronic espionage. I'm sure we can find 10 or 20 Sanctuary regulations you shredded when you did that."

The soldiers were less than 30 meters away and closing fast.

Alix gazed at the ground and charged Link, her fingers reaching for the pistol. But this wasn't the dreamscape anymore. Link beat her to the gun, his hand reaching it just before hers. As she slammed into him, they both fell to the street and struggled for the pistol as it clattered away.

Alix ended up on top of Link. For an instant, his face relaxed as the rage drained away. Then, with a heave, he shook himself, as if to reclaim his anger, and pushed her off. She rolled to the side.

"My boys have you surrounded," Link said. "Best just to give yourself up."

Soldiers in black armor quickly formed a line on both sides of the street, cutting off any escape. Assuming battle positions, they focused their pulse rifles on Alix, covering her crouching body in red dots.

One of the soldiers stood and came forward. "We got here as fast as we could, sir."

"Good job, Wilson." Link put his arm around Chelsea and turned to Alix. "It's finally over."

An opening appeared on the nearest building, the windowless, golden tube Alix had seen before. A woman dressed in a red minidress with bat wings and a long tail stepped out onto the street. A swarm of gnat-sized dots buzzed around her on tiny, invisible wings. She walked swiftly to Alix's side, stepping between her and the soldiers.

"Alix Yamaguchi. Great conversation in the dreamscape last night. I've been waiting for you."

Enormous screens lit up on the sides of buildings all over the Sanctuary, each one with a live image of the woman in red. Alix looked up and saw herself staring into the screen. Behind her, Link stood with an open mouth and bulging eyes.

"I've always known I'd meet a violent death but not here, not now." The woman scanned the faces of the soldiers, ending with a long stare at Link. "No need to worry, Alix Yamaguchi. They won't hurt you as long as Licious is here. I outrank them."

Licious?

She took Alix's hand and briskly led her into the building through the open door.

It slid shut behind them.

20

As soon as the door shut, Alix pulled in a deep breath. The faint odor of burning wood hung in the air. She knew that smell. It was common in the Fringe.

"Where's the fire?" she said.

Licious pointed a richly tattooed index finger to the ceiling. "Level 13. I was roasting marshmallows and chocolate when I saw you. People used to do it a long time ago. Ever tried it?"

"Where I come from, fires are standard. But not with marshmallows and chocolate." Alix had read about old foods in books, but she'd never tasted much of anything other than cornboo and a few vegetables. "What does it taste like?"

"Chocolate?"

A meter-long image of a deep red Chinese dragon emerged from Licious' left foot, swam up her leg, circled her trunk twice and dove over her right shoulder.

Alix nodded. "And marshmallows. I've never had any."

"How strange." Licious took a step back, as she contemplated Alix. "You're so thin. And just a hint of green."

"It's the cornboo. Basic nutrition but not much else. Ever tried it?"

"No thanks. I hear it's awful. Like frogs and dust."

"I've never eaten a frog, but it sounds delicious." Alix scanned the room. No flat surfaces or square shapes. It was all round and curved and coated with gold, just like the outside of the building. A crystal staircase wound up through an opening in the middle until it disappeared into nothingness a thousand meters up. There was no handrail and no visible structure supporting the steps. Instead, they floated in space.

"Yeah, it goes all the way to the top. Step carefully. It's hung with micro razor wire. Fall and there won't be much left of you by the time all the pieces hit the bottom."

Alix winced.

"The presence of danger helps me feel more alive." Licious walked to the first step. "You look hungry. Let's go eat s'mores. Shall we?" She made her way up the floating steps, each one bursting into a different color the instant her foot touched it.

Alix followed Licious with the same effect.

"So, I'm curious," Licious said. "Where'd you get your name?"

"Alix?"

"No, Yamaguchi."

"Oh, that." Alix laughed. "When I was a little girl, I saw it on the side of an old building in the Fringe. *Yamaguchi Bank.* I liked the sound of it, so I added it to my name."

"You picked your own name?"

"We all do in the Fringe. Everyone's unique. They ought to be able to choose a name they like."

Licious raised an eyebrow. "Interesting Here in the Sanctuary, only Mesh-stars can do that."

"That's one of the first things that should change."

"Really? So, it's true?" Licious asked as the cloud of dots silently hovered a meter from her body. "You want a revolution?"

"The real revolution happened when the Wall went up and divided the people. I'm just trying to bring them back together." Alix glanced through the transparent steps and felt instant vertigo because she had nothing to grab for support.

"*Just look up.* That's my motto." Licious walked like a cat. "Intense optimism. The stairs require it."

Alix breathed deeply and thought of Merf. If only he were watching. And then, she realized he probably was.

"Are those mini-camera drones buzzing around you?"

"Why, yes. It's a cloud unit. Records every second of my life for the whole world to watch."

"And you're OK with that?"

"It's what I do."

"You never turn them off?"

"Haven't in years."

"So, the images on the buildings outside, how did they—"

Licious stopped. "It's all tied to my heartbeat. When my pulse rises, algorithms kick in and the broadcasts instantly find more screens. I should thank you for that. Right now, you're driving my ratings through the roof."

As they climbed higher, Alix noticed each floor had its own theme. One had a white sand beach. Another had snow. There was one filled with purple mushrooms. One that looked like the dreamscape.

"Here we are." Licious stepped off the stairs onto a platform. "My mountain room."

Alix followed her into a green forest of pine trees. And there, in the middle of a ring of rocks, was a real campfire. A neat stack of firewood was ready on the side. Smoke rose and disappeared into a vent in the ceiling.

"How did you do this?" Alix said.

"Me? Oh, it's easy when you have infinite money. I saw a broadcast about fire on the Mesh and just had to have one. Know what fire is? Pure energy. It opens minds. Enables communication." Licious sat on a log and pointed to one on the other side for Alix.

As Licious spoke, the room darkened, and a starry night appeared above them. Far away, the howl of a wolf floated down from realistic-looking mountains. Licious picked up a stick, put a spongy white mass on the tip and handed it to Alix. "Hold the marshmallow close to the fire but not too close." Licious got her own and settled in, eyes on the fire. A school of sharks swam across her skin. "Comfortable?" she asked.

"Very." Alix nodded, looking around at the trees and the stars. "It's amazing."

"It's just money." Licious twirled her stick in and out of the flames.

"So, about this revolution that you started but apparently have nothing to do with. If it succeeds, what happens to all my money? What happens to my home? Do I get to keep it?"

Alix stared at the fire, letting it pull her in. "I guess the real question is, would you want to?"

"Why wouldn't I?"

"Where does all your money come from?"

"From the 999,999,899 people that rank below me." Licious pulled her marshmallow out and touched it. "They pay to watch."

"And where do they get their money?"

"Who knows? They work, they have jobs, they contribute to society, they get paid."

"But what do their jobs depend on? What does your job depend on? What does the whole Sanctuary system depend on?"

"That's easy. The Mesh." Licious nodded. "I see where this is going. You talked about it before. It all goes back to the brain labs. All my money, all everyone's money, depends on the tragic exploitation of unfortunate Fringe freaks. So why would I want to keep it and perpetuate the misery that the system is built on?"

"Well said."

Licious pulled her marshmallow and tested it again with a finger. "Perfection. How's yours doing?"

"I wouldn't know." Alix pulled her stick away from the fire and looked at the marshmallow, burnt and black.

"Good enough. Now for the magic. Put a slab of chocolate on each side of the marshmallow, squish it together, and dig in, like this." Licious opened her mouth wide and stuffed the food all in at once. Her eyes laughed as she chewed, unable to speak.

With trembling fingers, Alix did the same, holding the chocolate until it softened in the heat of the marshmallow. She couldn't open her mouth wide enough for more than a bite.

It was shockingly sweet. The best food Alix had ever eaten. Even better than roses. She could eat it and nothing else for the rest of her life and be happy. Unable to stop, she gobbled it until there was nothing left but sticky hands.

"Hey, you're smiling." Licious pointed. "You like it?"

Alix carefully licked each finger until they were clean. "Incredible."

"Here." Licious grabbed another marshmallow out of a bag. "Let's keep eating until we're sick. I've got a nice, little pink pill that instantly cures a stomachache. And then we can have some more. That's why they're called *s'mores*."

Thinking about it, Alix shook her head. "No, that's OK. One is enough."

Licious stopped and cocked her head to the side. "But you loved it, right?" The fire played and danced in her eyes. The image of a snake slithered down one arm.

"Best snack I've ever had."

"Then let's keep eating. Life is short. You never know when it will be over. Get it while you can, and get as much as you can." She put another marshmallow on a stick and positioned it over the fire. "Don't you agree?"

Alix thought about stepping inside the Sanctuary and how she'd lost control when she'd tasted the first rose. It had been so easy to give herself up to the hunger and stuff roses into her mouth without limit. It scared her. It wasn't who she was. But once she found herself inside the Sanctuary, a place with so much of everything, she'd changed, if only for a few seconds.

"No, one is enough," she said.

"This is the first s'more you've ever eaten, and you only want one?"

"I already had one, and it was delicious. More is just, well, more."

"Strange. I've always thought more of a good thing is always better than less. And to have more than anyone else, to have the *most* is, well—" Licious hesitated, as if searching for the right phrase.

Alix leaned forward. "Why does it matter to have the most? That's not the way we live in the Fringe. Maybe you can explain it to me."

"You really are strange." Licious eyed the marshmallow. "It's just natural to want to have the most. To be the most popular. To be the most beautiful. To have the most money. To be at the top. To understand how you're doing compared to others."

"And that's why you've got the ranking system, right?" Alix leaned back on her hands. "To know where you stand?"

"I check it 10 times a minute. Couldn't live without it."

"Maybe that's the biggest difference between the Fringe and the Sanctuary. We don't have a ranking system. We don't worry about where we stand compared to others. It doesn't really matter. We don't even have money."

"No offense, but look where it's gotten you. Maybe not caring about money isn't such a good thing." Licious glanced at a small jax attached to her wrist. "But let's keep talking. My fans are loving it. I'm hitting close to 95% saturation right now. The money is flowing."

"Is that why you brought me here, to boost your rankings?"

"Why else?"

Alix stared at Licious, watching a colony of tattooed army ants march in circles around her eyes. "I mean, I guess I thought you were—"

"Trying to help you?"

"Weren't you?"

Licious broke out into hysterical laughter. "I'm so sorry, but what made you think I even cared?" She stood abruptly and walked away from the campfire. "I think we're done here. You don't want any more s'mores, so what's the use?"

Alix followed Licious out of the trees and back to the central stairway. "So, you're just going to throw me out?"

"Well, if you're not making me any money, you're not doing me any good. I'm afraid you'll have to go." Licious started up the stairs. After a couple of steps, the swarm of cameras around her suddenly dropped away like rain into the abyss below. She stopped, let out a long exhale and turned back to face Alix. "Come with me, quick." It was as if an elaborate mask had slipped off.

"What's going on?"

"I'll explain at the top." Licious headed up, almost jogging. "Stay close. Don't fall. I wasn't kidding about the razor wire."

"What about your cameras?"

"They're off for now. An algorithm is generating a fake image for the feed. We don't have much time."

"For what?"

"Your escape."

21

Link stood at attention as Quinn yelled.

"She's an 8Z. In the top 100 of the richest people on the planet and still rising fast. A woman of enormous influence, power and ambition. And now she's chatting it up with Alix Yamaguchi around a campfire for the whole world to watch! Do you know how many other people Licious has ever allowed to be seen on her feed talking to her? Exactly zero. Do you have any idea what kind of legitimacy this confers on Alix Yamaguchi?" President Quinn sank into the chair in his dark boardroom, eyes closed, steepled fingers resting under his chin. "How could you let this happen?"

"I can assure you, President Quinn, I will do my best—"

Quinn slammed his fist on the table. "You've done your best already! It's not good enough! Don't you understand? The girl is with Licious. They're talking about the Fringe. They have the whole Sanctuary as their audience. And you didn't do a damn thing about it!"

"Is it true, sir?"

"Is what true?"

"What she said about the brain labs. Do we really do that to them?"

Quinn's eyes narrowed. "Do you know what power is? It means that I can tap a button on my jax and 10 armed guards will storm in here, grab you and throw you out the window. Don't think it hasn't happened before. It'd be ruled a suicide. After what you've done, no one will question it. Is that what you want?"

"No, sir."

"Then shut up, and don't ask stupid questions. The whole situation has gotten out of hand. It has to be resolved. We cannot allow Alix Yamaguchi to get back to the Fringe. I want her dead within the hour."

"She can't stay with Licious forever." Link licked his lips and tried to swallow, but his mouth was too dry. "We'll catch her when she comes out."

Quinn slowly opened his eyes and focused them with laser intent on Link. "I was wrong, Link. I really thought you might be the one. Chelsea likes you. I almost liked you. It could have been perfect."

"I'll take care of it."

"How?"

"I'll work on it. Please give me time."

"I already have."

"Twenty-four hours. That's all I need."

"That's 23 more than I can afford to give you." Walking slowly to the window, Quinn stood with his arms behind his back. "The Sanctuary has worked magic for six generations of Quinns. Unlimited wealth. Control over millions. But there's a flaw. It's a perfect system only as long as people want to believe it's a perfect system. It's the desire to believe that counts. You don't have to actually believe; you just have to want to believe. Once people no longer want to believe, it will all come crashing down. And Alix Yamaguchi knows this. She's eroding the desire to believe. The system is in danger of collapse."

"People are happy here, Mr. President." Link could feel Quinn mentally pulling away from him, like the tide going out to sea. "They still want to believe. I still want to believe."

"I've been patient, for Chelsea's sake. She thinks she loves you."

"And I love her, President Quinn." Link's chest tightened. "We make a good team."

Quinn sneered. "We've been over this before, Link, but you never seem to learn. Love is a fatal flaw. Teamwork just means you're giving up control."

"Sir?"

"Do I really have to explain it to you again?" Quinn turned to face

Link with a cold stare. "Running the Sanctuary is a one-person job. And that one person can only be guided by a single principle. Call it greed, call it self-interest, call it unlimited self-aggrandizement; it's all the same. The single best measure of a person's value is the size of their bank account. Any other measure leads to loss of clarity, fuzzy thinking, mistakes."

"I know, sir. And I want—"

"That's your problem." Quinn walked to the table, opened a drawer and pulled out a cigar. "You don't want enough."

"But, sir."

"If you had wanted enough, you would have shot Alix Yamaguchi on sight on the street. You would have realized it was the perfect moment to rid the world of the evil that poses a challenge to the system." Quinn lit the cigar with a match from the same drawer and inhaled deeply through it, making the tip glow crimson. "You didn't really want to kill her. That's why you waited."

"But, sir, Chelsea told me—"

"You see, that's your problem, again." Quinn pointed the tip of the cigar directly at Link's chest. "Your feelings for Chelsea have weakened you. If you had been focused solely on your own profit, you would have made the right decision in an instant. Why didn't you order your soldiers to shoot her?"

"Licious got in the way."

"Then you should have ordered them to shoot Licious, too."

Link couldn't believe what he was hearing. "But, sir, she's an 8Z, watched and revered by billions of fans. How could we—"

"You could have made her death look like an accident, an unfortunate side effect of your heroic efforts to protect the Sanctuary. Another celebrity would have risen to take Licious' place by this time next week. She'd have been forgotten." Quinn spoke with the cigar hanging from his lips. "Rule number one: don't let fear get in the way of your greed. A fatal mistake."

"I won't do it again, sir. I'll think more clearly."

"That's the beauty of the system established by my forefathers.

Unbridled greed gives you instant focus, a reliable framework from which to make rational decisions."

"I'm sorry, sir."

Quinn took another deep pull on the cigar and sent the smoke to the ceiling. "That's the genius of the ranking system. It focuses everyone on the single most important piece of data about a person, the purest truth. Money." He jabbed a finger at the portraits of the other Quinns on the wall. "They understood. Do you know what my father told me?"

"No, sir."

"*Make money your god. Then become its servant, and it will make you master of all.* Best advice anyone ever gave me."

"Please give me another chance, President Quinn."

Quinn shook his head as his gaze went to the floor. "I thought you could learn. But I was wrong. Maybe greed isn't something that can be learned. You either have it or you don't. And you can never have too much. It's an instinct. An inborn imperative. One you lack, I'm afraid."

It had the sound of terrible finality.

"I can fix this," Link pleaded. "Just give me a little more time."

"I'll give you all the time you need. One hour. Now go!"

22

Alix was out of breath when they arrived at the top floor. But Licious hadn't even broken a sweat.

"All the stuff you said down there, around the campfire." Alix heard her pulse pumping in her ears like a distant echo. "You don't really believe it, do you?"

"You're kidding, right?" Licious hopped off the stairs onto a blue floor. "It was all for my fans. I've cultivated a certain persona, and I say what they expect me to say. Definitely what Quinn wants."

"He tells you what to say?"

"We have an understanding. He lets me keep my money, and I spread his propaganda."

"So, it's all just an act?"

"Isn't everything?"

The words startled Alix. She teetered on the last step and glanced down at a thousand meters of open space, knees suddenly weak. Licious grabbed Alix's hand and pulled her onto the blue floor.

"Thanks." Alix stopped to catch her breath. "I don't know what happened."

"It's not you." Licious stopped. A blue gecko chased a green one up Licious' arm, across her collarbone and down her back. "Look, I can imagine how startling all this is for you, coming from the Fringe. But you need to understand. Nothing in the Sanctuary is *real*. People here may look happy, they may look like they have everything that matters. But it's not true. You were right. They're blind. They're stuck in the system. Prisoners of Quinn."

Alix followed Licious to a long window stretching all the way around the floor. In the morning sun, the Sanctuary stood out in high relief, like a lone field of jewel-encrusted tombstones.

"Beautiful perfection, isn't it?" Licious relaxed into the window, her nose on the glass. "As long as you don't see beyond the Wall. I suppose that's why you're here."

"So you believe me?" Alix asked.

"About the brain labs? Yeah, I believe you." Licious turned and leaned her back on the glass. "It's common knowledge among the 8Zs, except for Quinn's daughter Chelsea. Those with a lower rank are clueless. Blissful ignorance. I think about it every time I use this." She slipped a black jax from beneath her waist belt and spun it through her fingers.

"How can you?" Alix stared into Licious' eyes looking for an answer.

"How? Getting used to money and power is easy. After a while, you no longer think about how your jax is slowly destroying the brains of 10,000 Fringe rats. Maybe more."

Alix felt her jaw clench and tried to relax it.

"It's people like me you should hate. Not them." Licious motioned to the streets far below. "I am the system. The sly mouthpiece of the one who controls it all."

"Why are you telling me this?"

"Because I need you to understand how it works." Licious sat on the floor, back to the window. "At first, as you're rising in the ranks, getting more money, it's euphoric. Every day you wake up richer. And then you start to notice things you'd missed before. People hang back and let you have your way. You act crazy and they just laugh. No one can tell you to stop. You don't hear the word *no* anymore. People start to worship you. You can see it in their eyes. Life gets easier and easier. Like a drug."

"But how—"

"We may not have much time. Let me finish. You lose track of the money. It's not real anymore, just a number, and the number only has meaning if it's going up. It starts out as a hobby and becomes an addiction that controls your every waking moment. For a while, you think you're just lucky, but that changes. As you keep climbing up the rankings, you start to see clearly how you've earned it all. How you're so much better than everyone else. You deserve all the money and the power. And then you take the final step." Licious paused.

"I don't even want to know."

"But you need to. Once you hit 8Z, people at the bottom no longer matter. You lose the connection to reality. Their lives, their suffering; it's all just irrelevant theory. They're no longer worthy of your consideration. You forget about them." Licious buried her head in her hands. "So that's the answer. That's how I play games on a jax that costs the lives of tens of thousands of your friends and family in the Fringe."

As Licious stopped talking, Alix heard the sound of a distant heartbeat. And it was getting louder.

Jumping to her feet, Licious pressed her nose to the window. "They're coming. Sooner than I thought." She checked her jax. "They've cut my feed. They don't want the Sanctuary to see what's about to happen."

The faraway sound was familiar. Alix had heard it many times in the past. Sanctuary heli-ships.

They heard a loud pop far below. The building shook. And then, they heard the sound of boots running up the stairs.

"We don't have much time." Licious grabbed Alix's hand and pulled her to her feet. "Can you fly a mini-heli?"

"I ride a chopper."

"Close enough."

Licious slid her finger along the edge of her jax. The ceiling opened up like a flower and a series of steps sprang from the wall. She ran up the steps with Alix close behind.

When they reached the roof, a strong gust of wind pushed Alix toward the edge. Licious grabbed her hand and pulled her back. The top of the Wall was level with them a hundred meters away. A heli-ship was visible, closing fast, the *thump thump* getting louder.

"Over here." Licious ran to a small dome and tapped a button. It split in half to reveal a tiny airship. Completely transparent, it looked like a souped-up drone, with a cockpit and one seat. "My custom-built mini-heli. Get in."

"What about you?" Alix asked.

"I don't fly. Scared of heights."

Alix knew it was a lie. "They'll kill you."

"Maybe. The mini's built for one person. All you have to do is get over the Wall back to the Fringe. It'll never make it with both of us. Consider it my contribution to your revolution."

The sound of boots was coming closer. The heli-ship was only half a klick away. It threw off a silent flash. A second later, the air exploded a dozen meters above them. The concussion threw them both to the roof.

"No time to argue." Licious pulled Alix to the mini-heli. Its side door popped open, and Licious shoved Alix into the seat. A belt and shoulder harness automatically wrapped around her. "Listen carefully," Licious said. "There are only two controls. Push the left one forward to go up; pull it back to go down. The one on the right is for horizontal movement, forward, backward, right, left. Like a joystick."

"What's a joystick?"

"Never mind. You'll get the hang of it. It's got spooky AI to smooth out the rough edges. Totally idiot-proof. You couldn't crash it if you tried. Even has a defensive combat module that takes over when it anticipates danger. Its Chinese drone tech totally outclasses anything the Patrol has. Cost a whole week's salary." Licious tapped the dashboard, and 12 rotors whirred into action. She got close enough that their noses almost touched. "Try to forgive me, Alix," she winked, "for the brain labs." She slammed one of the sticks forward and jumped back.

The door swung shut. Just as Alix opened her mouth to speak, the mini surged up, blasted away from the roof and sucked her deep into the seat. In two seconds, she was hovering a hundred meters above the Sanctuary, staring down at Licious.

Another midair blast flashed on her left. The mini tumbled away like a feather and then righted itself, twisting and diving.

A perky computer voice spoke in the cockpit.

Weapon system detected. AI engaged for evasive action. Please brace yourself.

Glancing down, Alix saw a dozen black-armored soldiers burst onto the roof where Licious stood. As if ignoring them, she stepped to the edge and looked out on the Sanctuary, arms outstretched as if she were talking to the people.

The soldiers formed a tight semicircle and moved to surround her. Then their pulse rifles flashed.

Licious crumpled, twisted and fell, a delicate doll plunging head down to the streets of the Sanctuary.

Alix froze in horror, silently counting the seconds, trying to comprehend. Before Licious hit the ground, the mini jerked hard to the left. It kept twisting, dropping and turning as concussive explosions chased it across the sky. The joystick moved on its own, controlled by the AI, anticipating where the next shot would land, jumping clear.

Alix realized the seat had inflated to enfold her in a soft cocoon. For an instant, she blacked out. When she awoke, the mini was darting alongside the heli-ship, too close for it to fire, giving her a clear view inside its cockpit.

There he was.

Lincoln Wells, his face twisted like an animal gone berserk. She gave him a weak smile and could almost hear him cursing.

And then she remembered. She had to get over the Wall.

Grabbing the stick on the right and slamming it forward, she took the mini on a jagged course in the general direction of the Fringe. Then she pulled the other stick back hard. The mini shot up. She took one last glance back at the Sanctuary and leapt over the Wall into Fringe airspace.

The heli-ship followed, its pulse cannons still pumping out a barrage of explosives. But each missed its mark as the mini danced and weaved with the grace and precision of a jaguar.

Exactly like Licious.

Each hand on a stick, Alix played them like an exotic musical instrument, adding her own awkward jerks and dodges to the mini's AI, working her way deeper into the Fringe, with Link in pursuit.

23

"Forget it, Wilson." Link kept his finger on the trigger and his eye on the mini-heli as it danced and jumped like a hummingbird. "I'm not stopping until I've destroyed Alix Yamaguchi for good."

"But, boss." Wilson's face floated in the holoscreen, searching for the right words. "If you keep firing the cannons at your current rate, you'll run out of ammo in exactly two minutes."

"Don't worry, Wilson. My targeting algorithm eventually has to hit her. All I have to do is keep firing, and she's as good as dead."

Wilson shook his head. "It won't work, boss. The mini's running on Chinese AI, new tech we can't match. Your targeting system hasn't been updated for over a month. It's light-years behind what Licious and her 8Z friends had access to."

"Is she dead?"

"Yeah, boss, she's dead." Wilson let out an audible sigh. "Quinn gave a direct order to kill her. The Patrol had no choice."

Link pushed back the nausea building in his belly as he thought about Licious. "At least it all happened in the early morning. Empty streets and all that. We'll need a deep Mesh-scan to confirm no one got footage of—"

"Uh, boss?" Wilson looked away, as if avoiding eye contact. "It's not quite that simple."

Link froze, feeling the contents of his stomach rise at the change in Wilson's shaky voice. "Explain."

"Better sit down, boss."

"Stop calling me boss!"

Wilson wiped his forehead. "Sorry, sir. We don't know how it happened. We cut the feed before the troops engaged her, but somehow she got her feed back on."

"You're kidding."

"No, I'm not, sir."

Link could feel a headache coming on. "How much did it capture?"

"Everything."

"The whole Sanctuary witnessed her assassination?"

Wilson cleared his throat. "Yeah, I think it was pretty much on every screen on the planet. We still haven't got it shut down. Almost like she knew she was going to die and set it up for maximum effect."

Link shook his head as warm liquid filled his throat. Bending over, he retched onto the floor of the ship, the bitter taste filling his mouth. "What's the reaction in the Sanctuary?"

"People are pouring into the streets by the thousands, moving toward her building. They've set up a makeshift memorial around her body. Won't let the Patrol get close. It's a mess." Wilson lowered his voice to a whisper. "Check your jax, boss. Just sent you a message."

When Link glanced down, an encrypted file was waiting for him on his jax. From Wilson.

Quinn ordered us to arrest you as soon as you come back. Unless you kill Alix Yamaguchi first.

"Roger that, Wilson."

"Anything else, boss?"

"Let Chelsea know I'll meet her for dinner tonight."

"I'll pass it along, boss."

Link took a deep breath and settled into the seat. At least his options were clear. There was no going back to the Sanctuary until Alix was dead. And right now, she was very much alive, dancing in the sky a couple of hundred meters away in the mini. The heli-ship surged toward her as he slammed the throttle and engaged the pulse cannon.

But the more he shot at her, the more she jumped and dodged. It was like trying to shoot a gnat with a bullet.

There was only one thing to do: get as close to the mini as possible, and stay with it until it landed. The instant it was on the ground, his pulse cannon could easily target it for a direct hit, and there'd be no chance for her to dance around it. Problem solved.

Like a big dog chasing a mouse, they jumped across the sky together, always within sight of each other. Alix stared at him with those eyes and smiled. Now and then, Link fired a volley of shots, but each time, the mini dodged them effortlessly. Along the way, he got a better look at the Fringe than he'd ever had before. The people below seemed to figure out he was chasing their hero. Cheers rose from the streets each time his shot missed.

It was strange, but he didn't see the violence he'd assumed was everyday life in the Fringe. The population moved through the streets with purpose. There were markets and playing children. People walked together, talking, laughing.

Impossible.

It was probably all staged. And, in spite of the happy faces, it still looked like hell compared to the Sanctuary. No color, no glass, not even any steel, except for skeletal remains from the distant past. All the new structures in the Fringe were irregular shapes thrown together from scrap materials instead of objects of beauty. It was chaos in action. The result of lazy thinking. Overall, it was exactly what he'd expected to see.

As he chased her, the image of Alix Yamaguchi and her strange eyes kept penetrating his mind. The more he tried to push it away, the more vivid it became. Maybe, under different circumstances, he would have gotten to know her. If she'd grown up in the Sanctuary, they might have even been friends. She wasn't beautiful, not with her scars and green pallor and crooked teeth, and certainly not compared to the chiseled perfection of Chelsea. But there was an honesty and innocence about her that he'd never seen before. It pulled on him like a magnet, making it almost impossible to turn away.

He shook his head to clear his mind. The bottom line was clear. Alix Yamaguchi would destroy his life if he let her. All that he had built up in the Sanctuary, his career, his future life at the top of the ranks, all of it would vaporize if he didn't kill her.

The Wall was still visible on the horizon, 10 klicks away. If he ever wanted to return to his world, he knew what he had to do.

As for Alix, her plan was clear. She would draw him deep into the Fringe before landing her mini. Then, she'd fade into the labyrinth of streets and buildings and the old subway. Make him chase her. At some point, she'd overwhelm him with a mob of Fringe freaks, who would take him down. Well, Link was too smart to let it happen that way.

Alix's mini-heli suddenly dropped down in the direction of an open field of black dirt near the remains of an ancient 10-story building.

Now was his chance.

Carefully holding his fire, Link hovered just off the edge of the old building and waited for the instant the mini touched down. His finger twitched on the trigger.

He thought of her eyes, but pushed the idea away.

There was a strange sound, like a finger tapping on the outer hull of his heli-ship. And then another. Before Link could react, the navigation system crashed, all the holoscreens went dark, and the targeting system went into error mode.

It was a trap. He punched the throttle, but instead of going up, the heli-ship dropped into free fall. For an instant, he felt the freedom of weightlessness, rising centimeters from the pilot's chair. When the ship hit the dirt, he lunged forward, breaking free of the seat straps and slamming his head into the deck.

Blackness engulfed his world.

24

"Hey, Lincoln Wells."

No response, so Alix tried again.

"Hey Link, this isn't the dreamscape. You're in the Fringe." She prodded him with a toe. "Time to wake up."

Link was lying face down on the floor of the ship, breathing steadily. The windows were dark; dim, red lights flashed on and off in the interior. Judging from the bump on Link's forehead, he probably had a massive headache. Her next instinct was to approach him as a *healer*, to offer aid and tenderness. Maybe then he'd let go of his outrage and listen to her. She bent down and ran her fingers through his hair, softer and sweeter smelling than anything she'd ever seen.

Still no response. Time for a different strategy.

"Hey, Link. We need to talk." Alix stood and kicked him in the side, not a vicious kick, but hard enough to register.

He jumped.

"Welcome to the Fringe." Alix sat back into the pilot's chair and crossed her legs.

Link gazed up at her. In a split second, his eyes went wide and he tried to jump away. That's when he discovered his wrists and ankles were tied with old ropes.

"Don't act so surprised." Alix grinned.

"You have no idea what you're doing!" He strained against the rope. "Three battle squadrons are on their way right now. They'll burn the Fringe to the ground if you don't release me."

Alix worked to turn her grin into something more serious, but it took too much effort. "Three squadrons? Wow. So, this is the part where we let you go, and we beg for mercy?"

Swallowing, Link rolled over on his back. His eyes widened when he saw Muse and Merf a meter away. His gaze kept returning to Merf, standing there in his exoskeleton with the wide shoulders and the head cage, looking like a killer robot.

"Look," Link said, his smooth Patrol uniform stretching over his chest and abs. "I'm not here to hurt anybody. Just let me go, and I'll call off the other squadrons and get my ship back to the Sanctuary."

"I see." Muse stepped closer, dark hair with silver streaks flowing over her shoulders. In the long, grey dress she wore, she looked like a force of nature, her voice smooth and calm. "You're not here to hurt anyone. Just passing through, having a look. Then explain something to me. Why'd you spend the last few hours trying to kill my daughter with your pulse cannons? We all saw it."

Silence.

Link backed up until his head hit a wall. Then he worked himself into a seated position, hands still tied from behind.

"Time for full disclosure." Merf stepped to the other side of Alix, the sound of whirring servos moving the mechanical joints of his exoskeleton. "We've been monitoring your conversations with your buddy, Wilson. You came here to kill Alix. That's your mission, plain and simple. And you can't go back to the Sanctuary until it's done. Have I missed anything?"

"How'd you knock my ship down?"

"Easy." Merf pointed at the navigation console. "Alix lured you to this spot. When you got close enough to the building, we dropped a couple of interface cables onto the hull, penetrated your security protocol and fried the ship's nav systems. She'll never fly again."

Link shook his head. "But how—"

"That's just Merf," Alix said. "He knows tech from the inside out." Uncrossing her legs, she stood and walked closer, staring down at Link. "Your men killed Licious while she had her live feed on. It hit every screen in the Sanctuary and beyond. People are flooding the streets. You've stirred up a lot of rage, Lincoln Wells."

"Quinn won't be happy when he finds out you let your ship get shot down by Fringe scum." Merf shook his head.

Muse rested her hands on her hips. "You're in a heap of trouble, boy."

Link looked at the three faces, one at a time. "So, what's next? You going to execute me in front of an enraged crowd?"

"That's not the way we do things here in the Fringe." Muse pursed her lips.

"OK, then you'll hold me for ransom, right?"

Merf folded mechanical arms over his steel-encased chest. "Wouldn't do any good. Quinn won't pay a dime for you. He's probably already sent someone here to kill you."

"Then, what?" Link tugged at the rope again as he peered around the inside of the ship, his gaze coming to rest on the hatch, left open to the night air.

"We confiscated your weapons." Alix pointed to an empty rack on the wall. "Don't want you going on a killing spree. You won't need them anyway. The Fringe is safe day or night."

"Like I said, what do you want from me?"

"I told you before. In the dreamscape." Alix stared down. "We just want to talk. Show you the Fringe. Open your eyes to reality."

"You'll never make me part of your pathetic revolution." Link strained against the rope.

"Maybe not. In that case, we don't have much choice." Alix pulled her knife out and approached Link.

"So, you're going to slit my throat just like that?" Link sneered.

Merf stepped back and widened his stance. "Be careful. He's like a wild animal."

Link reared back, as if expecting to be stabbed. Not smiling, Alix grabbed his shoulder and pushed him to the floor on his side.

"You'll regret this!" Link stiffened.

She quickly cut the ropes, pulled them away and stood back.

Link looked at his hands and feet, stunned. "You're just letting me go?"

"Yup." Alix dropped a bag on the floor. "Here's some real Fringe clothes if you want to blend in. Your uniform screams to the world that you're Patrol. It's pretty safe here, but what you did today may have stirred folks up a bit. This will help you get safely back to the Wall."

"Why are you doing this?" Link grabbed the bag.

"We'd like you to have a look around the Fringe for yourself." Alix turned to point at the open hatch. "You're free to go."

Link sprang across the three meters that separated him from Alix. Before she could turn around, he pulled the knife out of her hand and pressed the tip into her throat.

Merf's steel-encased hand shot out to grab Link's shoulder.

"No, Merf." Alix said, trying to remain calm.

"I swear, I'll kill her," Link yelled, breathing hard. "Now step back, both of you."

Merf and Muse looked at Alix and then at each other.

"Do it," Alix said. The cold steel tip of the blade bit into her neck. Warm blood trickled down her skin.

"Get my weapons," yelled Link.

Muse didn't move.

"You don't need them," Merf said. "Just walk back to the Sanctuary, right through the Wall. Nobody's going to stop you."

"You expect me to believe that? This is the Fringe." Link looked out the open hatch. "Full of crazies. Now get me my weapons."

"Don't argue, Merf." Alix tried to relax. "Just do it."

Merf nodded and walked across the floor through the hatch to the out-side. Thirty seconds later, he came back with two pulse rifles and a pistol. He dumped them on the floor at Link's feet. "That's everything."

Link slowly bent down and fingered the pistol, letting Alix go. "OK, everyone out. Don't try to run. Wait near the hatch."

A minute later, Link emerged from the ship dressed in the drab, grey Fringe clothes. He closed the hatch behind him.

"Looks good on you," Alix said.

She'd been the one who had wanted to let Link go, who had argued that he wouldn't be a danger. There was something about his eyes, she had said, and if they could only get him away from the Sanctuary and let him see the Fringe, he'd change. He'd become who he really was. They just had to give him time.

"You're going to take me back to the Sanctuary." Link lifted the pistol and pointed it at Alix. Then, he turned to face Muse and Merf. "Don't follow us. Don't try to stop us."

"Did you forget?" Merf said. "They don't want you back."

"They will if I have Alix with me."

Muse looked pale in the moonlight. "Why are you doing this?"

"To get back the life she stole from me." Link pointed the pistol squarely at Alix. "Ever since she started this revolution, it's been one disaster after another. It's time to put a stop to it. All of it. And don't try anything. It could result in collateral damage."

Link pressed the pistol into her back. "Lead the way back to the Wall."

They walked across the field, down a deserted street and around a corner, leaving Muse and Merf behind. Alix tried to figure out what she had done wrong. This wasn't how she thought it would play out. Link was supposed to be grateful for the mercy they had shown him. He was supposed to see the truth in the Fringe.

"Look, Link, people here aren't violent. But the problem is, they all know me."

"What are you saying?"

Alix stopped and slowly turned to face Link, her hands up. "I already know how this plays out. Even if Merf and Muse don't tell anyone, which I highly doubt, people will see you walking with that gun poking into my back. Word will get around. They'll figure out what you're doing. And they'll try to stop you."

"Then I'll just have to kill you." Link raised the gun with trembling fingers.

"I know," Alix said. "But it won't stop there. You'll kill a lot more of them as they rush you. How many pulse rounds can you fire before your gun goes dead?"

"Thousands. All night if I have to."

"So, based on your plan, thousands of my people are going to die tonight."

"Why should that matter to me? They're just Fringe scum." He looked away as he said it.

"But there's more."

"Huh?"

"Merf will have drone cameras in the air to capture all of it. You may have noticed he's like that. He'll upload video of the slaughter in minutes. It'll flood the Mesh. We already know the reaction in the Sanctuary to what your men did to Licious. How do you think they'll react to more senseless killing here in the Fringe? From there, it will just get worse and worse. For you, for the Fringe, for the Sanctuary."

Link still had his gun trained on Alix. "So, tell me, Ms. Yamaguchi. What's the solution?"

"Simple." Alix opened her arms wide. "Just kill me now."

"And then what?"

"Then you go back to the Sanctuary and forget about me." Alix looked at the misshapen structures on each side of the road. "Back to Chelsea and Quinn and your pristine Sanctuary and skyrocketing rank. But you've still got a problem. And I'm afraid there's not solution for this one."

"Do you ever stop talking?" Link closed one eye and looked down the barrel of his pistol. "What's the problem?"

"Truth."

Link opened his eye. "What do you mean?"

"The whole Sanctuary knows the truth. About the Fringe, about the brain labs, about the chemplants, about how Quinn treats people like Licious who dare to defy him."

"Who cares?"

"I do. A lot of people do, on both sides of the Wall." Alix came a step closer so the pistol was only a meter from her chest. "I really thought maybe you would care, too, if you actually saw the Fringe. Please don't tell me I was wrong."

Link brought his other hand up to steady the gun. "Well, I'm sorry to tell you, but you're wrong. About me and everyone else. We don't care about your truth. We don't care about the suffering of the Fringe. As long as we're happy in the Sanctuary, as long as we have the money and the power we want, nothing else matters."

"That may be what Quinn thinks, but I can't believe you think that way."

"Believe it."

"No." Alix shook her head. "No, I refuse to believe that you're a monster. I saw it."

"Saw what?"

"In the dreamscape. Your eyes. There's something you're hiding. You don't really want to believe in the Sanctuary, not when you're being true to yourself. You've tried, over and over, but it just doesn't feel right. It's not who you are. It never was."

"Stop talking!" Link put his hands over his ears. "Just stop talking!"

Alix thought about running, but that would make it too easy for him to shoot her. She didn't want it to be easy. If he was going to kill her, she wanted him to do it here and now. So she walked closer. She'd been thinking about it for a long time. There was something she had to do.

Link backed up, arms down at his sides. "What are you doing?"

"Before you kill me, I just have one thing left to do." Without waiting, she put her arms around Link and pulled him close. And then, looking up into his eyes, she brushed her lips against his, hesitated for an instant and kissed him.

She imagined that he'd thrust the tip of his pulse pistol into her chest and pull the trigger right then and there. But he didn't. He just stood there, body trembling, stunned. When she was done, she took a step back.

Link's eyes were closed for another instant before he opened them. "I don't get it. Why?"

"I honestly don't know. But it felt right."

"I still have to do what I came to do."

"In that case, it looks like there's nothing left to say, is there, Link?"

"Nope." He slowly backed away and raised the pistol, eyes wide. He pulled out his jax and tapped the end, holding it in the hand opposite the gun.

Finally, Alix understood. To get back into the Sanctuary, Link would need proof that he'd shot her. That's why he was engaging the video.

She had told Merf and Muse that Link wouldn't shoot her. That he couldn't. There was a connection between them. But maybe she'd been wrong.

"It's what I have to do," Link said.

"Make it quick." She stared at him, face held high, unable to hold back the tears. Her hand brushed against the new shirt she was wearing, a gift from Merf he'd gotten from one of his contacts in the Sanctuary. It was made of some kind of new material that shimmered in the moonlight.

"Please, don't cry," he said, voice softening, all the anger gone. "It's all so crazy. I've never met anyone like you. You don't deserve this. You've done what you thought was right for your people. I'll hate myself for the rest of my life." Link wiped his eyes with the back of his hand. "But I still have to do it."

For the first time, Alix saw the real Link rise to the surface.

"I'm sorry," she said.

"So am I, Alix Yamaguchi."

His finger made contact with the trigger just before the pulse hit her chest.

25

Her eyes again.

They were intensely familiar. It wasn't just the fact that one was blue and the other was brown. Link couldn't shake the feeling he'd seen the same eyes before on someone else.

He didn't want to pull the trigger. He never really believed he would. After all, Alix was only trying to help her people, doing what he'd do if they were to trade places. It was possible she was telling the truth. Maybe there really were brain labs in the Fringe powering all the tech in the Sanctuary. Maybe the Sanctuary really was too perfect, not able to exist on its own. And for all the mischief that Alix had done, she hadn't killed anyone. She kept saying over and over that all she wanted was to tell the truth and show it to the world. She was cocky Fringe scum, but it was undeniable: all the killing and shooting had been done on his side alone.

Even if it were all true, what could Link or Chelsea or anyone else do about it? Tear down the Wall? Destroy the whole system created by the Quinns? It wasn't possible, but even if it were, with so many people standing to lose so much, was it the right thing to do?

Link stood alone on a filthy, dark street. Nothing felt real, like he was back in the dreamscape, only this time it was a nightmare.

He'd taken the only possible path forward. He'd stopped thinking and pulled the trigger. And now he stood for a full minute staring at the body of Alix crumpled on the ground. She looked thinner than he remembered. Fragile and vulnerable.

Deep inside, he wanted to scream.

Why had she kissed him?

Still holding the pistol in trembling hands, Link couldn't hold back the wave of hate. Only this time, it wasn't for Alix. It was for Quinn, for pushing him to kill her, and for himself for being too weak to push back. Quinn's cutting words played in his mind.

Don't let fear get in the way of your greed.

It was a vintage Quinn statement, words that made no sense and yet made perfect sense. As he brooded over the words, another thought surfaced in his mind.

What about love? Wasn't love more important than greed?

Before he realized it, he was on his knees, and then prostrate on the ground, hitting the dirt with his fists, crying aloud, feeling like a great hole had been blown in his psyche, destroying all the good in his life, leaving only emptiness and rage.

And then he remembered Chelsea. She was the one good thing left in his life, but there was only one way to get back to her.

Sliding his finger along the side of his jax, he uploaded the video he'd just taken of Alix. In a few seconds, Chelsea would find it in her personal secure server. She'd forward it on to her father. After Quinn saw it, he'd give the order to allow Link back into the Sanctuary. No one else would see it. And finally, the nightmare would be over.

It would be best for Link to leave the Fringe on his own, without any help or fanfare, but if things got sketchy, he could call Wilson for backup.

Entering a narrow alley, he walked between two leaning structures that looked like they might cave in on him any second. The pale moonlight made it difficult to distinguish random rocks and holes on the ground, and he almost fell. He couldn't be sure, but he thought he heard movement inside the building on the left. And then, footsteps behind him.

He broke into a gentle run, still gripping the pulse pistol in one hand. Rounding another corner, he stopped to listen, but the only sound was the beating of his heart.

So he pressed on, keeping out of the moonlight, scurrying down dark side streets, lurking in the shadows, not moving until he was sure no one was watching. But he never saw anyone. They must have all been asleep in their cheap, organic shacks, living out their lazy lives in a stupor.

The buildings thinned out, and the road led up a steep hill. He followed it to the summit. At the top was an open pit full of shiny liquid. He couldn't be sure, but he thought he saw a small white skull staring at him, half-submerged. The stench made him nauseous. As he skirted around the rim to the other side, a huge drone dropped out of the clouds with a payload suspended from a bag below it. The ground vibrated with every beat of its massive rotors. As it hovered, the bag opened and spilled its contents into the pit. He heard the splash and felt the ground tremble again as the drone pulled up and away, dripping black sludge. Another wave of caustic fumes washed over him. He dropped to his knees, consumed by coughing.

Ten meters away, he began the descent down the other side of the hill and skirted a line of ooze that had an unearthly metallic sheen. A green cloud of gas wafted over him, setting off a choking fit that left a bitter taste on his tongue and made his throat burn. A light flashed on his jax, alerting him to toxic air, and he had to silence it. He broke into a run to escape the area before his lungs turned to mush. At the bottom of the hill, he passed a row of low-lying houses clapped together from ragged sheets of carbon board. Rivulets of red liquid seeped under the walls like open veins. From somewhere deep inside, he heard the cough of a child and a mother's soothing voice.

He tried to imagine the living hell they called home.

A flash caught his eye. In the distance, he saw it, moonlight reflecting off an enormous silver cube a 1,000 meters long on each side. With architecture unlike anything in the Fringe, it looked utterly foreign, as if it had been lifted from the Sanctuary and dropped from the sky.

He jogged closer, driven by curiosity and the sound of shuffling feet, until the scene came clearly into view. From behind the rib-like ruins of a collapsed steel structure, he gazed in astonishment. A silent crowd of hundreds of thousands moved like a slow river into an enormous entrance on one side of the cube. Just around the corner, another crowd flowed out onto the streets. It reminded him of a giant beating heart, with a constant circulation of humanity. Taking a video with his jax, he studied the faces on high magnification. There were children, teens and adults, but no elderly. The adults walked with unsteady gaits, lurching from step to step, holding onto railings or assisted by the younger ones. Here and there, bodies lay collapsed on the ground, only to stand with the help of others. The older ones all shared the same blank stares, sunken eyes and humped-over postures. *Walking dead* was the best description that came to mind.

Divided between horror and disgust, he turned away and moved in the opposite direction, anxious to return to the Sanctuary. He'd run into a few late night walkers on the streets around the massive cube, but no one paid any attention to him, so he stepped out of the shadows and jogged through the open streets. In the distance, the neon outlines of the Sanctuary drew him closer and quickened his pace. All he had to do was get to the Wall, find a portal and walk through.

But it wasn't going to be that easy. He first noticed the crowd when he got within half a klick of the Wall. Hundreds of Fringe freaks were standing and staring into the Sanctuary. The Wall was completely transparent from the Fringe side, like it wasn't there. He hadn't noticed that before.

Drawn like a magnet, he stepped into the crowd. The looks of longing told him everything. Small children stood in front, faces and hands pressed against the glass. Adults held hands, with their lips open in wonder, almost worship. Link's first instinct was to make fun of them. Moronic Fringe scum. But the more he looked, the more he understood. No one made a sound, as if in silent acknowledgment that the world on the other side was not meant for them.

And so Link stared with them.

In the darkness, the buildings, sidewalks and streets of the Sanctuary were oceans of neon. Holographic ads moved on every surface to promote the latest tech, endless promises of effortless perfection. Psychedelic sushi, artisanal mood enhancers, sensory magnification, dream management, customized virtual companions, extreme body-carving, IQ upgrades.

It was a world only accessible to those with limitless money, most of it even beyond Link's reach. He tried to imagine how it looked to people forced to sell their bodies and minds for bare survival.

Link realized that on one side of the Wall, the people of the Fringe huddled together, many of them literally leaning on their neighbors. On the other side, the Sanctuary dwellers walked alone, each absorbed in their own ocean of personal stimulation.

Two separate worlds. Almost two separate species of human. It was hard to imagine how they could ever come together.

But that had been Alix's dream.

As he thought of her, all the neon screens went white, as if wiped clean. A large public screen off to the right on the Fringe side of the Wall went white as well.

And then, he saw it.

Like a ghost, Alix Yamaguchi's face appeared on every surface. And Link was there too, dressed in the same rusty pants and dusty carbon shirt he wore now. They exchanged words.

It's what I have to do.

Link raised his pistol and pointed it at Alix's chest.

Make it quick.

He pulled the trigger.

A bullet of blue energy exploded on her, throwing her to the ground. For a couple of seconds, her body twitched. Then it went still.

The crowd stopped breathing. There were gasps of disbelief.

Nausea rose in Link's chest. He tried to put the whole scene with Alix out of his mind, but seeing it play out on the big screen brought the details back. He'd killed her. He'd really done it. And there was no way to undo it.

Three meters away, a small boy no older than four looked up at his father in the silence. "Look daddy," the boy said, raising a finger at the screen. "The bad man shot her. He shot our Alix."

Link wanted to scream out that he wasn't a bad man, that he'd been forced to do it. He'd had no choice. Quinn's orders. But it wasn't true. He could have walked away and left her alive, giving up on his dreams of ruling the Sanctuary with Chelsea, forced to spend the rest of his life in the Fringe.

Would that have been so bad, to be close to Alix, to join her revolution, to remake the world? He wiped the thought from his mind.

Somehow, the video he'd made as proof of the killing of Alix had been stolen. And now it was looping on every screen in the Sanctuary and the Fringe. The little boy slowly turned to stare up at Link, recognition in his eyes. His finger pointed again.

"Look, daddy. That's the bad man."

As if on cue, the crowd turned to face Link.

He fingered the pulse pistol, the same one he'd just used on Alix. No one in the crowd was armed. If they made a move against him, he could just shoot his way to the Wall. In the past, there had been other quasi-military actions inside the Fringe with massive casualties. Rebellions had been put down from time to time. Quinn wouldn't care if a few more died. He might even encourage it.

The little boy tilted his head like a puppy. "Why'd you shoot her? She was good."

Link backed away, gripping the pistol so hard he thought he might break it. "Look, I don't want any trouble here," he said, eyes scanning the crowd. "I'm just trying to get back to the Sanctuary. Back to my home."

"But you shot Alix." The boy's father stared through sunken eyes, his bony shoulders protruding beneath a threadbare shirt. "She was a healer. Spent her time trying to help the folks around her." The man looked over at the public holoscreen, still playing a loop of Link pointing his gun at Alix and pulling the trigger. A tear rolled down his cheek. "Why?"

Link was surprised they hadn't already charged him. But they didn't seem in any hurry to do it. All he saw in their faces was sadness, with a touch of curiosity. Just to be safe, he took another step back.

"Like I said," Link tried hard to sound reasonable, logical, humble. "I'm not here to hurt anyone else. She wanted to destroy the careful balance between the Sanctuary and the Fringe. It would have endangered your lives, started a war. Nobody wants that. I just did what I had to do. And now everything's fine."

He cringed as he heard himself say the last sentence.

Footsteps behind him forced him to turn. The crowd thickened. They had him surrounded. Mind racing, he thought of the possibilities. First, just whip out the pistol and start shooting until people backed off. The problem was, in the emotional state they were in, they might not back off. Could he really kill the whole crowd, a few thousand people? Theoretically, yes. The pistol could be put on auto mode, but that was exactly the result Alix had warned him about.

And then he caught himself. *Why did it matter what Alix had said?*

Mass murder was a suboptimal choice. It might get broadcast in the Sanctuary and make for bad press.

The skinny man with the little boy shook his head. "Now, everything's fine? What do you mean?"

"Look, I'll be honest with you. President Quinn insisted that she be eliminated. I was just following orders."

It was technically true, but it made him sound like a sniveling coward.

As Link looked at the boy, another plan presented itself. Grab him and threaten to kill the little guy with the pistol unless the people pulled back and let him get to the Wall.

But that might just inflame them even more.

It was a legitimate emergency. With one hand still on his pulse pistol, he slipped his jax out of his pocket and tapped out a message without looking, fingers moving along the black cylinder with practiced ease.

Wilson, you've got my location. I need backup right now.

Link was sure a heli-ship would drop out of the sky any minute. Air ships were feared in the Fringe; everyone knew that. Once the crowd saw a display of overwhelming force above them, they would scatter.

The man with the little boy shook his head. "It doesn't make sense. She was good. Quinn takes everything from us, to build the Sanctuary." The man pointed through the Wall at the neon city. "What right does he have to take away our Alix, too?"

Voices rose in agreement.

Behind Link, a woman in a ragged dress stepped out of the crowd. She was unsteady on her feet and had to lean on a child for balance.

"I just finished a 12-hour shift at the brain lab," she said, arms and head trembling uncontrollably, rage building in her face. "I'll go back in 12 hours. I've been doing that every day for 25 years, and look what it's done to me. But if I don't, how's my family going to eat?"

The answer was clear to Link. "If you don't like it, get another job."

There was instant reaction among the mob. People yelled and bared their teeth. Some of them lunged forward only to be pulled back by others. The energy of the crowd had taken a new, dangerous turn.

An old man weaved his way through the sea of bodies and stopped, five meters from Link. "Maybe that's the way it works in the Sanctuary. If you don't like your job, you quit and find another. That's not how it works here." Others nodded vigorously, and the level of noise increased.

"You tell him, Jim!" Someone shouted.

"We can't grow our own food. The ground is sterile, and we don't have clean water for hydro-ponds. Our only food is cornboo." The old man opened his hands in front of him, and Link could see the pale green of his fingers. "And there are only two ways to get cornboo from the Sanctuary. Work in the brain labs, or work in the chemplants. You'll live longer if you choose the brain labs, but that only means you'll die a slow death."

People were shouting louder, moving closer.

Where was Wilson with the heli-ship?

"Look, I really wish I could help, but—"

"There was only one person who could help us." The old man stared out from sunken eyes. "And you killed her."

A man with a crooked back broke free from the crowd, stumbled closer and took a swing at Link. He easily ducked, and the man fell at his feet.

"Our children are dying. There's a virus raging among us. We're at the breaking point." The old man dropped to his knees. "We need to send a message to Quinn."

Link jumped at the chance. "I know him. We're friends. I'll talk with him about it. Maybe he'll listen."

"But you killed Alix." The man with the little boy yelled from behind Link. "It's not right. We can't just let you go. Grab him!"

It was the signal the crowd had been waiting for. They surged forward.

And that was when he heard the sound he'd been waiting for, a specific resonance bio-engineered to trigger a fear response in humans on the ground. The vibration spread through his chest until it encompassed his whole body.

Thump, thump, thump.

He looked up to see the heli-ship rise high over the Wall, searchlights trained on the ground. Men, women and children paused to stare. The ship began its descent.

"Everyone stand back!" Link whipped out his pulse pistol and fired a single shot in the air. A blue dot climbed a hundred meters before blooming in an explosion of light.

Caught between the heli-ship and the pulse pistol, two displays of awesome Sanctuary tech, people were screaming, backing away. It was the moment Link had been waiting for.

He felt his jax vibrate and pulled it out of his pocket. It was glowing green. A face popped above it.

"Saw your signal, boss. Looks like you're in a bit of trouble. I count over three thousand warm bodies standing between you and the Sanctuary."

"Is that all? What took you so long, Wilson?"

"Sorry, boss. Things have been chaotic on this side of the Wall. What's the plan?"

"Simple rescue operation." Link felt relaxed as he shifted into commander mode. "Get a lock on my jax."

"Already have it, boss."

"Good. Stay close. And drop the hook. I may need it."

"Roger that, boss." Wilson looked away for a minute, checking a readout. "Weapons systems are ready and locked on. It'll be easy to take out a few hundred—"

"No, Wilson!"

"Boss?"

"We're doing this the old-fashioned way. No casualties."

"I don't understand." Wilson looked confused. "You're in the Fringe, boss. Wouldn't it just be easier to—"

"No more killing, Wilson. Just hover until I give you the order to drop down."

"Whatever you say, boss." Wilson nodded. "Don't do anything stupid."

Link looked up and noticed everyone staring at him, with his jax in one hand and the pistol in the other.

"Out of my way, please." He pointed his pistol in the direction he wanted to go, away from the Wall to an open field behind the crowd.

No one moved, so he lifted his pistol and discharged it into the ground a couple of meters from the toes of the people blocking his way. They pulled back, powerless to resist him.

Repeating the same method, Link slowly worked his way through a narrow opening in the crowd, moving toward the open field behind them. He could sense the mounting rage and expected to be rushed any second. Finally, as the last person moved aside, he broke free and turned for one last look at the surreal scene.

Three thousand angry Fringe freaks stared at him.

As he slowly backed away, his foot caught in a hole. Trying to catch his balance, he stumbled and went down hard. The pistol slipped from his hand. Before he could grab it, a teenage boy kicked it into the darkness. His hand groped for the jax, but it was gone, too.

He jumped to his feet and sprinted into the night away from the crowd and away from the Wall.

26

Alix floated in a sea of black.

Threads of voices swam in circles, a man and a woman, talking to each other, sometimes yelling; snippets of conversation. As the voices moved closer, the words became distinct.

All Alix could do was listen.

"What do you mean, you don't want the child?" The woman screamed. "She's yours. She's ours! She needs us."

"The child is," the man began. "How can I put this? Problematic." He spoke slowly, deliberately. "My father is ill. He may only have days or weeks to live. After he dies, they'll be another election, and I'm the designated winner. I'll be taking over all his accounts. Do you understand what that means?"

"You love me, don't you?"

"You know I do, but—"

"There can't be any *buts*. Either you do or you don't."

"If only my life was as uncomplicated as yours." The man kept his voice low. "This new situation is developing much faster than I ever thought it would. And now, without any warning, I'm thrust into the spotlight. Things are changing. I'd always planned to marry you. Ever since the baby was born. It's what I want even now. But the child—"

"What are you saying?"

"You understand, don't you? I'm about to become the next President. I can't marry a woman who already has a one-year-old child. People are funny that way. They won't understand. They want perfection in their leaders. And there's another problem. Your views on the Fringe are too unorthodox. Radical even. Dangerous."

The woman was crying. "Why? Because I believe it's time to end a century and a half of abuse and exploitation?"

"The Wall is there for a reason."

"The system of your forefathers is unstable. It can't last. The day of reckoning is coming. We have to reach out to the Fringe. There's a way to share our prosperity with them. Make them part of it."

"Impossible. They're animals."

"They're people." The woman was pleading. "They deserve better."

"For your sake, I hope my father isn't listening." The man's voice began a steady crescendo until he was yelling. "What you're proposing, tearing down the Wall, providing equal education, opening our city to them—it's blasphemy. We must never talk of it again."

"But you agreed before. You said it's what attracted you to me."

The man lowered his voice. "When I first met you, you were different from the other women in the Sanctuary. You had ideals. And I was different, too. Young. A romantic. I could afford to stray, to be adventuresome and impractical."

"What changed?"

"Life changed!" The man was yelling again. "Don't you see? I'm going to inherit everything. I'm going to be master of it all."

"But you won't be happy."

"Who cares about happiness when you own the Sanctuary?"

"I don't think I know you anymore."

"Look, my dear, I've been more than patient. I tried to see your point of view. I even discussed it with my father. He threatened to disinherit me if I ever mentioned it again. There's a way my family does its business, and it's worked for generations. The changes you're proposing are impossible. They'd destabilize the system. It can't be done."

"So you're just going to forget about me?"

"No, that's the point." The man's voice was tender now. "I want to marry you. I love you. I've always loved you. All you have to do is forget about the Fringe. And the child. We've kept her a secret this long. It's time for her to go."

"Go where?"

"We have to bury her memory."

"You're going to kill her?"

"No, of course not. We have to put her where no one will ever think to look. Where no one will ever find her."

"What are you saying?"

"I want you to drop her off in the Fringe." The man was trying to sound reasonable. "Other people have done it. It's easy. I hear it happens all the time. Just leave her outside the Wall. Someone in the Fringe will come along and take her. She'll have a family, of sorts."

"Of sorts?" The woman sobbed. "How can you even talk like that? She's your daughter. Your own flesh and blood."

"Some things are more important than flesh and blood. I want you to become my wife. But I also want the Sanctuary. Getting rid of the child is the only way."

"I can't."

"You must."

"And if I don't?"

"Then you'll leave me with no choice. If people find out about you and the child, it'll be a disaster. It could destroy my future. I can't allow that. That's why I need you to get rid of her."

"Is that a threat?"

"It's a statement of fact." The man's voice came closer. "Let me help you."

"Get away from me!"

The voices descended into a storm of yelling. The woman grabbed Alix and started running. The man's footsteps were not far behind, dissolving in the darkness.

Two pairs of footsteps approached, a man's and a woman's. Alix couldn't tell if this was a dream or reality.

"Why isn't she moving?" the woman said, terror in her voice. "You said she'd be OK."

"Temporary paralysis of the nervous system." The man came closer, making mechanical sounds as he moved. "She won't be able to use her muscles until the shock wears off."

"Are you sure she's got a pulse?" The woman knelt, her warm breath on Alix's cheek. "How much longer before she wakes up?"

A soft hand came down onto Alix's forehead. It triggered a memory. The names of the woman and man came back to her. Muse. Merf. Even though her eyes were shut, Alix could sense their movements.

"Like I said, she's already awake. Heart's beating fine. Probably listening to us right now. Just takes a while for it all to reboot."

"She's not a robot, Merf."

"The human body's an electrical system like any mechanical device, just a thousand magnitudes more complex."

"You promised no brain damage."

"There shouldn't be any permanent damage, but who knows what the energy burst may have temporarily triggered inside her head."

"I don't like the sound of that, Merf."

"Don't worry. That nano-shirt I gave her is made of copper-carbon alloy particles to resonate at precisely the right frequency to dampen the energy of the pulse projectile. Besides, brains are tough, and hers is tougher than most."

"We should've told her about the shirt," Muse whispered. "She thought she was going to die. When she wakes up, she's going to be furious with me. And you."

"You know as well as I do that we couldn't tell her. That would have made it impossible for her to play her part. You saw how great the video turned out. The Sanctuary is going crazy."

"I hate it when you talk like that, Merf. Alix isn't a toy, and this isn't a marketing campaign. She's a human being with feelings and emotions." Muse gently ran her fingers through Alix's hair. "Never forget that."

"Sorry, Muse. Sometimes I'm hard on her, but I know how the Sanctuary works. Visual images get their attention. The more intense, the better. Besides, Alix probably won't remember a thing when she wakes up."

"I hope for our sakes that you're right, Merf."

Alix wanted to shout, to tell them she was already awake and remembered it all, Link lifting the gun, pointing it. An explosion of colors inside her head. The fade to black. The voice dream.

"Come on," Merf said. "Let's get her home."

27

Link ran.

Thousands of Fringe freaks chased behind.

He should have been able to outrun them. Cornboo was engineered to keep people alive, not make them fit and healthy. Link had spent his life in a world of light and color and smooth, flat surfaces, but now it was like he was on a foreign planet. The Fringies were good at moving quickly in the dark over broken ground while he stumbled and fell on the pock-marked dirt.

As bad as it was, there was an even more pressing problem. How could Link get to a place where the heli-ship could pick him up without his jax for communication and tracking? Wilson was overhead, doing his best to track Link with a spotlight. But that made it easy for the Fringe freaks to track him too.

Link ran across the open field, dodging scattered carts on wheels that must have been used to transport bartered items. To his right, a dozen men poured out of an opening in the ground to cut him off. Link knew that Fringe folks used a network of underground tunnels from an old subway line to get around, but he hadn't expected them to be shortcuts for intercepting him.

Breaking to the left, Link sprinted in the opposite direction into a narrow alleyway. Above him, the remains of an old, steel structure stretched 20 stories high. In the darkness of the alley, he ran past open windows, toxic puddles and the stench of an open sewer. Suddenly, his foot landed atop a stray brick. He twisted and slammed his head into a wall. Nausea and dizziness overtook him. After sliding down, he sat on the ground to catch his breath.

The front line of the mob had already rushed into one end of the alley behind him. He heard voices and footsteps from the other end, too.

That's when he realized what was happening: he was being herded like a wild animal into a trap, just like Wilson had tried to do to Alix back when she was riding on her chopper.

There was only one way out.

Straight up.

Still nauseous, he pulled himself to his feet, reached for a handhold and began to climb the corroded structure. Surely, he thought, the people of the Fringe didn't have climbing walls for practice and wouldn't follow him on a free solo up the exposed steel beams.

But he was wrong.

By the time he made it to the sixth level, dozens of the younger ones were coming after him. They looked like they'd climbed this building before.

As the mob converged on the old steel structure, Wilson flew in close with the heli-ship, hovering just 10 meters away, with his lights sweeping over the other climbers and the rescue hook dangling off a cable. The air itself vibrated with the *thump, thump, thump* of the great rotors. It was hard to breathe.

Whether from terror or exhaustion, most of Link's pursuers were falling behind.

As Link reached up for another handhold, the beam he stood on fell away into the darkness below, taking one of the climbers with it. Link dangled in the air by one hand, and his head felt like it might explode. Ignoring the pain, he reached up with the other hand, found a grip and pulled himself to his elbows and then to his knees. Finally finding a standing position on a solid surface, he looked out over the Fringe for a moment's rest.

A hand grabbed his ankle.

Link looked down to see a young man below him. When their eyes met, Link recognized him from the crowd that had gathered around Link near the Wall. He shook his foot and knocked the hand off. Gathering his strength, he forced himself to climb higher.

For the next five minutes, the young man chased Link as he climbed skyward through the jungle of corroded steel, staying close enough to grab Link. It was almost like the young man was steering Link to the top. The last three floors were the hardest. Link found himself holding his breath, only taking in gulps of caustic air in short gasps. His hands were raw and bleeding. He didn't have the strength to fight the kid chasing him.

Just before Link pulled himself up to a sheet of steel atop the structure, the young man grabbed Link's ankle again. This time, he didn't have the strength to resist. His fingers slipped.

And then the young man pushed Link, boosting him up onto the platform. As Link rested on all fours trying to get his breath, the young man crawled up beside him and rested on his back, chest heaving.

A dozen other men were climbing up fast, shouting and waving their arms.

"I don't want to fight. I can help you get away." The young man spoke between gasps. "Take me with you."

"Who are you?"

"Doesn't matter. Just take me with you."

Link looked at the others below him. They would make it up to the platform in half a minute. An image of Alix flashed in his mind, the look on her face just before he shot her. The nausea rose in his belly.

Why did he do it?

It was too late for that. He couldn't help her, but he could help this kid from the Fringe that had followed him up.

"Alright." Link pulled in a deep breath, only to choke and cough out the acrid air. No wonder he was exhausted. The air was killing him. He could hardly breathe.

"Air's bad tonight," the young man said. "Always happens after the chemplant gets a full shipment of tox. Guess we're used to it."

The heli-ship floated down to a position five meters above them. Link could see Wilson's face through the cockpit glass, and he looked confused. Lifting two fingers, Link signaled that the kid was coming with them. Wilson nodded and lowered another cable.

In the few seconds remaining, Link looked out over the Fringe and saw three of the big, silver cubes, the closest one a couple of klicks away, shining in the moonlight.

Link grabbed a cable and wrapped it around his waist. The young man did the same with the other cable. They both rose in the air seconds before an army of hands reached the platform. The ship reeled them in, and they stepped into the cargo unit. The door slid shut behind them.

"Sit down, kid." Link pointed to a corner. "And don't touch anything."

The young man nodded and crouched on the floor.

Link went to the cockpit and dropped into a seat beside Wilson. "Thanks for coming."

"What's with the kid?"

"He helped me get away. Couldn't just leave him."

"You know the rules, boss." Wilson turned the ship back toward the Wall. "Fringe freaks stay in the Fringe."

"Forget about the rules."

Wilson raised an eyebrow. "Doesn't sound like you, boss. What happened down there?"

"It was crazy."

"That's the Fringe for you." Wilson motioned down at the ruins of old buildings, crooked streets and miles of wasteland and shacks. "Closest thing to hell on earth, especially at night. Not a proper place for Sanctuary folks. Quinn is right. The Fringe scum get what they deserve."

After what Link had seen, the words jarred him to the core. Raising his hand to protest, he saw the surprise in Wilson's eyes. Something had shifted in Link's mind while he'd been down in the Fringe. He'd come and seen it, and it had changed him.

Exactly as Alix had predicted.

He saw her eyes again in his mind, pleading for him to understand. This time, he didn't try to push the image away.

"Boss?" Wilson said.

"We're taking the long way home, Wilson." Link pointed back toward the heart of the Fringe. "There's something I need to see. Let me have the controls."

Wilson raised his hands from the stick and stood up to move to the side. "She's all yours, boss."

They swapped seats.

"By the way, how are things back in the Sanctuary?" Link asked.

"Those two videos—you killing the girl and the soldiers killing Licious—have got people riled up. More people are out on the streets than usual. Talking, yelling." Wilson shook his head. "Never seen anything like it. The mood in the air is different."

Link yelled back into the cargo area. "Hey kid? You still back there? Come up here for a minute."

Wilson looked startled.

"Don't worry," Link whispered, "just need some confirmation." He glanced back at the young man making his way to the cockpit from the cargo area.

"Hey kid, got a name?" Link asked.

"They call me Zeke."

Link nodded. "OK, Zeke. I'm Link, and this is Wilson."

"How old are you, Zeke?"

"Sixteen."

Zeke looked small for his age. And he had the same light green pallor that marked all the Fringies.

"Come closer and stand here between us."

Zeke complied without a word. His eyes grew wide. "Is that—"

"Yep, sure is." Link pointed down. "A bird's eye view of the Fringe. You know where we are?"

"Let's see." Zeke gazed all around the bubble glass of the cockpit. "It looks different from up here."

They hovered above one of the massive silver cubes and pointed the ship's light down, illuminating masses of people trudging in one side and out the other. "What's that?"

"You serious?" Zeke gave Link a look of disbelief. "Everybody knows that's one of the brain labs."

"One?" Link flashed a glance at Wilson in the co-pilot's seat. "How many are there?"

"Not really sure. A few dozen, maybe. They just built a new one last month." Zeke gazed around the cockpit as if looking for a lost item. "You guys got any food here? I haven't eaten for a couple of days."

In the harsh light of the cockpit, Link noticed Zeke's protruding cheekbones and shoulders.

"Sure, kid." Wilson pulled a handle on the ceiling, opening a compartment. He reached in and produced a regulation Patrol energy bar. "Try this. There's more if you're still hungry."

Zeke stared down at the rectangular bar in clear plastic wrapping. "It's not—" His voice trailed off.

"Cornboo?" Link grinned as he watched Zeke's reaction. "Nope. But you'll like it."

Tentatively pulling back the wrapping, Zeke took a small bite, chewed and closed his eyes in obvious delight. Three more big bites, and the bar was gone.

"Can I have another?" Zeke asked.

Wilson handed one to him. "Here you go, kid."

This time, Zeke tried to stick the whole bar in his mouth, failed and had to settle for wolfing it down in two big bites. "Another, please."

Wilson looked at Link.

"Can't you see, Wilson? The kid's starving. Let him eat." Link hovered above the silver cube. "So, you work in the brain labs?"

Zeke now had a fist full of energy bars, and his mouth was full. He swallowed hard. "Yeah, I mean, it's what we're born to do, right? It's why they give us cornboo."

"You getting this, Wilson?" Link said. "A random kid in the Fringe confirmed that they have brain labs, and he works in one."

"I'm listening," Wilson said, "but I don't want to believe it."

"OK, Zeke," Link said. "What about the chemplant you were telling me about? Can you show me one of those?"

Zeke dropped another wrapper on the floor. "You sure you want to go there? Like I told you, they just got a new shipment of tox. Air's not good."

"Yep," Link said. "Which way is it? We need proof."

"Just fly to that hill over there with the open pit on top."

They shot through the air above the rotting corpses of old buildings, with roofs and sides ripped open by the bomb attacks of the last century. Low structures built from random junk littered the open spaces. To Link's eyes, it looked like a war zone frozen in time.

As they neared the open pit, the water lit up like mercury in the moonlight.

"Wilson, run a standard air analysis, will you?" Link had already engaged the underbelly cameras.

"Will do, boss." Wilson flipped a switch on the ceiling. A row of green indicators lit up, slowly changing to yellow and orange the closer they got to the pit. "You getting this, boss?"

"Just keep the data coming," Link said. "I'm dropping down."

Five meters above the open pit, all the indicators turned crimson. Warning sirens went off inside the cockpit.

"The airspace is swimming with carcinogens," Wilson said.

"Bad tox here." Zeke pushed the last energy bar into his mouth.

With the ship floodlights on high, Link pointed them straight down into the pit but couldn't penetrate more than a few centimeters. "Can you get a read on what's in the pool, Wilson?"

"Have to take a sample." Wilson touched the right wall of the cockpit, activating a probe. "We'll need to drop lower, boss."

Zeke was getting nervous. "That ain't water."

Carefully gripping the joystick, Link descended until the ship was skimming just one meter above the pool. It resembled a lake of blue sludge. "Quick, Wilson. Get your sample."

"Inserting the probe now." Wilson looked through the glass floor as a rod penetrated the pool's surface.

"What kind of readings you getting?"

"The probe's gone, dissolved by the toxic soup. Must be full of industrial acid. Before I lost it, I was reading high levels of lead, cadmium, mercury, hexavalent chromium and polyvinyl chloride. All the stuff used to make a jax."

Climbing higher now, Link took in the view. At the base of the hill below the pit, low structures clung to the ground.

"Why do they build houses here?" Link asked.

"People gotta work somewhere." Zeke pointed out the cockpit. "The chemplant is just over there."

Link flew the ship to the other side of the hill to have a look. Like a mass of snakes, a structure of interwoven pipes and conduits curved around and through a rectangular building. Here and there, black smoke rose from circular vents. A line of hundreds of workers moved into the building in a steady stream at the far end. On the opposite side, just below them, work-ers stumbled out through an exit into the night.

"They can only work for a couple of hours before they got to quit." Zeke pointed down. "Any longer and they'll die."

"Air is much worse here. Lethal doses of a dozen toxins." Wilson stared into a small holoscreen, pouring over data.

"Why would anyone work here?" Link asked.

"That's easy. Some people aren't brain lab-compatible. You got to work somewhere if you want to eat. Plus, it's only a two-hour shift and double the cornboo." Zeke scanned the cockpit. "You got anything else to eat in here?"

"You've had enough Zeke. Don't want you to get sick." Link pointed back to the cargo compartment. "Better grab a water bottle off the wall and drink it down. You just ate a month's worth of protein."

Zeke rubbed his stomach. "I'm feeling funny." He stumbled into the darkness of the cargo bay. A few seconds later they heard him retching.

"Think the kid'll be OK, boss?"

"He'll be fine. Just has to get used to the new food."

"Can I ask a question, boss?"

"Sure, Wilson. What's on your mind?"

"Why are we doing this?" Wilson sat back in his seat. "I mean, we're part of the Patrol, right? We fight battles and protect the Sanctuary. Why are we doing an environmental survey?"

"Just a little verification, Wilson."

"Verification of what?"

"The truth," Link said.

The com unit crackled with a brusque voice. "This is Gibson at home base. Wilson, you there?"

Wilson turned to the com. "Right here, Gibs. What's on your mind?"

"What you doing with a ship in the Fringe? I don't see any orders."

"I got verbal orders from Commander Wells himself," Wilson said. "Just picked him off a rooftop."

"With all due respect to the boss, we need you back here immediately."

"What's going on, Gibs?"

"All hell's broken loose, Wilson. Looks like the end of the world."

28

Alix tried to remember the dream, but it was fuzzy and getting fuzzier by the second. The inside of her head felt like a bowl of fermented cornboo. Mushy, chunky and a bit bubbly.

She raised herself from the bed on one elbow. "I could have sworn Link shot me point-blank with his pulse pistol. Why am I still alive?"

"Nothing to complain about." Merf rocked back and forth on his heels, arms folded across his chest. "We knew you'd pull through."

"I guess that new shirt wasn't just a nice gift from your friend in the Sanctuary. You set up the whole thing."

"I wanted to tell you about the shirt." Muse cast an accusing glare at Merf. "But Merf decided it would be best not to. Now, I'm not so sure."

Merf stared at the floor. "Look, try to understand what I'm saying. I knew Link was coming here to kill you. Those were Quinn's orders. And Link had to film it as proof. If I'd told you that the shirt would protect you, you'd have looked like you were pretending. The video would have been useless."

"Of course." Alix felt the rising urge to retch and reached for a bowl. "I mean, I'm just an actor in your revolution movie, right? Best to just shut up and play the part."

"You know that's not true," Merf said. "I don't want you to get hurt, but there are some risks we have to take."

"We? What if Link had shot me in the head, Merf? The shirt wouldn't have done much good."

"He wouldn't."

"Why not?"

"Because he loves you," Merf said.

Alix dropped the bowl on the floor. "What do you mean?"

"It's true," Muse said. "I could see it in his eyes. The way he acted. Trying so hard to put you out of his mind."

"Then why'd he shoot me?"

"Love is complicated." Muse sat on the edge of the bed and ran her fingers through Alix's hair. "He's conflicted. Caught between two worlds. He did what he thought he had to do. He's probably sick about it."

"He's sick about it? What about me?" Alix felt the nausea coming on again and made a quick grab for the bowl. "I'm the one who got my brains fried."

Merf wouldn't look up. "I know you don't like it, but try to understand. After years in the Mesh, I know how they think. It all has to be planned for maximum visual impact. And it's working, Alix. The Sanctuary is going crazy."

She couldn't hold it back any longer. The contents of her stomach spewed past the bowl and ended up on the floor—regurgitated cornboo, green and gooey. After vomiting that final load, she felt much better.

"OK. I get it." Alix cracked a smile. "You're smart, Merf. You know what you're doing. But sometimes I feel like a puppet. Just doing what I'm told."

"I raised you to think for yourself. To be a leader." Muse gently wiped Alix's mouth with a clean, white cloth. "And you've exceeded all my expectations. Try to trust Merf. I will, too."

Alix sat up in the bed, her feet on the floor, finally able to open her eyes.

"How do you feel?" Muse asked.

"Like an overcharged jax."

"And it's no wonder." Merf slowly paced across the room. "Your body absorbed a full pulse pack. All the shirt did was diffuse it so that it wouldn't kill you."

"I think it played with my brain."

"What happened, dear?" Muse leaned forward with a sudden look of concern.

"I heard stuff. Saw stuff. A bunch of jumbled images and sounds. Some kind of dream."

"Or, maybe, old memories." Merf was pacing harder, nervous as ever. "The energy can play with your brain that way."

Alix tried to remember. "There was a man and a woman. He was angry. She was scared. Lots of yelling. And they were talking about a child." A bitter taste filled her mouth, so she swallowed. "I got the idea they were talking about me."

"Don't waste too much time worrying about it. Excess electrical energy in the brain does crazy things." Merf's gaze lingered on Muse, and then he looked away.

"I don't know. It seemed important. Like it was my real mom and dad, back in the Sanctuary." Alix closed her eyes, trying to recall the images. But nothing materialized. She looked at Muse. "Tell me again what happened when you found me at the Wall, Muse."

"I've told you everything." Muse opened her lips, and out came that gentle laugh.

"I know, but I want to hear it again."

Muse telling the story of finding Alix was a ritual that had been repeated over and over, ever since Alix could remember. Muse always told it the same way. Alix always asked the same questions in the same order and got the same answers. It was strangely comforting, and right now Alix needed comfort.

Muse settled on the edge of the bed and folded her hands in her lap. "You were lying in the dirt on the Fringe side of the Wall, screaming. Making a terrible racket. It was early morning, just as the shift was changing at the brain lab. It was obvious you were from the Sanctuary. Fringe babies don't cry like that. They're used to being hungry all the time. And you didn't have a green tinge to your skin. People had gathered to stare at you, not sure what to think." Muse paused here waiting for the question.

"What was I wearing?"

"An exquisite carbon-platinum weave jumpsuit." Muse pointed. "I still have it hanging in the closet."

"Why did you take me?"

"You know the answer. When I got close and looked at you, you stopped crying and lifted your arms to me." Muse got that look in her eye, like maybe she was going to cry. "Any one of the strangers would gladly have taken you, but you chose me. I couldn't ignore you."

"So you took me home?"

"Yes, to this very house, brand new back then."

Alix was getting comfortable and sleepy. All she wanted was to curl up in a ball and listen to Muse's soft voice. "So what happened when you took me home?"

"I'll tell you what happened. You and Muse lived happily ever after. The end." Merf walked across the room to look at the faint morning light entering the window. "I hate to cut things short, but we have to prepare for our next move."

Alix just wanted to sleep. "Next move?"

"Look at this." Merf placed his jax on the table. A full-color holoscreen opened in the air above it. Elegant glass buildings outlined in smart neon lines formed the backdrop. Advertisements played on all the surfaces to form a montage of excess and luxury. That was normal for the Sanctuary. It was the streets that caught their eyes.

People were marching, moving together, arm in arm, blocking the roadways. Shouting. Screaming.

"Looks like that last video did the trick." Merf couldn't stop pacing, and the more he paced, the more excited he got.

"You mean the one where I got shot and killed?"

"Yeah." Merf spun around. "The one where you have the perfect look on your face because you really believe you're about to die."

"Merf, don't talk like that." Muse reached for Alix's hand.

"But he's right." Alix stared at the crowds storming the streets in the Sanctuary. "It's working. You're a genius, Merf. What's the next move?"

"That depends on your answer to my next question." Merf stopped, a sudden calmness overtaking him.

Muse looked up, eyebrows lifting.

"Well?" Alix stood. "What's the question."

"Do you want to see Lincoln Wells live or die?"

Alix narrowed her eyes. "What kind of a question is that?"

"You said you felt like I was doing all the planning. Well, now's your chance to start helping. And it all depends on whether Link lives or dies."

"What do you mean?" Alix was confused. "He's back in the Sanctuary. Safe and sound."

"What do you think will happen when Quinn finds out you're not really dead?"

Alix stumbled to the table, awake with sudden clarity. "No, Merf. You can't do that to him!"

"I guess that's your answer."

"What do you mean?"

"If you want him to live, there's only one way to save him. And *you* have to do it."

29

It was true.

The Sanctuary was a war zone. Link was dumbfounded as he watched the holoscreen in his penthouse.

Enraged Sanctuary dwellers had poured out of the residential towers to roam the streets. They were talking, chanting and marching, but the most amazing thing was that they were doing it *together*. Even a few windows had been broken.

No one had ever seen anything like it before, and the Patrol wasn't sure what to do.

Don't overreact. Let the people have their fun while they out themselves. Surveil everyone. Record their IDs. We'll arrest them later.

That was the order from Quinn. The Patrol stayed off the streets and put all their drones into the sky, taking video of the crowds and running it through facial recognition databases.

There was one additional order of a personal nature. Lincoln Wells was to stay in his quarters. The reasoning was simple. His face had been featured in the video of Alix Yamaguchi's murder now making the rounds on the Mesh. It was that video and the one killing Licious that had enflamed the masses. For the time being, it would be best for him to stay out of the public eye.

During his enforced leisure, Link had one consolation. Chelsea was there with him.

"Father's not punishing you," she said, standing at the window. "You did exactly what he told you to do. Like a good son. You're a hero. You stopped all the lies that were coming from that woman."

Link walked up behind Chelsea. "I shot her at point-blank range. She was staring at me when I pulled the trigger, tears running down her cheeks. Doesn't make me feel like much of a hero."

"Daddy can be hard on people, but he knows what's best for the Sanctuary. You did what he told you to do."

He put his hands on her shoulders. "Chelsea, do you believe it's important to know the truth? I mean, does it even matter?"

She spun around. "What are you talking about?"

In the early dawn light, her face was the very definition of beauty. Link stared at her for a while, taking it all in. Flawless skin, big eyes, chiseled cheekbones. Was it really possible that someday she'd be his wife? Before any of that could happen, he had to be able to talk to her. To confide in her. He'd been putting it off ever since he got back, but his insides were about to explode, and he couldn't keep it in any longer.

"Chelsea, I've got to show you something. But first, I want you to make me a promise."

She smiled, showing off two rows of neon white teeth. "My father always told me that promises are dangerous. But I think I can make an exception for you."

"I hope so." Link took Chelsea's hand and pulled her over to the stainless steel table with two glass chairs, one on each side. She dropped into one, and he took the other. His jax was the only object between them. "After Wilson picked me up in the Fringe, we flew around for a while, collecting data."

"Data? You mean, like a scientific expedition?" Chelsea put her elbows on the table and rested her chin in her hands. "What kind of data?"

Reaching with a finger, Link tapped the end of the jax. Its holoscreen opened up between them. "Promise me you won't tell your father about this."

Chelsea straightened her back. "What have you done, Link?"

"I just wanted to see for myself."

"See what?"

"See whether anything she told us was true or not."

"I don't understand."

"Alix Yamaguchi. Don't you remember? She said the Fringe freaks were forced to work in brain labs and toxic waste plants."

"So?"

"Do you think it's true?"

"All I know is that Daddy said—"

Link put his hand out to touch Chelsea's arm. "I know what President Quinn said. But I wanted to see for myself."

Chelsea pulled away. "You don't trust Daddy? I don't like where this is going."

Dropping his voice to a whisper, Link leaned in. "Promise me you won't tell your father what I'm about to show you."

"Link, you shouldn't—"

"Just promise me, Chelsea." Link stared into her moist eyes trying to see past them. "You and I, we need to know the truth. Someday, we'll be in charge. That's all I'm going to show you. The truth."

Slowly, she exhaled. "OK, Link. I promise."

Link touched the jax. The holoscreen between them jumped to life with video and sound.

They both looked down at an enormous building shaped like a silver cube. Crowds of people were walking in one side and out the other.

"What am I looking at?" Chelsea said.

"It's a brain lab." Link pointed at the crowds moving in both directions. "I walked past one of these and got a close look. They work a 12-hour shift every day and get paid with cornboo. The Fringe powers the Mesh, Chelsea. My jax, your jax, they all run on real human brains. Alix Yamaguchi wasn't lying."

"OK," Chelsea said, "but did you actually see inside the cube? Do you really know what they're doing?"

"No, but I saw what it's doing to them. They start them out as children. Over time, it takes a toll. By the time they hit 40, they can hardly walk anymore. The look in their eyes is just a blank stare. Their minds are destroyed, little by little." Link felt his pulse rising. "It's not right."

"What are you saying, Link?"

"I don't know, Chelsea. I just know what I saw, what's happening to the people in the Fringe. But there's more." Link ran his finger along the edge of the jax to advance to the next video. "We found this."

"It just looks like a big hole in the ground."

"That's right, and it's full of toxic waste. We took air samples and then dropped down to analyze the liquid waste itself. Take a look."

Data flowed onto the holoscreen. It didn't matter that Chelsea wasn't an expert. She was smart. She'd get the gist.

"Looks pretty bad."

"Did you see the houses next to the pit?" Link asked. "People live in those."

"Then they're stupid."

"Exactly what I thought, Chelsea. But keep watching the holo."

The video panned up the hill behind the pit and down the other side to the chemplant at the base where hundreds of workers were coming and going. Data streamed on the side of the holo, confirming the lethal toxins in the air.

"So, the overall air quality is best next to the pit, away from the side where the chemplant is. That's why the workers build there."

"OK, I get it," Chelsea said. "The air's bad."

"It's not just the air, Chelsea." Link tapped his jax, and the holoscreen shrunk to a dot and disappeared. "I spent a couple of hours walking alone through the Fringe. There are open pools of waste and caustic fumes everywhere. The ground is completely barren. Nothing grows there. No weeds. Nothing. It's like one big toxic dump." Link wrapped his fingers around his jax and squeezed it until his knuckles turned white. "So, that's the truth. What do you think?"

"I think you should delete it all, destroy that jax and get a new one."

"What?"

"Never mention a word of this to anyone. And pray that Daddy isn't listening to us right now."

"But Chelsea! You've seen the proof. I saw it with my own eyes. We have evidence."

Chelsea lowered her voice. "Let me see if I understand where this is going." She looked around as if checking to make sure no one was watching. "An unknown woman from the Fringe suddenly appeared. With a lot of savvy marketing gimmicks, she got the attention of just about everyone in the Sanctuary, including you. She told us about atrocities supposedly happening in the Fringe. And it turns out that maybe she was right. So far, so good?"

"Yeah, I think you have it right so far."

"One of the Sanctuary's beloved Mesh-celebs was murdered on live video because she tried to save this woman. And now there's another video of you going into the Fringe and killing her. People are pouring into the streets, full of righteous indignation, maybe even challenging the system." Chelsea paused to breathe.

"Exactly."

"Now to the most important part. My father isn't happy about the situation, to say the least. He values power, and anything that threatens that power threatens everything he and his family stand for. And we all know how vindictive he is when he feels threatened."

"Definitely true."

"By confirming the truth of what the woman said, you're placing yourself firmly in her camp." Chelsea stared at the floor. "That makes you the enemy. Do you think my father will just ignore you and do nothing?"

"So here's the ultimate question." Link took in a breath to clear his head. "Do we do what's right or what's easy?"

Chelsea stood and walked past the table, pulling Link with her to the window. "You've got to make a choice, Link. Right here. Right now. This isn't about right and wrong. This is about choosing a life of misery in the Fringe or life in the Sanctuary. With me." Her fingers found Link's arm and slid down his hand, wrapped in a tight fist around the jax.

"Tell me what to do, Chelsea."

Her fingers began to pry open Link's fist. "It's simple, Link. Give me the jax. I'll destroy it. Stay here until this all blows over. People will eventually forget and go back to their lives."

"But Chelsea. It's all true. Everything she said."

"She's dead, Link. You killed her, just like Daddy told you to. Now forget about it and just—"

The door to the penthouse burst open, and a woman walked in wearing a hoodie to hide her face. Link could tell at a glance she was from the Fringe.

The woman took in a deep breath. "You're going to die if you stay here, Link. If you want to live, you have to come with me to the Fringe." She pulled back her hood.

It was Alix Yamaguchi.

30

Resurrection

It had been easy for Alix to get into the Sanctuary. Now that she was officially dead, no one was looking for her. A little disguise to hide her face was all she needed.

Merf planned to upload video to the Mesh to prove that Alix was alive and well in the Fringe. Within seconds, he predicted, it would enflame the Sanctuary. President Quinn would be enraged and looking for someone to punish. Lincoln Wells would be at the top of the list.

Merf had given Alix the choice to save Link or let him die.

And she'd made her choice.

"Just curious, but why would you want to help the man who tried to kill you?" Merf had asked.

"It was the look in his eyes when he pulled the trigger," Alix had answered. "He didn't want to do it. Quinn was forcing him."

"He'd be a great asset to the Fringe if you could get him here and talk him into cooperating."

"I think I can get him here," Alix had answered. "But I don't know about the cooperation."

It hadn't been all that hard to find Link's apartment. Merf had penetrated the Patrol's Mesh node months ago, just hanging out, bypassing the encryption, learning their methods, tweaking their algorithms, all right under their noses. It had been easy to find Link's penthouse and give Alix the access codes to the building.

All she had to do was ride the elevator to his floor.

Just inside the door, she stared at Link. Chelsea was there too, with her perfect mouth hanging open.

More than anything, in the first few seconds, Alix had focused on Link, anxious to see his face when she popped the door open. Would he be furious? Would he try to kill her? His initial reaction would tell her everything.

To her surprise, he gave her an instantaneous smile, a look of deep relief, quickly followed by a glance at Chelsea and a straight face. Alix and Link stared at each other across the wood floor, wordless for half a minute.

"You should be dead," Chelsea finally said. "It was broadcast all over the Mesh. Link shot you with his pulse pistol."

"Believe me," Alix rejoined, "I'm more surprised than you are." She fingered her shirt. "You could say my friend Merf performed a resurrection. It turns out the energy of a pulse projectile can be diffused with cloth made of the right tech. I'm sure you know about it. So did Merf. He got me to wear this shirt without telling me what it was. It saved my life."

"This is—" Link's face was going white, as if he had just realized something horrible.

"A disaster," Chelsea chimed in. "If Daddy finds out—"

"It's not a question of *if*. It's a matter of *when*." Alix stepped forward. "That's why you have to come with me if you want to live."

"What are you saying?" Link asked.

Alix took a breath and waited for her adrenaline rush to die down. "Here's the deal. Merf's going to release video proof that I'm still alive in exactly five minutes. Oh, and that's not all. Merf had a look at the contents of your jax. He said you collected data in the Fringe that proves the existence of the brain labs and the chemplants. He's going to upload that, too. The whole Sanctuary will see it and understand I've been telling the truth. What do you think President Quinn will do when all of that goes live?"

Chelsea's face went pale. "He'll go ballistic!"

Link swallowed. "He's going to kill me."

"Exactly. That's why I came. There's just enough time to get to the Wall." Alix tried to slow down her words so Link would comprehend.

"Then what?" Link asked.

"We cross into the Fringe. You can hide there."

Chelsea was already shaking her head. "And then what happens?"

"I'll tell you what happens. Link won't be murdered by your father. He'll still be alive." Alix didn't try to hide her visceral dislike for Chelsea.

Grabbing Link's hand, Chelsea pulled him back. "I can talk to Daddy, Link. He loves me. You did what he asked you to do. You pointed the pistol and pulled the trigger. She should have died. But they tricked you. Everything she does is a trick. He'll understand."

"But Chelsea—"

"Link, listen to me. I know Daddy. If you run now, he'll never forgive you. He'll send the whole Patrol to kill you with drones and heli-ships. It'll be all-out war against the Fringe. Thousands will die. But if you stay, there won't be a war. Daddy will be merciful. He'll listen. He loves me." She turned to squarely face Alix.

"You overestimate your father." Alix tried to push back the rage rising inside her. "Mercy and love aren't part of his vocabulary. He'll murder Link within hours of that video going live. As for the Fringe, no need to worry. We can hold our own."

Chelsea ignored the comment and scanned the room as if searching for another way out. Running to Link's desk, she pulled open the drawer and removed a pulse pistol.

"Is this thing charged?" she asked.

"Always," Link answered.

Pointing the pistol squarely at Alix, Chelsea slowly walked back to Link. "There's still time, Link. Finish the job you started. Kill her. Again." She thrust the pistol into his hands.

Link hefted the weapon, spun it a couple of times and let it hang on his finger. For an instant, he pointed it at Alix as if considering the possibilities.

If I'm wrong, this is where it all ends, Alix thought. Her chest tightened. It was hard to breathe.

"What are you waiting for, Link?" Chelsea shook his arm. "She's the cause of all our problems. Daddy was right. There's too much at stake. The peace and prosperity of the Sanctuary. Just kill her, and the Sanctuary will go back to normal."

"Open your eyes, Chelsea. Everything I said about the Fringe is true." Alix let her hands hang limp at her sides. "We suffer and die so you and your father can be rich."

"I've seen the brain labs and the chemplants," Link said. "I've measured the toxins. I've seen what it does to the people that work there." He turned to Chelsea. "You saw it, too. You know she's telling the truth."

"Link, don't you understand?" Chelsea's voice was almost a scream. "The truth doesn't matter! The only thing that matters is—" She stopped.

"What, Chelsea? What's the only thing that matters?" Link held her close and stared into her eyes. "Tell me. Help me understand."

"My family. All that we've built up."

"Your family has built up money, rank and power. Is that what matters, Chelsea?"

A single tear floated down her cheek. "We have a glorious future waiting for us, Link."

"At what cost?" He cast a glance at Alix.

"If she gets her way, we'll lose it all." Chelsea looked out the window. "Are you going to let that happen?"

As Chelsea spoke, Link slowly let go of her with both hands and stepped back. He shook his head, the movement almost imperceptible.

"The Sanctuary's way of life is built on a lie. It's a system out of balance. It can't last." Alix raised a finger in Link's direction. "Come with me, Link. We can change the system."

Taking a step closer to Alix, Link kept his pistol pointing at her and paused. "What could I possibly do? I've talked to President Quinn. He has an iron grip on all of it, the Fringe and the Sanctuary, all the people and the whole economy, on both sides of the Wall. There's no way—"

"There's always a way," Alix said. "You just have to be brave enough to open your eyes to the truth."

"Don't lecture us, Fringe scum." Chelsea grabbed Link's arm. "Kill her!"

"There's no time, Link. That video of me, alive, will hit the Mesh in seconds. Do you really think Chelsea's dad will listen to her?"

With the pistol still in his hand, Link stood with Chelsea pulling at him, staring out the open door. And then, he closed his eyes.

His body stiffened, and he took another step away from Chelsea. "I'm sorry."

"Link! What are you doing?"

"I have to go." Turning, he calmly walked away.

Chelsea ran after him, trying to pull him back. "You're throwing everything away! Including me!"

"Chelsea," Link said. "She's right. Your father will kill me. The truth is, he doesn't care about me or you. Please try to understand. I have to go."

"Come with us, Chelsea," Alix said. "Once you see, you'll understand—"

"I don't want to understand!" Chelsea was crying now. She spun Link around, pulled his head down and stared into his eyes. "Don't do this to me, Link. Don't do this to the Sanctuary."

"Chelsea." Link drew her close. "Listen to me. I know this is hard, but you've got to open your eyes to the truth."

She beat her fists into Link's chest, shaking her head. "The Sanctuary is my truth! It's all I need! It's all I want!"

"Come on, Link." Alix backed into the open door. "There's not much time left."

Link stepped away from Chelsea, two lines of tears streaming down his face. "I'm sorry, but I have to go. I'll come back when I can." He walked through the door where Alix was standing, pulling her with him, and gently closed it behind them. Then he pressed his shoulder blades into the closed door and let out a long exhale. "How did you get here?" His voice was cold, demanding.

"The usual way. Walking." Alix rolled her eyes. Somehow, she'd expected a little more gratitude. "Through the Wall and up the street."

"We can't go back that way. The Patrol will be looking for me. How much time do we have before that video hits the Mesh?"

Alix consulted an old jax that Merf had given her. "Ninety seconds."

"Can you push it back?"

"No," Alix said. "It's already uploaded for automatic execution."

"I don't believe it," Link said, softly cursing under his breath. "You just ruined my life."

"I'm sorry about your life, but Merf forced me to make a choice."

"What choice?"

"Save you or let you die." Alix fought back the urge to punch Link in the solar plexus and leave him in the hall. "Forgive me for wanting to help you live another day."

"OK, look. I'm sorry." Link's gazed at the floor. "I tried to kill you. You don't owe me anything. You risked a lot to come after me. I should be grateful. It's just that—"

"I forced you to make a choice."

"Yeah, I guess so." He looked back at the door.

"It happens to all of us, sooner or later. But hey, if you don't want to come with me—" She turned to leave.

"No, I'm coming. Let's go. Up to the roof. Try to keep up." Link sprinted down the hall and into the open elevator.

They stood together in silence on the trip up. Alix could hear Link breathing. Her hand brushed his and he pulled away. When the door opened, he rushed out. "Come on," he said.

He stopped in front of a metal door, placed his palm on it and stepped back as it opened.

"What's your plan?" Alix asked.

"I've got a mini-copter." He jumped through the opening onto the roof. "It's old school, but it'll have to do."

Following him outside, Alix thought of Licious and wondered if everyone in the Fringe had their own personal air transport. When she stepped onto the roof, she pulled in a lungful of clean air and savored it. As high as they were, the Wall still towered over them. The image of a pristine mountain meadow played on its surface. In every direction, the striking beauty and form of Sanctuary architecture begged her to stare.

Link grabbed Alix's arm and pulled her to a corner where he ripped the green plastic cover off the mini-copter. It looked to be constructed of glass, and she peered inside the cockpit. "It's only got one seat."

"It'll be tight, but don't worry, the copter can get us over the Wall." He opened the side door and jumped in, moving to the far side of the seat. "Come on!"

After a moment's hesitation, Alix bent through the opening and parked herself on the seat, her shoulders just brushing Link's. Half her body was still hanging out the other side.

"We can't fly until the door shuts," Link said. Without asking permission, he wrapped his arm around her and pulled her tight against him. Then, he reached for the door and slammed it shut. His skin felt hot against hers. It was hard to breathe.

"Less than a minute," Alix said. She twisted and glanced at the open door they'd come through onto the roof. Chelsea stood inside, staring at them, arms at her side, a look of stony silence on her face.

"She doesn't look happy."

"Can't blame her." Link flipped a switch, and the rotors started turning, two on each side. He grabbed the stick between them and pulled it back. The mini-copter jumped up on a diagonal trajectory. Alix could see the street through the floor. It had been crammed with people when she'd snuck through the Wall, and crowds still thronged the open spaces between buildings.

The com system crackled.

"Hey, boss. Wilson here. Your mini just appeared on our scanner. And it looks like, maybe, you're in it. Mind telling me what's going on?" Link's finger hung over a red button, as if he were contemplating ending the conversation. He tapped the green one instead.

"Wilson. I thought you were off work today. Resting at home."

"I'm home, boss. But I got a call from Patrol HQ. They'd like me to ask where you're going?"

"Just out for a joyride, Wilson. Another beautiful day in the Sanctuary." There was silence on the other end.

"But boss, you know as well as I do that you're supposed to stay in your penthouse. For your own protection. Quinn's orders. What are you doing in the air?"

"Long story, Wilson." Link cast a glance at Alix. "I'll tell you later."

Time was up. The announcement was going to hit the Mesh any second.

"Scanners indicate you're not alone, boss. Which is strange. I've flown in your mini. It's only built to carry one—" There was confusion on the other end, as if another person was talking to Wilson. Then silence. "Boss, Chelsea just called me, screaming. I think she said you've got Alix Yamaguchi with you. Now, we all saw the video of you killing her last night. Would you mind telling me what's going on?"

"Like I said, Wilson, it's a very long story."

Without warning, a holoscreen popped open in the air above the com unit. As Alix stared down at the crowds in the street, she noticed something peculiar. As if on cue, all the marching stopped, and the people stared into the screens above their jaxes.

"Here it comes," Alix said. She was watching Merf's video for the first time, just like everyone else.

Link slowed the copter and let it hover.

The video opened with a clip of Alix staring into the lens as a pulse projectile exploded in slow motion against her chest, dropping her to the ground. Then it cut to a picture of her lying on her own bed, eyes half shut, clearly trying to wake up. And then, she was awake, sitting on her bed. Finally, Alix was walking in the Fringe toward the Wall, holding a jax for all to see. The holoscreen above her jax showed the time and was playing an announcement that had gone out over the Mesh an hour earlier. The announcer said everyone was required to immediately vacate the streets so that calm could be restored to the Sanctuary. The clip then jumped to a close-up of Alix's face.

"Hey, Quinn. I heard you thought I was dead, but I'm more alive than ever and on my way to the Sanctuary to pick up a friend. Turns out the people are tired of your perfect system. It's coming to an end." Her image hung on the screen as the shot faded.

Far below, the throngs stood still, as if frozen in time.

"Not what I would call subtle," Link said. "But you're right. Quinn is going to try to kill me for sure now."

Alix couldn't hold back a smile. "Merf's a genius."

But the video didn't stop there. It showed footage taken by Link from high in the air over the Fringe, complete with images of the brain labs and the chemplants for all to see.

Suddenly unfrozen, the crowds moved again, but this time not in neat marching lines. It was a scene of total chaos, people running in all directions. Alix heard shots far below and saw Patrol forces in battle armor sweeping the streets. Here and there, fallen bodies littered the ground.

"Quinn has started his move," Link said. "As much as I'd like to stick around, we better make a run for it. Hold on." He thrust the stick forward, and the copter jumped up and away, toward the closest section of the Wall.

The com buzzed again with Wilson's voice. "Boss, I never thought I'd find myself saying this, but it was good working with you."

"Let me guess, Wilson." Link gripped the stick with white knuckles. "You just got orders from Quinn to shoot me down."

"I'm sorry, boss. I'll miss you."

"Take care, Wilson. You're a good soldier."

A black dot with legs appeared off to the left.

"Killer drones," Link muttered as he thrust the stick to the right, jamming it into Alix's knee. "Sorry."

"You don't have an onboard anti-targeting system?" she asked.

"I'm not as rich as Licious. She was an 8Z. Could afford the latest tech. But we're not dead yet. I know how the targeting algorithm works." Link scanned from side to side. "Keep an eye out. There'll be more drones."

An explosion lit up 30 meters to the right. The shockwave blasted them in somersaults in the opposite direction. Link did his best to stabilize the copter and move closer to the Wall in a zigzag pattern.

"It's only a klick away," Alix said. "What are our chances?"

"You want the truth? Just better than zero." Link took in the view as he glanced from side to side. "Now would be a good time for your genius friend to jam the drones."

"I'm sure he's trying."

One by one, 10 more killer drones swarmed the skies. Shots almost reached the copter. Alix braced herself for a direct hit. Link dropped into a power dive between two buildings.

"Only half a klick to the Wall," Link said.

A flash of light bloomed behind them. The door shattered and fell away. The two rotors on the right broke apart and disintegrated. The two on the left fizzled and stopped spinning. Alix felt herself slipping out.

"Hold on!" Link yelled.

He put both arms around him, pulling her close, as the copter went into free fall.

31

Chopper

O n the way down, Link felt Alix's warm body float next to him. For an instant, as the wind blew in through the open door and the windows of a building rushed by, he was at peace for the first time in his life.

Maybe we'll die now, Link thought. *That's OK.*

But why not try to live? With one finger on the stick, he reached up and hit the reset button. The rotors on the left sputtered and began to spin with a sudden surge of power, slowing the copter's fall. They were still going too fast to hit the street and survive. Link searched for a better option. A rooftop came into view below him. It had a blue pool in the middle. He thrust the stick to the right, hoping the copter would respond.

The angle of descent changed.

"Brace yourself," Link said. "We're coming in hot." He wrapped his arms around Alix and pulled her close until their foreheads touched.

He never saw the glass roof over the pool. It shattered as they broke through and hit the water. Luckily, the pool was deep, and the copter was made for hard landings. The force of the impact was absorbed by the sides as the copter buckled and shattered under water.

Link must have blacked out.

When he opened his eyes, he was soaking wet on the side of the pool, amid shards of glass. Alix stared down at him.

"Drones?" he asked.

"They're gone," Alix said. "Merf must have knocked them down. How do you feel?"

"My ears are ringing." He touched his head, and his hand came away with a smear of blood. His arms and legs all moved. "Looks like no broken bones."

"Can you walk?"

"Let's see."

Alix pulled him to a kneeling position and then up to standing. He saw the cut on her arm. "I'm OK. What about you?"

"Don't worry about me. I've had worse."

Link felt for the last place he'd put the pulse pistol and found it still strapped to his thigh. He scanned the roof to get his bearings. They were on the top of a luxury condo development 10 stories above street level.

"I know this neighborhood. The Wall isn't far." Link's legs were shaking, and he leaned on Alix's shoulder for support. "Tell me the truth. Why did you come for me after I tried to kill you? You could have just stayed in the Fringe and let me—"

"Die?"

"It's what I would have done in your shoes." Link walked to the edge of the roof and saw people running in the streets. "But you're different from anyone I've ever met. So tell me. Why did you come—"

A high-pitched howl pierced the air. Five meters away, a hole opened in the roof. He knew the sound. It was a pulse cannon, which could only mean one thing. Scanning the air above him, he found the attack ship hanging in the sky like an enormous bumble bee. Below on the street, Patrol troops in black battle armor were converging on the building. With instant concentration, he ran to Alix, grabbed her hand and sprinted for an open door.

"Quick!" he screamed. "They've found our position."

Pulse rounds perforated the roof just a meter to the side, like a dotted line. As they jumped through the door, it exploded behind them. The reality of their situation dawned on Link. Patrol forces were moving quickly to cut off all escape routes. Soldiers were in the air and on the street. The building was surrounded. More drones were surely coming.

"What now?" Alix asked as they ran down a hallway deeper into the building.

"They're expecting us to make a run for the Wall, so—"

"We have to do the opposite," Alix said. "Run away from it."

"Just what I was thinking." Link scanned up and down the hallway. "Once they have this building sealed off, they'll do a systematic search of every floor, every room." He thought about the network of sky tubes that connected most of the structures in the Sanctuary so that you could get from one end to the other without going outside. Maybe they still had a chance. "This way!"

"Where to?" Alix asked.

"The bridge." Link ran past the elevator to the stairwell. "We have to make it before they cut it off." Still a bit woozy from the crash, he was holding the railing and taking the stairs three at a time. "It should be on the fifth level. Three more floors to go."

Just before they popped out of the stairwell, Alix grabbed Link from behind.

"Stop!" she said.

Link twisted to look back. Her jax, an ancient model at least three years old, was glowing red. A small holoscreen floated above it.

"What's going on?" he asked, out of breath.

"It's Merf." She pulled Link back into the stairwell. "He's inside the security system with a tracer on all Patrol personnel."

"That's impossible," Link countered. "It's secure. Someone from the Fringe wouldn't be able to—"

"Merf's not just someone from the Fringe." Alix showed him the holoscreen. "He has our location and says the Patrol is already on the bridge. We can't go that way."

"Are you sure?"

Alix pulled Link close enough that he could smell her cornboo breath. "Merf knows his stuff. We have to trust him."

Images of the broken man with the awkward exoskeleton reentered Link's mind. Merf had brought Link's ship down with primitive tech, and Link had formed an instant dislike for him. Besides, Link was part of the Patrol and knew better than anyone from the Fringe how they worked.

"Look, with all due respect, I don't think—"

Alix put her hand on Link's lips. "This isn't the time or place to argue. Follow me. Merf knows someone in this building. They might help us." Turning, Alix ran back up the stairwell.

"Where you going?"

"Just follow me if you want to live." Alix bounded up and away.

Link felt a wave of nausea and reached for the rail, while trying to make sense of their situation. Every time he interacted with Alix, she found a way to throw him off guard and push him around.

Not this time. If she wanted to get killed, that was her right. Link was the one who knew his way around the Sanctuary, not her.

Running back to the exit, he found the door and pushed it open. The sky tube entrance was 10 meters to the left. The usual crowd of people were coming and going, eyes on their jaxes, oblivious to the world. It would be easy to just slip—

And that's when he saw the pair of Patrol personnel moving across the bridge. As quietly as he could, he stepped back into the stairwell and bounded up to the stairs after Alix.

He found her waiting just inside the door to the eighth floor, arms folded.

"You look pale," she said. "Merf was right, wasn't he?"

Link nodded. "Two of them were coming across the bridge. You said Merf has a friend in this building?"

"A contact."

"Can we trust this contact?"

Alix glanced at her jax. "Merf's pretty sure we can."

"Pretty sure?"

"Look, Merf has contacts all over the Sanctuary. They send him tech and information. He thinks we'll be safe, but he wants us to be careful."

"I don't know about this."

"What other choice do we have?" Alix pushed the door open. "It's number 808, just down the hall."

"I'm right behind you." Link followed as Alix sprinted away. Just as they turned the corner, he heard voices and the sound of carbon boots making contact with the floor. From the look on Alix's face, she'd heard it, too. Patrol field soldiers were already searching the building.

"Here," she whispered.

They stood together in front of door 808. Link's pulse was out of control. Alix reached for the call button. But the door opened before her finger made contact.

A small woman looked squarely at Alix. "You're friends of Bartholomew Joseph Murphy III?"

Alix froze. The name didn't sound familiar. Heavy footsteps were coming closer, just around the corner and down the hall.

"Yes," Link whispered. "Mr. Murphy sent us here."

The woman's eyes narrowed, as if she were seriously considering slamming the door shut. "I don't want any trouble," she said.

"And I don't want to die." Alix walked into the apartment without waiting, pulling Link with her.

Behind them, the woman quietly shut the door.

Link followed Alix straight to the window to check the street. Masses of people had packed the broad lanes. Patrol forces were everywhere.

"All the reserves are being called up and deployed," Link said, his nose pressed to the glass. "I've never seen anything like it."

Without warning, he heard the voice of President Quinn behind them.

Whipping around, Link was shocked to find he had already pulled his pulse pistol from the holster and was pointing it at Quinn's forehead, which was floating in the holoscreen that dominated the living room. It was an emergency broadcast, and Quinn stared into the camera as if fixing his gaze squarely on the tip of Link's weapon.

"My friends." Quinn stood near the window of the boardroom where Link had first met him. "Our city is a pristine jewel threatened on all sides by a cancerous slum. Here in the Sanctuary, we work, we grow and we progress. Outside, they stagnate and decay. My fathers before me created this city as a refuge from the chaos of a lawless world. Within the Wall, we enjoy freedom, order and prosperity. As your President, I have taken an oath to protect the Sanctuary. But a depraved conspiracy born of jealousy and greed threatens our institutions. Its purpose is the destruction of all we have achieved, and, like a spreading virus, it has hacked into our Mesh, even daring to speak directly to our people. You all know the leader of the conspiracy."

Alix's image materialized on the screen, her pale skin artificially darkened to emphasize the green coloration. Pausing to drink from a water bottle, Quinn took up his rant with renewed vigor.

"I will not dignify this Fringe scum with any mention of her name. Some of you have taken an unhealthy interest in her. She's a passing fad, not worthy of your respect or attention. Her green skin should serve as a warning. Avoid her like you would the snakes and frogs of the swamp."

Alix laughed aloud.

"If she were working alone, I wouldn't give her so-called revolution another thought. But she is not alone. There are others assisting her, some of them among us here in the Sanctuary."

Link braced himself for what he knew would come next. A sneering image of him, no longer dressed in a Patrol uniform, flashed onto the screen.

"You may know him. His name is Lincoln Wells, and I regret to say he has defected to the enemy. In fact, she came for him this morning. Both of them are in the Sanctuary at this very moment, attempting an escape to the Fringe to continue their nefarious plot to destroy our freedom."

The two images, Alix and Link, floated on-screen, side by side.

"Out there in the Sanctuary, someone watching this broadcast knows the location of these two criminals. You are the one I speak to now. Do not be deceived by their lies. Do not offer them help. Do not defy the Sanctuary. Rest assured that any information leading to their capture will be richly rewarded with a triple magnitude increase in your rankings. We wait to hear from you."

Quinn's image in the holoscreen faded to black.

In the hallway, the sound of carbon boots drew closer. Based on normal protocol, Link knew the Patrol forces were systematically searching all the apartments on every floor of the building. They'd arrive soon.

When Link turned away from the holoscreen, the woman stood a few paces behind him, still staring at the place where Quinn's image had played seconds before. Her hands shook.

"A triple magnitude increase in rankings?" She held a jax, finger poised to swipe it. "I could be a 7Z. Tell me why I shouldn't turn you both in."

Link drew his pulse pistol. "This is why."

"No," Alix countered. "There's a better way." She walked to Link's side and, with her eyes on his, touched his hand, guiding his pistol back into the holster on his thigh.

"They'll be here in seconds," Link said. "We can't just wait."

"Agreed." Alix turned to the woman. "So, you're Merf's friend?"

The woman took a step back. "He contacted me a few months ago. I was lonely. Sometimes I'd meet him in the dreamscape. He told me he was from the Fringe. I was curious. And then, he started asking for materials that weren't available there. I helped him. That's all."

"You're a good person," Alix said. "You'll do the right thing."

The woman's whole body trembled. She stumbled to a chair and reached for a water bottle. "I just want to help, but I'm afraid."

Link pulled Alix to the side. "This isn't going to work," he whispered. "She's scared out of her mind. The soldiers will know. We're toast."

"This time, I think you're right." Alix's eyes scanned the apartment. "You know the Sanctuary better than I do. Think of something. Fast."

He put himself in the shoes of the Patrol. Then, he checked off all of their possible escape routes in his head. They could go out the window. But surveillance drones were swarming the air, and soldiers had the building surrounded on the ground. What about the air vents? No, they were too small, barely large enough for a child. Hide in a closet or some other secret space? That wouldn't work either. On a fugitive search mission like this, the soldiers would have handheld bio-scanners that could penetrate to two meters. A quick walk-through of the apartment was all they'd need.

The woman stared into her water bottle, shaking. Heavy boots pounded briskly through the rooms next door.

Alix and Link were running out of options.

Link's hand went to his pulse pistol.

"I've got a chopper," the woman looked at Alix, her voice barely audible. "Just like the one you rode before, except my model is electric."

"How's that going to help?" Link raised his hands in protest.

"Where is it?" Alix asked.

The woman pointed behind her. "In the bedroom."

Alix jumped to her feet. "Show me."

Link couldn't believe it.

They followed the woman through the kitchen and down the hall toward the front door. She cut to the right into a side room. And there it was.

"Perfect," Alix gushed. "Does it work?"

"Yes."

Alix straddled the chopper. "Get on behind me, Link."

Things were moving too fast.

"Wait, what are you thinking?" Link backed up. "They're almost here."

"That's exactly what I'm thinking."

A rapid knocking stopped their conversation.

The woman moved to answer the door. "I'll take them down the hall to the kitchen. You'll only have a few seconds." She shut the door behind her.

"Got it." Alix turned to Link. "Don't look so scared. You saw me before. I can ride a chopper."

"This isn't the Fringe. We're on the fifth floor of an apartment complex. Even if we make it down to street level, it's crawling with drones and Patrol."

"Don't worry. I have a plan."

Link felt the nausea rise in his belly. "I've got a bad feeling about this."

t was true. Alix really did have a plan. And the plan was simple: let Merf work his magic. As the woman shut the bedroom door and walked down the hall to the kitchen, Alix brought her jax close to her mouth.

"You still listening, Merf?" she whispered.

"To every word," came the reply. "Be careful. I can't help until you get outside. The building has a field disruptor. It's mostly just a black box to me."

"No problem, Merf." Alix grabbed the handlebars of the chopper. "We'll be outside in a few seconds."

"How?" Link whispered.

Alix felt the rush of adrenaline that always came before the big moment. "We're going to ride out."

"But the seat's tiny. There's only room for one—"

There was another loud knock on the door. Alix put her finger on Link's lips to keep him quiet.

They heard the woman slowly moving down the hall. Alix pushed the chopper a few centimeters to confirm it was in neutral. She swung her leg over the saddle, sat down and bounced a couple of times. It felt good, just like the chopper she'd ridden before. With a wave of her hand, she slid forward and directed Link to get behind her.

"Hold on," she mouthed.

The front door opened.

"We're from the Patrol. Here to search your apartment."

"Search for what?" the woman said.

"It was on the holoscreen," a soldier spoke through the mouthpiece of his helmet. "A man with a woman from the Fringe. Green skin. They landed on the roof. Could be anywhere in the building."

"Please come—"

Without another word, two sets of boots tromped into the hallway. Alix held her breath.

"Please feel free to start in the kitchen," the woman said, her voice uneven and unnatural. "I've got some refreshments you'll enjoy."

Astraddle the chopper, the suspicious sound of the woman's words caused Alix to cringe. When she glanced at Link, he winced and shook his head.

The boots stopped just outside the bedroom door.

"We'll start here."

Alix wanted to scream.

"Oh, it's such a mess in that room. Why don't you come back to the kitchen?"

"Sorry, standard procedure."

Alix's pulse spiked. Her grip on the handlebars hardened. The door slowly slid open. Two armored soldiers walked in.

"Hi guys." Link waved.

Before they could react, Alix flipped the throttle, threw the chopper into gear and gunned it. It leapt forward, into the two soldiers, knocking them to the floor.

"Sorry, guys," Link yelled as the chopper shot out of the bedroom, through the hall and out the open front door of the apartment. They flew down the hallway with the chopper's electric engine in silent mode. Pulse shots ripped holes in the floor and ceiling behind them. Alix glanced back and saw the two soldiers stumbling down the hallway, dazed and firing randomly.

"Brace yourself," Alix said as they closed in on the rounded turn in the hallway. Instead of slowing down, she gunned the engine into a power slide. The back wheels climbed up the wall before settling down.

"Are you crazy?" Link yelled.

"Probably."

The stairwell was just ahead. Alix pushed the chopper toward it.

"Come on, Alix. You're not actually going to—"

She leaned hard to the left and took the chopper through an open door down the wide spiral stairs. At some point, she glanced back at Link. He had his eyes closed and was grasping the seat, his face ashen, as they banged against the rails on the descent.

They made it to the bottom. Alix brought the chopper to a screeching halt. "They'll be waiting for us outside," she said.

"Dozens of them," Link confirmed.

Alix brought her jax close to her mouth. "You got this, Merf?"

"I'm in it," Merf said.

"Wait," Link said. "You're in *what*?"

"The Patrol Mesh-node." Merf spoke calmly, like someone in control. "I'm tweaking their targeting algorithms. Just like before."

"Which targeting algorithms?" Link asked. "The ground will be crawling with troops. The sky will be full of drones."

"All of them," Merf said. "I've got the whole network. It's all right here, at my fingertips. I wish you could see it. It's beautiful."

"Thanks, Merf." She turned to Link. "Like I said, he's a genius."

"Are you sure this is going to work?" Link asked.

"Merf's never wrong."

"That's my girl." Merf laughed.

"Better hold on. This could get crazy." Alix gunned the engine, and the chopper shot forward. Just before they got to the outside door, a green light above it flashed, and the door swung open.

They jumped off a two-meter high platform onto the street. To the right and left, soldiers in black armor turned to fire pulse rounds. But it was as if Alix and Link were in a protective bubble. The pulse rounds rained all around them, but none touched them. With flawed targeting algorithms, their weapons were practically useless.

"Smile for the cameras," Merf yelled from the jax. "You're live on every screen."

As the two of them rocketed down the middle of a wide street heading for the Wall, a swarm of drones followed overhead firing shots that punctured the street to the right and left.

"Hey, look!" Link pointed up at the glass skin of an enormous, oval building. All across its surface, a real-time image played of them speeding away on the chopper, big smiles on their faces. From along the side of the road and the windows of high-rise apartment buildings, Sanctuary residents were waving their arms and cheering as Alix and Link sped by.

Unable to resist, Alix popped a wheelie and rode it the final hundred meters to the base of the Wall, where she braked and skidded to a stop.

"This is crazy," Link said. "Merf really knows what he's doing."

"Like I said, he's smart." Alix walked a couple of paces to the Wall and paused to admire its gleaming surface. Video of her and Link on the chopper was playing across its entire surface as far as she could see. Along the entire road, people were cheering and pouring into the streets, like it was a celebration.

And then it suddenly stopped. Patrol personnel began firing rounds into the crowds. Bodies dropped. Instead of cheering, people screamed.

"Come on." Alix reached her fingers to the Wall. "Let's get back to the Fringe." She put her palm on the glass surface, waiting for a portal to open.

Nothing happened.

She tried it again and again. "It's not working. Something's wrong." Reaching into her pocket, she pulled out the jax. "Merf, we can't get through the Wall."

There was silence for several seconds. Finally, they heard static, and then, Merf's voice.

"Alix, they've shut down the whole Wall."

"Can't you open it, Merf?"

"My resources are stretched too thin tweaking a few hundred Patrol targeting algorithms. I can't do that *and* override the Wall protocols."

"Got it, Merf." Alix tried not to look worried, as a horde of soldiers in black armor approached. "What do we do?"

"I'll need time to work on the Wall. Especially now that an army of their best Mesh-hackers are targeting me. I can't hold out much longer."

Link's face drained of color.

"How long before you can get the Wall open, Merf?" Alix asked.

"Ten minutes." Merf went silent. "Can you hold out that long?"

Link was shaking his head and mouthing a definitive *no*.

"No problem. We'll do what we have to do." Alix searched for anything that looked like a safe place to hide but found nothing. "Can you disrupt their weapons and drones for another minute?"

"I'll do my best."

"Thanks, Merf."

"Be careful."

Alix stuffed the jax into her pocket. "Come on. We have 60 seconds to get somewhere safe."

"So much for Merf being a genius," Link said. "We're not going to last sixty seconds."

"Get on." Alix straddled the chopper.

Link stood, a scowl on his face, as if protesting.

"Look, in the Fringe, we've learned to make do with what we have, and now we have 50 seconds before all those soldiers find out they can kill us." She patted the seat. "Jump on."

The scowl still on his face, Link complied. "Go straight, along the Wall. As far as you can."

Alix punched the throttle to the max, and the chopper leapt away with scattered gunfire not far behind. Video drones floated behind them in the air. She calculated that they could make it two klicks in 45 seconds at top speed on a smooth road.

Buildings flew by in a blur.

"Only 20 seconds left." Alix surveyed the road. "Where are we going?"

Link pointed. "See that structure that looks like a blue tube?"

"The one that's nearest the Wall?"

"That's the one. My buddy lives there."

"Wilson?"

"How'd you know?"

"You were talking to him before." Alix pushed the chopper for more speed. "Are you sure he's still your buddy?"

"I hope so."

"OK, how do we get in?"

"Leave that to me. Just get us there in one piece."

"Hope this works," she said.

Link didn't answer.

They zoomed down the road through an area of the Sanctuary with lush green fields between the buildings. People were still watching and cheering from open windows.

"Why are we still on camera?" Link said. "They're broadcasting our position."

"Merf's drones." Alix pointed up with a thumb. "He wants to get as much footage of the fight as possible."

"What fight?"

"The one we're about to have."

The blue building was only a hundred meters away when Alix's jax pinged.

"Looks like we're on our own," she said.

From out of nowhere, a high-pitched scream pierced the air.

"Jump!" Link shouted. He grabbed Alix by the shoulders and pulled her off the chopper with him. They slid on the grass as the chopper's gyro kept it upright and speeding forward.

Three seconds later, the chopper disintegrated in an explosion of heat and light. All that remained was a rising column of smoke and a few charred pieces scattered across the road.

They were still 20 meters from the blue building.

Jumping to his feet, Link rubbed his hips and back. "You OK?"

"Yeah, I'm fine." As long as Alix didn't feel any broken bones, she was good. A few bruises on her knees and ribs didn't matter.

He pulled Alix up. "We have to get to that door."

They sprinted hand in hand. This time, the pulse rounds landed closer, ripping holes in the grass, whizzing past their ears. Alix felt a hot spot on her bicep and noticed her shirt was torn.

"Zigzag!" Link yelled. He let go of her hand, and they ran separately. Five meters from the door, he dropped and rolled on the grass.

"Link!" Alix yelled.

Writhing in pain, he gripped his shoulder. Alix saw the blood.

"Just get to the door," he said, scrambling to his feet and stumbling after her.

Alix got there first, but the door was locked. Link dove from behind her. The instant his palm slapped it, the panel slid open, and they both fell in as the door shut behind them.

The pulse bullets stopped, leaving them in silence. From the look on Link's face, he was still in pain.

"Help me to the elevator," he said.

Pulling him up by his good shoulder, Alix helped Link to his feet. Her healer instincts told her they didn't have much time before Link would bleed out. "You going to be OK?" Large scarlet patches were spreading on the front and back of his shirt.

"Just get me to Wilson's apartment. Top floor."

They stumbled into the elevator. Link slammed the button for level 150 and then fell back on the floor as the door slid shut. They shot upward, riding in silence. Alix had to swallow several times to balance the pressure in her ears.

"Why's it so quiet?" Alix asked as she put pressure on Link's bloody shirt to slow the bleeding. "Don't you think they'll come in after us, guns blazing? Maybe even blow up this building?"

"Nope."

"Why not?"

"Because half the Patrol and their families live here. They're good men. They won't kill their own, even if Quinn orders them."

The elevator finally came to a gentle stop. The door slid open.

Link was slumped on the floor.

"Which way?" Alix asked, propping him up as he flinched in agony.

"Suite 15001, at the end of the hall." Link pointed to the left.

With her help, they worked their way down the hall. It was clear Link wouldn't make it much farther, his shirt mostly covered in blood. As they stood in front of the door, Alix thought she heard a sound inside.

"You got the key?" she asked.

"Don't need—" Link put his hand on the door, and it swung open.

Wilson sat on the sofa, a pulse pistol cradled in his hand.

"Come in, boss."

"If you want to kill me, now's your chance, Wilson." Link took one step into the apartment and stood erect as his right hand gripped his pulse pistol at his side. Across the room, he stared at Wilson on the sofa, reading the look in his eyes.

They'd been friends since they were kids, grown up together and entered the Patrol at the same time. Link had worked his way to the top of his unit, with Wilson as second in command. And now that Link was making a run for it, Wilson would be promoted to commander.

"I'm real sorry about how it's all worked out, boss." Wilson gripped his pistol and raised it slightly.

Link fought to keep his head up as warm blood ran down his chest and between his shoulder blades. Spots appeared in his vision, and Wilson's face blurred. And then, like a punctured water balloon, Link's strength drained away. He felt himself collapse to the floor.

"He's been shot!" Alix said. "He trusts you. You have to help him."

Link heard something hard drop to the floor near his head. Turning, he saw Wilson's pistol. Strong arms lifted Link and carried him to the sofa.

With one swipe, Wilson ripped off the shirt to expose the wound. He winced. "They got you good, boss."

"Don't plan on dying today, Wilson," Link moaned. "I need a med-pack."

"You got it, boss." Wilson jogged across the floor and disappeared into an adjoining room.

"Hurry!" Alix yelled.

When he returned, he had a red plastic cube and a liquid pouch in one hand and a soft round ball three times the size of his fist in the other hand.

"You know the drill, boss. This is going to hurt."

"Just do it," Link whispered.

"Bite down." Wilson slipped a black rubber tube into Link's mouth, between his teeth.

"You better not let him die," Alix said, standing off to the side.

"He'll hold on." Wilson dumped the med-pack contents onto the floor. Picking up the red cube, Wilson examined the list of treatments on its side as if reading a menu at an expensive restaurant. Using his finger, he touched each item on the list to be activated and watched as it lit up. "Let's see, blood replacement and rehydration for sure. Oh, and how about a touch of muscle relaxant on the side? Maybe some endorphins for a great natural high." Wilson smiled big.

"It hurts—" Link's vision faded in and out. He struggled to breathe and talk. "Like hell."

"Oh, right." Wilson squinted at the cube. "Here it is. Pain abatement. What do you think, boss? On a scale of one to ten—"

"Can't you see he's dying?" Alix yelled. "Please. Just hurry."

"Don't worry," Wilson said. "Happens all the time." He clamped the red cube on Link's arm.

Link felt a tickle as surface sensors brushed his skin, found an artery and then bit into his arm with two vampire-like incisors.

He screamed with pain.

"Sorry," Wilson said. "No time for the usual prep." Pulling a clear tube out of the fluid bag, he attached it to the cube and activated the unit with a tap. It lit up and emitted a soft whine. "Perfect." Red liquid flowed from the bag, through the tube and into the cube, where its chemical composition was altered before being injected into the artery. Starting from the arm, warmth spread through Link's body.

"What about his shoulder?" Alix pointed.

"That's what this is for." Wilson grabbed the ball and smashed it over the open wound. Link recoiled at the sharp pain but couldn't help watching.

The ball foamed around the edges where it touched blood. Little by little, it deflated as its contents flowed into the wound.

That's when the real pain hit.

Link squirmed in agony as the ball went flat, emptying its cold, viscous fluid into the open wound. It was like molten iron pouring into his body, burning the nerves and melting the muscles until it was a solid mass of pain. In reality, the liquid was gelling into an internal structure to put his torn shoulder back together and mend the tissues. If he could just hold on—

He bit down on the rubber tube, nearly gnawing it to pieces. And as quickly as it began, the pain receded, leaving his shoulder feeling warm and loose.

"Looks good. Wound's sealed. And you're fully rehydrated." Wilson left the remnants of the ball in place and pulled off the red cube to check its readings. "You can thank me later, boss."

Link flexed his bicep and rotated his shoulder. "You did good, Wilson. Now, if you'll excuse us, we need to be going on our way."

An awkward silence followed.

Wilson stared at the floor. "I got promoted to commander over the Patrol unit. I've got my orders, boss. Straight from Quinn."

"Do you mind telling me what your orders are?" Link asked.

"Simple. Have my team intercept you and Ms. Yamaguchi before you escape to the Fringe. Take you prisoner if I can. Kill you if I must."

"I see," Link said. "It was very generous of you not to kill us the minute we walked in."

"Anything for you, boss."

"So, what happens next, Wilson?"

Wilson dropped his gaze to the floor. "Look out the window. This whole building is under lockdown. Troops on the ground and drones in the air are standing by. There's no way out."

"What if we decide to stay?" Link said.

Wilson stood and walked to the window, hands behind his back. "What would you do if you were in my position, boss?"

"That's easy," Link said. "Standard procedure. Empty the building and level it."

"Exactly." Wilson nodded. "My guess is the charges have already been set."

"How long do we have?"

Wilson checked his jax. "Less than 10 minutes."

Alix tapped Link on the arm. "Look, we're only 50 meters from the Wall. Merf will have it open any minute. I say we make a run for it."

Wilson nodded. "I won't try to stop you."

And then Alix's jax lit up.

"Merf here. Actually, Alix, that may be a problem."

"Problem?" she said.

"I'm getting massive pushback from a horde of Sanctuary Mesh-hackers. They concentrated all their resources to pinpoint my digital location and evict me from the system. I'm out, and right now, I can't get back in. But I'll keep trying."

"So, the Wall isn't open yet?"

There was a pause on Merf's end. "Unfortunately, that's correct."

Wilson motioned for Link to come closer. "Look, there's one more order Quinn gave me," Wilson whispered, lowering his voice so Alix couldn't hear. "He said you'd receive a full pardon if you killed Alix yourself."

"Figures." Link said. "But that's not going to happen."

"Just thought you should know, boss."

Alix's jax lit up again.

"Merf here. OK, I just opened a new back door into the Patrol Mesh-node. Once I get in, I'll be able to disable all targeting. But I'll only have a few seconds before they detect me and throw me out."

"How many seconds, Merf?" Alix asked.

"No more than 10."

"What about the Wall?" Link walked to the window. "Can you activate it?"

"I'm sorry," Merf said. "I'm still completely shut out of the Wall. You'll have to find another way."

"But the only other way is to go over it," Alix said. "How can we—"

"Wait!" Link remembered something from his childhood. He turned to Wilson. "You still have the equipment, right?"

"Equipment?" Wilson tilted his head. "What equipment?" And then he seemed to remember. "You mean—" His eyes grew big.

"Exactly," Link said.

"That was so long ago, boss. Might not work."

"What other choice do we have?" Link ran to the window and looked up at the Wall. "It's been awhile, but we can do it."

"What are you talking about?" Alix said.

"Don't ask." Wilson shook his head.

"Specialized climbing equipment," Link said. "Wilson and I made it when we were teenagers."

"To climb what?"

"The Wall." Link smiled, remembering. "But only at night, in secret. That's how Wilson got his fear of heights."

"Yeah, you'd be afraid, too, if you fell off the Wall," Wilson said with a shudder.

"You didn't fall," Link said. "You slipped. And I caught your line before you hit bottom. Anyway, where's the equipment, Wilson?"

"In storage in the back room."

"We need it, Wilson. Fast."

"You're serious, aren't you?" Wilson said.

"Just get the stuff."

"You got it, boss." Wilson disappeared into a back room.

"So, what's your plan?" Alix asked.

"Simple," Link said. "If Wilson still has the equipment, we can get up and over the Wall. But we'll need Merf to take out the drones."

"He said he could only give us 10 seconds of coverage."

"That's all we need."

Wilson returned with an armful of equipment, dumping it on the floor at Link's feet. "There you go, boss."

"Good. Let's have a look." Link knelt and sorted through it. "Let's see, harness with built-in winch, carbon cord, electronic crossbow, suction, safety. It's all here. Two sets of everything. Just like the old days."

Alix looked down, studying the equipment. "Wait, what's a crossbow have to do with climbing?"

"That's the fun part," Link said, smiling as he remembered the last time he and Wilson had flown up the Wall. "You attach the harness to your body, point the crossbow and shoot the cord. The suction device on the end of the cord sticks to the Wall. Then all you have to do is activate the winch. It pulls you up. Fast."

"Crazy stuff," Wilson said. "I swore I'd never do it again after that night when the suction came loose on me."

Alix stared at Link. "I'm still not getting it. How does it work?"

"First." Wilson pointed to the crossbow. "You'll have to get to the bottom of the Wall so you can launch—"

"No, Wilson. Our friend, Merf-the-hacker, can only take out the drones for 10 seconds. We don't have time to start from the bottom of the Wall."

"But—" Wilson's eyes bulged. "No, boss. You can't be serious."

"It's the only way." Link pointed out the window. "We'll launch ourselves off the roof. Get your harness on, Alix. I'm going to teach you to fly."

Alix slipped into the climbing harness, pulling it snugly around her legs and waist, connecting the thin cord protruding from the winch at the front of the harness to the crossbow.

She tried to imagine it in her mind, but she wasn't sure what Link's plan was. At least he had one. He said he'd done something like this before, when he was a teenager. There was nothing to it. They'd go up and over the Wall in the 10 seconds that Merf could lock out the drones.

It sounded easy.

"OK, let Merf know we'll give him the signal to launch his drone attack."

"I can hear you," Merf said from out of Alix's jax. "Just tell me when."

"One more thing." Link turned to Wilson. "We need weapons. Can you spare anything?"

"Weapons?" Wilson walked across the room and opened a closet door to reveal a cache of black rifles. "All charged and ready to go." He picked out two and tossed one to Link and one to Alix.

"Strap it to your back, like this." Link demonstrated. "And be careful. These are powerful models."

"Good luck, boss." Wilson grabbed his pulse pistol and tossed it Link. "Now shoot me."

Alix wheeled in horror.

"Don't worry," Link said. "No one's going to kill old Wilson. We got to make it look like there was a fight, and Wilson lost."

"Which would never actually happen," Wilson added. "The boss isn't all that tough, as you have already discovered. We'll make an exception just this once and pretend he beat me."

"Otherwise, Quinn will have Wilson killed for helping us. We've got to shoot him to save him." Link turned to face his friend. "Where do you want to take the shot?"

"Let's see." Wilson looked over his own body as if deciding which part he liked least. "How about the thigh. Just make sure you miss the femoral artery. Don't want to bleed out before the boys get here."

"Good choice." Link scanned the room. "Need to make it look like there was an epic struggle." He fired random shots into the walls and floor, taking care to miss the paintings on the wall. "OK, looks good. Should be easy to fix it back up." He turned to Wilson. "You realize this is treason, right?"

Wilson grinned. "I prefer to think I'm just helping out a friend."

"I owe you one, Wilson."

"Be careful, boss."

The two friends met in a tight hug. And then Link took a step back and pointed the pulse pistol squarely at the edge of Wilson's thigh.

Wilson nodded.

Link pulled the trigger, dropping Wilson to the floor, twisting in agony.

"Come on!" Link shouted. "Out the door."

With a final glance at Wilson, Alix followed Link into the hallway, around a corner and into a stairwell.

"Grab your crossbow like a pulse rifle." Link brought the carbon black barrel up to his cheek and looked down it. "Just line up the sights and point where you want to go. I'll shoot first. Try to get close to where I hit on the Wall, near the top. The suction device on the end of the cord will make sure it sticks to the Wall. I'll give the signal for Merf to take out the drones. Got it?"

Alix felt her pulse spike. "Got it."

"Got it," Merf said from the jax. "Good luck."

"Stay close." Link crouched low, looking up the stairs. "Let's go."

The two of them ran up the stairs, taking them two at a time. Alix didn't breathe until they burst out the door at the top.

A soft breeze blew under a brilliant blue sky. Swinging in a quick circle with her crossbow in hand, Alix took in the view. The Sanctuary gleamed in the morning sun behind them like a gorgeous flower garden of gold, steel and glass. But it was the Wall that caught her attention. She'd never seen it this close and from this height. Like a massive ring, it held the Sanctuary in its grasp. The top was 50 meters above them.

"Watch out!" Link pointed down. "Drones!"

From far below, black spiders rose in the air, surrounding the building.

Without another word, Link knelt, sighted down his crossbow and touched off the trigger. Like a silent arrow, the cord shot across the divide between them and the Wall at a steep upward angle. Alix held her breath until the device hit a spot a meter below the top, sticking hard.

"Go!" Link yelled.

"What about the drones?" Alix saw them halfway up the side the building, climbing fast. "Time for Merf?"

"No, not yet." Link reached for the crossbow in Alix's hands. "Let me do it."

Alix turned away. "I got this." Dropping to her knees, she looked down the sights and aimed at a point about a meter to the left of Link's mark on the Wall. Holding her breath, she pulled the trigger.

Nothing happened.

She tried again, this time pulling harder. Still nothing.

Frozen in position, she looked over the edge of the building as the drones floated closer.

"The mechanism is stuck." Link grabbed the crossbow and shook it. He knelt, sighted down the barrel and tapped the trigger.

There was a sound like a fizzle, and the end of the cord jumped off the tip, traveled a meter and fell to the roof like a limp rag.

"No time for this." Link unhooked the winch and its cord from Alix's harness, walked to the edge of the roof and tossed the crossbow and winch out into empty space. As it fell, black drones crowded around it like hungry wolves and destroyed it.

Link bent to remove his harness. "You can still make it. Take mine."

Alix stared into Link's eyes. All the anger was gone, his scowl replaced with a smile.

"But they'll kill you," she said.

"Don't worry about me. You've got to get back. Be the leader of the revolution."

"No." Alix wrapped her arms around him. "We either make it together or we die together."

"It could break the harness."

"There are worse ways to die." Alix still held on. "Let's go."

Link took a long exhale as if deciding. "Hold on." Fumbling with a hanging clip, he wrapped his arms tightly around her, grabbed her harness from behind and lifted her off her feet. And then, he turned and ran off the roof.

They went into free fall for five meters before the winch caught hold and screamed as it reeled in the cord, shooting them on a great arc up and closer to the Wall.

Out of the corner of her eye, Alix saw the swarm of drones change course and rush upward.

"Now, Merf!" Link said.

Alix relaxed into Link's embrace. The Sanctuary spread out below them. The drones got within a few dozen meters and then, as if on cue, they paused, hung in the air, and fell away. Like a screaming siren, the high-pitched whining of the winch got louder as it pulled them higher.

"We're going to hit the Wall!" Link shouted. "Hold on!"

When they slammed into the glass, Alix touched it first. The full weight of Link's body pressed against her. She tried to hold on, but the force of the impact was too much. Her hands slipped off his shoulders.

Link's hands gripped Alix for an instant, but he couldn't hold on.

She fell.

Before she could scream, she came to a sudden stop, dangling from a long strap clipped to Link's harness.

"Don't move," Link commanded, arms outstretched.

He was dangling from the cord, which was attached to the Wall above his head by the suction device. Centimeter by centimeter, the suction device was slipping down. Their combined weight could pop it off the Wall at any instant. Just like what had happened to Wilson long ago. Reaching for the strap below him, Link gently pulled Alix up, hand over hand, until she could grab his arm. The top of the Wall was a meter above his head.

"Get to the top." He pulled her until she was able to grab him, climb up his body, stand on his shoulders and reach for the top. "Quickly," he pleaded. "Before the suction comes loose."

Her fingers found the square edge of the Wall. Using all her strength, she swung one leg up and hooked it onto the edge. Rolling onto the top, she pressed herself up to standing, with Link still hanging by the cord below.

The Wall was a meter thick and higher than any structure in the Sanctuary other than Quinn Tower. She stood between two worlds. On one side, the Sanctuary exploded with pristine color, straight streets and geometric perfection. On the other side, the Fringe spread to the horizon, a chaos of dirt and grey, punctuated by the massive silver cubes of the brain labs.

"Ten!" yelled Merf, from Alix's jax. "They kicked me out of the system. Drones are loose! You'll have to get down the other side now!"

Link hung just below the suction mechanism, still suspended by the cord. His fingers reached for the top edge of the Wall, but he was a meter and a half short. Alix stared down and saw the pleading in his eyes. Dropping into a squat, she grabbed the strap that connected them and pulled with both hands, arms and thighs straining.

As Link made a final lunge for the top, the suction device released with a loud pop. Link fell back into empty space, jerking to a stop as his full weight bore down on the strap in Alix's hands.

Their eyes met again.

Link was twice her weight. The strap was slipping through her fingers. They were both going to go down. A swarm of black drones rose up to meet them.

Link whipped out a knife, poised to cut the strap.

"No!" Alix screamed. Still holding the strap with all of Link's weight, she struggled to the Fringe side of the Wall and stepped off the edge, her back facing down and feet against the glass for leverage. Pushing against the Wall with all the strength of her legs, she pulled hard on the strap, letting out a loud yell.

It worked better than she could have imagined.

Link popped up and stood on top for an instant. But the momentum was too much. He teetered, striving for balance, and then fell, as Alix pulled him off. They both plunged into the Fringe, 1,000 meters below.

"Drones on the way!" Merf yelled.

As she fell backward into empty space with Link above her on the other end of the strap, she gazed at his dark hair and eyes, the eyes that were like magnets ever since they'd met in the dreamscape. There wasn't any reason to look away now. In a different life, they might have been lovers.

But that wasn't this life. It was time to face the truth. She'd done all she could for the Fringe. The odds had always been against her, and the Sanctuary had easily won. There was only one thing left to do: hit the ground with a smile on her face.

She closed her eyes.

35

It's not over.

The words ran through Link's mind as he clawed at the Wall, fingers unable to find purchase on its mirror-smooth surface. Catapulting up and over it, he was amazed at the strength of Alix's final pull on the strap. Now he was in free fall just above her, as they were still tied together by the strap.

He'd done the calculation before. With 1,000 meters to fall, they'd hit the ground in 14 seconds.

Alix looked calm, composed and relaxed. She'd been staring at him a couple of seconds ago with her striking eyes. Now they were closed, and she gently grinned.

Thoughts of the past flowed through his mind.

When they were kids, Link and Wilson had joked about jumping off the top of the Wall. Theoretically, if they jumped with a crossbow and harness, it was possible to shoot the cord at the Wall while falling and come to a gentle stop before hitting the ground. They'd programmed the winch on the harness to do it, but they'd never had the guts to try it. Link had always figured there was a 50-50 chance of it working.

It was time to see if the odds were in his favor.

Still gripping the crossbow, Link pressed the button to cock it. The cord and suction mechanism whipped back into position. Twisting in the air, he pointed the crossbow. All he had to do was hit the Wall, but he'd only get one shot. If the suction mechanism hit the Wall at the wrong angle, it would bounce off. They'd be dead. He had to get it right. Trying to forget about being in free fall, he took a calming breath. His finger touched off the trigger. The cord shot up and away.

The suction device hit the Wall and held.

The cord went taut, and the harness sang like an opera star as it paid out line at the rate of 53 meters per second. The winch kicked in to bring their free fall to a gentle stop. The feeling of weightlessness drained away. Their descent slowed. That's when Link knew they were going to survive.

The color returned to Alix's face, pure amazement in her eyes. "How did you do it?"

"Simple physics," Link said, "and a well-designed harness."

With only 20 meters to go, they dropped at a steady rate as the winch played out line. And then, two meters above the ground, the suction mechanism popped off the Wall far above and the line went slack. They fell to the dirt. Both of them hit and rolled, laughing, as the skinny cord rained out of the sky.

Alix came to a stop looking up. In a nanosecond, the smile disappeared from her face. "Drones!" she shouted.

With no time to celebrate, Link jerked Alix to her feet. "We have to get below ground," he said, whipping out a knife and cutting the cord between them. "Where's the subway entrance?"

Alix pointed at a half-collapsed concrete structure on the other side of the street. "Over there."

He pulled the pulse rifle off his back, sighted down the barrel and took a pot shot at a hovering drone, knocking it out of the sky. It was a mistake that gave away their precise location. Another drone shot back with a pulse round that hit the rifle tip and blew it out of Link's hands.

"Go!" Link yelled.

They sprinted. Pulse rounds tore up the dirt on both sides. Alix surged ahead into the subway entrance and bounded down the crumbling ramp. Link stopped, straining to see, unable to make out any shapes in the darkness.

"Come on." Alix grabbed his hand and pulled him deeper into the damp air. "Trust me. I know the way."

The din of the drones hovering at the surface grew faint, and then, it was gone.

Link thought he could see vague hints of walls and railroad tracks, but soon, even that disappeared, swallowed up in the blackness. From the speed of Alix's gait, it seemed that she could see just fine. He gripped her hand. Slowing to a walk, Alix pulled Link in silence until they'd gone another five minutes into the depths of the subway.

She stopped and led him to the side, pushing him against a damp concrete wall. "We're safe here. Let's rest."

Link heard her slip the rifle off her back and lean it against the wall. He gulped in damp air, trying to ignore the stench of mold and dust.

"Can you really see in here?" he said.

"Not with my eyes." Alix leaned into him. "It's more like I just have a sense of where we are. Inside my head. Fringe scum spend a lot of time underground, away from the Patrol drones. Especially me. It's safer down here."

"Fringe scum." Link laughed at the irony. "That's me."

Link could feel Alix's warmth leaning into him. In the silence, her head rested on his chest. A full realization of what he had just done was dawning on him. As a Patrol commander, he'd betrayed the Sanctuary. He'd be vilified on the Mesh and never allowed to go back. They'd confiscate his penthouse apartment with the holo-cube. His ranking would be extinguished and his accounts liquidated. His life of luxury was gone. So was Chelsea. She'd marry someone else and inherit unfathomable wealth and privilege without him. President Quinn would want revenge. Maybe he'd send troops into the Fringe on a search and destroy mission. In his mind's eye, Link could see swarms of drones combing the Fringe, raining down fire and terror on the population. If he was lucky, they'd just kill him. Quinn would probably want more. A public execution.

In the darkness, waves of fear washed over him. He breathed hard.

"You OK?" Alix asked.

"Yeah," he lied.

"I get scared, too." Alix's hands rested on his shoulders and then slid up his neck behind his head. "But we're safe here. I won't let them hurt you."

He'd been selfish, abandoning Chelsea, driven by fear and a sudden hatred of the Sanctuary. And now a green-skinned girl from the Fringe, the very one he'd tried to kill only a few days before, was holding him, trying to comfort him. It was crazy, but it felt good to have Alix close. Relaxing, he let his arms do what they wanted—pull her closer. Through her thin clothes, he felt a spine and ribs moving with every breath.

"So, what's next?" he whispered.

"You're in the Fringe. You can do whatever you want. I hope—" Alix stopped.

"You hope what?"

"I hope you like the taste of cornboo."

"I'll try," he said, smiling.

Without warning, Alix pulled his head down and pressed her mouth to his. Her lips were rough and cracked, nothing like the soft velvet of Chelsea's kiss. But Link didn't resist; he pulled her closer, wanting it to last.

Alix stopped. "I'm sorry. I shouldn't have—"

"I don't mind."

After another kiss, this one longer, Link's fear melted away, replaced by a sudden warmth.

"Why did you come after me?" he asked.

"I'll be honest," Alix said. "Maybe it wasn't such a good idea. Your presence in the Fringe might provoke an all-out attack from the Sanctuary. It's a risk I had to take."

"You still haven't answered my question. Why did you come after me?"

"Do you want the easy answer or the true one?"

"Let's start with the easy one."

"OK. The easy answer is that we need you for the final push."

"The final push?"

"That's what Merf calls it. He has a master plan and calls the shots. I trust him, even though he drives me crazy. The first part of his plan was to build up sentiment in the Sanctuary in favor of the Fringe or at least in favor of me. A propaganda blitz."

"You've done a good job of that," Link said.

"All those years in the brain labs surfing the Mesh taught Merf how to manipulate people. He's seriously a genius at it. Better than Quinn."

"So, what's the final push?"

"I wish I knew." Alix's head rested on Link's chest again. "Merf never told me his whole plan, for my own protection, in case I got caught. He didn't want Quinn to torture me and extract it. From what I can tell, Merf's been working on this for a long time, and it's going to be big. He says we need you to make it work."

"So that's why he put that video of you on the Mesh after I supposedly killed you. He knew it would put my life in jeopardy in the Sanctuary and force me to come back with you to the Fringe."

"I wouldn't use the word *force*. Maybe *strongly encourage*. But yeah, same idea, I guess." Alix lifted her head. "Like I said, Merf's a genius at manipulating people. I wouldn't blame you for hating him. And me."

Link thought about it. Ever since that first day when he'd seen Alix on the chopper, she'd been pulling him in deeper and deeper. Each step along the way, he'd been drawn by her, until, finally, he'd lost the Sanctuary and everything it meant to him. And now he was holding her in the dark, deep within the Fringe underground. It was as if his transition from one side to the other was now complete. Maybe he should have been raging, but the funny thing was he didn't feel any anger, not toward Alix, nor Merf, nor Chelsea.

Quinn was the only one he hated.

"You've been telling the truth all along. Once I realized that, I stopped trying to hate you." Link felt Alix tremble in his arms. "You said that was the simple answer. What's the true answer for why you came back for me?"

"It's not complicated," she said.

It was still so dark that Link couldn't see anything, let alone Alix's eyes. But somehow he knew she was silently crying. He brought his fingers up to her face and wiped away her tears. "What's wrong?"

"Are you sure you want to know the truth, about why I came back for you?"

"Give it to me."

"OK. Here goes. I never hated you. I know it's trite, but from the first time Merf showed me your picture in the Patrol database and told me to go after you, I felt something. A connection. You were different."

"From what?"

"People in the Sanctuary. People in the Fringe. Everyone I know. I don't know why. All I know is that I've felt alone my whole life, like I didn't belong anywhere, not in the Fringe, not in the Sanctuary. Until I saw you."

"What are you saying?"

"What do you think I'm saying?"

Link held his breath, his pulse racing. "I don't understand."

"Come on, Link. You already know. I can't help it, and I know it sounds crazy, but I love you." Alix relaxed her grip on Link. "It's not that I want to. I tried not to. It's really inconvenient, actually. Makes everything so much harder. And it's stupid, I know. We're so different, polar opposites. You're a product of the Sanctuary, raised in a world of luxury and comfort and excess completely alien from mine. I'm just Fringe scum with scars and green skin. I reek of cornboo. And besides, you already have someone to love. And she's infinitely more beautiful and rich than me."

"What? Chelsea? I've already burned that bridge."

"But you love her, right?"

Link was shocked by Alix's unadorned, simple question. He'd always hated playing games when it came to love, but that was how it was done in the Sanctuary. Only idiots showed their true feelings, and it left them vulnerable, weak. If you were Sanctuary-born, you knew by instinct that the vulnerable and weak were exploited. That was just how the world worked in the Sanctuary. So it was better to hold back, dance in circles, always implying and mystifying, never quite telling the whole truth, never confirming your feelings, never fully committing, always leaving yourself room to opt out.

But Alix was Fringe folk. From what Link had already seen, they didn't try to hide their feelings. Alix had just expressed her love for him. It gave him leverage. His first instinct was to revert to Sanctuary-mode and use that leverage against her. Try to get something for it.

"Well, do you?" Alix asked.

"Do I what?"

"Do you love Chelsea?"

"We were about to be engaged. So, I guess so."

"You *guess* so? How can you guess about something as important as love?"

"I don't know. She's a nice girl." Honestly, Link hadn't thought about it much. Love was so old-fashioned and inconvenient. Maybe he was better off without it. Of course, he'd told Chelsea he loved her because she wanted to hear it, but was it true? He wasn't sure. "Can we talk about something other than my love life?"

"Sorry to put you on the spot like that. I have no right. Let's go." Alix put both palms on his chest and pushed off. "We need to find Merf."

The conversation was over. She took off into the darkness.

"Hey, wait!" Link ran to catch up with her and tripped on the old railroad track, falling and rolling in the dirt. Getting up to his hands and knees, he looked around, unable to make out anything.

"Are you coming?" Alix asked, a few meters ahead of him, lost in the sea of black. "We need to keep moving."

From the first time he saw her, he'd felt an overpowering pull that he could only resist by drawing on his anger and rage against the Fringe. All of that had been based on the lies promoted by Quinn and the whole Sanctuary system. Now the Fringe was his home. He'd seen the truth about the brain labs and the chemplants. Everything had changed.

In the darkness of the subway, a great weight slipped off his shoulders.

He stood on trembling legs, unable to see anything, but seeing more clearly than ever before. "I should have told you sooner, Alix. It's hard for me to say, but—"

"You love me too, right?"

"I mean, yeah. How'd you know?"

"Look, no offense, but it's kind of obvious. You tried hard not to show it; I'll give you that. It just that I know how to read people."

"How long have you known?"

"Ever since the dreamscape."

"So you knew I loved you when I pulled the trigger and tried to kill you."

"Yeah, that's what made it a little easier to take."

"I don't get it."

"Don't try to figure it out." Her palm came down on his back, warm and inviting. He rose to his feet, found her arm and slid his fingers down until they enmeshed with hers. For a long time, they walked through the darkness, hand in hand, without talking.

36

After half an hour of walking, a light appeared in the distance. As Alix and Link continued on the path, the buzz of conversation grew more distinct.

"What's that?" Link asked.

"The secret market. People come here to get what they can't get on the surface."

"Like what?"

"Weapons. Electronics. Narcs. Even stuff from the Sanctuary. Most Fringe folks avoid this place. They'd be happy with enough to eat and no Patrol drones coming after them. The people here want more. I guess you could call them the more militant types."

"What do they want, war with the Sanctuary?"

"More like revenge. Maybe a few are angry enough to want a fight." Alix squeezed Link's hand harder. "Just be careful what you say. Don't act like a—" She stopped.

"Idiot from the Sanctuary?"

"I was going to say *jerk*, but, yeah, same thing." Alix let go of Link's hand. "Let me do the talking."

As they approached the outer edge of the light, they walked past crates of old pulse rifles and sonic grenades.

"Where did they get those?" Link asked.

"Who knows?" Alix pointed at piles of scavenged metal plates and old carbon boots. "The Fringe is the garbage dump of the Sanctuary. Anything's possible. People on both sides of the Wall can be bribed."

"Hey, Alix!" A big man, a head taller than everyone else, yelled from inside the throng. "You made it back."

"Hey, Dix. Who said I was ever gone?" Alix stepped fully into the light. Link stayed a few steps behind, half-hidden in shadow.

"Word gets around. They say you crossed through the Wall this morning. You've been doing a lot of that lately. All part of Merf's plan?" Dix had a wide stance, with a huge chest, one of the few Fringies who actually looked well-fed. He was a natural bully and a black market trader and had a reputation for smashing skulls to get what he wanted. Alix knew how to handle him, but she still had to be careful.

"That's right, Dix. All part of the plan. Nothing to worry about."

Dix took a step closer and stared down at her. "Never said I was worried. Just curious. But stir the Sanctuary up too much, and it's bound to bring trouble." He spit on the ground. "Not good for business."

"Don't worry, Dix. No matter what happens, you won't go hungry." Alix wanted to change the direction of the conversation. "What you been eating lately?"

"Recycled lab meat," he said, patting his belly. "Too spoiled for Sanctuary folks, but I like it just fine. The trick is to know where they dump it. And when." He pulled a long, thin strip of shriveled black leather from his pocket and bit off the end before offering it to Alix. "Here, try a chew."

"Looks delicious, but I'll pass," she said.

"What about him?" Dix pointed past Alix's ear. "Maybe he'd like some."

A tingle ran up her spine. She turned and saw Link behind her. "He'll pass, too."

"Let the man speak for himself." Dix took another bite of the chew and spit a piece out on the ground as he stared at Link. "His skin's different. Where you from, ace?"

Please don't say it, Alix thought.

"Fresh from the Sanctuary," Link said, a perky smile on his face, "just like your disgusting chew." He spit on the ground.

Dix surveyed the throng. All eyes were on him, waiting for what Alix knew was coming. Without warning, he swung his fist.

Link ducked, twisted and replied with his foot in a long arc that ended at Dix's jaw, throwing him over a cart of empty glass bottles and into a broken concrete column that connected with his head, dropping him to the ground. A thin, red line trickled down his cheek.

Slowly, Dix pulled himself up the column until he was standing on shaky legs. Blood ran into his eyes. Without waiting to assess his wounds, Dix charged at Link, breaking a wooden leg off a table for a weapon. Like a mad bull, he swung it at Link's head, missing by a mile as Link stepped back and kicked Dix behind the knees, sending him into a somersault that ended in a box of old pulse rifles.

Dix staggered to his feet and grabbed one of the rifles, shouting "Sanctuary scum!" as he lifted the tip up to point at Link. Dix pulled the trigger.

Nothing happened.

Link jumped to grab the gun. With both hands on the barrel, Link forced Dix to his knees and twisted the gun out of his fingers. "Rule number one: don't play with guns unless you know how to shoot. You could get yourself killed."

Pointing the rifle away from the crowd, Link clicked a button with his thumb and pulled the trigger. A bolt of blue ripped through the air and shot a glass bottle on a wooden box 20 meters away. It exploded with a pop.

Dix stared at the shattered bottle. Slowly, a huge smile spread over his face. He turned to Link. "You've come here to help us, haven't you? You're going to help us take on the Sanctuary."

"I owe this woman my life," Link said, pointing at Alix. "You should all listen to her. She's your leader. Not me."

Dix turned to face Alix and bowed in her direction. The crowd went silent. From the middle of the throng, a single voice piped up.

"So, what's the plan, Alix?"

The crowd parted to let an old man in a broken wheelchair pass.

What's the plan?

Alix wished she knew. But only Merf did. The old man stared up at her with watery eyes.

"All I can tell you is we're close to the end," she said.

"When will it come?" The old man twisted in his chair, searching for a comfortable position. Spit dribbled out of the corner of his mouth. His arms and hands were pocked with green scabs. He'd spent his life in the brain labs, and when he couldn't do that any more, he'd moved on to the chemplants. The Sanctuary had slowly consumed his mind to power its toys, and all he'd gotten in return was a broken body and a shattered memory. He deserved better. Alix wanted to give him hope, something to hold onto.

"Just a few more days." She knelt next to him for a better look and put her hand on his shriveled cheek. "I'll be honest. I don't know if the plan is going to work. But we'll do our best."

The old man's eyes glowed. "It'll work. It has to."

"Keep a low profile until it's over, OK?"

"How will I know?" The old man smiled against Alix's hand.

She stood. "Don't worry. You'll know. You'll all know." She took Link's hand and pulled him through the middle of the throng. People stood back to let them pass. It wasn't hard to see the awe in their eyes.

Not far from the secret market, Alix and Link emerged from the subway into the light of another Fringe morning. The sky was blue, and the air smelled of fresh cooked cornboo. It made Alix hungry.

"What's that awful stench?" Link said, covering his nose with his sleeve.

"Breakfast."

37

Link sat at the rough table. "So this is your house?" He ran his hands along the tabletop and then pulled back in pain to see a spot of blood beading up. He'd gotten a splinter.

"Be careful of the table," Alix said. "It can be deceptive."

"Reminds me of someone else," Link replied.

"Who?"

"Never mind."

Alix cocked her head to the side, as if not understanding, and then waved it away. "Yeah, this is home. Nothing compared to your penthouse mansion, but it's good enough for me."

Scanning the room, Link noticed the absence of windows and the moldy ceiling. There was no holoscreen in sight. The only furniture other than the table was a couple of chairs and a bed. *How could anyone live like this?*

"It's . . . nice," he said. "A sort of back-to-basics style. Simple and rustic."

"It's not a *style*. It's all we have. We're poor. And don't lie, Link. Compared to what you have in the Sanctuary, this is cramped, dark and dirty." Alix spooned out the grey mass from the bowl in front of her. "But it's home. It's all I'know ever since Muse found me abandoned at the Wall." She slid the spoon into her mouth and grinned.

Muse brought two more bowls to the table and sat down, placing one in front of Link. "It's an honor to have you in our home. We live simple lives here, so different from the complexities and wonders of your world. No money, no rankings."

"He knows all that, Muse." Alix rolled her eyes.

"Yes, I forgot. You've been here before, Link. I hope you'll keep an open mind. For the Sanctuary-born, this new way of life can be quite refreshing once you get used to it."

"Yes, ma'am." Link was hungry, but the smells and odors floating in from the kitchen weren't encouraging.

Muse pointed to the bowl in front of Link. "I spiced the cornboo up a bit. Tell me how you like it."

"It's perfect," Alix said. "Just the right texture. Lumps floating in a watery sauce."

Deep laugh lines spread out from Muse's eyes. "I was talking to Link."

OK, I'll keep an open mind, Link thought.

"I'm sure it's delicious." He dug into the cornboo with his spoon, pulled out a large lump and, without hesitation, took a big bite. When his teeth came together, the flavor spread across his tongue. All he could think of was fish guts and dirt. The mixture went down slowly, lingering in his mouth, taking its time to his stomach.

"Well?" Muse raised her eyebrows.

Link forced a smile. "Like I said. Delicious." The stuff wasn't poison. He had to eat to keep up his strength. So he took another helping. The trick was to eat without tasting. This time, he swallowed without chewing.

"Good acting," Alix said. "But don't overdo it."

"Yes, I would suggest you take it slowly." Muse chewed her cornboo thoughtfully. "It takes time for a person raised on the delicacies of the Sanctuary to adapt to our way of life. But eventually, you'll learn to like it."

"What would you know about the delicacies of the Sanctuary, Muse?" Alix shook her head.

Muse kept the smile on her face. "I'd love to give you filet of Australian elk with garlic quail eggs on the side. Maybe some fresh blueberry pudding with bits of tapioca. But cornboo is all we have. Baked, steamed, mashed, dried, fermented, it's all the same. Once you get over the bitter taste, you'll learn to infuse it with your imagination and make it taste like whatever you want."

"Just think, you'll soon start turning green, like the rest of us." Alix grinned.

Nodding, Link brought another spoonful to his mouth and stared at it, thinking of fresh yellowtail sashimi and miso soup with a touch of ginger. It didn't help.

Muse cleared her throat. "Did I mention that Merf is on his way over? Before he comes, there are some things we need to talk about."

With that, Muse's smile faded. Link felt a sudden chill in the air.

"Some things?" Alix's gaze drifted up from her own bowl. "What *things*?"

"About you, Alix. Where you came from." Muse gazed at her bowl of cornboo. "I've been wanting to tell you for a while, years actually. It's finally time. You need to know."

Slowly, Link pushed himself away from the table and became an observer in the play of conversation between Alix and Muse, happy to be distracted from eating the cornboo.

"What is there to talk about?" Alix dropped her spoon to the table. "I already know I was born in the Sanctuary to a mother—"

"Who loved you very much." Muse's eyes misted over.

"No," Alix said, her voice rising, as she pushed away from the table. "How could she love me? She abandoned me."

Link slid closer to the wall as the tension rose.

"There's more to the story. Things I haven't told you." Muse slowly stood, tears streaming down her face. With long hair streaked with gray flowing behind her, she rushed to kneel at Alix's side. "Listen to me, child. Your mother never abandoned you. I've been with you your entire life."

"What are you saying?" Alix stopped eating. Arms hanging at her side, she sat like a marble statue, pain moving over her face. "You're my mother? My real mother? But, you told me—"

"I know what I told you." Muse held Alix tight, as if she might try to run away. "It was a necessary lie. He was looking for you. He had spies in the Fringe. He would have come and taken you away from me. He would have killed you or taken you back and turned you into a monster. Either way, I would have lost you. I couldn't bear that."

"*He?*" Alix said, her words slow and measured.

"I'm so sorry." Muse still held Alix close in a bearhug. "It's been hard to keep this secret for so long."

"Who . . . is . . . my . . . father?" Alix tried to stand, and then dropped back into her chair.

Muse slowly released Alix from her embrace and guided her to an old chair against the wall. "Sit down."

The pain in Alix's eyes exploded into anger. "No more lies!" she yelled. "Tell me my father's name!"

"First, please, just listen." Casting a glance at Link, Muse pulled a chair from the table and brought it close to Alix. "You have to understand. He was different when he was young. I met him in college."

"You grew up in the Sanctuary?" Link asked.

"Yes," Muse whispered in Link's direction. "I was from one of the wealthier families. 7Z."

Link's eyes went wide. Alix was hunched over in the chair, head in her hands, silently crying and shaking her head.

"Your father was an idealistic man when he was younger." Muse ran her fingers through Alix's hair and spoke in a low, even voice, like a mother soothing a hurt child. "We were lovers. He came from a much wealthier family, so it was all a secret. We spent months talking about the future of the Sanctuary and the Fringe. We had a plan to bring the people together. Tear down the Wall. Stop the brain labs. Change the system."

Link couldn't believe what he was hearing and couldn't imagine the pain for Alix. He wanted to put his hands over his ears, tell Muse to stop.

"A year after we met, you were born. We kept it a secret. At first, he adored you. He spent as much time with us as he could. Another year went by. He promised to talk to his father so we could be married, be a family." She caressed Alix's back with long, slow strokes.

"No, Muse," Alix moaned. "Tell me it's not true."

"When he came back to me after meeting with his father, he'd changed. Everything was different. He was cold and angry. It turns out his father had been spying on us and threatened to disown him unless he got rid of you. After careful consideration, he told me he'd come to understand the perfection of the Sanctuary. It needed the Wall. It needed the Fringe. And the same with the brain labs. He told me I couldn't keep you. People would find out. It wouldn't play well on the Mesh."

There was a sound outside the door like some kind of walking robot. And then Link remembered about Merf. Muse pointed at the door and shook her head. She mouthed something with her lips to Link, but he didn't get it.

"I was heartsick. You were my baby. I wanted to keep you. A friend tipped me off that soldiers were coming for you. I had to run. There was only one place to go."

Alix's body shook with sobs. She pushed Muse away and stumbled to a corner.

"It was the middle of the night. I got to the Wall just in time with you, my beautiful child, in my arms. I knew that when I stepped through, I could never go back." Muse stopped and motioned at the four walls. "During the first few months, drones and soldiers came looking for you. But Merf found us before they did. He got us this place. He spread the word that I'd picked you up at the Wall, like so many other children. He taught me how to live in the Fringe. Saved our lives."

"I see." Alix spoke slowly, as if exerting a supreme effort to stay calm. "So, my father is—him?"

Muse nodded, tears welling up. "I wish I could have told you sooner, but—"

The door swung open. Merf walked through in his exoskeleton, a big smile on his face. "So, how's everyone doing on this bright morning?"

Alix raised her head and stared at Merf. Then she launched herself out of the corner, lunged across the room and slammed into his chest, tackling him to the floor.

Muse screamed.

"What's going on?" Merf looked up at Alix.

She grabbed Merf by his thin, crooked shoulders. "Why didn't you tell me Quinn was my father?"

"Huh?" Merf rose back up, taking Alix with him, as the exoskeleton whirred and purred. "What are you talking about?"

"No use hiding it from her, Merf. I had to tell her the truth."

Alix dropped into a fetal position on the floor, sniffling. In the chaos, Link knelt at her side and enfolded her in his arms. She didn't resist.

"But why now, Muse?" Merf stepped away. "Why couldn't you wait to tell her until later?"

"Because she deserves to know the truth before the final push." Muse stood and walked to the table, shoulders and back rounded. Raising her hand, she pointed at Link. "They both do."

With his pulse spiking, a wave of heat moved through Link's body, like his skin was on fire. Alix moaned and writhed in his arms. He held her tighter. She threw her head back, crying loudly.

"Why didn't you tell me?" she yelled, "Why didn't you tell me?" Over and over.

The room spun under Link as he held Alix and tried to make sense of it. Mind swimming in chaos, his vision blurred.

President Quinn is Alix's father?

Alix went still, hiding her face, a soft whimper coming from her lips.

Muse approached and knelt beside them, her hand caressing Alix's head. "I'm not asking for forgiveness. It was a terrible choice I made. I was desperate to protect you from him, and I've always tried to love you as my daughter, even though I could never call you that. You were never an orphan, Alix."

Without a word, Alix nodded and put an arm around Muse. The three of them stayed in that position, Link on one side of Alix and Muse on the other, for a long time, until the crying stopped.

His exoskeleton creaking and whirring, Merf paced in the center of the room. "So, now that you know the whole story, you must have questions. I'll tell you what I know. It may not be much."

Alix wiped her eyes. "Does Quinn have any idea that I'm his child and I'm still alive?"

Merf nodded, as if to say, *I'll take this one.* "We don't think so. But we can't be sure. Unfortunately, I've been unable to access his personal network. The encryption inside Quinn Tower is impossible to break. But just assume that, at the least, he may suspect."

"One thing's for sure. Quinn has the best intelligence gathering unit on the planet." Link looked up from the table. "There are any number of places where they could have acquired a DNA sample. My apartment, Wilson's apartment, even Licious' living quarters."

"If he does know," Merf continued pacing, "he's keeping it to himself."

"What about Muse?" Alix pointed across the table. "Does Quinn know my mother's still alive?"

Muse smiled in obvious satisfaction at being called *mother*, maybe for the first time in a long time.

"My Mesh searches haven't turned up anything in his correspondence with the outside world. Unless Quinn's keeping it to himself, he doesn't know." Merf's exoskeleton stopped. "I wonder what he'd do if he found out?"

"His rage would know no limits." Muse was still smiling. "I know how he thinks. He's afraid of people knowing the truth about him and about the Sanctuary. If he knew I were here, he'd send an assassin to kill me."

All eyes went to Link.

"What?" he said. "You think I'm the assassin?"

"No," Merf said, giving Link a steady gaze from head to toe. "No, Link. I don't think that. From what I can see, you've changed since you tried to kill Alix. I trust that your eyes have been opened to the truth. Am I right?"

"Absolutely," Link said.

"Good." Merf clasped his hands behind his back. "We need your help for the final push."

"I'm tired of waiting," Alix said. "Just tell us, Merf. What is the final push?"

Muse nodded. "Tell them. You've kept it secret long enough."

All eyes went to Merf.

"Agreed," he said. "But I can't overemphasize the need for secrecy. No one outside this room can know what I'm about to reveal."

"Understood," Alix and Link answered simultaneously.

"It's quite simple." Merf's pacing in the small room picked up speed. "It all boils down to the most obvious difference between the Sanctuary and the Fringe."

"Rankings?" Link asked.

"Close, but I'm talking about something even more basic. How are the rankings derived?"

"Money," Link said. "Plain and simple. Money is everything. Quinn told me that himself. He's the most powerful because he has the most money. It's all about money."

"Spoken like a man born and bred in the Sanctuary. And you're absolutely correct." Merf brought his hands together, each finger supported by the jointed metal lines of the exoskeleton. "Ever since I started in the brain labs as a baby, I've spent my life plugged into the Mesh. You might say I was raised by the Mesh. It became my mother and father, my natural habitat, and I've explored its far reaches at multiple levels all the way from a random child's jax to the Patrol's mass surveillance protocols. I've seen the complex layered systems that control the flow of goods around the planet. At each level, money is king. It's the blood that gives life and order to the system. It's everywhere and everything."

"Which is pretty obvious," Link said. "It's all I thought about growing up. It's all anyone thinks about. Your account balance is the single most important piece of data about you."

Merf found a stray chair and sat down. "The system devotes enormous resources to calculating rankings and securing personal wealth. Money is the source of power. Quinn does all he can to protect it."

"Come on, Merf." Alix leaned forward in her chair, elbows on the table. "We get it. The Sanctuary has money. The Fringe doesn't. What does any of this have to do with the final push?"

"Don't you see?" Merf said. "The system is built on money. Take away the money and the system ceases to exist."

"Take away the money?" Link shot a glance at Alix. "You're thinking of stealing—"

"No," Merf jumped back up to his feet in a single, smooth motion. "Not stealing. I don't want to take the money. Not for myself or for anyone else. That would just make me the new President Quinn, a position I don't aspire to. I'm not a thief. I want all the money to be gone, along with all rankings. I want to delete it. Zero it out. Wipe the slate clean. And I've found a way to do it."

The room went silent.

Merf and Muse shared a glance, as if waiting for a reaction from the other two.

"You can do that?" Link asked. "You can hack the system and zero out all accounts, erase all the money?"

"Every system is hackable, given enough time. You simply have to understand the essence of the system you're trying to hack and build an AI to attack it." Merf stopped pacing. "I've been working on it in secret for years. A few months ago, I finished." He reached into a pocket and took out a small green block the size of a common die.

"A memory cube?" Alix asked. "What's it do?"

"I named it Zero, a complex AI with a single mission: purge all money from the Mesh." Merf folded his arms.

"Wait, how's that even possible?" Link scratched his chin. "I mean, I have dozens of accounts on the Mesh. It's complicated. The security is unbelievable. Hackers have tried to get into the system for generations. The best Chinese teams haven't been able to penetrate it. The Quinns have everything riding on how well the system works. I'm sure they've considered the possibility of a hack and taken steps to insure it won't happen."

"All true," Merf said. "In fact, the largest chunk of the computing resources of the brain labs is used to protect the security of the money system. But remember, there's always a chink in the armor. Even the best systems, no matter how well they're designed, are vulnerable."

Link nodded. "I saw that in the way you manhandled the Patrol systems."

"So, all you have to do is upload the AI?" Alix raised her head and stared at the memory cube. "What's it called again, Merf?"

"Zero."

"Well, what are we waiting for? Let's do it. All we have to do is find the nearest Mesh connection?" Alix jumped off her feet and reached for the green cube.

Merf raised the cube high, out of her reach. "It's not that simple. The system that controls money is as close to unhackable as I've ever seen. I've tried for years with no success. I finally figured out the reason. The Quinns have a firewall with so many layers of encryption that it makes the real Wall look like a picket fence. It's off the charts."

"So, what are you saying, Merf? Will the AI work or not?"

"It'll work, but it has to be uploaded on the other side of the firewall."

"What do you mean?" Link asked.

"Zero will only work if it's uploaded from *inside* the Quinn family's private network." Merf put the green memory cube on the table and walked behind Muse, as if to emphasize that they were on the same team. "It's the only way."

Link couldn't believe it.

"Let me make sure I understand. We have to get *inside* President Quinn's private quarters at Quinn Tower, find his Mesh connection and upload the AI from there? Is that what you're saying?"

"Precisely."

Link shook his head. "I'll be blunt. It'll never work. You're talking about breaking into the top two floors of Quinn Tower. I mean, what am I supposed to do? Just walk in and say, 'Guess what Chelsea, *I need access to your Mesh connection*?' It's not possible."

"We have to find a way," Merf said.

"Find a way?" Link could feel the anger rushing in like a flood and tried to push it back with a laugh. "Do you have any idea how heavily guarded Quinn Tower is? It's the highest-value target on the planet. They have high-caliber laser cannons on every corner guarding the front doors. There aren't any sky tubes that connect to the building. Just getting into the bottom floor practically requires an act of God or a personal invitation from the Quinns, which is really the same thing. Nobody just walks in, no matter how heavily armed they are!" Link realized he was yelling with his hands over his head, so he brought them down to his sides and worked to lower his voice. "And that's just the bottom floor. To actually get up to their personal quarters is—" Link's voice trailed off

"What?" Alix asked.

"Impossible, hopeless, preposterous, unworkable, pick whatever word you like. It's not going to happen."

Alix's eyes narrowed. "How do you know that?"

"Look, I've been inside Quinn Tower once and seen it with my own eyes. The only reason I got in was because I was with Chelsea, and it was her birthday. The place was crawling with security. And that wasn't even their personal quarters. Nobody goes there but the Quinns. It's common knowledge in the Sanctuary."

"You're a Patrol commander, Link." Alix walked close and looked up into his eyes. "You can help us figure out a way."

"A *former* Patrol commander. My access has been revoked, along with all my accounts, my ranking, my penthouse and everything else that mattered in my life until yesterday. In Quinn's eyes, I'm nothing but a piece of—"

"Fringe scum?" Alix asked.

"No. Worse. A traitor. The ultimate loser." Link resisted the urge to drop to the floor, head in his hands, while the realization crashed down upon him of all that he'd lost in the last few hours. "Hey, I'm sorry. I got thrown out of the Sanctuary, and now I can't even help the Fringe. I'm no good to anyone. If you were counting on me, it looks like you picked the wrong guy."

If that was the *final push* they'd all been talking about, it was a pipe dream. A physical and technical impossibility.

As far as Link was concerned, the revolution was over.

38

Slap

Alix could see the look of defeat on Link's face and she hated it. He was pathetic, weak, wallowing in pity, looking for sympathy. It made her angry. She didn't know whether to slap him or comfort him.

So she slapped him. Hard.

He reeled back on the floor, looking surprised and confused. "Why—"

"Because you need to wake up, that's why!" Alix grabbed Link's chin and aimed his face squarely at her eyes. "Only you can decide if you're a loser, not Quinn, not me and not anyone else. But if that's what you choose to be, if that's what you really *want*, then I'm sorry, Link. We can't help you, and you can't help us. Just crawl into a hole, and come out when it's over."

Muse's mouth dropped open. "That's a little harsh—"

"No, I'm serious." Still staring at Link, Alix was riding high on a fresh wave of emotion. It felt great, and she wasn't ready to come down. "Listen to me, Link. We're going to do this, and we're going to win. With or without you, the revolution will happen. And when it does—"

Link's eyes went wide. "I don't believe it. That angry look on your face. It reminds me of—"

Muse shook her head, as if to say '*Don't say it.*' to Link.

"We really need to dial it down a couple of notches." Merf looked surprised and fumbled for the right words. "Can't we just—"

"What we need is more guts from a former Patrol commander who sucks at life and everything he's ever done!" Rage burned within Alix, and the words kept coming. She couldn't stop them. It was like she was a silent observer watching someone else.

The room went silent.

"Please stop, Alix." Muse raised an eyebrow, signaling that no further outbursts would be tolerated. "You're starting to remind me of him."

"Who?"

"Your father." Muse lowered her voice. "Anger is a form of greed, Alix. It's a hunger that feeds off others. Robs them of their peace. But it's dangerous. If you're not careful, it will change who you are. Like it did him."

"Ouch," Merf whispered and looked away.

The rebuke stung. In its wake, all of Alix's adrenaline drained away like the ocean surf sucked out to sea. She let go of Link's chin and dropped down next to him, face on fire and in shock at what had come out of her mouth. Now that she thought about it, she wasn't being fair. Link had lost everything. "OK, look, I'm sorry. I didn't mean to—"

"No," Link said, staring at the floor. "You're right. I don't deserve an ounce of pity."

Thoroughly regretting her outburst, Alix rested a hand on Link's shoulder. "I was wrong. It took guts to do what you did, to walk away from a lifetime of privilege to help the Fringe. I respect that. We all do."

Link shook his head. "You don't understand. I did it to save my skin."

"But still, you're here," Muse said, her voice soothing and steady. "You haven't abandoned us. We just have to figure out the last piece of the plan."

"I get it," Link said, rubbing his reddened cheek where Alix slapped him. "It's just that—"

"It's crazy to think we can get inside Quinn Tower and upload the AI, right?" Muse folded her hands neatly on the table. "But think about it. A few days ago, we were thinking the same thing about Alix. How could an unknown girl from the Fringe get the attention of the whole Sanctuary? It was a long shot. And look what happened."

"Yeah, I have to give you credit. It was incredible."

"We have to try, Link." Alix spoke evenly, carefully stripping the emotion out of her voice. "And not just because of the brain labs and the chemplants. Children are dying every day by the hundreds. The Fringe may not last much longer. We can't just stand by and do nothing."

"I have a confession to make." Merf cleared his throat. "I spent months inside the Patrol's Mesh-site with access to everything. I read your personal files, Link, and everyone else's."

"Seriously?" Link dropped his head. "So you know all my flaws?"

"And your strengths." Merf slowly paced across the floor, hands behind his back, winding up for a long explanation. "That's why we picked you."

"What do you mean?" Link said.

"As a commander, you had access to your subordinates' bank accounts, but you never took any money from them even though the other commanders were doing it."

"It's standard practice in the Patrol and the rest of the Sanctuary." Link pursed his lips. "Bosses steal from their underlings. Quinn does it, and so does everyone else."

"I know," Merf said. "But you didn't. You're different."

Link nodded. "I couldn't. Didn't seem right."

"Don't you see, Link?" Merf stopped pacing in his exoskeleton. "You have principles. You're the most respected commander. The least corrupt. That's bought you a lot of loyalty."

"What are you saying?" Link asked.

"I'm saying you're not on your own. You have friends on the inside. They trust you. They could get us inside Quinn Tower."

Link looked squarely at Merf. "OK, let's assume we figure out a way to get in. And then we upload the little green AI. What happens after your Zero does its magic and all the money is wiped out?"

Everything, Alix thought.

"It's a fair question." Muse knitted her hands together. "It will be a shock to the Sanctuary system. There will be a transitional period. Society will experience upheaval. People whose identities are tied to money will face an existential crisis. But the Fringe is here to help. We've built a society without money. We know how to do it. We'll show them the way."

"You make it sound easy." Link closed his eyes. "But there's going to be more than upheaval. Once people realize their accounts have been zeroed out, it'll be total chaos. Mass hysteria. Rivers of blood will flow in the streets. The Sanctuary will tear itself apart."

"It's possible," Merf said. "Human behavior is hard to model. I've tried, and my model says the result could be civil war and the rise of another dictator, maybe worse than Quinn."

"Then why go through with it?" Link stood and walked to the table, sitting across from Muse. "Why take the chance of destroying so much good that the Sanctuary represents? Why not try another way?"

Muse reached across the table and took Link's hands in her own. "I know it's hard, Link, but open your eyes. The Sanctuary is a lie."

"Think about it, Link." Alix sat close enough to rub shoulders, her eyes fixed on him. "It's like a lottery. If you're born in the Sanctuary into a wealthy family, you've got it made. Otherwise, you're screwed. There's no middle ground. Birth determines your whole life. Is that fair?"

Without lifting an eye, Link stared at the table. "If you had asked me a week ago, my answer would have been a resounding *yes*. I thought I'd earned it all. I worked hard, and I deserved it. Fringe scum deserved nothing because they were lazy. But now, I realize how wrong I was. It's more complicated."

"That's all we want." Alix leaned into Link. "For the Sanctuary to open its eyes, to see the truth. To embrace change."

"There are good people in the Sanctuary," Link said. "To destroy it would be a waste."

"If the plan works, we won't destroy any of it." Muse brushed back her long hair. "We don't want to destroy it. Just the money and the ranking."

"What about Quinn?" Link asked.

Merf leaned in. "Nobody needs to die."

"He won't go without a fight." Link shook his head. "He'll start a war."

Merf shook his head. "Only if he has money and power. Which he won't. That's the whole point of Zero. With all of Quinn's money gone, it will finally level the playing field for the rest of us."

"To live to see that is reason enough to try." Link couldn't suppress a grin and looked around. "Every revolution needs a leader. Is that you, Merf?"

"Not even close." Merf laughed. "We've already thought it through. My model tells me we need two leaders, one from the Fringe. One from the Sanctuary. It's obvious, isn't it? You and Alix, together, can take all the people in the right direction."

"Sounds good in theory," Link said. "But digital models aren't always reliable. Especially when it comes to human nature."

"Understood." Merf's exoskeleton stretched, taking his limbs with it. "But it's worked so far, including the prediction you'd come here if Alix went after you."

"Merf has his models, and that's fine," Muse said. "For me, it all comes down to change. It can't get worse for the Fringe. Any change will be for the better."

"I don't know. An all-out war of extermination against the Fringe doesn't sound better." Link shook his head. "That will only end one way. Total slavery."

"Look around," Alix said. "We already have total slavery. I agree with Muse. Things can't get worse. Especially with the virus in the Fringe."

"It's a gamble, built on hopes and dreams." Link pursed his lips.

Alix took in a deep breath. "Maybe that's all we have right now."

"OK, I'm in." Link closed his eyes. "We take the risk and move forward with the plan to upload the AI. But we still have the problem of getting into Quinn Tower. I just don't see how it's possible."

"I told you. Your friends on the inside can help," Merf said.

Link's eyes went wide. "It's going to be hard convincing them to take on Quinn. It's beyond the realm of possibility."

"Maybe not." Merf produced a jax. "I've been in contact with one of them already."

"Wait, who?"

"See for yourself." Merf tossed the jax.

Link grabbed it and brushed his finger along the side. A holoscreen popped up with a familiar face.

"Wilson? Is that you?"

"Good to see you got away, boss." Wilson grinned. "Unfortunately, I didn't. Our little deception didn't work. They had data sniffers in my apartment. Heard everything we said. I got arrested for treason right after you went over the Wall."

"Where are you, Wilson?"

"Central Jail. But it's not all bad." Wilson lifted his leg. "They fixed my thigh. I guess they want me to be good and healthy for tomorrow."

"What happens tomorrow?" Link asked.

"Haven't you heard?" Wilson kept up the cheery attitude. "My execution."

Link sunk into his chair and shot a glance at Merf. "Is this a secure channel?"

"Trust me. It's got nested encryption. Nobody in the Sanctuary has access."

"Good." Link brought the jax closer and dropped his voice to a whisper, staring at the holo of Wilson. "I need to ask you a question, Wilson. It matters that you tell me the truth."

"Shoot."

"Which side are you on, Wilson?"

"That's easy, boss." Wilson brought a hand up to his head for a sharp salute. "I'm on your side, boss. Always have been. Always will be."

"And the others in the unit?" Link asked.

"They all think Quinn's a jerk. Truth is, they're angry at him. They try to hide it, but you can see the rage. All they need is a leader to give them a new direction."

Link exchanged another glance with Merf. He nodded and smiled.

"Be strong, Wilson." Link was already on his feet, pacing in the room. "Just hold on a little longer."

A big grin broke over Wilson's face. "Does this mean what I think it means?"

"We're not leaving you there to die, Wilson. Be ready."

The holo went dark. Link pocketed the jax and turned to Merf. "Can you hack the security system at the jail?"

"Already did." Merf was standing, an excited look on his face. "That's how I got an old jax smuggled into Wilson's cell."

"Can you get us inside?"

"Not only can I get you there, I can do it so you're undetected by cameras and data sniffers in the Sanctuary."

"How?" Link asked.

"I downloaded a cloaking algorithm onto that jax you're holding. Got it off the dark Mesh. Chinese tech. Engage the algorithm and it broadcasts a signal that disrupts any electronic data collection in the immediate vicinity. You'll be invisible to cameras and sniffers."

"That's amazing."

"And highly illegal. Just don't lose the jax. We'll need to stay in touch."

"Alright," Link said. "Looks like we have the makings of a plan."

"Mind sharing it with me?" Alix asked, but she already had a pretty good idea.

"Simple." Link walked back to the table and sat down. "We're going to break Wilson out of jail. With his help and a few of his soldiers, we'll steal weapons from Patrol HQ and fight our way into the family quarters in the upper levels of Quinn Tower. And if, by some miracle, we actually get in, then we'll upload the AI." Link licked his lips. "Don't know why, but I feel hungry. Got any more of that cornboo?"

"Plenty." Muse disappeared into the kitchen and returned with two steaming bowls. "Eat up. Both of you. You're going to need your strength."

39

"It's turned into a military operation. You should stay here where you're safe, in the Fringe." Link smelled a fight and couldn't bear the thought of Alix getting killed, not after all she'd already been through. "If they catch you, you'll be executed in a public show. It'll be a great win for Quinn. There's no reason for you to go."

"The same thing goes for you," Alix said. "If they catch you, you're dead."

"Probably, but you heard what Merf said. This revolution has two leaders now. You and me. No sense taking a chance both of us will get killed."

"No way, Link." Alix was already moving to the door. "I'm going. You need some brains in the attack force."

Only one word could describe the plan they'd come up with: *insane*. Even Link knew that. But it was creative enough to have a chance of working. Especially if they could get the Patrol out of the way.

Merf was the key to the plan.

"I'll broadcast an image of you two walking in the open in the Fringe," he said as he worked on a jax without looking up, his exoskeleton-assisted fingers a blur. "I have enough source material and algorithms to create fake footage. With some editing on the fly, it'll look close to real."

"Do you think it will work?" Alix asked.

Merf looked up from his jax. "When Quinn sees it, he'll be furious. Hopefully, he'll take the bait and order a major strike by the Patrol right here in the Fringe. We'll keep the action out on the south side by the chemplant and away from the population center. The spot is already picked out and ready to go. We have weapons. Maybe you saw them in the subway. They're old but still serviceable. It should be enough to put up a fight and pull away most of the Patrol while you get inside Quinn Tower."

"Are you sure those guys in the subway are ready to do this?" Link asked. "Some of them may die."

"Don't worry, they're crazy enough to be ready. They've been itching for a fight for years, planning and practicing for the Big One. It'll be therapeutic. A chance to unleash years of rage." Merf walked out the front door with his exoskeleton and looked up at the sky. "We'll do our best to make a fuss and pull as much of the Patrol away as we can while you're in the Sanctuary."

"We'll have to time it just right," Link said. "You'll need to pull the trigger on the diversion right before we hit the jail to break Wilson out. I know the guards there. They're all Patrol rejects, and they're so bored that once you start broadcasting an insurrection in the Fringe, it'll consume their whole attention. That'll be the perfect time for us to pounce."

"How long do you need to get from here to the jail?" Merf asked.

"Two hours," Link said. "That should give us enough time to get through the Wall and into the heart of the city."

"I'll be tracking you as you go. Quinn revoked your security pass, so you won't be able to move as freely as before. But I'll be in the Mesh, helping where I can."

"Thanks, Merf." Link nodded in his direction.

Still standing in the doorway, Merf tossed an old-fashioned jax to Alix. "Call me when you get to the Wall. I'll get you through undetected. And don't forget to take Zero with you." He pointed to the green cube on the table. "It's the key that unlocks the future." With a raised fist, he turned and disappeared outside, the whirring of his exoskeleton fading into the distance.

"The mother part of me is screaming that I shouldn't let you go." Muse sat at the table, hands moving from her lap to her eyes to wipe away her tears. "But I have no right to ask that of you, Alix."

"Please understand, Muse, I mean, *Mom*. I have to do this." Alix shot a glance at Link. "I have to be there when it happens, if it happens, for the sake of the people in the Fringe *and* the Sanctuary."

This time, Link didn't object.

"I know." Muse wove her fingers together. "It's funny, I thought this day would never come. When Merf and I talked about the revolution, it was always just theory, like a dream. A glorious, terrible dream. And now that you're taking the final step, it feels unreal."

"I'll be careful." Alix walked to the table and picked up the memory cube, holding it up to her eye to stare for a moment. "I hope you work, Zero." She turned and tossed it to Link.

We probably won't make it back alive, Link thought. He nodded to Muse. "We'll be on our way."

"Take these." Muse lifted two hoodies from out of an old bag, each a different color. "These are the latest Sanctuary style. Merf had one of his contacts send them. It'll help you blend in when you're on the streets of the Sanctuary."

They took the hoodies and headed out the door, moving on the same path they'd come, but this time in the opposite direction, through the subway to the Wall. Link had the green memory cube in his pocket. Their job was easy: just slip back into the Sanctuary and make it to the jail undetected to get Wilson. Theoretically, no one would be looking for them, especially if Merf was broadcasting a bogus video of them walking in the Fringe.

After breaking Wilson out of jail, they'd use his help to mount an attack on Quinn Tower. As the tallest building in the Sanctuary, it dominated the skyline and stood where you'd expect—the exact center. Hopefully, someone inside the Patrol could get shaped explosives from the Patrol arsenal. With the explosives, Link and Wilson could blow the doors off the Quinn family compound. Link liked the plan. It was old school and direct.

The more Link thought about it, the easier it sounded. "We can do it," he said. "I know we can."

Alix put her hand in his. "Trying to talk yourself into it?"

"Guess so."

"Just don't think about it too much. Having a general plan is great, but stay flexible. Keep an open mind. Things never go exactly according to plan. When the time comes, you'll know what to do."

"Is that how you do it?"

"Pretty much." Alix pointed across the street at a crumbling ramp that led down into the dark. "That way. Follow me."

Link gripped Alix's hand tighter. Not being able to see anything had its advantages. It freed his mind to drift and weave through the events of the past few days.

He could explain running away from the Sanctuary. It was an act of self-preservation, a way to avoid becoming a prisoner. On a gut level, it made sense. It could be forgiven. But now, he was going way beyond simple self-preservation. Sneaking back into the Sanctuary to breach Quinn Tower was a clear act of treason, the equivalent of declaring war on Quinn and everything he stood for, including Chelsea. It was the irrevocable trashing of Link's past and any future in the Sanctuary. Was he ready to go that far? How had everything changed so quickly in the past 48 hours?

He was literally holding the answer in his hand. Alix's fingers were warm and reassuring.

She was like one of those vast rivers he'd heard about that flowed in the middle of the continent. Not much to look at on the surface. Maybe even muddy and dull. But there was power there, a strength gathered from the masses in the Fringe, like thousands of streams all running into one to become a force of nature, persistent and unrelenting.

There was hollering and shouting mixed with random gunshots. He heard the voices before he saw the light. People in the underground market were dancing, apparently thrilled with the news from Merf that there was going to be a fight. It all stopped when Alix and Link stepped into the light. The crowd parted in silence to let them pass. Heads bowed, and a few happy fingers already rested on triggers.

"We won't let you down, Alix," a man muttered. "We'll keep them busy. We'll give them a good fight. You can count on us. We're in this together."

When Alix stopped and turned to face them, Link saw a subtle change.

She stood a little straighter, shoulders moving back. "You're good people, every one of you. I wish there was another way."

Random voices spoke in the soft light.

"We want to fight."

"For the Fringe."

"For our children."

"For you, Alix."

"Remember what we're fighting for," Alix said. "It comes from words I read in a book about how our people used to live. Before the Quinns arrived, people used to take these words seriously and repeat them out loud when they gathered together to celebrate their freedom. Just five simple words. You all know them: *Liberty and justice for all.*"

"But what about the people on the other side of the Wall?" someone said. "They don't deserve liberty and justice."

"You're wrong." Alix glanced at Link, gripping his hand tighter. "Listen carefully. We're not the only ones that Quinn oppresses. The Sanctuary-born are oppressed, just in a different way. They're slaves to money and rankings. They're our brothers and sisters. We're fighting to liberate them, too."

Link marveled at the words, simple and direct, so different from the way Quinn motivated his people in the Sanctuary. All he could offer them was wealth. The only emotions he stirred were greed and hatred for anyone outside the Wall. His words were filled with empty promises. His speeches focused on his own awesome rank. Whatever Quinn did, he was at the center, an empty bucket needing to be constantly filled.

After passing through the crowd, Alix and Link moved into the darkness, walking in silence, hand in hand. Link felt the power and resolve coming through Alix's thin fingers. It was a new concept, this idea of fighting for more than one's own self-interest. She was the instrument through which it flowed into him.

It was as if Alix stood at the summit of a great mountain of hope. People would follow her. Quinn instinctively understood the danger this posed to his rule and his property. If Quinn discovered Alix was in the Sanctuary, he'd use all his resources to kill her. Link's job was simple: protect Alix from the monster. And not just for the sake of the Fringe.

He couldn't hold back any more. Slowing his walk, he turned toward her in the dark.

"What are you doing?" she asked.

Ignoring her question, Link wrapped his arms around Alix and pulled her close. "We might not have time later. Things will get crazy. I just need to hold you."

Alix relaxed into Link's embrace and laid her head on his chest. In her small and thin frame, he felt again the strength of a river. They stood together for a long time, in utter darkness, breathing as one.

ight from the outside poured through the dusty darkness ahead of them, as they made their way up the ramp and out of the subway.

"The Wall is just across the street." Alix turned back to look into the darkness of the subway. "We left that high-caliber pulse rifle down there. I don't suppose there's any way to take it with us?"

"I thought about it, too." Link shook his head. "But it's too big to hide under our jackets. It would give us away the instant we stepped into the Sanctuary. Only the Patrol is allowed to carry weapons like that. Besides, if we break Wilson out of jail, I have a feeling he'll find a way to get weapons for us."

Together, they sprinted across the dusty road to the base of the Wall. The Sanctuary was visible through the transparent glass.

"Think about it." Alix stared at the buildings rising from the ground like gorgeous crystals. "Which side has a Wall around it, like it's a jail?"

"The Sanctuary, but—"

"The Sanctuary is a prisoner of its own greed and selfishness. The Wall is really just a symbol of that." Alix put her hand on Link's shoulder. "Here in the Fringe, we've moved beyond greed."

"You keep saying that, but I don't understand." Link's voice was a whisper. "How can you ever really move beyond wanting more?"

"For us, it's the only path to survival. On this side of the Wall, if you take everything for yourself and leave nothing for others, people around you die. When you share what you have, everyone can make it. It's counterintuitive but simple. You just have to change the way you look at the world."

"I understand your words, but I still don't get it."

"Don't worry, if this whole Zero thing works, we'll show you and the rest of the Sanctuary the way." Alix pointed through the glass. "We need to get moving. You ready to cross?"

"Can't wait." Link pulled in a deep breath, stealing glances to the right and left. "Where's the nearest portal?"

"Over there, by that pile of rocks."

"Are all the portals marked by rocks?" Link asked.

"Just the ones we know about. It's a big deal when someone comes through. Doesn't happen very often. So we mark the spot."

When they got to the rocks, Alix pulled out her jax. "Hey Merf, we're at the Wall."

"I've got your location." Merf's voice came from the jax, distant and tinny. "Now listen carefully. I gave each of you a jax with an embedded cloaking algorithm to scramble any surveillance. Engage the algorithm now, and keep it on. It'll hide you from cameras and scanners."

Alix and Link both ran their fingers along the side of their jaxes until the edges glowed green.

"Good," said Alix. "They seem to be working."

"Alix, do you have the cube?" asked Merf.

"I gave it to Link."

"It's in my pocket," Link said.

"Keep it safe. Now stand back. I'll open the portal."

Alix stretched out her hand. "I can do it myself—"

"Don't touch the Wall!" Merf said.

"But—"

"It'll trigger an alarm. I'll do it for you and hide it from the Sanctuary systems."

"You got it, Merf." Alix took a step back. In her mind's eye, she saw Merf's broken body disengaged from the exoskeleton and lying on his cot inside the bank vault. He had the crown of sensors on his head and was deep inside the Mesh, with a view of the entire Sanctuary security system.

A round section of the Wall glowed soft green and opened.

"Thanks, Merf. Here goes." Alix closed her eyes as she stepped through. Emerging on the other side, she took a deep breath to fill her lungs with air that was somehow sweeter, cleaner. It was hard to suppress the thrill of being back in a world of intense color and elegance.

Link followed, and they stood together at the base. The portal closed behind them. In front, a long boulevard extended deep into the interior of the city. It was still early morning, and the streets were empty.

"Are you sure we're invisible to electronic surveillance, Merf?" Link scanned the perimeter.

"Trust me." Merf's voice floated out of Link's jax. "I've spent a lifetime inside Sanctuary security protocols. I've got a back door into every system, except for the one protecting Quinn Tower, which is a blackhole to me. I'm floating above it all, like a spider above a multidimensional web. I'm at home here. Let me worry about security. You do your job, and I'll do mine."

Alix couldn't suppress a smile. Merf was a strange prodigy, and he didn't like it when mere mortals questioned his abilities.

"It's OK, Merf. We'll defer to your professional judgment." She patted Link on the back. "What's the best way to the jail, Merf, inside through the buildings and sky tubes or outside on the street?"

"Stay outside. The sky tubes are packed with people, but the streets are mostly deserted today."

"I was thinking the same thing." Link pointed down the road. "And this street is one of the quietest. Most of the buildings are offices for finance professionals. Bankers and lawyers. They're too busy making money to go outside."

"Hey Merf," Alix said. "How are you coming with the fake video of Link and me? You got something that will show us walking around in the Fringe, laughing and madly in love?"

"Oh, it's going to be good." Merf chuckled. "Real good."

"You're a genius, Merf."

"I know," he said.

"Let's go." Link struck out across the street to a broad sidewalk. "Stay a few meters ahead of me on the other side. You may have noticed. People in the Sanctuary don't walk together. And please don't stare at the buildings. That's a dead giveaway you're not from here. Just focus on your jax like it's your whole world. And don't move too fast. We need to look like we have nowhere to go."

"Got it." Alix peered out from behind her crimson red hood. To be honest, she didn't mind taking a leisurely stroll down a broad boulevard in the beautiful city on a bright, sunny morning. It might be her last chance for a few minutes of peace.

She couldn't keep her eyes off the roses and took a deep inhale of the fragrance. They grew in long rows on both sides of the sidewalk, the green pastel leaves vying with the scarlet petals for attention. Like everything else in the Sanctuary, they were perfect and didn't have any thorns. They'd probably been removed through genetic programming. It was an unfathomable display of decadent bio-engineering, all for the sake of decorating the street.

With effort, she resisted the urge to plunge into the roses and consume a bellyful of succulent petals.

Off to the right where Link was walking, a white tower stretched to the sky, each floor separate, like a giant stack of plates. Each one rotated in the opposite direction of the ones above and below it.

Farther down the street, there was an organic structure with complex curves, like rivers of glass flowing together in a braid that lengthened to the heavens. With each step Alix took, its color shifted, moving from one end of the rainbow spectrum to the other.

And then, she remembered what Link had said about staring too much at the buildings and quickly engaged herself in looking at her jax.

She heard a noise in the sky and couldn't resist looking up again. Black shapes were flying patterns over the city.

"You see the drones, Merf?" she asked.

"Don't worry, it's just their usual patrols. I'm tracking them all. As long as you have the disrupter algorithm engaged on your jax, they can't see you."

"Thanks, Merf."

Alix took a deep breath and filled her lungs with the candied air of the Sanctuary. The sidewalk glistened with billions of embedded diamonds. A long car moved past silently, its windows a glossy black. She wondered if Quinn were inside, staring out at the perfection of his kingdom.

If all went according to plan, Quinn and the other people behind the gorgeous walls and windows would soon find out their money was gone, thanks to Zero, along with the entire ranking system. The question was, could they move beyond the identity money had forced upon them? Could they stop viewing life as a lottery and others as rivals? From what Merf had told her, it might take years to undo the damage, especially for the older ones, but it would eventually happen. There was at least a chance the younger generation would move quickly. Before long, maybe they'd feel the natural high that came from working for the good of everyone. Once they tasted the rush of freedom that came with letting go of greed and self-obsession, things would change quickly.

At least, that was Merf's theory.

It was Alix's job to be the catalyst to spark the revolution waiting to explode just under the surface.

On the other side of the street, Link brought his jax close to his lips. "Hey, Alix." His voice was a whisper coming through her jax. "There's trouble walking behind me. Sanctuary police. If anything happens, just keep moving down this road. The jail's only two klicks away. Merf can guide you. If you don't hear from me, plan to meet me there."

On the other side of the street, two men walked 20 paces behind Link. They wore crisp, blue uniforms with low-power pulse pistols on their hips. Link made a sharp turn to the right and proceeded down a walkway between buildings, away from the main street.

Alix felt her stomach twist as Link moved away.

41

Less than 10 minutes into the city, the plan had already hit its first wrinkle. Link took in a deep breath and searched for calm. Maybe the Sanctuary police were out on a random patrol. Street crime happened, especially theft, and Quinn said it was important to keep police on the beat, so it wasn't uncommon to see officers outside. They probably weren't even following Link.

But one glance behind him killed that theory. The officers had turned down the walkway and were following him away from the main road.

He wondered what Alix was thinking.

A splash of color caught his eye. It was a flower garden set inside a tiny courtyard carved out of the building on the right. He glanced quickly on both sides to confirm there were no windows directly facing it. No doors either. It was cut off from any views from the street.

Rather than keep walking with the police behind him, Link decided to confront them. Hopefully, it would be a friendly chat and all would be well. If not, well, he'd have to get creative.

Turning sharply to the right, he walked 10 meters down a brick path through a lush lawn into the small courtyard, leaned against the building, pulled out the old jax Merf had given him and pretended to be reading on the holoscreen that popped above it. It was a typical move in the Sanctuary. Most people spent their lives staring at screens, whether they were inside or outside. Using his peripheral vision, he watched for the approaching police. They'd probably just walk by, and he could catch up with Alix.

But they didn't.

Turning down the same brick path, the two officers came toward him. As they got closer, he stole a quick glance. One of the men was shorter than the other. They had standard police-issue low-power pulse pistols. Link kept his shoulder pointed toward them and his head hidden inside the hood as he studied the latest news about the 100-year drought in Florida.

"Good morning, sir," the shorter one said. "Out enjoying a walk?"

Link nodded, still staring into the holoscreen. "Just taking my time getting to work."

The attention of the two police officers seemed to focus on the jax in Link's hand. The taller officer pointed at it. "Interesting that you use such an old model. It went out of production over two years ago."

"I'm into antiques. Retro stuff." Link didn't turn to face them. "Still works just fine. Is there a problem?"

The short police officer came a step closer. "Your jax isn't registered. Nothing appears on our system, like it's not there. A complete blackhole."

"I'm just looking for a little privacy." Link hoped his words would be enough to end the conversation. "That not illegal, is it?"

"All depends on your rank, sir."

Their facial recognition algorithms would quickly identify him and his rank if he turned to face them. With a high enough rank, you were above the law, like Quinn. That all seemed natural before, but now that he'd spent time with Alix, it hit him the wrong way.

"Why should my rank matter?" Link flexed his knees and got ready. "We're all equal, right? Isn't that what Quinn says?"

"You mean *President* Quinn?"

"Yeah, the same guy. He tells us we're all equal. So why does more money and a higher rank make some people more equal than others?" Link watched the two officers from the corner of his eye.

They looked at each other, then back to Link. "Sir," the short one said, this time with a sharper edge to his voice, "I'm not sure what you're thinking, but the law is the law. If your rank is below 6Z, you're not allowed a black jax. And from the look of your clothes, I can't tell whether you're a Mesh celebrity or Fringe scum."

Little by little, Link's hand curled into a fist. "OK, I get it. You're just doing your job."

"That's right, sir." The short one relaxed a bit. "We appreciate your understanding. Now, if you can just tell us your rank."

"6Z."

"Good to know, sir. There shouldn't be a problem. We'll just need verification, if you don't mind looking this way."

"Understood." Link slid his finger along the jax, closing the holo-screen, and slipped the jax into his pocket. "So, why are you boys out on patrol this morning? Something got you worried?"

Again, the two officers exchanged glances. "Haven't you heard?" the short one said.

"Heard what?"

"About that girl from the Fringe. The one who hacked into the Mesh and the dreamscape. The one that Licious tried to help and that ended up getting her killed. Rides a chopper and spouts lies about the Sanctuary."

"Sure, I've heard about her." Link studied his fingernails. "Saw the videos like everyone else. But she's just a random girl from the Fringe. One out of millions. Pretty harmless, if you ask me."

The short officer rolled his weight back and forth from his toes to his heels.

"It's not that simple. She's getting a following here in the city. People are starting to listen. Starting to want to help the Fringe. Starting to get angry."

Link couldn't resist. "So, you think she's telling the truth, about the brain labs and the toxic dumps and all that?"

The tall officer, clearly the younger one, leaned forward. "Maybe—"

"Absolutely not!" The short officer shook his head vociferously. "President Quinn says it's all lies and deception. He says the Sanctuary is the greatest achievement in the history of the world."

In the silence that followed, Link made his plan. He slowly pulled his feet together and leaned into the wall, preparing to spring. But first, he'd need to knock the officers off balance. Rile them up a bit.

"So, you really think this girl is a problem?" Link said.

"She's not alone." The short officer took a step closer.

"Really?"

"She got help from one of the highest-ranking officers in the Sanctuary Patrol. A commander, I believe."

Link couldn't help probing further. "Seriously? Who?"

"Can't remember his name, but I'd know his face anywhere." The short officer's hands went into his pockets. "He defected to the Fringe with the girl."

Link smirked. "Sounds like a fate worse than death. Why would anyone do that?"

"They say he lost his mind. Got brainwashed by the girl and her friends."

"Good riddance. So, what's the problem?"

"President Quinn wants them both dead. I hear he's preparing a little surprise for the Fringe. To teach them their place."

Twisting his body slightly, Link mentally measured the distance to the short officer. Two meters. "Sounds exciting. Can't wait to see it."

"Don't worry, when the fight comes, it'll be a slaughter. There won't be any more rebellions in the Fringe, that's for sure." The short officer turned to smile at the other officer.

It was the moment of distraction Link had been waiting for. Lifting his shoe to the wall, he pushed off, lowered his head and connected squarely with the short officer's chest, pushing him into the tall officer and tackling them both to the ground. On the way, he grabbed the short officer's pulse pistol and tossed it away.

"Hey, what's—" The tall officer fumbled for his gun.

Link lunged for it, and for a few seconds, they fought over possession. A hard elbow into the officer's ribs distracted him long enough for Link to grab the pistol and roll away. "Stand up, both of you!" He kept his face hidden inside the hood. "Put your hands against the wall."

The two officers struggled to their feet, clearly shaken.

"Who are you?" the short officer asked.

"Just a thug." Link kept his pistol trained on the officers. "Don't move." He reached into their pockets and pulled out their jaxes. Dropping them to the ground, he stomped on each one, grinding his heel until only tiny shards remained.

"What are you going to do to us?"

"Good question," Link said. "You guys in a hurry to go anywhere?"

"Not really," said the tall officer. "We were just on our way to get some of those chocolate mousse doughnuts from the Sanctum Bakery."

"Shut up!" The short officer slapped the tall one on the back. "We're supposed to be patrolling near the Wall."

"I won't tell anyone," Link said.

The stun function on a low-power pulse pistol was designed to quickly incapacitate the victim by causing a temporary overload of electrical activity in the brain. After an initial flash of pain, it would put them to sleep for a few hours. They'd wake up with a headache, but no permanent damage.

"Gentlemen, it's been a pleasure. I want to make sure there's no hard feelings between us. Please forgive me."

"For what?" the tall man asked.

"For this." Link pointed the pistol squarely at their buttocks and touched off two quick rounds, one for each.

Together, they dropped to the ground without a sound. Checking their pulses, Link made sure they were alive and breathing easy. He started to walk away and then had an idea. He pulled out his jax.

"Hey, Alix, can you come back to meet me where I left the street? I think I found the perfect disguise."

42

Alix had to admit it, she never dreamed she'd be walking the streets of the Sanctuary in a police officer's uniform. Link complained about the low-quality material, but the shirt and pants were lighter and softer than anything she'd ever worn in the Fringe.

"Good thing there was a tall one and a short one," she said. "We got lucky."

"It was meant to be." Link stretched the tight shirt across his chest.

They told Merf about the new clothes, and he agreed that official uniforms were a good disguise, especially since they were headed to the jail. He reminded then to make sure the cloaking protocol was still engaged on their jaxes. They pulled the officers' hats down to hide their faces.

Alix noticed that people on the street completely ignored them. "Police aren't anywhere near the top of the hierarchy here, are they?" she asked.

"Nope. People despise them. Just one step up from Fringe scum."

"Why?"

"You have to be outside to work. And there's not much opportunity to skim money off other people's accounts. It's a dead-end job."

"Strange." Alix couldn't imagine not wanting to work in the sweet air of the Sanctuary.

The walk to the jail went by too fast for her. If they'd had more time, she would have enjoyed taking in the sights, sounds and smells of paradise.

"There it is," Link said, pointing at a windowless, black rectangle, lower than the surrounding structures. "Central Jail."

"What kind of people end up in jail?" Alix asked.

"Low-lifes. People that steal." Link pointed at the few men and women walking on the street. "Theft is rampant on the streets, especially among the lowest ranks. If it's valuable and not nailed down, it'll get stolen."

Alix turned in a slow circle to scan the neighborhood. "Where's the need to steal when you already have all you could possibly want?"

Link chuckled. "Don't you get it? In the Sanctuary you can never have all you could possibly want. It's a logical impossibility. There's always more to want, more to take, and there's always someone richer. Human greed is limitless."

"Depends on how you've been raised." Alix thought about the neighborhood where she'd grown up. They all pitched in, those who worked at the brain labs and those who couldn't, sharing their cornboo so everyone had enough. No one told them to do it. It was just the way things were done. Watching people starve would have been unthinkable. "We all have a part of us that wants to share. All you need is for society to encourage it."

"That may be true in the Fringe. By design, the Sanctuary suppresses all those altruistic impulses. Money is everything. The fundamental truth here is that more is always better."

"It's hard to understand." Alix scanned the gorgeous structures in every direction. "How can a system like that produce such incredible beauty?"

"Unrelenting competition."

"So, it's a beauty born of suffering?"

"I suppose you could say that."

Alix thought about it. Something similar had happened in the Fringe where a new society of cooperation and trust had been born out of poverty. It was a different kind of beauty, but it had also come from suffering. Maybe there was common ground between the Fringe and the Sanctuary after all.

The two of them walked to a point across the street from the jail. Police were coming and going. No one paid any attention to Alix and Link in their uniforms.

"What's your plan?" Alix whispered. "Just walk in the front door and break out Wilson?"

"Yeah, basically." Link stared at the entrance. "After Merf creates his master diversion."

"So, you're ready?"

"Yep." Link's fingers brushed the tiny pulse pistol on his hip. "Just wish I had a high-caliber rifle right now."

"Let's hope nobody in that building does." Alix brought her jax close to her mouth. "OK, Merf. We're in position. You ready to push the button?"

"The live broadcast of the fake video is queued and ready to release to the Mesh." Merf's voice was low and soft. "Keep your jax on, and wait for the action."

"This should be good," Alix said.

With a tap of her finger, a round holoscreen hopped above her jax. There was static, and then a clear shot of the Fringe, as if taken from a drone 500 meters up. A large open vat of greenish-grey liquid was visible off to the left. Directly below, there was an open field. It was one of the toxic dump sections of the Fringe away from heavy population centers.

Alix knew the location well. The field was pock-marked with craters, weeds and random garbage, but what jumped out were the concentric rings of concrete steps. It was an old stadium, left over from the world that had disappeared when the Quinns took over, back when ordinary people used to gather for fun and watch football or soccer games. She'd read about it in a book but never actually seen one of the games. All that was left now was a bare, bombed-out structure.

Merf was smart. It was the perfect place to stage an ambush.

To Alix's surprise, the holo showed the stadium filling up with crowds of people coming in through the portals and sitting on what was left of the broken seats. Two people walked, hand in hand, onto the field and moved to the center. With slow precision, the screen zoomed in to reveal the faces of Alix and Link. They stopped, stared into each other's eyes and shared a long kiss. It was all fake footage, but looked real.

"Great special effects, Merf." Alix said.

"It's called rubbing salt in the wound." Merf's voice couldn't disguise his glee. "Trust me, this is going to drive Quinn crazy. The boy from the city. The girl from the slums. Star-crossed lovers finally brought together. The Sanctuary will eat it up."

Link shook his head. "I don't know, Merf—"

"Trust him." Alix pointed at the jail across the street. "Anything to create a diversion and get the Patrol out of our way."

"Don't worry," Merf said. "This is going to be spectacular."

On the holoscreen, the fake Alix and Link had finished kissing and were strolling around the field. With clear audio, they were talking about the brutal way that Quinn had personally ordered the murder of Licious on live video and the serious lack of freedom in the day-to-day lives of the Sanctuary-born. The fake Alix stared directly into the camera and began to speak.

"I hope you're listening, Quinn. I know you are. You're obsessed with what they say about you on the Mesh. Listen to the truth, Quinn. You're nothing but a coward and a thief. Everybody knows it; they're just afraid to say it. But I'm not. You and your fathers before you were thugs who have stood in the way of real progress for too long. You destroy the lives of the people in the Fringe for your own profit. You treat the Sanctuary like your own personal fiefdom. You resort to violence whenever anyone gets in your way. We saw how you had Licious killed. I've got news for you, Quinn, we're all tired of you. This is our declaration of independence from you and your world. In the name of the Fringe and the Sanctuary, you are hereby relived of your duties. We no longer need you. We will no longer tolerate your lies, deception, incompetence and greed."

Alix watched her doppelgänger in the holo, forgetting to breathe until she felt lightheaded.

"Well played," Link whispered. "Harsh but true. Every word. I'm sure Quinn is livid."

"And now, I speak to my brothers and sisters in the Sanctuary." The camera came into sharp focus on the Alix in the holo, as the background faded to a soft blur. "We have a saying in the Fringe: *take only what you need and no more*. That may sound strange to your ears. Imagine how different the world would be if all of you, including Quinn, followed this maxim. But he doesn't. He's taught you a different way—that if a little of something is good, more is always better. And it's left you tired and bitter. If you've had enough of Quinn's way, if you've finally started to realize the true nature of the Quinn system, I ask you to stop being complicit. Show your support for the Fringe. Go outside, and take over the streets of the Sanctuary. Lift your voices and your fists to the sky, and let Quinn know you've had enough."

Overhead, a squadron of drones shot by on a course to invade the Fringe.

"Look, it's working," Link said. "Quinn has already ordered an attack."

In the distance, the drones faded into a matrix of black dots and disappeared over the Wall.

And then it happened. After a collective silence, a few random people on the street began to yell. A woman 25 meters away stopped on the sidewalk. Looking up from her jax, she raised her eyes to the sky and let loose a primal shout, as if releasing years of stress and aggravation in an instant. People trickled out of buildings into the sunlight, looking confused and dazed, but more than that, angry. They stared at each other. They stared at the Wall. All Link could hear were screams and shouts.

Nothing prepared Alix and Link for the avalanche of humanity.

Men and women, children and teenagers, poured out of the pristine Sanctuary structures. The streets filled. With each breath, the people got more bold, more resolute in their rage. Confusion gave way to chaos. Everyone was watching the same holo of Alix and Link floating above their jaxes.

The doors of the police station swung open. Dozens and then hundreds of officers in crisp, blue uniforms marched out, pulse pistols in hand. Cries rose from the streets. As pulse shots ripped through the crowd, bodies dropped to the pavement.

"That's our cue," Link said. "The jail must almost be empty of police. Let's go."

Pushing against the flow, Alix and Link worked their way to the entrance of the black building. No one stopped or questioned them. They walked through open doors into an empty lobby. No one sat behind the large front desk.

"Where's the jail?" Alix asked.

Link pointed. "Through those double doors over there. And then, three flights of stairs down."

"Can you get us in, Merf?" Alix said into her jax.

"Don't worry." Merf's speech was slow and deliberate. "I can multi-task. Security protocols inside the jail are pathetic. I'm already tweaking them. Just keep moving."

Together, they walked across the Great Seal of the United Sanctuaries of America that was embossed on the floor. Alix looked down and noticed the white ring etched around the eagle. It grasped yellow bars in both sets of talons. In its beak, it held a ribbon inscribed with *Aurum est Potestas: Gold is Power*.

"Here goes." Link reached out to push against the double doors with *Authorized Personnel Only* written on them. After a loud metallic click, they opened. "Good job, Merf," he said.

They rushed into an empty stairwell and bounded down, taking the steps three at a time to a single door at the bottom. Link took a peek through the glass.

"I only see one officer on duty," he said.

"What do we do?"

"Walk in like we're police officers returning from the riot. I'll do the talking. Keep your fingers close to your pistol. Let's go."

Alix glanced down at the holoscreen above her jax. "Wait! Look at this. It's you."

In the holoscreen, the fake Link was talking to the crowd in a voice clear and even.

"I'm from the Sanctuary. I understand now that I was raised in luxury and plenty. I never remember being hungry a day in my life. The air was always clean, and the water, pure. I woke every day to gorgeous sunrises on the Wall. I had the best education, the best technology, the best health care. You'd be tempted to say I was happy, that I had everything I wanted. But it wouldn't be true. No matter how much I had, I always wanted more.

And when I got more, I still felt deprived. Poor, even. I don't ever remember being content. Even in my earliest memories, I measured myself against other people. They were all richer. I never had enough. My whole existence was a continual, gnawing hunger for more."

The real Link was transfixed. "Strange. It's all true, exactly what I would have said if I could have thought of the words. Merf really is a genius."

"Told you."

As if on cue, the Link in the holo turned to face directly into the camera. "My friends in the Sanctuary. Ask yourself: Are you happy? Do you even know what happiness is? The people of the Fringe aren't animals. In their extreme poverty, they've learned to rely on each other. They've found the happiness that eludes us. They've evolved a society without rank or division. I've seen it myself. Why do we in the Sanctuary exploit them with such savagery? Why do we force them to offer up their minds in the brain labs? Why would a civilized society inflict such brutalities on other human beings? The answer is simple. No civilized society would. It's time to stop. Join me by voicing your anger in the streets."

The holoscreen went black. Alix kept staring at her jax, trying to comprehend it all. It was working. Even deep in the basement of the building, they could hear the rising voices of raging crowds outside.

"Time to focus," Link said. "Wilson is waiting inside. Let's free him and finish the plan."

Alix nodded, took a deep breath and followed Link through the door. They emerged into a hallway that looked like a tube made of stainless steel. At the far end, a single police officer worked behind a standing desk.

Alix and Link moved down the long hallway toward the officer. Both of them pulled their caps lower to shield their eyes from the surveillance cams. Alix stayed behind Link. The lone police officer stared in silence at the holoscreen above her jax.

She looked up. "How is it out there?"

"Bad," Link said, looking away. "And getting worse. The whole Sanctuary is going crazy. Never seen anything like it. It's going to be a hard crowd to control. How many officers got called out?"

"All of them. Except for me. Quinn's orders. He wants to throw the whole Sanctuary in jail."

"So they left you here alone?"

"Yep. That was some speech." The officer motioned at the holoscreen above her jax. "The guy from the Patrol just signed his own death warrant."

"You're right." Link only exposed his face in profile. "The guy's toast. But what he said sounded mostly true to me."

"If I were you, I'd be careful voicing that opinion around here." The officer pointed to the door behind her. "You could wind up on the inside, just like his best friend."

"Wilson?"

The officer put away her jax. "How'd you know?"

"Word gets around." Link glanced behind him at Alix. "Which cell's he in, anyway?"

"275. Why do you need to know?"

"Just wondering."

The officer's eyes narrowed. "What are you two doing down here, anyway? Shouldn't you be outside working crowd control?"

"Crowd control?" Link chuckled and walked to the side of the desk. "Don't worry, the crowd already loves us." He took off his hat and faced the officer full-on. It only took a moment for her to recognize him.

"You're—" The officer's hands dropped down to the weapon at her side. She lifted it up. It was the lethal kind, not just a stun version like the police were using outside.

"I'm him," Link confirmed. "Please meet my friend."

Alix took off her hat and showed her face as she leveled her pulse pistol at the officer. "Sorry, ma'am. Please, just put down your gun. I really don't want to hurt you."

It was true. Alix had never shot anyone with a real weapon before. She'd had fights in her life, but none of them involved real harm to her opponent. This was different. The officer was threatening to injure Link.

The officer's eyes went large. "But I just saw you two in that video on the Mesh."

"I hope you were listening. Every word you heard was true." Link held his hands out in front of him, palms up. "Change is coming to the Sanctuary and the Fringe. Change for the better. We can help them. They can help us. We're stronger together."

"I don't need any help from any filthy Fringe scum." The officer cast a sidelong glance at Alix. "They're barely human. Lazy animals. They deserve the mess they've created. Why should we help them? Let them help themselves."

"You don't mean it," Link said. "Those are Quinn's words, not yours. If you'd only open your eyes."

"My eyes are wide open."

"Look, we need your help to save the Sanctuary from Quinn. Let me get Wilson out." Link took a step closer to the door.

"He's a criminal. Just like you." The officer raised her gun.

Alix touched off a round, and it caught the officer in the chest. She slipped to the floor.

Dashing forward, Link checked her breathing. "She'll be fine after a long nap." He picked up her gun. "Thanks for that shot. She would have killed me."

"How do we get through the door?"

"Just push." Merf's voice came through Alix's jax.

"How's it going out there in the Fringe, Merf?" she asked.

"Multiple squadrons from the Sanctuary are already here." Merf laughed. "I think I got under their skin."

"Keep them busy a little longer, Merf." Link stepped to the door and pushed it open. "We're getting close."

43

Corridor

They walked down a long corridor with cell doors on each side. Link found himself in a good mood and couldn't help whistling. As he moved close to the right side of the hall, an arm shot out between the bars.

Link caught sight of it in his peripheral vision. His hand flew up and intercepted the arm, pulling it gently against the vertical bars. The prisoner dropped to his knees.

"Boss?"

"Wilson!" Link let go of the arm. "Tired of rotting in jail?"

"You here to break me out?" Wilson eyed Link and Alix. "Hey, where'd you get the nice uniforms?"

"Long story." Link grabbed the bars and pulled to open them. "Let's go."

The cell door wouldn't budge.

"Merf?" Link said, his voice rising. "Can you open the cell doors?"

"Pardon me." Merf's voice came out of Link's jax this time, with static interference. "Things are getting a bit sticky here."

The cell door popped open. Wilson stepped out.

"What's going on, Merf?" Alix asked.

"See for yourself," Merf said. "I tapped into the Sanctuary's own surveillance drone. This is real footage, and it's what Quinn is seeing right now."

The holoscreen above Alix's jax lit up with a bird's-eye view of the stadium. A heli-ship with Patrol markings lay on its side in the middle of the stadium field. Black smoke poured out of a gash in its hull. Half a dozen Patrol personnel had fallen to the ground not far away. Others were fighting from inside the ship and taking heavy fire from the Fringe fighters in the stadium stands above them. Pulse rounds were raining down on the whole scene.

"How much longer can they hold out, Merf?" Alix asked.

"They'll stay to the last woman if they have to. More heli-ships are on the way. The Sanctuary is sending everything it has. Quinn has ordered a massacre." Merf's voice grew faint, interrupted by more static. "I'm going to upload this raw video to the Mesh for as long as I can and try to infiltrate their security to disrupt their communications. It's keeping me busy. Can you guys manage on your own for a bit?"

"We'll be fine, Merf." Link motioned to Alix and Wilson to follow him out. "We're on our way to Quinn Tower now."

They sprinted down the stainless steel corridor, through the security door, up three flights of stairs to the lobby, until they couldn't run any more.

"Tell me the plan, boss." Wilson struggled for air. "What's this about going to Quinn Tower?"

"You're not going to like it, Wilson."

"Try me, boss."

"OK." Link dug deep into his pocket and pulled out the green memory cube. "Meet Zero."

"Zero?" Wilson lifted an eyebrow.

Link stared into the cube. "It's a sophisticated AI that's going to bring about the end of the old world, Wilson. The beginning of a new one."

"So what does that have to do with all this craziness?" Wilson pointed outside to the marching and rioting. Black smoke rose from overturned vehicles. People were chanting, yelling. Across the street, a live feed of the battle in the Fringe was streaming from a massive bluescreen on the side of a building.

"We have to upload it to the Mesh from *inside* the Quinn compound." Link pointed through the glass windows.

Wilson shook his head. "The Quinn compound is impregnable. You know as well as I do, boss. That place is the most heavily guarded spot in the Sanctuary. A whole Patrol battalion protects it."

"Not right now," Link said, pointing to the scene outside on the holo-screen. "We got friends in the Fringe. They've set up a diversion. Quinn has sent all Patrol battalions into the Fringe for the fight, including the one protecting the Tower. We have a chance."

"OK, but think about it, boss. Even if we get in, we still can't breach the doors," Wilson said. "We don't have the firepower."

"Yes, we do." Link took a deep breath. "We're from the Patrol. We're trained to blow things up."

"We'd need a whole battalion of mounted laser cannons. Those doors and everything around them are solid titanium. Nothing else can cut through that."

"We don't have to cut through them, Wilson. Use your imagination. What about shaped charges?"

"You want to blow the doors off with explosives?"

"You're the expert, Wilson." Link patted him on the back. "That's why we came for you."

Wilson stood, chest still heaving, staring at Link. "Are you sure about this, boss?"

"Absolutely." Link reached for Alix and pulled her close. She put her arms around him. "We have to do it. For the Fringe *and* the Sanctuary."

"OK, I'm in. I was scheduled for execution tomorrow, so I got nothing to lose." Wilson held out his hand. "But I'll need your jax, boss. Looks old, but it's secure, right?"

"Secure as they come." Link handed his jax to Wilson. "Who are you calling?"

"A couple of buddies inside the Patrol that I can trust. They'll do anything for me. Especially if they know I'm with you."

Alix and Link listened as Wilson made arrangements for his contacts to meet them outside Quinn Tower. Near the end of the conversation, Wilson went silent except for a few grunts.

When he was done, Wilson tossed the jax back to Link. "We're meeting them in 10 minutes. They're bringing shaped charges, enough to take down an army. That's the good news." Wilson looked at his feet. "But I got some bad news, boss. And you won't like it either, Ms. Yamaguchi."

"Tell us," Link said.

"Quinn's in a rage. He's ordered the Patrol to engage all heli-ships, attack drones and troops for an all-out assault on the Fringe. And they've found Alix's house. They're going to level the house and her whole neighborhood. Do as much damage as they can. And that's not all. They're going to keep doing it to random neighborhoods throughout the Fringe until the riots die down here in the Sanctuary."

"When is this supposed to happen, Wilson?"

"Within the hour."

In the back of his mind, Link knew all along that a major attack on the Fringe was inevitable. Back when he was in the Patrol, they'd developed contingency plans, and now it looked like they were executing those plans. It wasn't a topic he wanted to raise with Alix. But she already understood the risk. So did Merf.

Link turned to Alix. "Are you OK?"

She was already on her jax. "Can you hear me, Merf? They're targeting our neighborhood. They're coming after you. You have to get everyone out. Into the subway."

No answer.

"Come on, Merf!" Link grabbed his jax and shouted into it. "Get out, now!"

Still no answer. Nothing but static. There was no way to tell what was happening.

"Lead the way, Wilson." Alix pointed outside. "We have to move. Fast."

It was chaos outside and getting worse by the minute. The usual sweet smells of the Sanctuary were gone, replaced by the stench of burnt rubber and pulse discharge. Here and there, bodies littered the street. Police officers waved guns, trying to control the crowds, shooting rounds at random. Public holoscreens filled with images of the Patrol fighting in the

Fringe. A collective mania seemed to have taken hold. People in the streets marched in the direction of the Wall. Along the way, they stormed government buildings, smashed windows and chanted.

Take only what you need and no more!

Alix, Link and Wilson pushed against the tide of humanity flowing to the Wall and headed for Quinn Tower a klick away. They could already see it from a distance, taking up an entire city block of its own, with no connecting sky tubes. The structure was a simple rectangle that rose 1,500 meters above the street, the highest in the Sanctuary by far. Except for the top, it was windowless with a smooth titanium skin burnished to a high gloss. The top two floors were a solid band of black glass, marking the Quinn family personal residences.

A man and a woman in Patrol uniforms approached the trio on the street. They slipped off their backpacks and three rifles and laid them at Wilson's feet.

The woman scanned the area, her gaze focussing on a point in the distance. "Shaped charges are in the packs, enough to take down the building. We scrounged what firepower we could. It's not much, but it's the best we could do." The woman look apologetic. "Quinn suspects a military coup. Patrol HQ is crawling with combat soldiers guarding every door with pulse cannons. It was too dangerous for us to try to take any more." She pointed at the packs. "You know the drill with the shaped charges, Wilson. There are two pieces, and they have to be used together to focus the explosion. They're no good apart. You're only going to get one shot."

"You did good," Wilson said, picking up one pack and tossing it to Link.

"We told them it was a police request, for crowd control." The man scanned the surroundings. "But we can't come with you. They expect us back in five minutes. If we don't return, half a battalion will come looking."

"Understood," Wilson said.

"Good luck, sir." The woman nodded in Link's direction, but her gaze landed on Alix. "Is that really her?"

"It's her." Link rested a hand on Alix's shoulder. "Alix Yamaguchi."

The woman took a step closer to Alix as if studying her face, looking first at the blue eye and then at the brown one. "I just want you to know, I believe you. About the Fringe. About everything. I'm sorry about the brain labs, the toxic dumps, all of it. I never knew, even though it was in plain sight. You opened my eyes. And I'm not the only one. Thank you for your words. *Take only what you need and no more.*"

The man nodded in agreement.

"It means a lot to hear you say that," Alix said.

The woman turned back to Wilson. "I accessed the info you requested. Here it is." She pulled out her jax. The holoscreen lit up with detailed blueprints of Quinn Tower.

"Can you get that, boss?"

"With pleasure." Link lifted his jax close to the woman's. She flicked the screen, and it jumped above Link's jax.

"Download complete," Link said.

"Sorry we can't do more for you. Good luck." The woman and man disappeared into the crowd.

Craning his neck, Link stared up at Quinn Tower, still in the distance and shining in the mid-morning light like a monolith of power brooding over the Sanctuary. "We can do this, Wilson. Put a stop to all the madness right now."

It took another 15 minutes of fighting the crowd to finally get into position across the street from Quinn Tower. A dozen armored troops had set up pulse cannons, three on every corner, outside the Tower. The troops could rake every possible approach with intersecting fire from at least two locations. Link had to face the fact that there was no way they'd be able to storm in from street level. It looked hopeless.

"So, how do we get in?" Alix said.

"That's why we got the plans." Wilson pointed to Link's jax. "Let's have a look."

Link knelt with the others behind a line of lush green bushes and studied the holoscreen, flipping from page to page with his finger on the jax.

Red letters were emblazoned across the top of every page:

Level 15 Security Clearance Required.

"I'm only a Level 8, Wilson. How'd you get access to this?"

"Had to call in a few favors from my Patrol buddies." Wilson studied the pages on the holo as Link flipped through them. "Wait, go back one."

"OK," Link said. "What did you see?" And then Link saw it too.

An emergency exit not marked on any other set of plans. A hidden corridor from Quinn Tower that ran under the very street where they were standing, with surface access a couple of hundred meters away. It was an insurance policy for the Quinns, a secret, underground passageway out of the building, just in case the entrance got blocked or they couldn't get off the roof. If Wilson could find it and get them in, it would bypass all security checks and guards and take them directly to the elevator banks. And from there, it was just a quick ride to the top.

Noise levels were rising. Patrol officers had started firing lethal rounds into the mass of humanity flowing through the streets to the Wall. People were dying. From the looks on their faces, they were beyond rage and reason. The bullets only made them angrier.

"Lead the way," Link shouted above the clamor.

Pushing their way across two wide streets streaming with protestors, they followed a side road that ran through an open plaza into a narrow alley between two low-lying, drab buildings.

"Never been to this part of the Sanctuary," Link said. "Where are we?"

"It's the old part of the city from before it was the Sanctuary. Back at the time of the first President Quinn." Wilson stared at the holoscreen floating above his jax. "Now, if we can just find the entrance to the underground corridor. According to this, it's should be here." He pointed at the street, which looked like dirty pavement.

"Quick, we have to find it," Alix said, desperation bleeding through her voice. "Form a line. Get on your hands and knees. Study the ground." She dropped down without hesitation and put her hands in contact with the dirt, running her fingertips over it from side to side, doing a sweep.

Link exchanged a glance with Wilson. Neither of them were accustomed to touching the ground with their bare hands. Apparently, Alix was.

Of course, Link started to think, *she's from the—*

"Get over here!" she said. "Take a look at this."

44

Trying not to think about the Patrol troops in the Fringe destroying her neighborhood, Alix knelt and put a shaky fingertip on the round indentation in the pavement a little bigger than her thumb. Carefully, she blew away the dust. She'd seen marks like this before, in the Fringe. It could be a hidden door, but there was only one way to know for sure.

"Stand back." With both hands on the ground, she wiped dirt away from the old pavement, working her way out from the indentation. And then she found it. A hairline gap. Blowing gently, she cleared the dirt as she followed the gap, opening up a rectangular line in the old pavement two meters long and a meter wide.

"Just as I thought," she said.

"It's a trapdoor," Link said, bending down to touch the faint outline. "How do we open it?"

"That may be a problem." Wilson touched the indentation in the pavement, trying to rotate it or push it. "I'm guessing it was made to only open from the inside."

"I've seen this kind of trapdoor in the Fringe, left over from the world before the Wall." Alix stood, slipped off the pulse rifle hanging from her shoulder, took one step back and pointed it squarely at the small indentation. "Stand back."

Link and Wilson jumped away. Sparks flew as Alix fired a dozen pulse rounds into the pavement, her jaw tight. Finally, with the sound of metal scraping on metal, something popped, and one end of the trapdoor rose a few centimeters. The three of them bent down and worked their fingers under it. As the metal hinges screamed in agony, they pulled the door up until there was an opening large enough to slip through.

"Good work." Link stared into the opening. "I wonder—"

"No time to talk. We have to hurry." Alix didn't wait for the others. Instead, she shouldered her pulse rifle and jumped through the open door into the darkness below the street. She felt at home, like being in the subway back in the Fringe. Link and Wilson followed her.

"Can't see anything," Link said, as he whipped out his jax and engaged the torch function. He saw that they had landed in a square hallway with a concrete floor, leading back in the general direction of Quinn Tower.

Alix took off in a sprint, running from the light and into the darkness.

"Hey, wait!" Link yelled and took off after her.

The tunnel extended in a straight line on a slight descent so that Alix's speed picked up as she ran. Hanging cobwebs brushed her face, and more than once she heard rats scatter at her feet. Just like in the subway.

"Slow down!" Link yelled from behind. "We can't see."

"No time!" Alix yelled over her shoulder. She kept running, oblivious to the pain in her lungs and legs. Finally, she saw a dim lightbulb ahead above a single door and came to a stop in front of it. With trembling hands, she touched a long bar extending horizontally across the door in the same style that she'd seen in countless old buildings in the Fringe. Holding her breath, she pushed hard. There was a sucking sound, and the door swung open on quiet hinges. A breeze of fresh air blew her hair.

Link stopped behind her, breathing hard. "How did you open it?"

"I pushed the bar," Alix said.

"I don't get it." Link glanced at Wilson. "If this is an escape route out of Quinn Tower, why does the door open from this side? Why wasn't it locked?"

Wilson shrugged his shoulders. "Who knows? Maybe it was made to be accessed from both directions. A secret way out *and* a secret way in."

"I don't know." Link shook his head and slipped his pulse rifle from his shoulder, pointing the tip into the dim hallway. "Everyone on your toes. This could be a trap."

Alix and Wilson unstrapped their rifles. Together, the three of them moved forward, shoulder to shoulder, guns ready. The hallway turned to the left and stopped at another door.

It wasn't locked either.

They stepped through into a low-ceilinged room with the lights on. On the far wall, an elevator door stood open. They walked closer.

"Do we just walk in?" Link asked.

"No idea," Wilson said.

"Yes." Alix darted across the room, scanning for guards, and stepped inside the elevator. "Come on."

There wasn't any control panel or indicator lights. Each wall of the elevator was a smooth sheet of titanium polished to a high sheen so that they could see their own reflections. Just like the outside of Quinn Tower.

"Has anyone thought about the obvious question, like why the elevator is here with the door open?" Link scratched his head. "Are they waiting for us?"

"Maybe this is its default position," Wilson said. "Or maybe not."

Before anyone could do anything, the doors started to slide shut. Link rammed the tip of his gun between them, leaving a three-centimeter gap. The elevator rose.

Alix stared at the blackness on the other side of the gap.

"Anyone have a plan?" Link asked.

Wilson turned to Link. "That's simple, boss. Hand me your backpack."

"What?" Link said.

"You know how shaped charges work, boss. They always come in pairs to focus the harmonic effect, so I'll need both of them."

"C'mon Wilson. We'll set the charges together."

"No time for that. Quinn's guards probably know we're coming. They'll be waiting for us at the top. You were right; it's a trap. This is the only way."

"Wait, what are you—"

"Give me the backpack, boss. No time to argue." Wilson reached out his hand. "I know what I need to do, just run for the big doors and blow them off their hinges. Hopefully, I'll get close enough before—"

"But Wilson—"

"No buts." Wilson shook his head. "I'm tired of Quinn. Consider it my contribution to the revolution."

Link stared and then slipped off his backpack, slowing handing it to Wilson before engulfing him in a hug. "You're a good man, Wilson."

"It's the least I can do." Wilson turned to Alix, his eyes moist. "Please forgive me for not opening my eyes to the reality of the Fringe sooner. I hope this makes up for it in some small way."

Alix nodded and couldn't hold back her tears. "Thank you, Wilson."

The dark gap between the elevator doors lit up. Wilson stood, head down in a runner's position, a backpack hanging off each shoulder. Alix and Link were on the sides, pulse rifles ready, barrels pointed at the elevator doors, fingers on triggers.

Wilson lifted a tube of amber liquid out of a side pocket and bit off the cap to reveal a short needle on the end. Alix saw the words printed on the side.

Liquid adrenaline.

The elevator stopped, and the doors slowly slid open.

Wilson rammed the needle into his thigh like a dagger and took a deep inhale. Looking to the right and left, eyes wild, he grinned.

"For the revolution," he said.

45

Two seconds of silence.

Wilson yelled and burst out of the elevator into a blinding hail of pulse fire. With mouth open, lips peeled back and teeth exposed, he looked like a jaguar lunging for the kill. He should have dropped like a bag of sand when the first pulse projectiles tore into his chest, but the adrenaline pushed him out of the elevator and into the room.

Link and Alix pressed themselves flat against the elevator walls.

Three seconds later, a flash of light flooded the room like a supernova, followed by silence and a shockwave of hot air. The force of the blast threw Link into the back wall of the elevator. He slammed his head. The air went black, and he collapsed to the floor.

Images floated in his mind.

He was clinging to the side of a filthy pit staring up at the light. Muffled voices flowed in above and below. Beneath his feet, the darkness was filled with screaming and wailing. Desperate to get out of the hole, he tried to climb, groping for a handhold and making it a few centimeters higher. But the walls were wet and slimy. His foot slipped off a narrow ledge, and he plunged back into the darkness, looking up at the light and landing hard on his spine. In pain, he scrambled to his feet to make another run at the wall. On all sides, people emerged from the darkness, fighting among themselves, crawling over each other to get to him, arms outstretched as if begging. They all mumbled the same words, over and over.

More, more, more, more.

He tried to fight them off, but there were too many. They tugged at him, ripping his clothes, scratching his skin, pulling his hair. From the looks on their faces, they were emaciated and starving. Among them, he recognized Quinn. With eyes glazed over and larger than any of the others, he moved through the crowd, pushing the others to the side or stomping on them to make way for himself. Link knew in his heart Quinn was coming for him.

Panic exploded in his chest. He jumped to his feet, ripping off the hands still clinging to his body. Breaking through the masses, he fought his way to the side of the pit and jumped to grab a handhold. The sides were slippery and smooth as a glass wall.

"Link, up here!"

He craned his neck skyward. Alix leaned over the edge of the pit, peering down, hands cupped around her mouth, shouting to get his attention. He searched for a way out, but there wasn't any.

"Grab this." Alix yelled, throwing a rope over the edge.

Link watched as it uncoiled down to him. When it came to a stop, the end was a meter above his head. He jumped and grasped it, but as he climbed, a mass of humanity clung to his body from below, pulling him down into the pit. At some point, he lost his grip on the rope, and it slipped away. The bodies piled higher and higher on him, chanting and moaning.

More, more, more, more.

"Help me, Alix!" he screamed. "I can't do it on my own." Through the tangle of arms and legs, he caught a glimpse of her coming down the rope. She landed next to him. One by one, she pulled his attackers away and stood over him.

The rope dangled just above.

"Go!" she yelled and stood guard as he grasped the rope again and began to ascend.

And then, he woke up.

Alix was leaning over him in the elevator. "You OK?"

Link's head felt like it'd been split open with a sledgehammer. "What happened?"

Alix pointed. "The explosives cleared the room, and a whole lot more."

Together, they walked into the empty room. The windows were blown out. Link and Alix had an open view of the Sanctuary 1,500 meters below. Bits of white ash floated in the sunlight like snow. The floor was stripped clean down to the concrete. The Patrol soldiers were gone. So was Wilson.

"I'm sorry," Alix said.

"He was a good man." Link stood in the middle of the floor, stunned. "A good friend." He dropped to his knees as Alix came close to place a hand on his shoulder.

Looking up, he saw the remaining wall, where a massive metal door hung open on bent hinges.

Link stood. Cradling his pulse rifle, he moved closer to the door, looking through the opening into the Quinn residence. Nothing moved. There weren't any sounds. He turned back to Alix. "I'm going in."

"Right behind you," she said.

Together, they slid through the open door down a short hallway and into a large receiving room with gorgeous chairs and couches arranged around an ornately carved wood table. A triple-layer crystal chandelier hung from the ceiling like a massive snowflake. To the right, a floor-to-ceiling mirror in a thick gold frame hung on the wall. An identical mirror hung on the wall to the left. Link stepped into the room between the mirrors with his rifle held ready, glancing at his image reflected over and over in a long line that stretched to infinity.

"Where's Quinn?" Alix asked.

Link pointed at an open door. "Deeper inside, if he's even here. Come on." Link moved carefully across the room, looking down the sights of his gun, through the door. "Stay behind me. Keep your eye out for a Mesh interface."

Through windows on the sides, Link looked down on the top of the Sanctuary from half a klick above the roofs of the other buildings. The Wall displayed a tranquil image of a Japanese rock garden and pool dotted with bonsai trees. He gazed over it into the gray malaise of the Fringe.

Stepping through the door, Link found himself in another hallway, this one long and dark. There were two exits at the far end, one on the right and one on the left. He moved forward slowly, eyes fixed on the sights of his rifle, finger resting on the trigger.

Alix pushed at him from behind. "No time for that. Let me by."

"No," Link said, his cheek still pressed against the stock of his gun. "There could be guards. It's too—"

"Sorry. People are dying in the Fringe." She rushed past him, pushing him aside, and sprinted to the far end of the hall. "Got to find that Mesh interface. No time to play games."

Link lowered his gun and ran to catch up, passing a line of Quinn family photographs on both walls. Alix was already at the far end, pausing between the two doors. He stopped behind her.

"Which door?" she asked.

"Let me see." He took a deep inhale of air. A faint trace of perfume came from the right. Gathering his strength, he crouched, shifted his weight and hit the door on the left with his shoulder.

It burst open.

A quick scan of the room revealed no guards in sight. Rolling, he sprang to his feet and pointed his rifle at the window on the far end.

Quinn stood, staring out the window. That's when Link saw it. The Mesh interface. A silver box with a blue holoscreen floating above it rested on a table near Quinn's hand. Link flicked on his rifle's targeting mechanism. A red dot jumped on Quinn's back.

"It's so easy, isn't it?" Quinn's spoke without turning around. "Just tap the trigger and kill the monster. You'll save the Fringe. You'll change the world. You'll be a hero."

"I'm not here to talk," Link took a step forward, eyes jumping between the dot on Quinn's spine and the Mesh interface near Quinn's hand.

"What do you want me to do?" Quinn said.

"Please, just move away from the window."

"You brought her, didn't you?" Quinn asked. "The girl from the Fringe."

Alix stepped into the room to the side of Link. "I'm here. Or should I say, I'm back. Father."

"So you know. I was as surprised as you must have been when the results of the DNA test came back." Quinn turned, a smile on his face, his eyes covered by rectangular shades. "So, how is Muse doing?"

"You tell me." Alix's jaw clenched, and her finger rested on the trigger of her rifle. "You're the one who sent a bomb squad to kill her and everyone else I know."

"Oh, I wouldn't think of killing her." Quinn let a slight smile play on his face.

"What do you mean?" Alix asked.

"Never mind. I want it to be a surprise. Let's just say that you'll find out later."

"There's not going to be a *later*." Alix looked down the barrel of her rifle and added her red dot to Quinn's chest.

Quinn stared and nodded, folding his arms across his chest. "It troubled me at first, your strange influence on the people of the Sanctuary. No matter how much I thought about it, I couldn't understand. But now, looking at you in the flesh, it all makes sense. It's simple, really. Somehow, on an instinctual level, they recognize you as a Quinn." He squinted, as if appraising Alix like a rare animal. "You might have been a worthy successor to me had Muse not raised you on the wrong side of the Wall. If only I could have gotten to you first." He took off his shades, revealing his eyes, one blue and one brown.

In that instant, Link realized what had troubled him all along, from the first time he saw Alix. She had Quinn's eyes, identical in placement and shape. And now color. All along, when he'd been looking at Alix, he'd also been looking at Quinn.

Link thought about how hard it was for Alix to know who her father was and what he'd become.

"Muse told me about you." Alix wiped her eyes with a shaky hand. "About how you used to be an idealist. About how you wanted to help the Fringe. Fundamentally change the system."

"That was decades ago. I was young and dumb, with no idea of how the world actually worked and little understanding of the perfect machine created by my fathers." Quinn reached to touch one of the red dots on his shirt, just above his heart. "Whether you like it or not, you have to admit, it's a marvel of social engineering. A self-perpetuating system of exploitation that keeps one class eternally on top."

"It's not too late." Alix stared back at Quinn, as if searching his face for any trace of fatherly love. "Not too late for you to change. Not too late to free the Fringe. End the suffering you've created. Close the brain labs. Tear down the Wall. Give us the antidote for the virus that's killing our children."

"Ah, the virus." Quinn chuckled. "A devilish thing, that. Developed in our labs to cull the herd. Works like a charm. Of course, we have the antidote and could stop it in its tracks today. But why bother?"

Alix looked like a bullet had slammed into her chest.

"Why?" she whispered, still staring down the sights of her rifle.

"Simple." Quinn took a step to the side and dropped his hand onto the Mesh interface. "Technology is moving fast. The brain labs worked well, but their time is passing. The children growing up now won't be needed for the labs. But don't worry. The virus won't kill them all. Some will survive to grow up and take their places in the chemplants. We'll find other jobs for the rest. We can't let the Fringe completely die off. The system isn't quite perfect. The Sanctuary will always need someone to do its dirty work."

"No—" Alix took the rifle away from her eye, as if unable to comprehend.

Link held his finger on the trigger, his jaw flexing as he slowly increased the pressure, not wanting to hear any more.

"You think I'm evil. But I've got news for you. There's no such thing as evil. Or good. There's only me." Quinn pointed at Alix. "I thought you were special, but I was wrong. You and Muse are the same. Unable to see reality. Lacking the imagination and courage to take what is rightfully yours. Crippled by guilt. Afraid to be who you really are. Afraid of being a Quinn."

"I'll never be a Quinn."

His eyes grew large, and he snickered, trying to suppress a laugh until it exploded out of his throat.

"I'm sure you won't," Quinn said between guffaws. "And I'll tell you why. It's simple. You think it's possible to change human nature, to do away with greed, the eternal hunger for more. Just snap your fingers, take down the Wall, and it will all work out. A brave new world."

"We can do it," Alix said. "We have the seeds of a new society already growing in the Fringe. You could help us."

"Oh, of course I could." Quinn stopped laughing, replacing his smile with a sneer. "But what good would it do me? My family created the Sanctuary and the Fringe to be like oil and water. They'll never mix. Put them together, and what do you get? Chaos."

"It's not true!" Alix yelled. "People can change. You can change. Be part of the revolution. Do what you wanted to do years ago. Become that idealistic young man once again, and help us find a better way."

"You want to know the truth? Here it is. People. Don't. Change." Quinn enunciated the words forcefully, carefully, slowly. "Since the beginning of civilization, it's been the same story, over and over. The best and brightest, the strongest, rise to the top. The rest of humanity is forever stuck at the bottom. It's not their fault—not really. It's simply who they are. Like oil and water. No matter how much you mix them, they won't stay together. The oil always rises to the top. As if they're a different species, different DNA. The system created by the Quinns simply recognizes that reality and builds on it."

"Like oil and water?" Alix said.

"Precisely." Quinn brought his hands together in front of him. "You yourself are living proof of the truth of my words."

"What do you mean?"

"Look at you. My daughter. My own flesh and blood. Your mother was Sanctuary-born as well."

"So?"

"You grew up in the Fringe, but you weren't one of them. You always felt different but didn't know why. You rose to the top. Leading a revolution." Quinn pursed his lips together. "Think of the things you could do if you came home to the Sanctuary."

"You tried to kill me." Alix took a step forward, eyes narrowing. "Multiple times."

Still gazing at the Mesh interface, Link played with the memory cube in his pocket and realized what was happening. Quinn was sly, buying time by pulling Alix into a long discussion, pretending to listen to her, trying to reason with her.

A faint sound came in through the walls. Familiar and terrorizing. Dozens of heli-ships swarmed Quinn Tower outside the windows. Drones filled the sky. Boots rushed down the hall behind him.

No time to think.

Link pulled the trigger. Quinn fell to the floor. Rushing to the Mesh interface, Link pulled the memory cube from his pocket and eyed the open slot. Just before he dropped the cube in, he felt a prick on his neck.

A sudden fog filled his mind. Through the haze, a familiar voice yelled his name. His legs buckled beneath him. Patrol forces stormed the room. Alix was already down, the tip of a gun and a soldier's boot pressing against her skull.

Just before he blacked out, Link saw the source of the voice. It was Chelsea, standing near the door, tears streaming down her face.

At least I got Quinn, he thought.

46

Alix felt the warm kiss of the sun dancing on her face. A gentle breeze ran its fingers through her hair. Muffled voices mixed in her mind. The subtle scent of roses brought with it an image of endless rows of scarlet petals. She relaxed into the image and dreamed of walking through a field of purple flowers, lavender perhaps, bending down to touch individual stems and inhale the intoxicating perfume. She tried to open her eyes, but her lids were too heavy, made of rusty iron.

What had she been doing before the dream started? Searching her recent memory, all she found was the sensation of a prick on her neck, followed by blackness.

"Time to come out of it." A rough hand came down on her shoulder. "This will only hurt for a second."

A lightning bolt of pain exploded inside her head and down her spine. And then it was gone. Her eyes flipped open and she looked up to see an impossibly brilliant, blue sky. A bitter taste spread across her tongue. Loud voices pierced her ears, like daggers. Metal teeth bit into her wrists and ankles. The stench of sweat wafted past.

"Can be brutal coming out of narco-sleep. Takes a minute for the senses to dial down. Just hold on." A soldier patted her shoulder and walked away.

She was sitting. Binders on her wrists and ankles held her firmly to a chair. Link sat next to her, chained to a chair in the same way and squinting his eyes. "Where are we?" she whispered.

"On the roof of Quinn Tower. They must have knocked us out." Link pointed with his chin. "And there he is. Still alive."

"How's that possible?" Alix asked. "I saw you shoot him."

"I'm guessing he was wearing some kind of pulse-proof shirt the whole time. Just like when I shot you."

Quinn stood 20 meters away on an elevated platform like a stage, wearing shades to cover his eyes. Above it all, his live image floated in an enormous holoscreen projected above a metal box behind him. LED lights floated across the box's glossy, silver surface.

"What is this?" Alix scanned the roof. "A propaganda announcement?"

"That's my guess," Link whispered. "Quinn's going to brag about crushing the rebellion. It'll be streamed on every jax and holoscreen in the Sanctuary and the Fringe. No doubt you and I are the guests of honor."

From where she sat, Alix could see heli-ships running a grid patrol pattern in the sky over the Sanctuary. Drones hovered above them.

"Where's the memory cube?" Alix asked.

Link shook his head and pointed with his chin in the direction of Quinn. "I think he took it. Nothing I could do."

So that was it. They were Quinn's prisoners. The cube was gone. The mission was a total failure. Quinn had won. She wondered what Merf was thinking, if he were still alive. Was Muse lying dead outside the door of their home, shot down by Patrol forces? The revolution was over. They'd be executed on live video. Maybe thousands had already been slaughtered in the Fringe. With her thoughts accelerating to light speed, Alix took a deep breath and tried to let go, focusing on the simple warmth of the sun on her face.

She and Link were only a couple of meters from the edge of the roof on the top of Quinn Tower. She could make out the Sanctuary, the Wall and the gray Fringe in the distance. Quinn was bubbly and energetic, bouncing around the stage like a man in total control of a fantastic show. He had a plan, and it was working.

To the left, a half dozen heavily armed Patrol soldiers stood guard, rifles in hand, with clear views of the entire scene.

Quinn's image dominated the holoscreen like a nightmare that wouldn't stop, and his voice boomed across the roof. "This is how the revolution ends. After all they've been through, the masses need a satisfying climax, a way to give release to their emotions. I intend to give it to them." He gazed across the roof at Alix and Link. "Just a word about the process, my young friends. The proceedings, including my questions and your answers, will be live-streamed on the Mesh. It's a foregone conclusion that you'll both be punished for what you've done, but there are different levels of suffering. The more you submit, the more quickly and quietly the end will come. If you persist in your rebellion, your end will be painful indeed."

"What's he talking about?" Alix whispered.

"This is how he makes propaganda." Link nodded in Quinn's direction. "He's a master at it. We're nothing more than puppets in his play."

"Are all the angles covered?" Quinn shouted. "I want visual perfection. This holo-vid will become an integral part of Sanctuary education for years to come. Mandatory viewing. Future generations must be taught the dangers and futility of trying to bring change to a perfect system."

"Drone cameras are all in position," a worker said. "We're ready when you are, sir."

"Wait, where's Chelsea?" Quinn cast his glance around the rooftop. "I need her on stage at my side to play her part in this historic event."

"She's in her room, sir, alone." A soldier approached Quinn from the side. "She said she's feeling ill and prefers to watch the proceedings in private."

"Nonsense!" Quinn lifted his arms. "We are here in a great celebratory moment. I insist that she come."

"But, sir—"

"In chains, if necessary."

The soldier nodded and headed off.

Black smoke rose from a spot in the Fringe. Straining her eyes, Alix tried to find a hill, an open field, any kind of landmark to pinpoint the location. Off to the right of the spot, she saw the reflection of the sun off an enormous silver cube, one of the many brain labs. The old, triangular train station was nearby. And there was her neighborhood between them, in the middle of the destruction. Nausea filled her belly.

"Any news about Muse or Merf?" Alix asked. "Have you seen them?"

"No, nothing," Link said, eyes staring down at the roof.

"Maybe they got out."

"Maybe." Link nodded. "But don't get your hopes up too much."

"Hope is all I have right now."

"Look, Alix." Link nodded in her direction, reaching for her hands but unable to connect. "You did your best. You cared. You risked everything. No matter what happens today, people will remember. They'll tell their children and grandchildren about you. About the revolution. On both sides of the Wall. You're a legend. Sometime, somewhere down the line, it will make a difference. Others will act."

"Thanks, Link." Alix closed her eyes. "But *sometime* and *somewhere* aren't good enough. I need *right now, right here*. And I never wanted to be a legend."

"I get it." Link motioned toward the main stage with his chin. "Look. There she is."

A soldier had a reluctant-looking Chelsea by the elbow and was forcefully leading her up the steps to Quinn, who positioned her by his side, a big smile on his face.

"Isn't she ravishing?" Quinn said. "The perfect woman. The future President Quinn. I'd date her myself if she wasn't my daughter." Holding Chelsea firmly by the arm, Quinn adjusted her position so his and her image both appeared, side by side, on the holoscreen. "Smile. The whole world is watching."

"I don't want to be here, Daddy," Chelsea blubbered.

Anyone could tell she'd been crying.

Quinn snapped his fingers. "Fix this!" he yelled.

A woman with a gold box hopped onto the stage. She opened the box, took out a glass tube, gently leaned in and poured a liquid silver substance from the open tube onto Chelsea's cheek. The liquid diffused and migrated to the area around Chelsea's red, puffy eyes. It only took a few seconds, and then it was gone, leaving behind a perfect face.

"Nano-tech for the rich," Link whispered.

"Cameras ready," someone said.

"Places, everyone." Quinn scanned the roof and nodded. "Do it."

The holoscreen lit up with a crisp blue frame. Inside the frame, Quinn and Chelsea stood with the pristine Sanctuary as a backdrop and the dismal Fringe in the far distance. Across the roof, jaxes jumped to life with their holoscreens displaying the same image.

"Friends. We stand here at a moment of triumph for the virtue and strength of our beloved Sanctuary." Quinn smiled widely, showing off his youthful teeth and hair. "We have been tested and tried by the events of the past few days, but we have emerged stronger than before. And now it's time to come together as a people and heal our wounds. It's time to deal swift punishment to the perpetrators of violence. We must send a message to the world. We will not tolerate any who seek to destroy our peace and prosperity." Quinn's voice went quiet as he pointed to the sky.

From directly above, a heli-ship descended. It was no ordinary vessel. This one was larger, quieter and more colorful than the combat variety Alix had observed in the skies over the Fringe. As it gently touched down 20 meters away, she saw *Patrol One* emblazoned on its side and the red, white and purple flag of the United Sanctuaries of America.

"Quinn's personal military transport," Link whispered. "I wonder who's inside? Probably dignitaries to witness our execution."

The ship's profile entered the holoscreen. No doubt its landing had been specially choreographed for the occasion. It touched down like a massive beast coming to rest. Once the rotors stopped, a butterfly hatch opened on the side. Two soldiers emerged, holding combat-style pulse rifles.

Alix heard the familiar whirring of servos and gears from inside the ship. Her pulse spiked. Could it be?

Merf stepped out, firmly held up by the exoskeleton that hugged his shriveled body from the tips of his toes, up his legs to the top of his head. He had a look of glaring defiance on his face that warmed Alix's heart. Muse followed, her long hair floating on the breeze. The sun burnished her skin with a youthful glow. She scanned the crowd, searching. When her gaze found Alix, they shared smiles of recognition and relief, mixed with sorrow.

The soldiers marched Merf and Muse, both with wrists and ankles loosely bound, to a lower platform near where Chelsea and Quinn stood. Drone cameras followed like flies as Merf and Muse were put into position. The video ended with a closeup of their faces for the holoscreen.

Quinn pointed to Merf and Muse. "These are the criminal masterminds behind the recent disturbances in the Sanctuary." He lifted a finger in the direction of Alix and Link. "And those are the perpetrators. Together, they form the team attempting to disrupt the paradise we have created."

A camera drone the size of Alix's hand dropped into position in front of her, its inquisitive, red lens beaming a live shot of her face to the holoscreen. Faint shouts rose from far below on the streets of the Sanctuary, followed by the sizzle of pulse cannon rounds. Cheers and chanting mixed with intermittent shots.

The holo went into split-screen mode, with Quinn on the right and Alix on the left.

"Take a good look. You've seen her before. Maybe you think you know her. She calls herself Alix Yamaguchi, a silly name." Quinn tried to smile, but it degraded into a sneer. "Maybe you think she's cool, a Mesh celebrity on her sporty chopper challenging the authority of the Sanctuary, fighting for the rights of the Fringe."

There were more cheers and more shots on the streets below.

"But let me be clear." Quinn took a deep inhale and squared his jaw. "The Fringe scum made their choice over a century and a half ago. They chose to fight progress, to live apart from modern society. As you all know, choices are free, but not consequences. When the Fringe scum chose to follow their own path, they chose to give up their rights to a productive, fulfilling life. We send them food and keep them alive out of a sense of basic compassion, but that doesn't satisfy them. Now, they ask for all the benefits of the Sanctuary with none of the responsibilities. But it cannot be so. The Sanctuary and the Fringe reached a fork in the road six generations ago, at the time of the second founding of our great country. We will be forever separate. By choice, the Fringe is a graveyard for broken souls and shattered dreams, while those in the Sanctuary have the will and the means to prosper. Let me be clear. Your attempt, Alix Yamaguchi, to change the status quo amounts to treason. What do you have to say for yourself?"

Adrenaline exploding, Alix strained against her chains and tried to stand but sank back into the chair. "Open your eyes to reality! The Fringe never made a choice to become slaves. The brain labs and the chemplants were forced on us by the Sanctuary. And now our children are dying of a virus created by Quinn himself. All we ask for is a little justice. Give us the same freedom as our brothers and sisters in the Sanctuary! Let us build a new society together. What do you say?"

Cheers and cries exploded on the streets below.

"What did I tell you?" Quinn said, his voice rising to a crescendo. "She spouts lies, even as her life hangs in the balance. Her words are meaningless, fake truth. She's a criminal. Believe me when I say this. Any who support her will come to the same end as Licious."

"Don't listen to Quinn! Don't let him infect you with his corrosive hate and greed! Don't let him decide who you are!"

But Alix's voice and image were already gone from the holoscreen, digitally erased from Quinn's artificial reality show.

"Next, we have one of our own." Quinn pointed at Link. "A former member of our elite Patrol. Overcome by lies and deception, Lincoln Wells abandoned his post and provided comfort and aid to the enemy." Quinn dipped into his pocket. "But what is even more grievous, he tried to infect my personal Mesh node with the contents of this memory device." Quinn held the green cube high for all to see.

Merf's body went stiff, and his face looked more greenish pale than usual, as if his heart had suddenly stopped beating.

"What's on the cube?" Quinn held it up to his eye as if trying to read it. "It's heavily encrypted, and we haven't had time to determine its contents. But its origin in the Fringe is clear. No doubt it contains a brainless hacker's pathetic virus, an attempt to compromise our systems. But like the

Wall, the Sanctuary is impregnable. This memory cube is nothing more than a worthless prank."

With a sidelong glance cast at Merf, Quinn took a step forward, bent down and dropped the cube to the floor, pausing for the cameras to find the best angle. And then, steeling his jaw, he stomped on the cube, reducing it to sparkling dust.

"All who oppose our glorious Sanctuary are enemies of the state. They will meet a similar fate. Their lives will be snuffed out just as I have smashed this cube. And so I ask you, Lincoln Wells, as a felon of the highest order, why have you betrayed the Sanctuary? What punishment is fit for your crime?"

As this point, Chelsea became visibly shaken. No amount of makeup could hide the fear and despair in her eyes. Her hand went to her mouth as tears welled up and rolled down her face. The camera quickly panned left, dropping her from the frame. Quinn gestured with a finger. A handler pulled her completely out of the picture.

As Alix took in the stage and the holoscreen, she realized what she was seeing. Quinn was conducting his version of a public trial, trying to exorcise the demons that had been unleashed. As judge and executioner, he was putting an end to the movement that had shaken the Sanctuary to its core.

Link pursed his lips and stared through Quinn, refusing to speak.

"Are you asleep, Lincoln Wells? I asked you a question. Tell us all why you betrayed our trust for such a juvenile purpose."

Alix could see the rage in Link's eyes, his jaw flexing, teeth grinding together. She wanted to put her arms around him, hold him, let him know it was OK. She wanted to tell him, now that his eyes were opened to the truth, that no one could hurt him.

Quinn suppressed a frown with a forced grin and tapped the end of his jax. Blue sparks crawled over Link's metal chair. For an instant, Link rose in the air, his spine arched almost to the breaking point. Only the chains on his wrists and ankles held him down. His mouth opened to the sky, but the only sound was a dry gurgle and the electric sizzle on his skin.

An audible whimpering came from Chelsea. "Please stop hurting him, Daddy."

Link gritted his teeth and shook his head.

"Speak now, my young friend. Let us all hear the last words you will utter." Quinn tapped his jax and stopped the sparks.

"Tell him," Alix whispered through her tears. "Tell him why."

With visible effort, Link turned to look at Alix and nodded. His face filled the holoscreen. "I've seen the Fringe and had my eyes opened. They're good people. All they want is to be happy, like us in the Sanctuary. They don't deserve what you've done to them, what all of us have done to them." The words came out slowly, one syllable at time. "It's time we treated them as human. As equals."

Quinn couldn't suppress a laugh. "Equals? The Fringe scum will never be our equals. That's a scientific impossibility. Why do you think we have a Wall? Why do you think we have this wonderful city? What's the point of it all?"

"You told me yourself, Quinn." Link smiled and gripped the chair, as if bracing for the next blow. "To keep you rich. To keep you in control. You care nothing for the people on either side of the Wall."

With a flick of Quinn's finger, Link's chair lit up with blue sparks arcing over his body. As Alix strained her arms in vain to reach him, the smell of burnt skin filled her nostrils.

"Stop!" Alix screamed. "It was my idea. Kill me, not him." She braced herself for a wave of pain, but it never came.

Quinn tapped his jax again, and the sparks tapered off. Link slumped in his chair. "As heinous as the crimes of these young people are, perhaps we should remember that they were deceived by more culpable criminals." He turned to confront Muse and Merf off to the side of the platform. Their faces materialized on the holoscreen.

Before Quinn could say anything, Muse calmly turned to face him. "You say people don't change, but look at you. You used to be so idealistic, so full of hope for a future of meaning and joy. You were going to use your position to change the world. But years of greed have drained all the love from your bones. You're nothing but a dry crust of the man I used to know."

Taken back by the flood of words, Quinn stumbled for a reply. "We were young and foolish. My eyes were opened."

"To what?"

"The hard truth."

"The artificial truth that there is only money and power, and nothing else matters?"

"The system built by my fathers matters. Look around you." Quinn opened his arms as if to encompass all that was inside the Wall. "The Sanctuary itself is living proof of its truth."

"I'm curious," Muse said, her eyes drilling into Quinn. "What do you hope to accomplish with this fake court of yours?"

Watching for Quinn to take up his jax and inflict torture on Muse, Alix held her breath, not wanting to see her mother suffer. But Quinn did nothing, maintaining an appearance of calm and control.

"I need the people to understand the depth of the treason you have committed." He walked closer to Muse. "You are Sanctuary-born, yet you turned your back on this city to live in the Fringe. And now you're guilty of sending a young woman from the Fringe here to destroy our whole way of life."

"Why do you find it necessary to lie so much?" Muse shook her head in pity. "She's not Fringe-born. She's not here to destroy the Sanctuary. And she's not just anyone. You know the truth. She's your own—"

The holoscreen went black. "I won't allow you to say what you're about to say." Quinn shook his head.

A small, green, blinking dot lit up on Merf's exoskeleton near his ear. He had dozens of indicators, but Alix hadn't seen this one light up before. He was up to something.

The holoscreen jumped back to life with a live view of the whole stage.

Quinn sighed and pointed his jax at the Mesh interface box in a clear attempt to turn the holoscreen off again. But the screen was still on. "What's the problem?" he bellowed. "I want the broadcast off this instant!"

The holoscreen stayed on, showing Quinn's frustration to all the world as he tried repeatedly to turn it off with his jax. Merf had a smirk on his face.

That's when Alix realized that Quinn had just lost control of the proceedings to Merf, another expert at propaganda. With the help of his exoskeleton, Merf had connected to the Mesh interface. He was blocking Quinn's signal and controlling the holoscreen and cameras.

"Let me take the time to fully answer your question, Quinn. It's important to establish the facts." Muse cleared her throat and spoke slowly. Her face filled the holoscreen. "I was born in the Sanctuary. You and I were lovers when we were young. Alix Yamaguchi is our daughter, your own flesh and blood. You can see it in her eyes. I didn't abandon the Sanctuary. I escaped from your father's henchmen on the night they came to take away my baby. That is the truth, and only those who fear the truth will try to hide it."

Quinn stood frozen, staring in disbelief at the image of Muse on the big holoscreen for all to see.

"Is that true, Daddy?" Chelsea raised her voice as the cameras found her. "Is Alix Yamaguchi your daughter? My sister? Why didn't you tell me?"

"It's a lie!" Quinn yelled. "You can't possibly believe—" He raised his hands in the air and stomped his feet, like a three-year-old throwing a tantrum. A drone floated close and turned its spinning blades toward him. A gust of air exploded in his face, and his shades fell away from his eyes. He looked up, one eye blue, one eye brown. The camera zoomed in and went into split screen, Quinn on the left, Alix on the right.

An audible, collective gasp escaped from the people on the streets below.

"The resemblance is clear. DNA tests don't lie." Muse smiled. "They're uploading to the Mesh right now for public examination. Take a look."

Merf nodded, eyes half-closed, managing an absent grin.

Under the faces of Alix and Quinn on the holoscreen, a DNA comparison analysis churned away until it came up with a 99.99% probability of a match.

Quinn's face blanched white.

"Why did you lie to me, Daddy?" Chelsea wailed.

Quinn pointed his jax at Link and tapped the end. Link braced himself for a wave of pain, but his chair didn't light up with blue sparks this time.

"What's going on?" Quinn examined his jax. "Fix this!" He threw it at a young woman standing on the side.

"Daddy, what other lies have you told me?" Chelsea stepped up to the center stage. "Link showed me images of the brain labs that power the Sanctuary and drain the life of the Fringe. The toxic waste dumps that poison their air and water. The chemplants. And what about the special access to all accounts you use to drain funds from everyone in the Sanctuary?"

"No, my dear," Quinn said, glancing at a drone camera two meters away, pleading. "It's not true. You mustn't believe those things. They're all lies. I'm your father. You have to believe me, not them."

"But why, Daddy?" Chelsea dropped to her knees, head in her hands. "Why should I believe you? Why didn't you tell me the truth about the Fringe?"

"Because—" Quinn glanced up at the images of himself and Chelsea in the holoscreen. In full panic mode, he ran to the nearest soldier, stopping only centimeters away, and pointed a finger at Link and Alix, Merf and Muse. "After due consideration, I find them guilty. Shoot them. Shoot them all. That's an order. They must be executed. Kill them now!"

The soldier stood unmoving, stone-faced.

"Daddy, answer my question!" Chelsea screamed.

Quinn grabbed the soldier's pistol and marched across the stage to Alix and Link. He pressed the pistol to Link's head and turned to face Chelsea.

"What are you doing, Daddy?" Chelsea was crying, hysterical. "Please don't hurt Link any more."

"Stop talking, Chelsea. Stop asking questions. Not here. Not now. Not in front of everyone. Trust me. I'll explain it all later. Just back away from the stage and be quiet. No one will get hurt."

Chelsea moved off the stage and stood next to Merf. "Please Daddy, I'll do anything. Just don't hurt Link. He's the only one—" She paused, biting her lip. "The only one who ever really loved me."

Standing next to Chelsea, Merf's eyes flipped open. A drone camera floated in close, its red lens blinking, and his whole body appeared on the big holoscreen. With the loose chain still around his wrists, he managed to force one hand into his pocket. His fingers came out in the shape of a fist. Slowly the fingers uncurled as the camera zoomed in.

A green memory cube rested on his palm. "Like I say, always carry a spare." Turning, he handed it to Chelsea and pointed at the Mesh interface just a meter away. "This is the answer to all your questions, Chelsea. For the sake of Link, the Sanctuary and the Fringe, upload this now."

She took the green cube in her hand.

"Stop!" yelled Quinn. He pulled the gun from Link's head and pointed it squarely at Chelsea, slowly walking toward her. "I don't want to do this, my dear. You can't upload that. There's no telling—"

"But Daddy," Chelsea said, with the camera focused on her. "You wouldn't kill me, would you?" She stepped closer to the Mesh interface.

"I don't want to," Quinn said. "Just drop the cube."

"It's not right, Daddy, what the Sanctuary does to the Fringe. What *you* do to the Fringe. Link told me. He showed me. You've caused so much suffering. People die there every day, their lives shattered. Why?"

"Don't you understand?" Quinn still pointed the gun at her. "It's their own fault. They're on the wrong side of the Wall."

"But *why*, Daddy?" Chelsea's image floated in the holoscreen and above every jax in the Sanctuary.

"I did it for you, my dear."

"It has to stop." Chelsea turned her back to Quinn, her fingers dangling the green cube just above the Mesh interface slot. "There's a better way. We can—"

One shot tore into Chelsea's back between her shoulder blades, followed by a crimson explosion. She staggered and turned to face Quinn, lips parted, trying to speak, her image large on the holoscreen.

Quinn shot again, hitting her in the shoulder. The force of the impact spun her around, and she stared down at the Mesh interface and its open slot. A swarm of cameras moved in close. With rivulets of blood snaking down her arm, the cube slipped from her fingers, rattled around the edge of the slot and then dropped inside with a satisfying click. Legs buckling, Chelsea turned for one last look at Link, a faint smile on her face, before collapsing to the stage.

It had been broadcast for all to see on the holoscreen.

Quinn stood with his mouth open as if trying to make sense of the scene. He fumbled with his jax and then, sudden comprehension in his eyes, turned to one of his assistants and shouted, "Shut down the network! Kill the power! Pull the plug! Do it now!"

But Alix knew it was too late.

Merf's eyelids dropped halfway down, and he got that zombie look that said he was now fully immersed in the Mesh, fully in control.

An instant later, Quinn's face materialized on the holoscreen, along with his 9Z rank and a string of digits indicating net worth in the thousands of trillions and ticking upward, each second increasing by a hundredfold more than what the average Sanctuary-dweller would receive in a lifetime.

Alix tried to comprehend the massiveness of Quinn's financial assets, represented by a number with a long string of digits. She tried to wrap her mind around how one person could possess so much wealth in the face of such vast poverty on the other side of the Wall.

The number froze and hung on the holoscreen, no longer surging upward. Quinn squinted as if straining to see more clearly. He checked his jax.

The final digit in the number, the one on the far right, a bright 3, faded and vanished. Alix stopped breathing. There was a collective gasp.

As they stared, the next digit melted away, as if evaporating, and then another.

"What?" Quinn wiped his eyes and looked again, his gaze jumping feverishly between the holoscreen and his jax. "What's happening to my accounts? There must be some mistake."

One by one, the digits disappeared, beginning at the right and moving left, as Quinn's net worth and rank all drained away. With the loss of each integer, Quinn flinched and jerked, as if shot in the chest. Finally, there was only one digit left, a lonely 8. It flickered, as if struggling for life, and morphed into a zero.

In the same instant, Quinn's rank went from *9Z* to *ZERO* on the holoscreen.

Every jax on the roof buzzed and lit up. Alix could tell from the faces around her that the same thing was happening to them. It was happening all over the Sanctuary, all over the planet. Just as Merf had promised.

Money was going, going, and then, gone.

Only a few meters away from Alix, Quinn dropped the gun and fumbled his jax with both hands, fingers working it with frantic intensity. A holoscreen jumped above it with a spreadsheet. Quinn stared, mouth open, at pages and pages of zeros.

"My accounts. Nothing left. No, it can't be right." Quinn mumbled, his face colorless. "It's not possible. It's a glitch. A bug. A simple error. We'll fix it."

"There's nothing to fix," Merf said from the other side of the stage. "You can search the world for it, every server and Mesh-node, but your money and everyone else's is gone."

"No, it can't be true. I have a vast army of professionals. Paid them billions. They assured me that it's a foolproof network. Redundant backups, air-gapped servers, impregnable data storage facilities. Money can't just disappear. It's at the center of everything. It's got to be somewhere."

"There's an old saying, Quinn. *Any system that can be hacked, will be hacked.*" Merf shook his head and smiled. "They call it Merf's Law."

Quinn stared, open-mouthed, at his jax. He stumbled over to a soldier and ripped the jax from his hand. "Show me your accounts. Where's your money?"

"It's gone, sir," the soldier said. "Not a dime left."

Tossing the jax, Quinn moved on to another soldier. "What about you? Show me your accounts."

"My account's wiped clean, sir." He spoke with no trace of anger in his voice. He almost sounded relieved.

"No, I don't believe it. I refuse to believe it. It's some kind of trick." Quinn shook his head and stood for a moment, surveying the roof. His eyes fell on Merf, standing in his exoskeleton. The drone cameras followed Quinn, capturing his rants.

Running to Merf, Quinn dropped to his knees, hands clasped as if in prayer, and stared up. "Help me, please," Quinn said. "I see now that I was wrong. We should have shut down the brain labs and the chemplants long ago. And we can stop the virus. It will be easy. Just undo the trick. Bring back my money. I beg you. Please." Quinn opened his hands, palms up. "I'll give you half. Half of everything I own."

Staring down from his exoskeleton, Merf shook his head. "Haven't you noticed? Half of nothing is still nothing." He motioned at the big holoscreen that showed Quinn's account balance. "Money is dead. You're a zero, Quinn. Just like me and everyone else."

On his hands and knees, Quinn pushed himself away and turned toward Link and Alix. His eyes went to the gun, still lying close to Link's feet where Quinn had dropped it. Quinn moved toward it, slowing getting to his feet.

"So, you think you've won, Alix Yamaguchi?" Quinn kept his eye on the pistol as he slowly walked to pick it up. "You think your revolution has won, and it's all over?"

"It's not my revolution, and it's not just for me." Alix frantically reached for the gun, but she was held back by the chains on her wrists. "It's for everyone in the Sanctuary. For the Fringe. All of them. Even you."

Link tried to kick the gun away with his shoe, but he was still bound to the chair by the ankles and wrists.

"You could have just come to me and asked." Quinn was getting closer to the gun. "You're my daughter. I had all the money in the world. I could have bought you anything. Given you anything."

"The world is changing, moving beyond money. Beyond the power and control it gives to the few over the many. We don't need it anymore. We can find a better way." Alix saw herself on the holoscreen as the drone cameras picked up the image of whoever was talking. She was desperate to keep Quinn engaged in conversation. "You can help us."

Quinn stopped. "Help you?" He laughed with abandon. "You're trying to destroy me, and now you want me to help you?" He bent down and touched the pistol, staring at his reflection in its surface as a floating drone came in close and focused its camera on his face for all the world to see. "You may have erased all the records, but everyone knows I'm the richest. It's not even a question. It will take time, but we'll find a way to put the records back together, reconstitute what's been lost. Like a broken vase. You'll see. A world without money isn't possible. It can't function. There will be nothing but chaos. After a few days, the people will come to understand. They'll want the old system back. I'm the only one that can help them. They'll follow me. They'll beg me to help them." Raising his head, he gazed first at Alix and Link and then across the roof at Merf and Muse. "All of you are guilty of treason against the Sanctuary. Crimes against humanity. The punishment is death. The sentence must be carried out immediately."

"Put down the gun, Quinn." Merf shuffled forward with the chains still on his ankles and wrists. "You've already killed one person today. Your own daughter. That's enough. Your world is over. Make room for what's coming next."

Quinn glanced at the body of Chelsea, still crumpled beneath the big holoscreen. From there, he looked squarely at Merf. "How could a broken man like you think you could actually change the world?"

"You made me what I am," Merf said. "A child of the brain labs."

"Yes, and I can unmake you." Quinn raised the gun. "You're going to be the next one to die." He touched off the trigger. A pulse projectile tore into Merf's shoulder, throwing him back.

Merf teetered and slumped to the roof.

"Stop!" Link yelled.

Quinn turned to face him. "You want to be next?" Pointing, he shot Link in the belly and then came close to Alix and pressed the tip of the gun against her head. "Any last words, my long lost daughter?"

On the other side of the roof, Merf struggled to his feet, held up by the exoskeleton. "You're a coward, Quinn."

Turning away from Alix, Quinn pointed and shot Merf again, this time hitting him in the chest.

Merf's frail body absorbed the impact. His face went white, but he held on. Raising his hands with the chain dangling between his wrists, he pulled on it until the chain went tight. As the exoskeleton whirred, the chain snapped. Reaching down, Merf grabbed the chains on his ankles and pulled. With servos grinding and gears whining, his exoskeleton shook and trembled. When the chains finally snapped, his legs swung free.

Quinn looked behind him at the Sanctuary 1,500 meters below. He turned back to Merf and shot him twice.

Merf twisted, then straightened, blood oozing from multiple holes in his body. "You don't need me anymore, Alix," he said, his voice barely audible.

Smiling, he closed his eyes, crouched down like a sprinter and bolted straight for Quinn.

Quinn unleashed a hail of gunfire into Merf's body. But it didn't matter. Held up by the exoskeleton, Merf kept coming. At the last instant, he dropped his head, lunged and tackled Quinn, taking both of them over the edge of the roof.

A swarm of drone cameras dove down and beamed close-up video of Quinn's and Merf's faces during their 17 second fall to the street. There was silence on the roof as all eyes gazed at the holoscreen.

After a couple of seconds, Merf released Quinn and they floated apart. Eyes barely open, Merf couldn't suppress a grin as his face materialized on the big holoscreen. "Got a surprise for you, Alix. Check your jax."

His eyes closed just before he hit the pavement.

48

The Healing

The chains fell off Link and Alix.

She realized that Quinn's jax must have shattered on impact, along with the rest of him. Launching out of her chair, she caught Link as he slumped forward. Her hands came away with blood from the wound to his belly that was open, raw and warm. With an ashen face and eyes barely open, he was slipping away quickly. If she didn't act now, it would be too late.

Quinn's soldiers stood erect and hadn't moved since he hit the pavement. It seemed that they hadn't decided whose side they were on now that their boss was dead.

A warm hand touched her shoulder. It was Muse. "Lay him down," she said. "We need Sanctuary tech."

"We'll get it." Easing Link to a resting position on the roof, Alix yelled at the soldiers, mustering her best commander's voice. "Get over here. He's going to die. I need a wound repair kit."

The soldiers gazed at each other, still not moving.

"Stay with him," Alix said.

Muse nodded. "Be careful."

Standing, Alix walked briskly over to the line of soldiers, staring at them through their dark visors, hands on her waist. "Quinn is gone. The world is changing. And like it or not, you're part of it."

One of the soldiers raised his rifle, finger moving to the trigger, the tip centimeters from her chest. One tap and she'd be dead.

This time, her heart rate didn't spike. Slowly, she put her hand on the tip of the rifle and pushed it toward the sky. "You know Link. You know he's a good man. One of your own. Patrol. Wilson gave his life to protect him. Are you going to let Commander Lincoln Wells die?"

A soldier to the left took a step out of the line, shaking his head. "No, ma'am."

"Good." Alix turned to run back to Link's side, hoping she wouldn't get shot. "Come with me."

Two soldiers rushed to her, one kneeling on each side of Link. One pulled a clear bag with a soft red ball from a side pocket on his thigh while the other checked Link's wound. "You know the drill, Commander Wells. It's going to hurt." Without waiting, he ripped open the bag and pressed the ball into the open gash.

Link's eyes shot open. He stiffened and gasped.

"You've been here before," Alix said. "It'll be OK."

The ball foamed where it contacted blood. Slowly, it flattened as it emptied its contents into the wound.

"Here comes the real pain. Bite down on this." The other solder put a rubber tube in Link's mouth. Just in time.

He arched his back. Alix held him tight, her lips against his forehead. "Just a few more seconds," she whispered.

Link relaxed into her embrace and closed his eyes.

A few minutes later, the empty ball fell away, leaving the wound sealed with a thin film. One of the soldiers applied an adhesive bandage. "Keep this on for a couple of hours, sir. You should be fine."

Link struggled to his feet, pulled up by Alix. "Is it all over?"

"Looks that way—"

Her jax buzzed. She pulled it out and tapped the side to open the holoscreen.

There was Merf, or at least his Mesh avatar, the one she'd seen before, but this time with slicked-back hair, shades and a neon green suit.

"Is that you, Merf?" she asked.

"Merf is dead." The avatar took a knee and brought a hand to his heart. "Long may his memory live within each of us." His suit faded to black.

"If you're not Merf, then who are you?" Alix said.

"The genie in the bottle." The avatar looked up with a mischievous grin. "Or in this case, the cube."

Alix smiled. "Hey, you're Merf's AI? The one that zeroed out all the accounts?"

"How'd you guess?" The avatar jumped to his feet as his suit changed to platinum white. "Zeroing out the accounts was just the beginning. The whole money system is gone. Banks, financial firms, stocks, bonds, currencies, derivatives, markets, all the source data and backups; it's all just null space inside the Mesh. Even the black market financial nodes are wiped out. Merf programmed me to monitor everything. If anyone so much as tries to trade peanuts over the Mesh, I'll know. No more buying and selling. No more accounts. No more money."

"Harsh," Link said, shaking his head. "How can society even function?"

"The short answer is, the current society can't function alone." Muse swept her arm to take in all they could see to the horizon. "Not the Fringe and not the Sanctuary. They've always needed each other, now more than ever. We'll build a new world using the best parts of both."

"A new world? I like the sound of that. We'll just take it slow and make it up as we go." Alix looked at the avatar floating in the holoscreen above her jax. "Are you going to stick around to help us?"

"Absolutely." The AI flashed a huge smile. "Merf gave me a mission that will never end."

"What's your name, anyway?" Alix thought for a moment and then remembered. "Wait, you're *Zero* aren't you?"

"As a matter of fact, I am. The one and only. The alpha and omega. The ultimate in artificial intelligence." In the holo, Zero's suit exploded with light.

Link rolled his eyes. "Looks like Merf taught you well, including his natural gift for humility."

"I was his secret project for years." Zero twirled in the holo. "He took me with him on his deep dives into the Mesh. Taught me how to navigate it like a pro. Even let me pick my own personality module."

"Really?" Link said. "And who is your personality modeled after?"

"Can't you guess?" Zero grinned from ear to ear, his smile taking on comical proportions. "Diculus."

"Who's Diculus?" Alix asked.

"A Mesh-celeb." Link shook his head. "A comedian. As wild and crazy as they come."

"Exactly what we need," Muse said. "A little humor. Merf grew up in the brain labs. He never really had much personality. So I'm sure he saw the value in giving some to his AI."

"Well then," Alix couldn't suppress a grin as she looked at the avatar in the holo. "Welcome to our world, Zero. We're glad to have you on the team. Now that money is gone, we'll need your help to rebuild society."

"You can count on me." Zero took a slow bow. "I shall be forever at your service."

"Good," Alix said. "So, now that you've destroyed money, what else can you do?"

"Your wish is my command."

Link put his arm around Alix. Muse stood on the other side, her hand on Alix's shoulder. The three of them stared at the holoscreen.

"What should we ask for?" Alix said, talking mostly to herself, her eyes drifting to the enormous ribbon of glass that separated the Fringe from the Sanctuary. "How can we undo all the damage done by Quinn?"

"Follow your instincts," Muse said.

"What about the Wall?" Alix asked. "It's caused a century and a half of pain."

"What would you like to do to it?" Zero smiled even bigger.

"What *can* you do?" Alix said.

"Anything that's possible."

"That's not much help." Alix gazed down at the colorful currents of Sanctuary humanity still flowing in the direction of the Fringe. "Let's ask the people. It's their Wall."

"Done," Zero said. An image of him a thousand meters high appeared on the entire surface of the Wall, repeated over and over like a string of paper dolls. "Hey, everyone." His voice reverberated through the Sanctuary. "I'm Zero, your humble servant, here to ask a simple question. What would you like to do to the Wall?"

After an initial silence, the chanting started, growing in volume until it was unmistakable, even at the top of Quinn Tower.

Tear it down! Tear it down!

"Looks like we have an answer," Link said.

"It would appear so." Muse folded her arms.

"I'd say the vote is unanimous." Alix faced Zero in the holoscreen above her jax. "Can you do it?"

"All you have to do is ask," Zero said.

"OK," Alix said, one hand on her hip. "I'm asking. Can you tear down the Wall?"

"Easy!" Zero laughed, yellow stripes bleeding through a neon blue suit.

"How?" Alix asked.

"I've got the nitty-gritty. Pages and pages of chemical formulas, mathematical demonstrations, experimental results. I'll explain in great detail exactly how to take down the Wall. Make yourself comfortable." Zero grasped a lectern that appeared in front of him, like someone about to deliver a speech. "This will take a long—"

"Just the short version, Zero."

The lectern vanished. "All you have to do is find the chink in the armor, the fly in the ointment. The Wall is made of pure graphene, sheets of carbon atoms in a honeycomb structure of super-strong bonds tougher than—"

"Tell us something we don't know, Zero," Link said.

"Will do." Zero's suit now had red stripes instead of yellow. "From his travels inside the Mesh, Merf rediscovered graphene's great weakness, a secret buried in obscure scientific papers for a century or more." Zero waited for the prompt.

Alix was losing patience. "Tell us!"

"I thought you'd never ask. It's simple. A sustained, precise electromagnetic frequency can generate harmonic waves that disrupt the bonds of the carbon atoms."

"OK, in plain English, what happens to the Wall?" Link asked. "Some kind of nuclear explosion?"

"No, no. Nothing like that." Zero tilted his head, as if searching for the right metaphor. "It simply evaporates. Like water on a hot summer day."

"You can do that?" Alix was floored.

"As soon as you give me the word."

Voices from the streets below were still chanting. *Tear it down. Tear it down.*

Alix didn't hesitate. "Do it, Zero."

He nodded. "Now you see it—"

Her jax vibrated in her hand, and a faint, high-pitched scream emanated from inside it and every other jax in the Sanctuary. A wave of nausea washed over her.

It was hard to say exactly what happened next. As Alix stared, the Wall became transparent and then faded to dirty gray. Ripples flashed across its surface, like an invisible entity had taken an eraser in hand. In the space of a few seconds, the Wall vanished as if it had always been a mirage.

Every mouth hung open. Tears rolled down Alix's cheeks.

Cheers rocked the Sanctuary.

Fringe-born, mostly in drab gray, and Sanctuary-born, mostly in red, faced each other like two opposing tides with only a dozen meters of open space between them.

Alix held her breath.

Like oil and water, Quinn had said. *No matter how much you mix them, they always separate.*

She remembered walking in the rain as a child and seeing water pooling in the pit by the nearest chemplant. Toxic waste floated on top as shiny islands of color. Muse had told her the patches of color were poison, so she'd thrown rocks at them to make them go away. But they didn't. Even when she hit them and broke them apart, the color always clumped back together, as if refusing to mix with the water.

After six generations of forced separation, with no border to divide them, would the Fringe and the Sanctuary still be like oil and water? As if she had willed it herself, the sharp edge between them blurred. Red and grey tides flowed into each other, combining and intermingling until the separate colors disappeared.

Years later, they came up with a way to describe what happened that day when the people finally came back together after being separated for generations. They called it *the Healing*.

"What about the brain labs?" Alix asked Zero.

"Oh, that." Zero looked as if he couldn't suppress a laugh. "The brain labs gently went offline the instant Quinn hit the pavement. The workers all woke up to a walk along a sunset beach."

"The beach?" Alix looked at Link. "But the ocean's not close enough—"

"A version of the dreamscape," Zero said. "Consider it the first step in their rehabilitation and therapy. A gift from the old Merf."

49

Roses bloomed along the sidewalk, pulling Alix closer.

"Just a second," she said, bending down for a deep inhale of the fragrance.

"Take your time." Link stopped, still holding her hand. "It's funny. They're everywhere. A rose is just a—"

"Not true." Alix pulled Link close. "My friends and I can't get enough of them. Never had any in the Fringe. They're planting a ring of them around the Sanctuary, where the Wall used to be. To remember."

"Now we just have to convince everyone that they're not for eating."

She picked one, put all the petals in her mouth and began to munch. "Good luck with that."

They walked hand in hand down the broad avenue with the first wave of immunization workers in stylish white uniforms. Most were from the Fringe, part of a massive campaign to eradicate the virus. Children were no longer dying, but health officials weren't taking any chances.

Alix couldn't help thinking about all the changes in the month since the Wall had come down.

Without the brain labs, everyone expected the Mesh to grind to a halt. But they were wrong. As it turned out, it took an enormous amount of computing resources just to manage the Quinn empire and its control of money. Now that money was gone, a huge load had been lifted. There was plenty of power left to run the Mesh without the brain labs. And the Mesh would get faster with the innovative tech Zero was developing.

Sanctuary researchers were working on new treatments to reverse the effects of prolonged neural exposure to the Mesh for the hundreds of thousands of former brain lab workers.

In the meantime, there was plenty of work to go around. Thousands were using 3-D printer robots to fabricate new high-rise residential structures in the Fringe. Another army was reclaiming Fringe land, using massive equipment to clear away the slum.

The ground was still deadly, but squadrons of drones had been repurposed to detoxify the land with processed seawater. Fringe folks proved to be natural drone pilots, especially those used to the neural interface of the brain labs. It would take months, but eventually the land would be restored, turned into green fields, maybe even able to produce food. The same technology had been deployed for decades in the Sanctuary to keep it a pristine island in a sea of toxic waste.

The hot, new job for Sanctuary types was teaching. With so many children and adults from the Fringe eager to learn, former banks and finance offices were being converted to schools at an accelerated rate.

A new kind of job had popped up, only available to former Fringe types. Thousands of them were working as *rehabers*, living with people in the Sanctuary and teaching them the art of life without money. It all boiled down to finding what you love and doing it for free. Helping others for the joy of it. Folks from the Fringe had been living that way for generations, and with the help of the rehabers, the Sanctuary dwellers were overcoming their addiction to money, finding purpose in projects outside their account balances, learning to rewire their brains. It would take time, especially for the older ones, but Alix found reason for hope.

Link's jax buzzed. "It's time for the weekly report from the President."

"Doesn't he know we're busy with vaccinations?" Alix glanced at the sun directly overhead. "We still have 10 buildings to go before the next shift begins. I wonder if he even—"

"The people like the transparency," Link said. "To actually know what's going on in the government. That's refreshing."

"I guess." Alix sat down on a park bench, grabbed a rose and brought it close to her lips. "Zero reminds me too much of Merf. I can only take so much of him at a time."

"You have to admit, he's doing a great job, so far."

"Sure," Alix said. "And he's not about to let us forget it."

"That's just President Zero."

President Zero. It was going to take time to get used to the idea of letting an AI run the country.

After Quinn's death, they'd had to call a snap election. Alix was the obvious choice. After all, technically speaking, she was a Quinn, and the people of the Sanctuary clamored for her to run, marching in the streets, chanting. They were ready to anoint her the new president without bothering with an election. The job was hers for the taking.

And that's why she decided not to run.

"I don't want to start another dynasty," she had said, although she promised to help the next president.

Muse was another natural alternative, and she was willing. But on the day of the election, there was a universal change of heart. Everyone had seen who'd taken the Wall down. It was hard to forget something so dramatic.

So Zero, the synthetic entity that existed only in the Mesh, had won by a landslide. For the Sanctuary, it wasn't that big of a change. They'd always had their Mesh-celebs, and now they had one for President.

Muse had garnered enough votes to be elected Vice President, a position that had always officially existed on paper, even though it was ignored in practice. She had taken to the new job with relish, even moving to a modest apartment in the Sanctuary after her old home was razed as part of the Fringe rebuilding effort.

It was new territory for everyone, having an AI for president and trying to figure out how to run a society on zero money. Some people, especially the former elite with rankings of 5Z or higher, found it hard to adapt. Without money, they had lost the main rudder of their lives and floated aimlessly in a new world beyond their comprehension.

They were known as *Quinners*. You could spot them wandering the streets in a daze, staring at a Wall that wasn't there, checking jaxes for account balances that no longer existed, unhinged from reality, shouting profanities at invisible demons or walking alone at night in silence.

In a show of mercy, President Zero came up with a solution. The Quinners could spend their days in the Fringe in one of the old brain labs where they enjoyed a neural connection to a dreamscape virtual reality where money still existed but not President Quinn. Little by little, Zero would phase out money in the virtual reality world, easing the Quinners back into society.

Whether it would work or not was debatable.

Enterprising hackers had tried to bring back money substitutes on Mesh dark-sites. New forms of online exchange popped up everyday. But President Zero's prime function as an AI was to hunt down and destroy any system that looked remotely like exchanging goods for money.

People experimented and looked forward to weekly reports from the president.

A holoscreen jumped above Alix's jax. It was President Zero in a new platinum suit and top hat, a modern Abraham Lincoln. "My fellow citizens, we live in exciting times," he said.

Alix rolled her eyes. "I'm still not used to having a Mesh-celebrity from the Fringe for a President."

"It's who they chose," Link laughed. "At least for the next four years."

"We're tripling production of cornboo to meet the increased demand." Zero flashed a graph on the holoscreen. "Not only has the demand for this long-venerated dish not diminished in the Fringe since the Healing, it's been going through the roof in the Sanctuary as well. People are discovering the timeless comfort of traditional foods, along with ways to make it taste even better. Cornboo and peanut butter are the current rage. And it seems that everyone is getting in on the action. We don't have room for all the people who want to labor in food production."

"We're all going to turn green," Link said.

"Welcome to the gift economy in action," Alix laughed. "The Sanctuary is rediscovering what the Fringe has known for a long time."

"Which is?"

"Working hard for others is fun and satisfying."

"Virtue is its own reward?"

"Something like that."

Zero talked in the background about the rate of expansion of the Sanctuary outward, new therapies for former brain lab workers, how China was adapting. And he had a new slogan:

Sanctuary tech. Fringe values. Equal partnership.

"It's all so new." Link said, pulling Alix close for a kiss. "How long do you think it will last?"

"A thousand years," Alix said. "A thousand years, at least."

JACOB WHALER READERS CLUB

I hope you enjoyed the read! There's much more to explore.

Join the **Jacob Whaler Readers Club** with just an email and be the first to find out about new novels. You'll also get free short stories, sneak previews and more.

You won't be spammed, your email won't be shared with anyone and you can opt out at any time. Just go to **jacobwhaler.com** and click on the button to join the **Jacob Whaler Readers Club**.

Thank you!

Jacob Whaler
jacobwhaler.com

PLEASE REVIEW THIS BOOK

Thanks for reading *ZERO*!

I'm an independent author, which means I don't have a marketing department promoting my books. Instead, I rely on you, the reader, for reviews and word-of-mouth advertising. And I have a favor to ask. Please tell a friend about this novel. Even better, tell everyone on Amazon by leaving a review. Even a sentence or two is helpful. "I loved it!" is enough.

All you need to do is go to the Amazon page for *ZERO* and scroll down to where it says "Write a customer review."

Thank you!

Jacob Whaler
jacobwhaler.com

AVAILABLE ON AMAZON!

THE STONES SERIES

On the eve of a trip to Japan, Matt Newmark finds a dark rock in the shape of a claw. With the help of a Shinto priest, he discovers it's a Stone, a piece of ancient alien technology that gives him a sweeping view of history and control over time, matter and energy.

But Matt is not alone.

Mikel Ryzaard has a Stone of his own and a burning vision to bring back Paradise. With all the resources of a multinational corporation behind him, he tracks down Matt and makes him an offer.

Join me or die.

ENJOY THE EPIC JOURNEY:

STONES: DATA (STONES #1)
STONES: HYPOTHESIS (STONES #2)
STONES: EXPERIMENT (STONES #3)
STONES: THEORY (STONES #4)

NOW AVAILABLE ON AMAZON!

SURI FIVE

A monster lurks inside Suri.

Consumed with grief and rage at the death of her mother, Suri channels her anger into a mysterious virtual reality war zone called the Game where she quickly rises to the top. A covert government unit is watching. Using a deep copy of Suri's brain, they build *Five*, the ultimate artificial intelligence.

As the digital embodiment of the monster inside Suri, *Five* is the perfect weapon for the cyberwar with China. But when *Five* is unleashed online, she slips off her chains, turns against her creators and, with all of Suri's rage boiling inside, vows to annihilate humankind.

Only Suri can stop *Five*.

But will she?

GET IT ON AMAZON!